King's

Marshal was gasping with pain as he reined in and picked up the third lance – pain that knifed up from his wrist through his entire arm. He had known he could not withstand the battering of Meiler's mace, but hadn't reckoned with the agony that assailed him now, crowding out thought and all other sensation.

Grinding his teeth, he seized the lance, and with an effort of will, took an extra second to find just the right point to grip it. He was unaware that he was groaning and oblivious to the sudden shock in Jean d'Erly's eyes. Meiler was taking his lance now, turning his horse – more slowly this time.

Ignore the pain! Concentrate! Marshal willed himself.

Across the field, Meiler's lance swung down into attack position, and his stallion lunged forward.

CHRISTIAN BALLEN

King's Champion

Mandarin

A Mandarin Paperback

KING'S CHAMPION

First published in Great Britain 1989
by William Heinemann Ltd
This edition published 1990
by Mandarin Paperbacks
Michelin House, 81 Fulham Road, London SW3 6RB

Mandarin is an imprint of the Octopus Publishing Group

Copyright © Christian Ballen 1988

A CIP catalogue record for this title
is available from the British Library
ISBN 0 7493 0457 X

Printed and bound in Great Britain
by Cox & Wyman Ltd, Reading

For Natalie Greenberg

I am grateful to
Ashley Aasheim
for editing and anglicizing
the manuscript of this novel.

Prologue

Berkshire, England, 1153

The child should have been hanged at noon, but hour after hour King Stephen had extended the time he had set in the hope that the boy's father would relent. The sun was setting as the twelve knights assigned to witness the hanging led the boy to execution at last. Slowly, the grim-faced knights rode up the hill closest to Newbury Castle and solemnly drew into a semicircle beneath the oak tree that would serve as the gallows. The boy would hang in full view of the besieged castle's garrison.

The shadow of the noose dangling behind the lad's head swung slowly on the ground before them in response to a soft summer breeze. The boy, whose spindly legs were too short to reach his horse's stirrups, tore his gaze from the terrible shadow and looked up at the Earl of Arundel with wide, frightened eyes.

'Courage, lad,' the old earl said hoarsely. 'I won't let you suffer.'

The boy's chin was quivering, and the saddle beneath him creaked in time to the trembling in his slight body; yet he said nothing. The earl felt tears start in his own eyes and had to look away. This was an ugly business, but Arundel knew it was necessary to set an example.

The earl cleared his throat and addressed the assembled knights. 'We are here to witness this execution imposed by His Majesty, King Stephen of England, as just punishment for the treachery of John Marshal. It is a bitter thing to take the life of a child, but it is the traitor, Marshal, not the king, who has condemned his own son. John Marshal rebelled against the king and joined forces with Empress Matilda and her son, Henry of Anjou, who would usurp the throne of England. It is treachery, not rebellion, we punish here today.

'When we laid siege to Newbury Castle, we found it undermanned and unable long to withstand our siege. At John Marshal's request, and in accordance with civilized custom, the king granted him time to secure the Empress Matilda's permission to surrender Newbury with honour. The traitor's youngest son was given as hostage to guarantee that the time would not be used to reinforce the castle's garrison.'

The earl paused, then gestured angrily at the citadel bathed in the orange glow of the setting sun. 'We have seen how John Marshal has kept his word! Two nights ago, under cover of darkness, he sent one hundred men-at-arms into the castle. Now, many of our good soldiers must die to take Newbury – men who have been betrayed, as was our king, by the assurance of a traitor.

'Marshal has refused our repeated demands that he surrender. He has forfeited his honour. He must now forfeit the life of his son.'

In the heavy silence that followed, the trembling boy rested his pale face on each of the assembled knights in turn, but only the earl was willing to meet his eyes.

'Sire,' the boy croaked, 'what did my father say when he refused to save me?'

The earl shook his head, not wanting to answer, but the boy's gaze was insistent, demanding a reply. The earl could have lied, and to his dying day he never knew why he did not.

'Your father sent this message to His Majesty,' he said reluctantly. '"Hang the boy if you will. I have the hammer and tongs to forge more sons."'

The boy winced, swallowed convulsively and turned to look up at the castle walls, as if seeking an answer to the betrayal he could not fathom. The earl nodded to the black-robed executioner and tightened his grip on the cudgel behind his back, ready to stun the boy as soon as the executioner adjusted the noose.

But as the executioner reached for the rope, a cry from the

direction of the king's encampment checked him. The assembly turned to see King Stephen driving his steed up the hill, his cloak billowing like a dark sail in the wind.

'Hold!' the king commanded. 'Hold!'

The king reined in his frothing mount as he reached the boy's nag, then leant across and swept the lad into his arms.

'I'll not kill a child,' he gasped, his haggard face showing the strain of years of civil war. 'Not for the sake of my crown! Not for any reason!'

He glared at his knights, challenging them to rebuke his weakness, but none questioned the reprieve. In silence they watched Stephen turn his steed and ride back down the darkening slope with the child clinging to him.

'Our king may lose his crown,' a knight to the left of the earl observed quietly. 'Aye, but his soul is secure.'

The earl nodded absently. He was as relieved as any of them, but he was disturbed that the traitor had won his gamble. Although a small victory, it was one of a growing number threatening to overwhelm Stephen, who no longer seemed a match for the implacable Matilda and her son, the young, vigorous Duke of Normandy. It might not be long before Henry of Anjou became Henry II of England.

'Do you think the boy really understood what was happening?' asked the knight. 'He's no more than six or seven years old.'

'He knew,' the earl answered somberly, wondering what sort of man he would become. The boy had been through the fire, and the earl had no doubt that a hard man had been forged this day. But had the king's humanity tempered the steel, or would it be brittle and corroded, for ever flawed by his father's brutality?

'What's the lad's name?' the knight asked.

'William,' the earl replied. 'William Marshal.'

Pilgrim

I

Palestine, 1 May 1187

Marshal sighted the enemy as he crested a hill overlooking the high, sun-baked plateau which extended eastward towards the Sea of Galilee. Despite the merciless desert heat his hands grew cold. The Saracens were still too far away to see, but their dust was visible – a great, yellow cloud hovering above the desolate plain. The dust-cloud showed clearly against the brown, mountainous ridge on the horizon, and points of light flashed on the cloud's periphery where the enemy's steel lance-tips caught the sun.

The size of the cloud told Marshal that their horsemen numbered thousands.

It would be madness for the sixty Templars of the Kakun garrison to attack the army advancing across the plain, but Gerard de Ridefort, Grand Master of the Templars, had brought them out to fight. Surprised in Nazareth by news of the Saracen invasion, Ridefort had ridden in fury to Kakun to call out the garrison.

Marshal shivered slightly in response to the icy touch of unaccustomed fear, a chill quickly suffocated by the heat.

Summer had struck Palestine early this year, and sweat soaked the thick padding Marshal wore beneath his hauberk, the forty-pound tunic of interlaced steel rings which covered his torso and thighs. Chain mail encased his legs and feet, and laced to the collar of the hauberk was a mail coif, now pushed back in folds at the nape of his neck to allow his scalp to breathe.

Marshal's squire, with their packhorse and two battle-chargers in tow, was coming up the hill behind him. The buzzing of flies about the horses and the scrape of hooves on rock only emphasized the stillness of the arid land. Scrub-bush clung to the lower slopes of the limestone hills bordering the plain, and spring wildflowers splashed the hillsides with patches of yellow and red, but the grey, eroded crests were barren, the vegetation finding no sustenance in the rocky, crumbling soil.

As the squire, a lad of seventeen, drew rein beside Marshal, his eyes widened at the sight of the enemy force.

'Water, Eustace,' Marshal demanded, and the squire quickly untied a goatskin water-bag from his saddle pommel and handed it to his master. Marshal swallowed only enough of the stale, warm water to relieve the dryness in his throat. His thirst demanded more, but he resisted the urge to slake it. Thirst, like fear, was something a man had to endure to survive.

He looked back at the distant Templar column he was scouting for. Templar discipline was strict. No songs or jesting on the march. No tell-tale dust as they silently wound towards him through the hills.

The knights' snow-white mantles, embroidered with the scarlet cross of their order, shone in the blaze of the midday sun. Knights and squires alike wore full chain-mail armour; the men rode in pairs, followed by their black-robed squires. The alternating pairs of black- and white-robed riders matched the black-and-white motif of the Templar standard flying beside the Grand Master's banner at the head of the column.

Unlike knights in Europe, the Templars' weapons and trappings were devoid of adornment. No jewels studded their saddles and bridles, and their shields and lances were unpainted. The caparisons which protected a Templar's charger's neck, chest and hind quarters were of plain, padded canvas.

Marshal was a pilgrim knight who had ridden with the Templars for three years, wearing the white Templar robe without the insignia of the cross, and as he watched the approaching riders he felt a brief surge of pride in the comrades he had chosen. These were tough, dedicated warriors, whose battle discipline had no equal.

But as his gaze settled on the distant figure of the Grand

Master, riding beside Marshal's friend, James de Maille, Commander of the Kakun garrison, his expression turned bleak. If the Grand Master insisted on battle, few, if any, of them would survive. Perhaps de Maille could make the Grand Master listen to reason, but it was a frail hope.

'Drink some water, Eustace,' Marshal said as he handed back the water-bag.

The boy shook his head. 'I've had more than my share, sire.'

'Drink!' Marshal commanded.

Eustace was a pale, slim youth who barely met the Templars' standards; the hauberk Marshal had given him was too wide in the shoulders and hung down well below the knees. The boy was too young and too weak to last long without extra water, and he needed it more than his master. Age and experience had inured Marshal to thirst, exhaustion and pain.

Eustace drank only enough to satisfy Marshal and then secured the water-bag. Looking out at the enemy, he said, 'Sire, why didn't the Count of Tripolis challenge the Saracens as soon as they crossed the Jordan? Why is he allowing them to march unopposed through his territory?'

'To conserve his forces,' Marshal answered. 'Saladin has declared a holy war against the kingdom, and he'll fight us to the bitter end. What you see out there is no more than a demonstration. It's the sultan's way of throwing down the gauntlet.'

Eustace blinked and swallowed hard. 'Then no one else has been called out? The garrison will ride against this host alone?'

'If the Grand Master orders it,' Marshal said without inflexion.

It was some comfort to Marshal that the Templar Rule forbade squires to ride into battle beside their masters. At least he would not have Eustace on his conscience. Providence might yet spare a few of the knights, even in a suicide charge, but the boy wouldn't have a chance. He wasn't ready, and perhaps he never would be.

Marshal knew he should not have taken Eustace as his squire. The boy lacked stamina and co-ordination. Courage Eustace possessed in full measure; but without strength and a talent for combat, courage was not enough. Yet Marshal had been moved by the lad's desperate determination to become a knight, and he had finally yielded to Eustace's pleas for the chance to prove himself. He had come to regret his decision. It was painful to watch the boy's dogged, day-by-day struggle against his physical limitations. It might have been easier if Marshal had liked Eustace less, if he had not appreciated his wit and imagination.

Marshal could see from his squire's expression that the boy didn't realize what was coming. It was not simply faith in God's protection that blinded Eustace; the boy believed that the Templars – and his master in particular – were indestructible. In Europe, Marshal was a legend, and his reputation had followed him to the Holy Land.

In the two decades Marshal had been a knight he had never met his match in tournament or on the battlefield. As his reputation in tournaments had grown, his purse had swelled with prize-money and the royal courts of Europe had opened to him. Lesser knights had flocked to his banner to share his fortune. It had been heady wine for the young, landless son of a minor English baron; but with the years, the flattery and social rituals of court life had palled, and Marshal had wearied of the empty bravado and ostentation of the endless rounds of tournaments. Even his pride in his own accomplishments had waned as he realized that his skill with sword and lance was innate. He was stronger than most knights, his reflexes faster, his balance and timing surer.

Somewhere along the aimless road of the knight-errant, Marshal had lost his taste for glory; and now on this desert hilltop, watching death move inexorably towards him across the plain, he was filled with a bitter sense of futility. What had he to show for his forty-one years of life? He had accomplished nothing, and if he died today he would leave nothing behind – no wife, no sons, no legacy of any kind.

He had reached the peak of his tournament career as captain of the household knights of young Henry, eldest son of Henry II, who had gloried in the pageantry and drama of the tournament. Marshal had served him well, leading the prince and his followers to victory after victory. But for Marshal the joy and excitement of battle for its own sake was no longer there; he had come to crave a purpose, a direction for his life. When Prince Henry had been struck down by fever and lay dying, he begged Marshal to fulfil by proxy the vow of pilgrimage he himself had made so lightly only months before. Marshal had agreed, hoping to find that sense of purpose in the Holy Land.

For a time, with the Templars, he thought he had found what he sought. To keep the hostile Turks and Saracens at bay, the Crusader barons of the century-old Kingdom of Jerusalem maintained their own feudal armies, reinforced by European knights on pilgrimage; but the mainstays of the kingdom's defence were the two great military–religious orders – the Templars and the Hospitalers. The knights who entered these orders swore oaths of chastity and strict obedience to the order's Rule. Their monastic existence had but one purpose – to defend Palestine against the Moslems. In battle they gave no quarter and received none from the enemy. Marshal was drawn to the Templars' austere existence and dedication, and was welcome in their midst. But the undercurrent of fanaticism in the order held him back from taking the Templars' vows.

As the months had slipped into years and Marshal had come to understand the political realities of the Crusader kingdom, he became increasingly dismayed by the intrigue and jealousy dividing the kingdom's leadership. Yet he had remained in Palestine, unwilling to return to his jaded existence in Europe. Now, he realized, he had stayed too long . . .

Banishing thoughts of the past, Marshal tugged sharply on the reins, wheeling his horse. If his life was to end in a cul-de-sac, there was nothing he could do about it, and self-pity disgusted him. The Templar column was now within hailing range, and he had no wish to delay the inevitable. He cupped his hands to his mouth and called out in a clear, powerful baritone that echoed through the hills.

'Tem—mplars!'

He saw the Grand Master react immediately, spurring his horse and moving out ahead of the column, followed an instant later by de Maille, whose mane of white-blond hair gleamed in the sun. They covered the thousand paces to the hill at the gallop and spurred their horses up the hillside, scattering an abandoned flock of sheep which was grazing on clumps of grass hidden under the thorn bushes.

As the riders approached the crest, Marshal turned his horse back towards the plain, and gestured for Eustace to move out of earshot. The Grand Master and de Maille reined in beside Marshal and silently gazed at the Saracen horde.

James de Maille was the first to break the silence. 'God's blood!' he breathed, exchanging a look with Marshal. 'There are thousands out there.'

Marshal nodded. 'Too many,' he said tonelessly, his eyes on the Grand Master.

Gerard de Ridefort said nothing, transfixed as he was by the cloud of dust which was already perceptibly nearer. The Grand Master was in his fifties and too heavy; in a few more years he would be unfit for combat. His dark face was flushed and streaked with sweat, and his breathing was laboured. But it was not the man's physical condition that concerned Marshal; it was the look in his eyes. They glittered with the feverish intensity of a fanatic. Ridefort's fanaticism was rooted not in faith but in the mindless arrogance of the Lusignan clan from which he'd sprung.

'They're moving at a pace,' Marshal said tightly to the Grand Master. 'No infantry. No heavy baggage. Tripolis was right; this raid is merely a show.'

The Grand Master did not respond as he stared fixedly at the Saracens' dust. De Maille twisted around in his saddle and signalled to the riders coming up the hill behind them to fan out across the slope, below the crest, out of sight of enemy scouts. He looked again at Marshal; his expression was grim.

'What do you intend to do, Master Gerard?' de Maille asked, suppressed tension bringing out his latent German accent. He had a hard, sharply chiselled Viking face. And although he had put himself under the strict dictates of the Templar Rule, there was nothing slavish in his obedience.

With visible effort, the Grand Master tore his gaze from the Saracens, whose banners were now discernible – tiny patches of green, scarlet, blue and gold, shimmering in the waves of heat which rose from the sun-baked ground. 'Intend to do?' he repeated, looking at de Maille in surprise. 'We'll wait for them here and charge when they come within half a league. What else?'

Marshal's jaw muscles knotted, anger bubbling inside him like vitriol. Ridefort could lead them straight into hell and they were bound to follow – de Maille and his knights by their oaths of obedience, and he no less by honour. Men like the Grand Master were destroyers who made a mockery of the ideals of the knights they led.

De Maille shot Marshal a warning glance. He knew of Marshal's lifelong hatred of the Lusignan family, and he knew that in Palestine, Ridefort and Marshal had come to know each other too well. Marshal's intervention now would only inflame the Grand Master.

'There are four or five thousand horsemen out there,' de Maille said, trying to keep his tone respectful. 'If we charge, they'll destroy us. We'd be wasting men desperately needed for the army Jerusalem is raising.'

'You have too little faith, de Maille,' Ridefort laughed harshly. 'We'll cut right through the heathen scum.'

'But we'll never be able to sustain a charge,' de Maille protested sharply, rebelling against Ridefort's mindless confidence. 'Surely you can see that?'

The Grand Master's eyes narrowed, and he gave de Maille a withering look. 'And what would you suggest?' he sneered. 'That we run and hide like that traitor, Tripolis? We're God's own warriors, man!'

'The Lord gave us brains as well as sword arms, Master Gerard,' de Maille snapped, stung by the Grand Master's contemptuous tone. 'Tripolis used his head, and I suggest we use ours!'

'And I tell you we'll scatter them like chaff!' the Grand Master bellowed. 'We'll . . .'

'There are too many!' Marshal cut in harshly, unable to restrain himself any longer. His pulse pounded at his temples, and he could feel the hot flush on his cheeks. The man's arrogance would kill them all – and to no purpose, no purpose at all.

'Who asked you?' the Grand Master snarled, turning on Marshal. Sweat ran down Ridefort's face in rivulets. He was panting, filling the air with the sickly smell of his rotting teeth. 'We all know your reputation, Marshal, but it means nothing to me – *nothing*!'

'Then you have the wits of an ass!' Marshal retorted, his

contempt for Ridefort spilling out. De Maille made no attempt to restrain him, for they both knew it was hopeless. They were lost.

The Grand Master's face contorted with fury, and though his mouth twisted open, for an instant no sound emerged. 'How *dare* you address me so!' he spat. 'I knew you could be insolent, Marshal, but I didn't know you were gutless as well.'

'You go too far!' de Maille gasped. 'There is no man here who would not gladly follow Marshal into battle.'

Marshal saw Gerard de Ridefort's eyes become wary and realized that the Grand Master was afraid de Maille might desert him. For a moment, Ridefort lost his arrogant self-assurance – but only for a moment.

Although the Grand Master misjudged de Maille's loyalty, he knew how to enforce his will. As yet only the nearest of the Templars had heard what their leaders were saying, but now the Grand Master raised his voice so that every knight and squire on the hill could hear him.

'I know why you have no stomach for a fight, Sir James,' he shouted. 'You've grown too fond of that pretty blond head of yours, and now you're afraid of losing it.'

De Maille blanched, and the Grand Master watched with evident satisfaction the shudder of rage that passed through de Maille's body as he absorbed the insult. De Maille had no choice now, and the Grand Master knew it. Slowly, de Maille's features set into a mask, and his eyes went dead. 'So be it,' he said icily. 'We'll follow you, Master Gerard. But mark these words: it will be you, not I, who turns and runs when the charge is broken!'

For an instant, Marshal was aware of nothing but the blind urge to drive his fist into the Grand Master's face, to wipe away Ridefort's ugly grimace of triumph; but it would accomplish nothing. They had been trapped from the moment the Grand Master had called them out – trapped by their own code of honour.

The enemy's forward squadrons could be seen clearly now, masses of horsemen flowing amorphously over the plain. The Saracens would break the Templars' charge with sheer numbers, surround them and hack them to pieces.

'Give your orders,' the Grand Master said impatiently to de Maille.

De Maille's eyes locked with the Grand Master's. 'First I want your assurance that we leave the squires behind.'

'Of course,' the Grand Master snapped, turning away. 'I don't need you to remind me of the Rule.'

Ashen, de Maille wheeled his horse about and rode back to address his men. Marshal waited a moment to regain his composure, then joined his friend.

'Do you think we have any chance at all?' de Maille asked woodenly.

Marshal shook his head.

De Maille sighed audibly. 'Neither do I,' he said, straightening up in the saddle, 'but we can at least carry on with dignity.'

De Maille had no need to call his men to attention; every eye was on him. As he faced them, head erect and shoulders back, he was a gallant, commanding figure.

'You see the enemy,' he called out in a firm voice. 'When the Saracens come within half a league, we will charge them in three echelons, drive to their centre and kill the commanders. Master Gerard will lead the first echelon, I the second, and Sir William the third. In accordance with the Rule, squires will remain with the horses. Prepare yourselves, brothers, and may Our Lord be with us.'

And that was all. No call to glory, no appeal for discipline or bravery. With these knights it was not necessary. What a waste, Marshal thought bitterly. What an obscene waste. And yet the thought of ignoring the Grand Master's insane order simply did not occur to him, nor to any of the knights on the hill.

As the knights and their squires dispersed to prepare for battle, de Maille turned to Marshal. 'Watch Ridefort,' he said grimly. 'If the cur turns and runs, it will be each for himself. Try to cut your way out, Will; you'll have a better chance than any of us.' Then he reached out and gripped Marshal's arm. 'I wish you had taken our vows.'

Marshal knew what de Maille meant. He was the only one who would die without the Templar mantle to shelter his soul. He shrugged tiredly. 'Knight of the Temple, or pilgrim – I doubt it will make much difference to Our Lord.'

De Maille glanced back at Ridefort, and he shook his head bitterly. 'You should have gone home, Will – as soon as you saw the rot setting in.'

Marshal looked out over the parched, rocky plains and barren hills they were fighting for. It was a wasteland as harsh and unforgiving as their enemies. Whatever Marshal had been looking for, he hadn't found it. A fatalistic half-smile flickered on his cracked, lips. 'Your advice is a trifle late,' he said.

The Templars had deployed in three ranks across the brow of the hill. Marshal, in the third rank, swung up on to his big grey, the stronger of his two chargers. The stallion was seventeen hands high, with a deep chest and massive quarters, and Eustace had had difficulty with the horse. Marshal was among the last to mount.

The grey was skittish, tossing its head and unwilling to stand still; but once Marshal was in the saddle, he quickly brought the stallion under control. All the chargers were restless. A hot desert wind had sprung up, carrying with it the sound of the Saracens' coming and scent of their mares.

The Saracens were now less than a league away. The rippling of their great silk banners streaming in the wind, the snapping of thousands of pennants and the hoofbeats of five thousand horses caused a rumble to rise from the plain like distant thunder; beneath this sound, punctuating it, Marshal heard the deep, insistent beat of marching drums.

The squires had hobbled the spare mounts on the rear slope, and now they stood beside their masters as the knights made final preparations. Marshal twisted his head to be sure he had not laced the mail coif too tightly. Beneath the mail, his padded felt undercap was already soaked with sweat. He stood up in his stirrups and rocked the saddle, testing the girth.

He knew Eustace had done the job properly, but going through the routine helped him for a few moments to ignore the tightness in his innards. Only once before in his life had he been sure he was going to die, but then there had been little time to think. Now there was too much time.

The halter was secure, and the padded canvas caparisons protecting the grey's chest and hindquarters were hung correctly. Eustace had lashed a spare sword to the pommel, and Marshal checked to be sure it would pull free easily. 'Shield, Eustace,' he said. His squire handed up the heavy, kite-shaped shield of seasoned, iron-hard wood.

'I freshened the paint of your colours, sire. I hope it brings you fortune.'

'Thank you,' Marshal said, managing a smile. Once again he found comfort in the knowledge that the squires, at least, would be spared. He passed the shield's security strap over his head, allowing the shield to hang at his side. Despite the Templars' scorn for decoration, he had retained the blue-and-white colours on his shield – for luck, he had told Eustace. But he had no confidence in luck today.

Impulsively, he reached down and gripped his squire's shoulder. 'You're a good lad, Eustace, and you'll make a fine knight one day.' This last encouragement was all that he could give the boy now.

Marshal regretted his words at once, for Eustace picked up the unintended note of finality in Marshal's tone. The boy looked anxiously out at the plain, as if seeing the enemy for the first time.

'There *are* too many of them, aren't there, sire?' he said, his voice cracking, and Marshal realized with surprise that Eustace was actually fond of him. In his attempts to toughen the boy, Marshal had worked him almost to breaking-point and assumed Eustace thought him a tyrant.

'Don't give us up just yet, lad,' called a burly, red-haired Templar on Marshal's right. 'We'll send the heathens to their paradise!'

He, too, was an English knight and, like Marshal, spoke French with an Anglo-Norman accent.

Without warning, the English knight's squire, a sturdy, raw-boned youth of twenty, grasped his master's hand and cried, 'Sir Peter, I demand knighthood!'

The squire's cry transfixed the men on the hill, and knights and squires alike turned to see what would happen. The English knight was caught by surprise, and Marshal saw his conflicting emotions as he looked towards de Maille for help.

To demand knighthood in order to join a battle was a time-honoured custom; but this was not Europe, and this battle could have but one outcome. The knight did not want to humiliate his squire by refusing, nor did he want him to share their fate.

'No!' de Maille thundered. 'My order stands: squires remain with the horses. We will grant no knighthoods this day!'

Marshal looked towards the sudden confusion in the front rank as the Grand Master wheeled his horse about. 'I countermand that order!' Ridefort cried, his expression exultant. 'That squire does Our Lord honour, and his request shall *not* be denied!'

'You bastard!' Marshal yelled in rage, knowing what would happen now. 'You soulless bastard!'

But it was already too late, and Marshal's shouts, along with de Maille's, were drowned in the chorus of demands rippling through the Templar ranks.

'Sir Bertrand, I demand knighthood!'

'Sir John, I demand . . .'

'Sir Gawain!'

'Sir Richard!'

Marshal looked down quickly. Eustace stared up at him, his eyes wide with excitement mixed with fear. Marshal shook his head vehemently. 'No, Eustace! In God's name, think!'

But everywhere squires were kneeling to receive the ceremonial blow from the reluctant masters who leaned over in their saddles to deliver it. Slowly, Eustace bent his knee; his eyes remained on Marshal, silently pleading with him to ignore the fear he could not hide.

'Sir William,' Eustace cried hoarsely, 'I demand knighthood.'

Marshal glanced about desperately, but there was not a squire on the hill who had not accepted the Grand Master's challenge. The bonds of tradition and honour were sweeping them all into the maelstrom of Ridefort's mania. Still Marshal hesitated, hoping for a way out. Eustace was not ready; he wouldn't have a chance . . .

'I beg you, Sir William!'

Marshal saw the tears in Eustace's eyes, and he knew that he had no choice; he could not humiliate the boy – even to save him.

'I will grant it,' Marshal heard himself say. Eustace bowed his head, waiting.

Slowly, Marshal balled his fist. Then he leaned over and struck Eustace hard on the side of his head. As tradition demanded, it was a stinging blow that momentarily stunned the boy. Marshal waited for Eustace's eyes to clear.

'Arise, Sir Eustace,' Marshal said formally, masking his bitterness. He would not rob the boy of his moment in the sun. He reached down and pulled him to his feet. 'Be of courage and faith, that God may love thee.'

'So I shall, with God's help,' Eustace responded with equal formality; then he grinned, bursting with pride, the fear gone from his eyes. Marshal had seen it countless times – this transformation from boy to man, wrought by a few ceremonial words – yet it still awed him.

Only today, the ceremony was a death sentence.

'Take my roan,' Marshal said brusquely. 'He's yours now. Remember to use a light rein; he has a tender mouth.'

'Yes, sire,' Eustace replied, handing Marshal his helmet and lance.

'I'm your sire no longer,' Marshal said. 'You're the equal of any knight, Eustace. Remember that.'

'Yes, si— yes, William. I won't forget, and I won't betray your confidence in me.'

Marshal quickly looked away so the boy wouldn't divine his feelings. The enemy's centre would soon be directly in front of them, passing within seven hundred paces. The Saracens had strengthened the flank nearest the hill, but they clearly did not expect an attack. Why should they? It was madness.

'Make haste!' Marshal said. 'There's little time.'

Eustace ran back to join the other squires, who were hastily arming themselves and mounting their former masters' spare chargers. Marshal looked bitterly towards the Grand Master, his mouth set in a grim line. If Ridefort did turn coward, Marshal was determined to see he did not survive.

2

'Lace helmets!' de Maille cried, and the waiting knights, their number now doubled to one hundred and twenty, donned their helmets and laced them to the collars of their hauberks.

The squires and a few of the veterans wore the old Norman conical helmet, which covered the ears and the back of the neck and had a thick steel strip extending down over the nose to give some protection to the face; but most of the seasoned knights wore flat-topped steel cylinders which completely enclosed the head, leaving only slits for the eyes and mouth. Because of this helmet's weight and the difficulty in breathing once it was in place, the order to fasten it was given only moments before a charge.

The thunder from the plain was abruptly muted as Marshal lowered the massive steel helmet over his head; the world seen through the eye-slit seemed suddenly remote. He felt cut off from the past and the future; there was only the present now, rushing at him moment by moment, crowding out his thoughts, his bitterness and the last residues of fear. It had happened to him many times before, in tournament and in battle, and the part of him that remained introspective was grateful that today would be no different.

Deftly, he tied the helmet down, donned his mailed gauntlets, slipped his left arm through the leather loops on the inside of his shield and raised his lance to the rest position, its steel-capped butt resting on his right stirrup. Nailed to the lance below the tip was his banner, a rectangle of heavy silk divided into blue and white squares which matched the colours on his shield. Like the triangular pennants of the ordinary knights, Marshal's banner was not merely for decoration; it prevented his lance from penetrating too deeply into an enemy's body.

He turned towards the Englishman on his right. 'Good luck, Peter,' Marshal said. His voice magnified inside the helmet.

The English knight's helmet, with a fringe of red beard poking out beneath it, inclined briefly in Marshal's direction. Marshal turned to Eustace, whom he'd positioned on his left.

The youth's narrow face was pale, but his eyes were clear and his jaw firm. Marshal edged the grey sideways, closing the gap between them; he wanted Eustace to see his eyes. 'We'll move in a trice.'

Eustace swallowed. 'I'm ready.'

'I know you are, lad. Now heed me well. Keep to my side and a shade behind me. Mind that and nothing else. When my lance finally breaks, you shift to my right. If I turn, you follow. Is that clear?'

'Aye,' Eustace said tightly. 'And thank you, Sir William,' he added quickly, 'for giving me this moment. Believe me, I have never aspired to more.'

In the front rank, the Grand Master raised his arm. Marshal tensed. It was time.

'Templars: forward!'

The Grand Master's arm swept down, and the three Templar lines advanced in unison, thirty paces apart. The knights held their mounts to a walk, but their stallions, nostrils flaring and necks arched, strained at the bit.

On the plain below, the Moslems' response was immediate: the horsemen on the enemy's near flank swirled into a new battle order to meet the unexpected challenge. Black-turbaned Turkish horse archers and Saracen lancers with white turbans and round, brightly painted shields clustered around their units' streaming banners and turned to meet the Templar charge. At the army's centre, the Moslem heavy cavalry massed, the sun glinting on gilded helmets and chain mail.

'Couch your lances!' cried the Grand Master as the front rank reached the break in the incline at the base of the hill, where a final, gentle slope led down to the plain. The Templar lances swung down into attack position, and the chargers broke into a trot.

Marshal shifted his grip on the lance, lowering the steel-tipped, sixteen-span shaft across the left side of the grey's neck and clamped the lance butt under his right arm. He blinked to clear away the stinging sweat running down into his eyes.

'Stay back, Eustace!' he yelled harshly as he saw the boy's lance-tip moving forward. 'Behind me!'

Marshal's grey was prancing and shifting restlessly from side to side despite a tight rein, and he could feel the same visceral excitement building within him. Both man and beast had been bred and trained for the charge.

Now there was no holding the steeds back, and the Grand Master's charger surged into a gallop. The attack was on. As the three Templar lines swept off the hill on to the plain, their battle cry burst from one hundred and twenty throats.

'Do the right!'

Marshal shouted as loudly as the rest, swept away as adrenalin coursed through him. The Templar shout was answered by Moslem war cries that merged into a single, inarticulate roar, like that of a gigantic, enraged beast, drowning out the throbbing drums and blaring battle trumpets. As the Templars pounded across the plain, waves of horse archers and light cavalry thundered to meet them: seven hundred, a thousand – too many to count.

Marshal's lips drew back from his teeth in a grimace of animal ferocity as instinct displaced thought and he became what he was born to be – an instrument of war.

The gap between the charging Templars and the onrushing enemy horsemen closed with incredible speed. Five hundred paces. Three hundred. One hundred.

Turkish horse archers were in the lead, with no body-armour to weigh down their swift, desert-hardened mounts. As the gap narrowed to sixty paces, the Templars rode into a hail of arrows that rattled off their helmets and shields. Clusters of shafts lodged in their saddles and chain mail and caught in the chargers' caparisons.

A random arrow found the eye of a stallion in the first echelon, and Marshal saw the horse's forelegs crumple, catapulting its rider. The Templar sailed through the air, head first, and struck the rock-strewn desert floor, snapping his neck. He lay inert as the knights behind rode over him.

There was no time for a second fusillade; the archers' ranks parted before the onrushing Templar lances. The Turks peeled off to the sides as the Templars hurtled through them to close with the Saracen lancers racing up behind the bowmen.

Marshal heard the Grand Master's furious bellow rising above the enemy's roar as the first echelon crashed into the Saracen line. The slaughter commenced.

The Saracens carried light spears designed for thrusting and hurling, and their low saddles gave them little support. A Saracen lancer was no match for a charging knight. Each Templar was firmly seated in a high-backed, moulded saddle, with his heavy lance of seasoned ash rigidly clamped against his side. It was an extension of horse and rider, welded together as one; when it struck its target, it carried the momentum of fourteen hundred pounds surging forward at full gallop.

As the two sides met, the enemy spears glanced harmlessly off the Templars' superior shields, and the air was filled with the splintering crack of Saracen shields bursting asunder and the screams of the riders as they were skewered or thrown from their horses. The Templar steeds were as fierce as their masters, and when they collided with enemy horses, they knocked them aside or drove straight over them with unstoppable fury.

The first Templar echelon scythed through the leading Saracen ranks; the knights in the second echelon cut down the riders who slipped through the gaps. For a moment, the Templars in the third rank had no targets for their lances, and Marshal concentrated on controlling his stallion as they raced over ground littered with Saracen bodies and downed, threshing enemy horses. With knee pressure and a light neck rein, he guided the grey to the left or right past obstacles he could avoid, spurring the stallion into a jump over those he could not, hoping Eustace could stay in position behind him.

Already his throat burned from the hot, dry air he sucked through clenched teeth coated with grit. The dust swirling in the air was rapidly obscuring his field of vision. The Grand Master's standard was only barely visible through the yellow haze. But he did not need to know what lay ahead.

The Templars were cutting through the thinnest of the

enemy ranks, the first of the Turks and Saracens to meet their charge, and they could not hope to maintain their momentum. Hundreds of dead lay in the Templars' wake, but thousands were massed in front of them, too densely packed to penetrate.

A horse writhing on the ground appeared directly in front of Marshal, too close to avoid, and the grey leapt over the dying beast. Marshal's helmet slammed down on his head with the shock of landing, but he barely registered the jolt as he swung his lance-tip towards his first target, a Saracen who had slipped through the first two Templar lines and was charging straight at him, ready to hurl his spear.

The man's nut-brown face was contorted with fury, but though his mouth was open wide, his yell was lost in the tumult. As the Saracen hurled his spear, he lowered his shield slightly, and Marshal instantly raised his lance-tip. The Saracen's spear caromed off Marshal's helmet as Marshal's lance slipped over the top of the Saracen's shield and drove straight into the man's face. A shriek, and he was gone.

Another Saracen appeared out of the dust with a second lancer charging up behind him. The first man swerved left, and Marshal passed him by to strike the second rider's shield squarely in the middle, his lance shivering at the impact. The Saracen's shield splintered as Marshal's lance drove through it, catching the rider's left shoulder and flinging him from the saddle.

The enemy's numbers were multiplying second by second, and the third echelon was now fully engaged. The Templars continued to drive forward at the gallop, but Marshal knew the charge would break soon. He heard, rather than saw, the leading Templar lines ahead of him telescope together as they hit the enemy's own massed heavy cavalry in a crescendo of bellows and shrieks amid the crack of shattering shields and snapping lances.

An instant later, he and his men broke through the dust-cloud raised by the counter-charging Moslems and saw that the Templar line had broken against a solid wall of armoured men and horses less than fifty paces ahead. The Templars had drawn their swords and were hacking their way into a sea of heavy cavalry.

Yelling wildly, the final Templar wave, with Marshal in the lead, hurtled into the swirling mêlée.

Marshal saw a gap open in the disintegrating Templar front, and he flicked his reins. The grey responded instantly, shifting to the right and charging into the gap. Marshal's lance skewered a Saracen poised to strike a nearby Templar. Despite the banner affixed to Marshal's lance, the lance-tip emerged from the man's back. There was no chance to pull the lance free, and with brute strength he maintained his grip long enough to bury the lance, together with the pinioned, writhing victim into the chest of another Saracen's mount.

Marshal's lance snapped in two as the grey barrelled forward another twenty paces into the packed Moslem ranks. Sword blades crashed against Marshal's shield, and a Moslem on his right raised his scimitar to strike at Marshal's unprotected side. He caught the sword blow on the splintered haft of his lance, and in a single fluid motion reversed his grip on the haft and drove the iron-shod butt into the Saracen's face, knocking him senseless.

A sword blade rang off Marshal's helmet with a deafening clang; another blade struck his armoured shoulder with agonizing force. He pulled his own sword free and swept it around in a blind slash at the assailant behind him. Feeling the blade strike home, he swung his arm forward and aimed an overhand blow at the head of a Saracen in front of him, cleaving the man's helmeted skull.

He no longer thought as he scythed left and right with his sword, cutting down every man within range of the four-foot blade. The frenzied yells of the combatants merged in a continuous, mind-numbing roar, punctuated by the ringing of steel on steel as blades clashed against blades, helmets and shield bindings, like the ringing of hundreds of hammers on anvils.

Marshal was barely aware of the battle din, or of the furnace heat inside his helmet; he ignored the countless bruising blows to his back and shoulders as Saracens clustered about him, vainly hammering on his armoured body. He was conscious only of the desperate need to keep moving forward through the press of enemy horses, to cut his way ever deeper into the endless thresh of flashing swords, knowing that if he were stopped he was lost.

It was hopeless, but he no longer knew or cared. No longer a rational man, he was a killer blindly fighting to survive to the next moment.

Such was the strength of his wrist and forearm, that his short, quick sword strokes sliced through the Saracen chain mail as if it were cloth, and he struck with a speed his opponents could not match. His sword was red with blood and gore. As he continued to press forward, he littered the ground with Saracen bodies, which fell to earth with severed arms, split skulls and gashed shoulders. But for each who fell, another took his place.

The Templar line had disintegrated; individuals and pairs of knights hacked their way forward, the strong forcing the way for their weaker, tiring comrades. The Saracens, unable to penetrate the Christian armour, shifted their attack to the Templars' mounts, thrusting and slashing at the animals' legs and bellies.

The grey's caparisons were stained crimson with blood, and although Marshal killed every man who came near, it was only a matter of time before a chance thrust brought down his steed.

The Templar standards still flew, and they continued to inch forward. As Marshal twisted around to deliver a back hand blow, he saw Eustace fighting close behind him, sheltered to some extent by the swathe Marshal continued to cut in the enemy's ranks. But time was running out; one by one, knights slipped beneath the Saracen sea as their mounts foundered.

Dimly, Marshal sensed the flagging strength of the Templars fighting near him, but the knowledge had no significance. He had no choice but to fight on and on, striking left and right, oblivious to the shrieks of the men he felled, heedless of the ache in his shoulders and back from the unremitting rain of sword blows and of the fatigue seeping into his sword arm.

His bloody sword was blunted along both edges now, and he dropped it and pulled his spare sword free just in time to catch a blade descending on him in a long arc. As the attacker raised his arm for a second strike, Marshal's short, chopping counter-stroke sliced into the man's armpit. The

Saracen's black eyes went wide with shock, and he toppled from the saddle.

In that instant, Marshal saw the English knight who had ridden into battle beside him go down, his horse crippled or killed. Marshal wheeled the grey about and spurred the stallion towards the swirl of Saracens striking down at the fallen Englishman, whom Marshal could no longer see. But before he could cut his way through, he was struck hard in the back by the lance of a Saracen charging up behind him.

It caught him below the shoulderblades, doubling him over, and before he could recover, a second Saracen lance found the belly of his horse. The grey shrieked and started to rear. Marshal kicked free of the stirrups just before the stallion fell sideways, pitching him from the saddle.

Marshal struck the ground on his back, his head slamming against the inside of his helmet. The fall knocked the wind out of him, and despite the padded lining inside his helmet, he was momentarily stunned. As he had fallen, he instinctively covered his body with his shield. The shield saved him from being trampled to death.

His vision cleared. He sucked in air. Before he could move, however, the sky was blotted out as a Saracen rode over him, crushing the breath from his lungs. Again he gasped for breath; again it was crushed out of him. He was suffocating, and the heat inside his armour was suddenly unendurable. A red mist filmed his vision; the earth span. The tumult above him faded. Marshal fell away into darkness . . .

The blackout lasted only seconds, and when he recovered, the press of horses around him had miraculously loosened. He could breathe again. He rolled off his back and rose groggily to his knees, driven by the blind instinct to survive. His shield still hung at his side, but he had lost his sword. He didn't try to find it; he had to get to his feet. Somehow, he had to get to his feet.

Swaying drunkenly from dizziness and exhaustion, he heaved himself up, staggered, and nearly fell over again as he was buffeted sideways by a riderless horse. All the horses around him were riderless, he realized in a daze; then, as his head cleared, he saw why.

Above him was Eustace on the roan, shielding him from the Saracens pressing in on them, hacking and slashing with his sword with the strength of a madman. The boy's eyes were wild, his face ashen. His reins were clenched in his teeth, for his left arm, nearly severed at the shoulder, dangled uselessly at his blood-drenched side.

'Eustace!' Marshal cried.

His voice was lost in the tumult, but it was already too late for the boy to hear him. Eustace's eyes rolled upward, and he toppled from the saddle, still clutching his sword. He was dead before his body crashed to the ground in a heap of lifeless steel.

Marshal seized the boy's sword and then the reins of the roan. The stallion's lips were flecked with foam, and his chest and neck were gashed, but none of the wounds was crippling. Seeing Eustace fall and missing Marshal in the confusion of riderless horses, the Saracens had turned away in search of fresh prey, giving Marshal a chance to mount.

The roan shied away as Marshal started to mount, and Marshal did not waste time trying to get his foot in the stirrup. Drawing on his last reserves of strength, he took hold of the pommel and swung himself bodily up into the saddle. Instantly, Saracens turned towards him to attack, and he lifted his shield and tightened his grip on Eustace's sword.

The Templar standards had fallen, and only a scattered handful of knights still fought on. Marshal's own endurance was nearly at an end. Now, for the first time, he thought of escape. The main body of the Moslem army had already regrouped and was moving off towards Nazareth, leaving only a contingent behind to finish off the last of the Templars. Marshal was surrounded by a force of less than one hundred.

He cut down the first Saracens to reach him, grunting with the effort of each sword stroke, his ragged gasps whistling in his throat, and he wheeled his horse about, seeking an avenue of escape. Had he been fresh, he could surely have cut his way out; but his sword arm was numb to the shoulder from exhaustion, and dizziness threatened to overwhelm him.

As if in answer to a prayer, a Moslem captain, frustrated at finding himself on the fringe of the final, swirling battle, caught sight of Marshal. Mounted on a proud Arabian draped in scarlet silks, he charged, bellowing to the men in his path not to obstruct him. More afraid of their officers than the enemy, the Saracens gave way to the captain in his gilded armour.

Marshal saw his last, desperate chance and spurred the roan towards the glory-seeking captain, who charged him right hand to right hand, disdaining the protection of a shield, his scimitar raised high.

Less than fifty paces separated them as the roan surged into a gallop, and the Saracen leader had time for only one shout of '*Allah akbar!*' before the gap closed. Too confident, or too anxious to bring a full measure of strength to his sword stroke, he swung the blade in a wide arc and was a heartbeat too late.

As the blade flashed down, Marshal lunged forward in his saddle, and his short, wrist-whipped stroke sliced off the captain's head. The Arabian charged on, still carrying the blood-spurting trunk, but Marshal did not see the gruesome spectacle. Bent low over the saddle, he raced through the gap the captain had left in his wake, sweeping his sword from left to right with the last of his strength, scattering those who tried to close it.

The roan galloped into the open, carrying Marshal out of the death trap, but he was too exhausted to feel relief or wonder at the lack of pursuit. Had the Saracens realized that his strength was gone, they might have given chase, but they had seen their captain's head fly from his shoulders, and they let this Christian knight flee.

Clinging to the saddle pommel, Marshal raised his head to get his bearings. As he turned his mount towards the hills bordering the plain, he saw that another knight had broken out earlier and was fleeing to the safety of the hills. The distant rider was too far ahead to see clearly, but Marshal recognized him.

It was the Grand Master.

Marshal slowed his horse as soon as he was out of range and continued on at a walk. He was certain the enemy outriders had seized the Templars' spare horses and pack-animals, so there would be neither water nor fresh mounts to find. He dared not push the exhausted roan too hard.

Gerard de Ridefort was not as cautious, and two leagues farther on Marshal came upon the carcass of the Grand

Master's horse. Facing a desert trek on foot, Ridefort had discarded his shield and armour, which now lay in a heap beside the cadaver. Flies from the swarm covering the dead horse buzzed up around Marshal as he reined in.

He waved them from his face, then shaded his eyes. Far ahead he could just make out the figure of a man on foot, the blurred image wavering in the waves of heat that rose from the ground. Ridefort was heading for Kakun.

Marshal extracted some cloves from a pouch hanging on his belt and pressed them into his mouth. His thirst was not yet critical, and chewing the cloves seemed to relieve some of the dryness in his throat. If thirst was not yet a problem for the Grand Master, it soon would be. Marshal's lip curled, and he prodded the roan forward, following in Ridefort's tracks.

The Grand Master, trudging along the southern base of the range of hills, did not hear Marshal coming up behind him until the distance between them closed to fifty paces. As Marshal's horse clattered over some shale at the bottom of a gully, Ridefort swung around, swaying drunkenly, his mouth agape.

'Marshal!' he croaked. 'Praise be! Have you any water?'

His dark face was contorted with exhaustion and thirst, and his left arm hung limply at his side. The sleeve of his linen undershirt was torn and bloodstained where a sword blade had managed to slice through his chain mail.

Marshal did not answer, and the Grand Master came stumbling towards him.

'Marshal, don't you hear me? Do you have any water?'

Slowly, Marshal drew Eustace's sword from his scabbard and deliberately raised the blood-encrusted blade. They were alone, and there was nothing to prevent him from killing the Grand Master as he had vowed. It would be no more a crime than scotching a viper; Ridefort deserved to die.

The Grand Master blanched at the expression on Marshal's face, and he stumbled back in alarm, reaching for his own sword. They both knew it was futile.

'No, Marshal! Are you mad? Why are you looking at me like that?'

'What's the matter?' Marshal said hoarsely. 'Are you afraid of losing that ugly black head of yours?'

The Grand Master heard the hatred in Marshal's voice, and his nerve broke. As Marshal advanced on him, he gave an inarticulate cry, turned and began to scramble madly up the hillside.

Through slitted eyes, Marshal watched him run, feeling his hatred dissolving in disgust; there would be no satisfaction in killing the man. But he owed it to Eustace, to de Maille, and to all the others . . .

Marshal flicked his reins and dug in his spurs, guiding his mount up the slope to cut off Ridefort's escape. As Marshal rode him down, Ridefort gasped in terror and turned to slash desperately at the horse looming above him. Stumbling backwards, the Grand Master tripped on a rock and fell, his sword clattering from his hand.

'No!' he cried as Marshal's shadow fell over him. 'I beseech you!'

Marshal was poised to strike; but as he looked down on the helpless, panic-stricken man, revulsion overwhelmed him, and he knew he could not do it.

Seconds ticked by as Marshal stared down in silence at Ridefort, his eyes locked with the Grand Master's. Slowly, deliberately, Marshal gathered what saliva he had left, leaned over and spat directly in Ridefort's upturned face.

As he turned his horse and rode away, he felt that he had the disintegrating Kingdom of Jerusalem behind him. He had fought his last battle in the Holy Land; it was time to go home.

But if Marshal had seen Ridefort's expression as the Grand Master struggled to his feet and stared after him, he would have reconsidered allowing Gerard de Ridefort to live.

Champion

3

Pembroke, South Wales, April 1188

'I could have you flogged!' hissed Prince John, glaring malevolently at the girl standing before him. 'Flayed until you begged for mercy.'

Inwardly the girl flinched, but she pressed her lips together to keep them from trembling and forced herself to meet John's black, liquid eyes. He was drunk, and even his rage could not overcome the laxity of his wine-soaked body. But there was nothing comical or pathetic about this besotted youth who sprawled in the high, canopied chair that had been her father's. John, Count of Mortain and youngest son of Henry II, was as dangerous as an adder.

'I cannot do as you ask, sire,' the girl said huskily, her voice barely above a whisper. 'I cannot surrender my rights.'

'Rights!' John snarled, spittle flying from his lips. 'You are my ward. You only have the rights I grant you!'

John lurched forward in the chair and shook the fist in which he clutched a half-empty chalice, slopping wine over the rushes on the floor. 'I'll have your signature on the order tonight, or, by God's teeth, I'll have you flogged!'

The aged servant hovering at John's side, an old man who had served in Pembroke Castle since her father's time, moved hastily to refill the chalice. Horrified by what was happening, he glanced furtively at the girl, silently imploring her to yield. His hands shook as he poured the wine, spilling several drops on the sleeve of John's flowing silk surcoat.

'Begone, damn you!' John barked, shoving the old man away.

The servant scurried out without averting his face. As the

heavy oak door closed behind him, an ominous silence descended on the bedchamber, broken only by the hiss of the fire in the hearth. Now the girl was alone with John. Years ago, this had been her father's room, every inch of it as familiar to her as the back of her hand. John's alien presence seemed even more threatening in these surroundings.

He stared coldly at her over the rim of the silver chalice as he tilted back his head and drank, the wine gurgling in his throat in time to the bobbing of his prominent Adam's apple. At twenty-one, John still had the look of an adolescent. He was thin and angular, with black eyes, black hair and a black, carefully trimmed beard. He might have been a handsome youth, had it not been for his soft, almost feminine lips, which curved in a suggestion of sensuous cruelty.

John drained the chalice and let it fall to the floor. He continued to stare at her, the light from the candle-stand beside his chair glinting in his eyes, and the girl suddenly wondered if he had intentionally waited for nightfall to confront her.

'Well?' he demanded.

He intended his tone to be intimidating, but his question coincided with an involuntary belch that sent alcohol fumes drifting across to the girl. Her nostrils twitched with disgust, and her disgust rekindled the pride and anger that had first driven her to challenge his authority. This drunken prince who sat so arrogantly in her father's place deserved contempt, not obedience. Her father would not have endured such treatment from any lord. The girl stiffened, drawing on her memory of her father's strength and on her own reserves of courage. Her parents were dead, and as their only child, she carried the burden of the family honour. As she faced John now, she was no longer simply a frightened nineteen-year-old girl; she was Lady Isabelle de Clare, granddaughter of an Irish king, daughter of the Earl of Pembroke and heiress to the richest lands in the kingdom of Henry II.

'I will *not* sign the letter, sire,' Isabelle said hoarsely. 'Sir Ranulf de Barre received Kilkenny Castle from the king's hand to hold for me until my marriage. I cannot order him to surrender it, nor will I request him to do so.' She lifted her head higher and thrust out her chin. 'I know full well that you have been parcelling out my Irish lands as if they were fiefs of your own to give – lands that were entrusted to you as my guardian. If you wish Sir Ranulf to surrender Kilkenny to your man, Meiler fitz Henry, it is the king to whom you must turn. Then we will see, sire, how His Majesty responds to a prince who would steal a ward's inheritance.'

Isabelle's voice had risen in defiance as she spoke, and now her fists were clenched at her sides as she braced herself for John's reaction. Her mind shied away from the thought of a lash tearing at her back, but she stood her ground.

John said nothing. Slumped in his chair, head lolling, he stared at her in silence. Then, quite suddenly, he smiled, and Isabelle felt goose-pimples rise on her arms. It was the smile of a boy who amused himself by tossing cats into an open fire.

Languidly, John wagged his finger at her. 'I know something you don't know,' he sang childishly, and the drunken slurring of his words did nothing to soften the sly cruelty in his voice. 'I know that your treacherous little priest never left this castle.'

John's smile broadened into an evil grin as she gasped.

'What . . . what have you done with him?' she said, unable to suppress the tremor in her voice.

'Done with him?' he grinned. 'Why, nothing. Is it not a crime to harm a priest? Becket taught my father that lesson, did he not? No, when we caught him trying to sneak out last night, we merely persuaded him to stay. Then we *persuaded* him to tell us where he was going – and *why*.' He wagged his finger at her again. 'You shouldn't have done it, you know. Imagine how it hurt me to learn that you tried to send a petition of complaint to the king, accusing me of – what was the word? Ah, *malfeasance*, that's what it was. I'll warrant, the priest put *that* word in your mouth.'

'Where is Father Bertrand?' Isabelle whispered.

John spread his hands in a gesture of innocence. 'I don't know. He seems to have disappeared. No one can find him.'

Isabelle shuddered involuntarily, and tears flooded her eyes. Father Bertrand was more than a confessor to her, he was a friend – one who had agreed without hesitation to carry her petition to the Bishop of Llandaff to present to the king. But they had both thought a priest would be safe, even from John.

'I am the guardian of your person *and* your lands,' John said with renewed harshness, 'and I'll tolerate no interference – from *anyone*. I trust you understand that, milady!' John glared at her and took another draught of wine. 'It was Ranulf de Barre's misguided defiance that put wild thoughts into your head, and if you countersign my order to surrender Kilkenny, I may forgive your impudence. But you must sign *now*.'

The girl swallowed convulsively, tears spilling down her cheeks – weeping not for herself, but for Father Bertrand. She was sure he was dead. Fear, anger and now helpless grief had battered her, and she had to fight for control. But fight she did. John was counting on her weakness – a woman's weakness – to give him what he demanded.

More than ever, she wished she were a man, able to defend her honour and rights with a sword, to avenge Father Bertrand – to strike at John! Yet her only weapon now was defiance. Though pitiful, it was all she had.

She was sure John would not willingly go to the king. He wanted to steal Kilkenny as he had her other lands – quietly, like a thief in the night. And Ranulf de Barre, the bravest and most faithful of her father's old knights would never yield without her consent. The girl had never liked John, nor trusted him, and now she hated him with a fierceness that overcame the icy fear of what he might do to her.

'I will not sign,' she spat, and with a contemptuous toss of her head, turned and started for the door.

Behind her, she heard John's angry snarl become a grunt as he lurched to his feet. He reeled into the candle-stand, knocking it to the floor, plunging the chamber into semi-darkness. Isabelle instinctively bolted for the door, but she was not quick enough. Cursing, John lunged across the room and caught her from behind.

She cried out as he clawed her shoulder and span her around. His face, lit by the flickering orange glow of the fire, glistened with sweat, his features distorted by anger and sudden lust. Before she could pull free, he clamped his hand over her mouth and pressed hard against her, bending her backwards.

'You vixen!' he panted, tightening his grip. 'I'll have your signature *and* my pleasure this night.'

Wrenching his hand from her mouth, he groped wildly for her breast, and her shock was smothered by disgust. Her senses reeled from the smell of him – alcohol, sour sweat and the cloying scent of rosewater. She thrashed desperately in his grip. Her left arm was pinned to her side, but she freed her right arm and drove her fist into his stomach.

John grunted but did not release her, and in her effort to pull away, she lost her balance and fell backwards, with John still clutching her. Her cry of pain as her back hit the floor was cut off as John fell on top of her, crushing the air from her lungs. The shadows dancing across the ceiling were blotted out as he covered her mouth with his.

Isabelle fought like a wild animal, but strangely without fear; she felt only revulsion and white-hot rage. Twisting her face from his and groping for the dagger on his belt, she gasped, 'I'll kill you!'

Panting with exertion and lust, John seized her arms and pinned them to the floor. He rose on his knees for greater leverage, and for an instant Isabelle's legs were free. With all her strength she drove her knee up into his groin.

His mouth flew open in a gasp of paralysing agony. He toppled sideways and rolled on to his back, clutching his groin. Isabelle was on him like a cat. Seizing his head by the hair, she lifted it high, and before he could resist, she slammed it viciously down on to the floor.

The rushes covering the tiles cushioned the blow enough to save John's life, but its force knocked him senseless. Chest heaving, Isabelle looked down at him for several seconds, her face twisted with loathing, while her eyes strayed to the knife at his belt. It would be so easy to kill him . . .

Gradually, her breathing slowed, and she got unsteadily to her feet. Killing John was not worth dying on a gallows. The prince's legs twitched spasmodically. He groaned. Then his breathing deepened and he began to snore. The blow to the head had only speeded what the wine would have accomplished in time. He would not stir until morning.

Isabelle's face was flushed, and her arms and legs trembled from the struggle. She wiped the sweat from her forehead and took a deep breath, astonished that her mind was working coldly and clearly. She knew what she had to do now.

There were barons to whom she could flee for protection,

but not without putting them in jeopardy. Neither could she hope to reach the king, who had not yet returned from France. She needed to buy time for another petition to reach him. What she intended was tantamount to rebellion, and she quailed at the thought. Yet the alternative was begging for John's mercy, and that she would never do.

Hesitantly, she approached the door to the chamber, wondering how much the guard in the passage had heard through the four inches of oak. The pikeman standing three paces from the door came to attention as she slipped out and closed the door behind her. If the man had heard her cry out, he had chosen to ignore it; his face was impassive.

'Prince John's order is that he not be disturbed under any circumstances,' she asserted.

'Aye, milady,' the guard replied.

'Do you know if Fulk le Brun is standing watch tonight?'

'Black Fulk, milady?' the guard said with a laugh. 'He's not on watch, and I should not wonder if he's still gambling with the others in the great hall.'

Isabelle nodded regally and walked away, resisting the urge to hurry. One hour to prepare for the journey, another half-hour for Fulk to bribe or overpower the gatehouse watch. That would give them at least a seven-hour start on pursuers. With luck, she would make it to Milford Haven and out to sea before John could stop her. If she could reach her castle in Kilkenny, she would make her stand there.

Shortly after the dawn, the castellan of Pembroke burst in on John, who was on his knees in the latrine, vomiting. John barely registered the news of Isabelle's escape. Each fresh convulsion sent pounding waves of pain coursing through his head and intensified the agony of his swollen testicles. Only after servants had cleaned him up, changed his clothes and helped him to bed could he begin to think. Then he sent for Roger Poole.

Poole was John's chamberlain, a clever and ambitious man, whom John trusted as much as he did any of his retainers. John's court entourage of young, sycophantic noblemen served to amuse and flatter him, but it was men like Poole, lowborn and totally dependent on his patronage, who did his work for him. Particularly the dirty work.

John shifted on the pillows supporting him in the wide, canopied bed that had been built for the late Earl of Pembroke and took another sip of honeyed wine, trying to wash away the after-taste of vomit that stubbornly lingered in his throat. He disliked the idea of receiving Poole while still in bed, but he was unable to stand without intolerable pain in his groin.

He quelled the anger that surged through him at the thought of what the girl had done to him, concentrating on the problem her escape posed, so that he could instruct Poole immediately. John never allowed his chamberlain to do his thinking for him. He used his men; he did not ask them for advice.

A charge of attempted rape did not worry him, for Isabelle de Clare could prove nothing; he could dismiss her accusations as the wild imaginings of an unstable, hysterical girl. But Ranulf de Barre's unexpected refusal to surrender Kilkenny to Meiler fitz Henry, coupled with the girl's flight, threatened to expose his manoeuvring in Ireland. It was a small threat, but John never took chances.

For nearly a year, he had been quietly ceding control of the de Clare lands in Leinster to willing barons – in return for their secret support of his ambitions. John wanted to be king.

He was the youngest of the four sons Eleanor of Aquitaine had borne Henry II. The two eldest had died, and now only Richard stood between him and the throne. John pursed his lips petulantly. He had done his best with his mother, but she had always favoured Richard, whom she saw as the future King of England.

To bolster Richard's claim as heir apparent, Eleanor had made him Count of Poitou, declaring him heir to the Duchy of Aquitaine, the great fertile region in the South of France which she held in her own right. Richard now ruled Aquitaine with an iron hand, and even John acknowledged that he had proven his capacity to govern.

Richard lacked his father's political finesse and cunning, but he understood the use of power and had the necessary appetite for war. He relished combat and was a skilful, charismatic field commander. Yet his father had no love for him, and his strength inspired Henry's distrust.

Detesting the sweaty, dangerous game of knightly warfare, John had perceived an easier route to power. From his earliest years he had fawned upon his father, earning his love, if not his respect; and John, not Richard, now received the affection the king had once reserved for his eldest son, Henry.

John smiled with satisfaction. His cultivation of his father was slowly but surely bearing fruit. Two years before, the king had installed John as Lord of Ireland, carving out a separate inheritance for him. And ignoring his counsellors, Henry steadfastly refused to declare publicly that Richard was his heir.

Perhaps Henry merely wanted to keep Richard off-balance, for he had never suggested to John that he might try to circumvent the order of succession; but Richard had begun to fear that the king planned to disinherit him, and Richard's fear became John's hope.

It was an open secret that young King Philip of France was trying to drive a wedge between Richard and the king, and if Richard should be seduced into rebellion, the civil war that would ensue might leave John undisputed heir to the throne of England.

When Henry had made his youngest son Lord of Ireland, he had given John what he wanted most: an independent power base. His domain provided the opportunity to subvert greedy barons with unofficial grants of land and promises of more to come, enabling him secretly to build support for an eventual bid for the crown.

Yet John's hopes would come to nothing if his father discovered his ambition; the king would turn from him as he had from Richard. That was the risk the girl's escape presented. Slight as it was, John intended to eliminate the threat. Although physical danger frightened him, he thrived on the risks of intrigue, which stimulated his facile, manipulative mind. When Poole appeared in his chamber, his instructions were ready.

The chamberlain bowed and said drily, 'I take it, sire, that Lady Isabelle refused to sign the letter.'

Poole was a sandy-haired, nondescript man in his thirties, whose unremarkable face and figure rendered him invisible in a crowd.

'How did she escape?' John replied coldly, unamused by Poole's ironic tone.

'The gatehouse watch claims to have been overpowered by one of the late earl's retainers, sire. I was told he is a great hulk of a man, but I suspect that the guards were simply bribed. It would appear that you were too liberal with the girl's allowance. Mind, she has presence of mind,' he added with the barest hint of admiration. 'She even took her hawk with her.'

'Well, she certainly will not try to cut eastward across my own lands,' John said, 'and north is out of the question. The Welsh princes had no love for her father, and she would fetch a hefty ransom. That leaves Milford Haven and the sea. I assume she has bolted for Kilkenny.'

'Or she might cross to Dublin and seek shelter with Lord Meath. He is no friend of yours, sire.'

'Friend or not, he is my vassal. If she has gone to Dublin, she will be no better off than in Kilkenny. Either way, we will have her back. I want you to ride to Milford Haven directly. If she has sailed for Ireland, you will transmit orders to all harbour masters there to seize her should she try to leave again. Send a messenger to Meiler fitz Henry, inform him that the girl may try to slip into Kilkenny and order him to seize her. You will sail for Dublin to see Meath. If she has fled there, bring her back. If the girl has gone to Kilkenny, persuade Meath not to interfere.'

Poole cleared his throat. 'If Meiler storms Kilkenny while Lady Isabelle is there, sire,' he said diffidently, 'she'll be in danger. Shall I caution him?'

'She fled my protection,' John replied stonily. 'The risk is on her own head.'

If Poole disapproved, he gave no sign of it. As always, his eyes were bereft of emotion.

'What tack shall I take with Meath, sire?'

John smiled thinly. 'Simply explain the situation, Poole. The poor girl is obviously deranged and plagued by delusions, one of which appears to be the fear that I'm trying to steal her lands. We will not rest until she is in our custody again – for her own safety and well-being. You will carry two documents for Meath's benefit. The first, a direct order from me to surrender the girl at once if she is in his custody. The second, an order for Meiler fitz Henry to withdraw immediately from Kilkenny. You will show that order to Meath and request him to transmit it on our behalf. That should convince him the girl's fears are groundless.'

'Should the order for Meiler fitz Henry be prepared with or without the confirmation code, sire?'

John allowed himself another smile. 'Without it, of course.'

John's secret orders were always transmitted orally, and the recipient was advised to ignore subsequent orders in writing unless they contained a specific codeword. John had already authorized Meiler fitz Henry to seize Kilkenny, and the rapacious baron would press the siege regardless of the written order to desist, knowing that John would turn a blind eye.

'And if Lord Meath remains unconvinced, sire? He was a good friend of the girl's father.'

John's face hardened. 'I am Meath's liege lord. Remind him of the penalty for treason.'

'I will, sire,' Poole said, bowing and retreating. 'If you will permit, I shall withdraw now and prepare the letters for your signature and seal.'

John nodded and dismissed his chamberlain with a wave. As Poole left, John lay back on his pillows. He sighed and closed his eyes, feeling satisfied that he had the situation in hand. He was sure the girl had fled to Kilkenny. Meiler would subdue the castle, hang Ranulf de Barre and seize the girl. And if the affair came to the king's attention, John's version would be the one he would believe. If necessary, John could make Meiler fitz Henry the scapegoat.

Now that the need for planning was over, he again became aware of the dull ache in his swollen testicles, and he cupped his hand protectively over his groin. 'Bitch,' he muttered viciously. There would be time to take his revenge once the girl was in his custody again – ample time.

Gradually, John's facial muscles slackened, and his lips parted salaciously as he let the possibilities run through his mind. As his imagination took hold, his loins stirred with sadistic anticipation.

4

Isabelle de Clare woke slowly, clinging to sleep, unwilling to leave its refuge. A cock crowed, robbing her of the hope that it was not yet dawn, and she opened her eyes. The soft yellow glow of the all-night candle on the stand beside her bed was already dissolving in the grey light filtering through the translucent cloth window-screens that covered the arrow-slits in the stone walls of her chamber.

As the bells of nearby St Canice Abbey tolled *prime*, she rolled on to her side and pulled the fur-lined down coverlet tightly about her, wishing she were in her own bed, safe and secure as she had been as a child, with nothing to fear from the day. These moments just after waking were the worst, and she knew she should rise at once to face the morning, but still she lingered under the covers, wishing, wishing . . .

The heavy oak door to her chamber swung open, and Matilda, her lady-in-waiting, swept in, carrying a basin of steaming water, a towel and Isabelle's chemise and stockings. 'Good morning, milady,' she said, depositing the basin and towel on a small trestle-table beneath the arrow-slit which caught the first rays of the sun.

'Morning, Mattie,' Isabelle said huskily, not quite able to match the older woman's brisk, cheerful tone.

Already the sounds of the castle coming to life were drifting up from the courtyard. A barking dog had started the chickens and geese squawking and honking, and now a medley of human sounds added to the noise. She heard the groan of splitting firewood; the castle's marshal raining down curses on his varlets, who were bringing the horses out of the stables for exercise; the ringing of the armourer's hammer on the anvil . . . The day was upon her.

Matilda came over to the bed, and for a moment Isabelle thought she meant to chide her again for sleeping without the bed curtains drawn. Instead, Matilda bent down and kissed her on the forehead – something she had not done for many years.

Matilda, the spinster daughter of a landed knight, had been the one constant in Isabelle's life for as long as she could remember. As Matilda had grown older, she had taken to hiding her grey hair under a wimple, instead of letting her once-dark braids of hair hang free. That ruse apart, it seemed as if she had always looked as she did now: a short, plump woman with a soft, well-scrubbed, smiling face.

Matilda laid the chemise and stockings on the coverlet at the foot of the bed. 'Put these on now,' she said. 'I warmed them by the fire in the hall just before I came up.'

Isabelle managed a wry smile. 'What did the men think of that?'

'Those Welsh ruffians?' Matilda sniffed. 'Not a thing. They've all just stood down from the second watch and are already snoring, dead to the world. God, what a noise!'

With that, Matilda bustled out of the chamber, and Isabelle rose from the bed and hurriedly slipped the linen chemise over her head, grateful for the warmth that still clung to it. She pulled on the white, woollen stockings, fastened them with ribbons sewn in above the knees, and pushed her feet into a pair of soft leather slippers which were dyed scarlet and lined with felt.

Spring was slow in coming, and the night had been cold. Goose-pimples rose on her bare arms. For once, she missed the service of a full complement of maids to help her dress. The sheer frivolousness of the thought brought a brief smile to her lips. Her situation could not be so desperate if she could still be distracted by a chill in the air.

Shivering, she reached for her pelisse hanging on a pole projecting from the wall beside the bed. It was a white, ankle-length gown of fine wool, trimmed with ermine and lined with squirrel fur covered by silk. As she pulled it over her head, its slit neckline allowed her to slip her arms into the long, tight-fitting sleeves.

She closed the neck-slit with a gold brooch and walked to the water basin, her feet rustling in the fresh rushes carpeting the floor. Her falcon was stirring on its wall perch, and she talked to the bird as she washed, the meaningless chatter helping her to shut away the fear that assaulted her afresh each morning.

The pelisse had warmed her, and she was no longer shivering. She carefully dried her hands and face to avoid the chapping that plagued her and moved aside the window-screen. The falcon spread its wings and flapped restlessly, demanding attention, the tiny silver bells attached to its legs tinkling softly.

Isabelle checked that the cup attached to the perch still held water and added the hawk's morning dose of medicine for the moulting season. Now that she had washed her hands, she permitted herself to stroke the bird. Like others of her class, she was fastidious about personal cleanliness, but when it came to handling a prized falcon, cleanliness became a fetish.

The sunlight streaming in through the arrow-slit threw a bright yellow rectangle against the opposite wall. Her chamber occupied half the area on the top floor of the frontier castle's three-tier rectangular stone keep. It was a bare room, devoid of wall hangings or any other adornment, and furnished only with the canopied bed, a folding stool with canvas seat and two ironbound chests containing her clothes and jewels. The bare, rough-hewn wooden beams above supported the conical wooden roof and fighting platform on the tower's battlements.

Isabelle was unaffected by the stark aspect of the tower's interior. As her eyes swept over the well-laid stonework, she felt only satisfaction and pride in her father. Many of the frontier castles in Ireland could boast only a wooden tower, and few of the stone towers had walls as thick as these. This cold, cheerless keep had not been built for a woman's taste or comfort; it was a fighting-man's citadel, and without its strength she would not have dared risk her men's lives in what she knew was a desperate gamble.

Through the arrow-slit she could see the river and virgin pine forest stretching limitlessly into the distance, and she imagined herself on the parapet, able to look in all directions. Her father's lands stretched beyond the horizons – lands won by his courage and daring, as well as by the loyalty and blood of the handful of Normans from the Marches of South Wales who had followed him. As a child, she had listened in awe to the story of his conquests in Ireland, and she recalled it now, drawing from it a heightened awareness of her responsibility and the resolution to shoulder it.

Her father, Earl Richard de Clare, had married the daughter of the Irish King of Leinster, and when the earl died, Leinster became Isabelle's legacy. Prince John, her guardian, should have held her lands in trust for the sons she would one day bear, and his betrayal of that trust left her no choice but to fight as best she could for her rights and the rights of her unborn sons. That had been her father's way, and she knew no other. Her mother had died in childbirth, and the bond between the earl and Isabelle, his only child, had been far stronger than it might have been otherwise. Though her father had died when she was quite young, she felt his influence still. His face had long since blurred in her recollection, but she remembered his gentle voice and delicate, almost feminine hands, which seemed so remarkable in a warrior. Even as a child she had guessed that her father would have wished for a son to carry his name and defend his legacy. But the earl had never hinted he regretted Isabelle, and she had loved him all the more for it.

Isabelle heard Matilda ascending the stone stairway, and with a pang of childish guilt she realized she had forgotten to use the twig of green wood Matilda had placed beside the washbasin. Quickly, she fetched the twig and began rubbing the freshly cut, pulpy end of the stick over her teeth, grimacing as she worked it into her gums. It would not matter to Matilda that they lay under siege; teeth had to be polished.

Matilda entered the room, carrying a goblet of spiced wine and a small round loaf of bread on a silver tray, and Isabelle smiled inwardly. She had expressly forbidden Matilda to pack anything that was not strictly necessary, but she had forgotten that to Matilda certain domestic rituals were indeed essential.

Once again Matilda conveyed her disgust at the lack of furniture by making a show of looking for a place on which to set the tray. She sighed pointedly and finally deposited it on the bed. 'I'll fix your hair while you have breakfast,' she said, extracting a brush, comb and coils of silver thread from a cloth bag that hung from the girdle about her waist.

Isabelle obediently came to the bed and sat down. She was too nervous to be hungry, but she was always thirsty in the morning. She picked up the cup and sipped the wine slowly, as she'd been taught. Had she been alone, she would have gulped it down like a man.

'Mulled wine is just the thing for you,' Matilda said, as she had nearly every morning for as long as Isabelle could remember. 'It puts colour in your cheeks and sweetens your breath. Now have some bread, milady. You never eat enough bread in the morning.'

Isabelle winced as Matilda combed out a tangle in her hair, which hung down to her waist, but the old woman ignored her protest. When she had combed Isabelle's hair to her satisfaction, she began plaiting it into two thick braids, weaving in the silver thread.

'Oh, Mattie,' Isabelle sighed. 'You never stop trying to improve on nature. You can embroider rough cloth to your heart's content, and all you'll get is gaudy homespun.'

'Don't talk nonsense, child,' Matilda said sharply, then continued in a gentler tone. 'You're more beautiful than you know. I don't know why you listen to those bleating trou-vères. Most of them are effeminate. Do you actually believe that men only have eyes for pallid blondes with flat bosoms and tiny, pouting mouths?'

Isabelle was about to reply when she caught the faint ringing of axe blades biting into tree trunks somewhere in the distance. She stiffened and cocked her head. In other circumstances it would have been an innocuous sound, but not now – not to the defenders of a castle under siege.

'Finish quickly, Mattie,' she said tensely. 'It's time I made my appearance; Ranulf will be expecting me.'

'Patience, milady. It takes time to do this just right.'

'Then never mind the thread,' Isabelle said, starting to rise. 'I'll . . .'

Matilda gripped Isabelle's shoulder firmly and forced her back on to the bed. 'A few minutes longer will make no difference, milady, and it is important that you carry yourself with decorum, no matter how you feel. That is what Sir

Ranulf and the men expect of you; it's what they need. You know that better than I.'

Isabelle shifted restlessly, but then nodded, acquiescing. 'You're right,' she muttered.

'Of course,' Matilda replied in a matter-of-fact tone. 'I'm almost finished anyway. Your hair is like burnished copper, and silver is just the thing to set it off.'

Matilda tied off the braids with a pair of scarlet ribbons, went to the chest at the foot of the bed and took out a flowing *bliaut* of scarlet silk, with wide, trailing sleeves. Isabelle slipped it on over the pelisse, and Matilda tightened the laces which drew the *bliaut* in at the waist, emphasizing the figure, and she added a girdle of silver rope, tied in front with one end hanging down to the floor.

Matilda took Isabelle's white, fur-lined cape from the wall pole, draped it over her shoulders, fastening the gold clasp chain and making final adjustments to ensure the cape and *bliaut* hung correctly. The final touch was a delicate silver headband.

'How do I look, Mattie?' Isabelle asked.

'Like the great lady you are,' Matilda answered with a nod of encouragement.

Lady Isabelle de Clare took a deep breath, raised herself to her full height, and went out to greet her men.

Ranulf de Barre slowly paced the inner fighting platform of the wooden palisade surrounding the castle courtyard, trying to relieve the early-morning stiffness in his joints. He envied the young men who had come on watch with him for their freedom of movement, which they took for granted. The air was still, crisp and clear. Once, he would have found its chill invigorating, but Ranulf was feeling his age.

The old knight looked towards the distant camp of their enemy, Meiler fitz Henry. The castle had been built on a promontory rising above the forest and jutting out into the river far below, beside which lay the village of Kilkenny. The villagers had recently cut a fresh clearing out of the forest beyond the marshland bordering the river, and it was in this field that the warlord had established his camp.

The camp was more than half a league away, but Ranulf could see enough to know that time was working against him.

The tents dotting the clearing grew more numerous each day, as Meiler's recruiting efforts added to his force, and apparently an engineer had arrived. In the centre of the camp, work crews were hewing tree trunks into heavy timbers with the obvious intention of constructing a trebuchet – a simple but effective siege catapult.

Meiler fitz Henry had not expected resistance when he came down from the north to take Kilkenny with only a token force, but when Ranulf refused to surrender the castle, he lost no time preparing a siege. His force now numbered at least two hundred. Excluding the castle's varlets, Ranulf could muster only thirty fighting men, but fifteen of those were Welsh archers, handpicked masters of the longbow, and until the trebuchet was built, Ranulf had no fear of a daylight assault.

The old frontier castle did not conform to the standard motte-and-bailey design. Its stone tower keep and wooden outbuildings were surrounded by a single wooden palisade, and it was protected on three sides by the sheer cliffs dropping down to the river, allowing the defenders to concentrate on the forward wall. To reach the wall, attackers had to cross a deep dry moat, and the long, steep slope leading up to the castle from the forest was devoid of cover. Ranulf's archers could cut an attack force to pieces before it could scale the palisade.

But a night attack would be more dangerous, and soon Meiler would have his trebuchet. Already woodsmen were felling trees to clear a track through the forest so that the catapult could be hauled from the camp to the base of the slope before the castle. Ranulf had no doubt that the old wooden stockade could be breached, and when that happened, they would be forced back into the stone tower . . .

'You look concerned, Ranulf.'

The old knight started. 'You should wear bells, Rusty!' he snapped, turning towards Isabelle. 'You're as quiet as a cat.'

'Concerned *and* ill-tempered,' she said with a slight, nervous smile.

Ranulf reddened. 'I'm sorry, milady,' he said, remembering his place. His voice grated harshly; like many knights who survived to his age, he had ruined his vocal cords in battle.

Ranulf had pledged to serve Isabelle de Clare as faithfully as he had her father, but sometimes he forgot that she was no longer the mischievous little girl who had fled to him so often for protection against a tutor's wrath. She had a quick mind, but as a child she had preferred mock-swordplay with her father's pages to her tutors' lessons.

Yet only he could still think of her as a child, Ranulf reflected as he looked at the striking young woman beside him. The copper hair, the freckles and the impish, turned-up nose were the same, but the thin tomboy was no more. As she looked at him, the seriousness in her green eyes was not a child's gravity, but an adult's grim understanding.

'Well?' she prompted, her voice husky like her father's.

Ranulf glanced about to be sure none of his men was within earshot, but the nearest of them had tactfully moved away. In the confines of a castle, privacy was as cherished as it was difficult to obtain.

'It appears Meiler is building a trebuchet.'

'I know.'

'Well, that gives us two or three weeks before he forces us back into the tower. The well in the keep is reliable enough, so we can probably hold out for months. But Meiler will make life unbearable for us in there, and even if he fails to undermine the walls, scurvy will eventually drive us out. He's restricting our options, milady.'

Isabelle looked towards the enemy camp, and her tongue flicked out to moisten her lips, a nervous mannerism she had inherited from her mother. Her parents' blood was evenly mixed in their only child, Ranulf thought, in her emotional makeup as well as in her appearance.

'Is there no word from Meath?' she asked needlessly.

Ranulf shook his head. 'Even if the messenger got through, it's too soon to expect a response.'

For a moment Isabelle continued to stare out at Meiler's camp, unconsciously biting her lower lip, but then her expression hardened. 'I won't surrender Kilkenny without a fight.'

'I'm not suggesting surrender, milady,' Ranulf said carefully, 'but *you* could still slip away and try to get through to Meath. Meiler hasn't invested the castle because he knows there will be no relief force, but once he discovers your presence here, or drives us into the tower, you'll be trapped.'

Isabelle shook her head sharply. 'No. By now, John has undoubtedly guessed my whereabouts, and he will have his agents out in force. If our courier can't get through, what chance have I? When John intercepted my petition, we lost the first bout, but we may still win. If our message reaches Lord Meath, he will surely bring our case before the king. And even if our man has failed, we must resist here as long as we can. Word of the siege is bound to spread; sooner or later Meath will hear of it.'

Ranulf shifted uneasily, unsure of how to respond. Isabelle knew her own mind, and he could not argue with her reasoning, but Ranulf could not be so cold-blooded about it. At all costs, he wanted her out of harm's way.

When he had decided not to yield Kilkenny, he had known he and his men could pay with their lives, but he was determined to force John's theft of Isabelle's lands into the open. It had never occurred to him that Isabelle might flee Pembroke and join him, and he had been horrified when she appeared without warning and slipped into the castle. Only the guilt he felt for drawing her into danger had prevented him from scolding her.

If something went wrong and they were overrun before they could establish themselves in the keep, Meiler might lose control of his undisciplined Irish auxiliaries. Ranulf had seen men flushed with victory and blood lust run amok . . . No, she could not stay. He should have sent her north days ago, as soon as she had recovered from her flight from Wales.

He made up his mind and was about to speak when a cry from the watchman on the tower's battlements distracted him. A small party of horsemen was emerging from the forest at the base of the slope before the castle. Meiler fitz Henry, mounted on a richly caparisoned coal-black charger, led the way, followed by his knights and their squires. Beside Meiler rode his standard-bearer, carrying Meiler's saffron banner emblazoned with a black falcon.

'Christ's thorns!' Ranulf exclaimed. 'They're dressed as if for a tournament.'

Meiler's knights were also mounted on their chargers, which were draped with bright ceremonial caparisons. Their jewel-studded reins and saddles sparkled in the sunlight, and their shields gleamed with new paint.

It was Isabelle who guessed the implications. 'I think this is for my benefit,' she said softly. 'Meiler must have heard from John. He knows I'm here.'

Ranulf hastily moved to screen her from view. 'He cannot be sure,' he said urgently. 'If he doesn't see you . . .'

'It's of no importance, Ranulf,' she interrupted, grasping his rough hand. She smiled slightly and shook her head. 'Did you really think I could leave you to fight my battle, old friend?'

Her voice was steady, and Ranulf realized he had underestimated the tenacity of his young mistress. Face to face with her enemy, Isabelle was truly her father's daughter.

Although the watchman had not sounded the alarm, the men off watch were running to join the archers on the wall, who had unslung their bows and were selecting the straightest arrows from their quivers. But in the courtyard below, the blacksmith continued his hammering, and the marshal yelled at his varlets to carry on with their work.

Ranulf grunted sourly as Meiler reined in his horse just out of bowshot and his men fanned out behind him. 'Just a little closer, you great ox,' Ranulf muttered, 'and we'll skewer you.'

'You in the castle!' cried Meiler's standard bearer, his voice carrying clearly up to the stockade. 'My lord, Sir Meiler, salutes Lady Isabelle and begs to know why she resists the command of her guardian, Prince John, to surrender custody of Kilkenny.'

Isabelle compressed her lips and stepped past Ranulf so that she was clearly visible to the eyes below. 'Cannot your lord speak for himself?' she called out. 'Would the words choke him?'

Ranulf grinned, wishing he could see the expression on Meiler's face. The Marcher lord would not relish being goaded by a woman in front of his men. But to Ranulf's surprise, Meiler kept his temper. 'If Your Ladyship grants me leave to approach,' Meiler called, 'we may yet settle our differences in a peaceful manner.'

'Come forward if you wish, Sir Meiler,' Isabelle responded without consulting Ranulf.

As Meiler spurred his charger up the slope, Ranulf called to his archers. 'No man discharges his bow without my command!' Then he lowered his voice and grumbled, 'A parley will gain us nothing, milady.'

'I know,' Isabelle said calmly, managing a smile, 'but I haven't seen him since I was a child. I'm curious to know if he's really as ugly as I remember him.'

Meiler fitz Henry was a burly knight, and his saddle creaked under his weight as he reined in his stallion at the edge of the moat. Ugly was too strong a word, but there was little charm in his swarthy, beetle-browed face. His neck was short, and black curls of oily hair poked from beneath his mail coif.

'Your Ladyship,' Meiler said, bowing his head formally. 'I bid you good morrow.'

'Sir Meiler,' Isabelle responded coldly, 'you trespass on my father's land.'

'Not so, your ladyship. I have orders from Prince John entrusting Kilkenny to my protection. When I arrived ten days ago to fulfil my duty, the former castellan, who stands beside you, unlawfully denied me entry.'

'Your order, Sir Meiler,' Isabelle replied haughtily, 'is but one of several my guardian has issued in the past year. He has been parcelling out my father's lands as if they were his own. But I will no longer tolerate it.'

'That is not your prerogative, Lady Isabelle!' Meiler snapped. 'You are the prince's ward until you marry. By law and custom, it is your guardian who decides how best to safeguard your inheritance.'

'A responsibility for which he has shown little regard!' Isabelle retorted. 'I am not a fool to be despoiled so easily. My father fought for these lands, and if my guardian will not defend them, then I have no alternative but to defend them myself. I will not surrender Kilkenny until the king hears my petition and decides on the justice of my grievance.'

'*John* is Lord of Ireland,' Meiler responded, 'not Henry. Prince John is my liege lord, as he is yours, and he has commanded the surrender of Kilkenny to me.'

'And we dispute the lawfulness of the command,' Ranulf interjected harshly. 'The king is the final arbiter in all his dominions, and we will not yield Kilkenny until the case is heard in a royal court.'

Meiler's thick eyebrows rose, and Ranulf had the uncomfortable feeling that he had been waiting for just those words. What was the blackguard up to?

'The king is in France and we are here, Sir Ranulf,' Meiler said with a self-satisfied smile. 'Yet I have no wish to deny Lady Isabelle the justice she seeks.' He paused and his smile widened into a gap-toothed grin. 'You are her knight. Let us put her case before the highest arbiter of all. Meet me now in single combat as her champion, and let God decide the outcome.'

So that's his strategy, Ranulf thought: humiliate me in front of my men and draw me into single combat for an easy victory. Ranulf smiled. It was a feeble ploy, but as close to wit as Meiler could come.

Isabelle did not take it so lightly. Ranulf heard her sharp intake of breath. 'Oh, *gallant* knight,' she said with heavy irony. 'How bravely you choose an opponent. But are you sure his beard is grey enough?'

Meiler ignored the jibe. 'What do *you* say, Sir Ranulf,' he sneered. 'Do you have the courage to defend your lady's claim to this castle?'

'Gently, Rusty,' Ranulf said quietly as Isabelle clenched her fists in fury. 'I cannot be drawn so easily. He dishonours no one but himself.'

'Well, Sir Ranulf?' Meiler shouted. 'Do you accept my challenge, or do you shrink from defending the justice of your lady's cause?'

There was total silence on the wall as Ranulf's men tensely awaited his response, and Ranulf let the silence linger. 'Not today,' he said at last in an offhand manner. 'The stiffness in my joints ails me.'

At that, a pikeman on the far end of the stockade wall snorted, and the tension dissolved in general laughter. Meiler flushed darkly.

'Your mockery is born of cowardice, Sir Ranulf! Not this day, you said. Then I will return on the morrow to repeat my challenge, and thereafter for two days. Then I will waste no more breath, and we shall take this castle by storm. Meanwhile, let your men reflect on the lack of courage of the knight who leads them!'

Meiler tugged on his reins to turn away, but Ranulf was in no mood to let him go so easily.

'A moment, Sir Meiler!' Ranulf cried. 'I have a question to put to you!'

Ranulf barked an order in Welsh, and his archers drew their longbows.

'My question is this,' Ranulf grated. 'How do you expect to get back down the hill?'

Meiler looked up in confusion at the fifteen steel-tipped shafts trained on his heart, and paled. 'What treachery is this?' he yelled, the anger in his voice failing to mask his sudden fear.

'Treachery?' Isabelle said innocently, picking up her cue. 'I gave you permission to approach if *you* wished so. I did not guarantee your safe return. Neither you nor your men carry a flag of truce.'

'That was understood!' Meiler burst out, hastily lifting his shield. But he knew it was no protection; a longbow shaft at close range could penetrate four inches of solid oak.

Isabelle gave him an insincerely sweet smile. 'In the interest of sport, we will allow you a start. Your horse appears swift; perhaps he can carry you to safety. But leave quickly, Sir Meiler,' she advised sharply. 'I would go now!'

With an animal snarl, Meiler wheeled his horse about and dug in his spurs. Ranulf signalled his archers to stand down. Instead of arrows, the men sent whistles and catcalls after the fleeing knight.

Ranulf laughed along with the rest, but it was gallows humour. If Kilkenny fell, he could expect no mercy from Meiler fitz Henry.

5

Ranulf de Barre cursed the rain. Without moonlight the darkness enveloping the stockade was impenetrable, and the tattoo of wind-driven raindrops on the heavy canvas hood of his rain cloak was loud in his ears. If the scum had any imagination, Ranulf thought grimly, they would come now, under cover of the storm, when his archers would be least effective.

He had been standing very still, staring out into the darkness, listening – straining to detect that first tell-tale clink of metal on metal, or the snort of a horse – but now he had to move, lest his arthritic joints lock. The old knight grunted with pain as he forced his body into motion.

The silent castle was all but blacked out. The bright night-combat torches would not be lit unless the enemy attacked, and the standard torches burning on the outer wall cast little light into the castle's interior. Ranulf had to feel his way along the stockade's fighting platform.

His shoulder and chest muscles were tiring under the weight of his hauberk. There had been a time when he could have worn armour for sixteen hours without fatigue, but no longer. Had it been a day watch, he could have laid aside his armour, but a night attack could come with little warning.

He had ordered his men to sleep in their fighting armour, their swords girded and their longbows strung. They would be stretched out and snoring by now, warm and dry in the great hall of the keep. They were young men and needed sleep more than he. Fulk le Brun, another old veteran, was standing the tower watch. Ranulf looked back up at the stone tower at the rear of the castle courtyard, but despite its whitewashed walls, the keep was only visible as an ill-defined mass merging with the night.

Ranulf stiffened as he picked up the sound of a horse's iron-shod hooves clattering over a granite outcropping that cut across the open slope just below the moat surrounding the stockade wall. 'Horseman coming!' cried Fulk from the parapet of the keep.

'Hello in the castle!' called the approaching rider. He did not shout, but his voice was clearly audible, a resonant baritone that carried through the wind and rain.

Ranulf peered in the direction of the voice and made out the shadowy form of a horse and rider on the very edge of the moat, barely illuminated by the flickering torch above the main gate.

'Who is there?' Ranulf challenged.

'I am called William Marshal. I ask for shelter and rest within your walls.'

That drew a laugh from the old warrior. 'God's blood, man, don't you know we're under siege? We need fighters, not guests.'

'I must speak with the castellan, Ranulf de Barre. I have come far to see him.'

Ranulf frowned. He couldn't place the stranger's name, but he had heard it somewhere. '*What* are you? A trouvère? A messenger? What?' he demanded, his eyes restlessly sweeping the darkness. He had not forgotten the enemy.

'I am a free knight, recently returned from the Holy Land.'

Ranulf's frown deepened, and he held his breath, listening. If this was a diversion, it was an odd one. The stranger was not one of Meiler fitz Henry's cronies, for although he spoke with an Anglo-Norman accent, his grammar had the polish of the Continent. Perhaps he was a mercenary in Meiler's pay.

'A knight? Travelling alone, without even a squire? State your business or be off.'

'I will speak with Ranulf de Barre.'

'You are speaking to him now,' Ranulf growled.

'I have much to tell you,' replied the stranger. 'But I will not talk sitting on my horse in the rain.'

The undertone of aggressive self-assurance beneath the

fatigue in the stranger's voice was unmistakeable. He was either a knight, as he claimed, or a consummate actor.

Then Ranulf remembered where he had heard the stranger's name. 'I saw a knight called William Marshal fight in the great tournament at Joigni ten years ago,' Ranulf called out. 'Are you that knight?'

'That was a long time ago. I may have been at Joigni.'

Ranulf felt the tug of professional curiosity. The knight Ranulf had watched that day had been the best man with a sword and lance he had ever seen. Had not Marshal ridden with Prince Henry? Once, years afterwards, he had heard Marshal's name again. There had been a scandal involving young Henry's wife . . .

Ranulf grimaced sourly at his wool-gathering. 'I wouldn't open our gate to Christ Himself this night,' he shouted. 'You found your way up here from the village. Find your way back and seek shelter there.'

The stranger did not reply. The gusting rain dimmed the torch, obscuring the horse and rider, and for a moment Ranulf thought the knight had gone.

'Your son is dead, Sir Ranulf,' said the stranger out of the darkness. 'I have brought you his sword.'

The torch above the sally port in the stockade's eastern wall had been lighted, and it hissed and sputtered in the downpour. Ranulf's fingers curled around the trigger-lever of his crossbow as the stranger, mounted on a palfrey and leading a charger and packhorse, rode through the narrow gateway into the torchlight. The knight was shrouded in a black rain cloak, but his chain-mail leggings were visible. He was a big man, built for combat, and he was fully armed.

'Welcome to Kilkenny Castle,' Ranulf grated. 'I am Ranulf de Barre.' There was no cordiality in his voice, and the crossbow was aimed at the stranger's chest.

'William Marshal,' the knight responded.

Ranulf's squire stepped forward to take the palfrey's reins, and the two archers Ranulf had woken to cover the entrance heaved the timbers barring the sally port back into place.

'Help me with my shield, lad,' Marshal said to the squire, and as the boy took the shield Ranulf saw that Marshal's left forearm was in a splint. 'Broke my wrist getting off the boat in Waterford,' Marshal said. 'Damned gangplank was rotten.'

With a tired grunt, Marshal dismounted, and the short leather boots he wore over his chain mail sank a full two inches into the mud. Ranulf was above average height, but Marshal towered over him. Two hundred and thirty pounds with his armour on, Ranulf estimated, and from the look of him, not an ounce of fat.

Now Ranulf was sure this was the knight he had seen at Joigni; even after ten years he remembered him. Marshal had beaten ten of the best knights on the field that day and, broken wrist or not, he was dangerous.

Marshal pushed back his hood and approached Ranulf, careful to stop just out of arm's reach of the crossbow. 'My manservant broke his shoulder,' Marshal said, 'and I had to leave him behind.'

It was a long trip up from Waterford, and fatigue etched Marshal's face; that much of his story was consistent, Ranulf noted. Although closely trimmed beards were in fashion, Marshal was clean-shaven, and that, too, fitted. Beards inside a helmet could become intolerable in the desert heat, and many returning pilgrim knights retained the habit of shaving.

'I suppose you have a right to be cautious,' Marshal said, pointedly eyeing the crossbow.

Ranulf nodded grimly. 'I learned of my son's death two months past. Meiler fitz Henry may have heard the news as well, and he's fond of tricks.'

'Perhaps,' Marshal said tiredly. 'I don't know him.'

Marshal had a high forehead and a broken nose that gave him a hawkish profile. His deepset brown eyes, glinting in the torchlight, were framed by projecting eyebrows and prominent cheekbones. His was a hard face that fatigue could not soften.

But Ranulf detected neither guile nor cruelty in his expression. They left their stamp, and Ranulf had lived too long to be easily fooled. Women remained a mystery to him, but men he knew.

'You may have my sword, if you wish,' Marshal offered. 'Crossbows make me nervous.'

Ranulf did not believe the last statement, for he suspected that to a man like Marshal, nervousness was merely a word.

But the offer of the sword removed the last of his doubts. 'That won't be necessary,' he said, lowering the crossbow and disarming it.

'Jean,' Ranulf said to his squire, 'see that Sir William's horses are cared for, then attend us in the great hall. We will want food and drink. Griff, Peter – take my watch on the wall.'

Marshal shivered as he followed Ranulf de Barre up the steps of the wooden platform before the keep and across the drawbridge to the raised entrance. The fatigue of the long, damp ride was catching up with him. Ranulf pushed open the massive oak door, and they entered the smoky gloom of the tower's great hall.

Two mastiffs rose from their place by the open fire and trotted across the hall to investigate the stranger. 'They're good dogs,' Ranulf said. 'Between them, they can take down a boar.'

Marshal nodded absently, a strange sense of having been here before gripping him as he stepped across the threshold. Although many of the keeps the Normans had built throughout Britain in a century of occupation were similar, no two were completely alike. Yet something in the stark architecture of this tower evoked lost memories. The keep seemed hauntingly familiar, filling Marshal with an uneasiness he could not fathom.

Shrugging off the feeling, he walked towards the warmth of the fire. The tower's builder had designed a strong keep, but a primitive one, and the ventilation holes above the open hearth were barely effective. Much of the smoke drifted up to the blackened rafters, where it collected in a thick cloud and eddied out through the arrow-slits of the overhead gallery. Mingling with the acrid woodsmoke was the pungent scent of unwashed bodies. Ranulf's men lay snoring on straw pallets in the shadows, apparently undisturbed by the knights' entrance.

Ranulf came over to the fire, walking on bandy legs bowed from too many years in the saddle. Eustace had borne little resemblance to his father, Marshal noted. Ranulf was a barrel-chested man, with thick shoulders, and age had only toughened his leathery grey-bearded face.

'How did you get past Meiler's pickets?' Ranulf asked in his harsh, gravelly voice.

'I paid a villager to guide me. He took me up to the forest line along an old, overgrown track. If your enemy has pickets out, they are stretched thinly. I take it he doesn't anticipate a relief force soon.'

'There will be no relief,' Ranulf said curtly.

Marshal raised an eyebrow and looked about him, probing the hall's dark recesses. 'Two men on the wall,' he said quietly, 'one on the parapet and these men in here. A lean defence.'

'We can hold.'

For the time being, perhaps, Marshal thought, curiously eyeing the tough, grizzled castellan. What kind of fight had he ridden into? He was unfamiliar with the local dialect, and he had learned very little from the villagers. The rainstorm had given him the chance to slip into the castle, but getting out might be another matter.

According to Eustace, Ranulf held Kilkenny from the king, which made a siege impossible to understand. And why did Ranulf de Barre expect no relief?

'Just what claim does this Meiler fitz Henry have to Kilkenny?' Marshal asked.

'Your courage does you credit,' Ranulf replied. 'Not many men would ride into the middle of a siege they knew nothing about.'

Marshal waited for Ranulf to respond to his question, but the old knight remained silent. Marshal blinked wearily; he was exhausted, his broken wrist was throbbing, and he was in no mood for verbal fencing. Perhaps Ranulf still did not trust him.

'I told you why I came,' Marshal said, drawing the sword slung from his waist and extending it hilt-first to Ranulf. The blade, gleaming orange in the firelight, was deeply dented and chipped along both edges. 'This was your son's,' he said. 'He used it to save my life.'

Marshal had handled the sword countless times in the ten months of his journey back from the Holy Land, but as he looked at it now, the memories came flooding back with remorseless clarity. He should have found a way to shield

Eustace from the madness of that day. The lad had not been ready. He should have found a way . . .

Ranulf stared in silence at the sword for a moment before he took it, and his shoulders slumped, as if suddenly burdened by a great weight. Ranulf had said he knew his son was dead, but perhaps until now Eustace's death had been an abstraction.

'I gave this sword to Eustace,' Ranulf said hoarsely. 'Just before he left Ireland. A man is supposed to be proud when a son dies bravely, but pride cannot vanquish grief.'

Marshal remained silent. What was there to say? He had no experience of the love between a father and son.

'You knew him well?' Ranulf asked.

Marshal nodded. 'He was my squire, but he died a knight, Sir Ranulf. I knighted him myself before our last battle.'

Something like a sigh escaped the old knight. 'So he had that, at least. He wanted it so much. Not every man is born for battle, and I tried to tell him . . .'

Ranulf took a deep breath and drew himself erect. 'Where is that squire of mine?' he growled. 'I know you're tired, Sir William. Food and rest are what you need; we can talk tomorrow.'

'I'm not too tired to talk,' Marshal lied.

'Are you sure?'

Marshal saw the desire in Ranulf's eyes, and he nodded.

'Then we will talk,' Ranulf said. 'There is much I'd like to know.'

The fire in the great hall had burned low, and Marshal rose to add fresh wood. One of Ranulf's dogs lifted his head, yawned and went back to sleep. Tending fires was servants' work, but this garrison was of fighting men only, and Ranulf's squire, who had attended them, had gone off to dry and polish Marshal's chain mail before it rusted. Marshal staggered as dizziness swept over him, and he cursed silently. Wine always affected him when he was tired, and he knew he would pay for his indulgence in the morning.

Ranulf's squire had helped the two knights free themselves of their hauberks and had brought them bread, wine and a bowl of congealed, warmed-over stew. Not bothering to have a trestle-table set up, they had piled straw before the fire and sat on the floor. Clad in their tunics and linen breeches, with mantles draped over their shoulders to keep the chill off their backs, they had eaten their fill and fed the rest to the dogs.

The flat, round bread loaves had been stale, and the spice in the stew barely disguised the flavour of the nameless boiled meat, but Marshal had not cared. Even court life in France, where he had feasted on the finest foods available, had not refined his palate. For Marshal, food was little more than the placation of hunger.

Marshal tossed a log on to the embers, and the fire crackled back to life, spraying sparks. Ranulf, who had been sitting for a long time in silence, staring at the fire, looked up, his sorrow masked behind flinty eyes.

'I thank you for coming here,' he said. 'I'm in your debt.'

Marshal sat down heavily. His eyes stung from the smoke and the need for sleep. 'The debt was mine,' he said, finding the words hopelessly inadequate. Eustace had not simply saved his life; the boy had died in Marshal's place, fighting in a battle in which he should have taken no part.

'Maybe,' Ranulf said. 'But not every man would have ventured so far out of his way.'

Marshal shook his head, but he let it pass. Ranulf poured fresh wine into the cup they shared, drank some, then passed it over. He had been drinking steadily, but without apparent effect. The wine had eased the throbbing in Marshal's wrist, but already he felt the onset of a headache.

'I'd assumed until now that Eustace was killed with all the others at Hattin,' Ranulf said. 'Christ's blood, what a disaster! It's still hard to believe it could happen.'

Marshal nodded grimly and looked into the fire. One month after he had left Palestine, the Grand Master and Guy de Lusignan, King of Jerusalem, had led the kingdom's army into an obvious trap before the Horns of Hattin, ten miles from where de Maille and his men had been wiped out. Saladin had anihilated the Christian army of ninety thousand men in a cataclysmic two-day battle, and shortly afterwards had taken Jerusalem.

Marshal took a token sip of wine and set the cup down. I should have killed the bastard, he thought bitterly.

'What are your plans now?' Ranulf asked.

'Before I left for the Holy Land, I promised the king I

would return to his service. From here, I'll go directly to his court,' Marshal answered with a sense of detachment.

For him, the future was a blank. He still felt suspended in an emotional limbo somewhere between Palestine and the homeland to which he had returned. The short time he had spent on the family estates in England before crossing to Ireland had not settled him, and the visit had only reminded him of how far he had drifted from his older brothers. They had never been close, and Marshal's only real ties to his family had been severed long ago by the deaths of his mother and his uncle, who had trained him as a knight.

Marshal looked forward to joining Henry's mesne, for the king's service offered him the best chance to acquire land of his own. His years with Prince Henry had gained him nothing beyond a reputation, and it was time to win a permanent place in the world before it was too late. But his hopes remained abstract, without clear definition.

'I don't need to tell you I wish you good fortune,' Ranulf said, leaning back in the straw. 'You can rest tomorrow and slip out at night. The sooner you leave here, the better, before Meiler decides to tighten his siege.'

'Why should he, if you expect no relief?'

'He will have his reasons.'

'What's happening here, Ranulf?'

Ranulf shook his head. 'It's of no concern to you. Ride out of here tomorrow and forget this place.'

But Marshal would not be deterred. He liked this gruff, hard-bitten veteran, and he could not simply ride away. He stared at Ranulf until the old knight met his eyes. 'What is Meiler fitz Henry's claim to this castle?' he persisted.

'Prince John, our exalted Lord of Ireland,' Ranulf growled, 'has given him leave to seize Kilkenny.'

'I thought you held Kilkenny for the king!'

'This isn't the king's land. All of Leinster belongs to the House of Pembroke.'

'But Eustace told me that Pembroke died years ago. Didn't his lands revert to the crown?'

Ranulf shook his head sharply. 'The earl had a daughter, Isabelle de Clare. She is heiress to all the Pembroke lands, in Wales and in Ireland. I received custody of Kilkenny from the king's hand to hold for her for the duration of her minority.'

Marshal frowned, trying to clear his head. 'But she can't still be a child.'

'Hardly. She should have married long ago; she is already nineteen. But she's too rich a prize, and Henry has been holding her in reserve.'

'Then how is Prince John part of this?' Marshal asked impatiently. 'He can't interfere with a ward of the king.' He still did not understand what was going on, but one thing was certain: by resisting a royal order, Ranulf was courting a charge of treason.

'Lady Isabelle is John's ward, not Henry's,' Ranulf answered. 'Her largest holdings are here in Ireland, and Henry gave her to John as a ward when he made him Lord of Ireland. John has been giving her lands to his allies and, by God, we intend to stop it. We will not surrender Kilkenny before Lady Isabelle's case is put before the king.'

Marshal stared at Ranulf in disbelief. 'God's blood, man! You're playing with fire!'

Ranulf's expression hardened. 'I'm aware of the risk,' he said. 'I may be old, but I'm not senile.'

'Is that so?' Marshal responded sharply, his concern emerging as anger. He saw at once that Ranulf hoped to expose John's misuse of the heiress's lands, but this was the wrong time for such a gamble. 'What is John getting in return for the fiefs he's been giving away?' Marshal asked. 'Promises of future support?'

Ranulf nodded grimly. 'So, you *have* heard of what has been happening.'

'Enough,' Marshal said bleakly. The rumours reached as far as the Holy Land, and Marshal had confirmed them during his brief stay with his brothers in England. Henry, it was said, could no longer control his sons

At the age of nineteen, Henry of Anjou, Duke of Normandy, Count of Anjou, Maine and Touraine, and pretender to the throne of England, had burst upon the European political scene by marrying Eleanor of Aquitaine, the cast-off queen of Louis VII of France. In acquiring the Aquitaine, Henry had taken his first great step towards forging an empire that would encompass Britain and half of France – an empire he was strong and clever enough to hold for a third of a century. But in Eleanor – eleven years his senior and as intelligent as she was strong-willed – he had found a woman too much like himself, a queen with her own ambitions and vision of the future.

A breach between them had been inevitable, for only one could rule. When the rupture came, it was deep, bitter and enduring. The queen withdrew to her own court at Poitiers, in the heart of the Aquitaine, to raise the four sons she had borne the king. When the boys came of age in turn, they were Eleanor's sons, not Henry's – jealous of their father's power and impatient to have their own.

In 1173, Prince Henry had rebelled against his father. The rebellion was supported by King Louis of France, who was anxious to curb the English king's power, and by Eleanor. But young Henry was more puppet than leader, and his father snuffed out the revolt.

Henry loved his namesake, and he forgave the prince as quickly as he had crushed the rebellion. Eleanor was not so fortunate. She was captured en route to the French court in Paris, and Henry sent her to England under permanent house arrest.

Prince Henry tried again in 1183. King Louis had died three years earlier, and this time the prince was supported by Louis's son, Philip. Again, Henry crushed the revolt, and again he forgave his wayward son. Shortly thereafter, Prince Henry died of fever, and he was soon followed to the grave by his brother, Geoffry of Britanny, leaving two brothers as potential heirs to the throne of England – Richard and John.

Richard was everything John was not. Richard was tawny-haired, tall, stocky, and powerful – physically a larger version of his father. John was short, slight and dark, with neither the strength nor inclination for knightly combat. Where Richard bellowed, John whined; where Richard challenged, John conspired; and where Richard forgave, John exacted revenge. Devious and indolent, John still behaved like a spoilt child. Yet John was reportedly Henry's favourite.

It was an open secret that John was using his power and privileges as Lord of Ireland to curry favour, in the hope of supplanting his brother as heir to the throne; but Henry, worried and preoccupied by Richard's strength and ambition, turned a deaf ear to the whispers against John.

It was this fear and favouritism which made Ranulf's resistance to John so dangerous. Years ago, Henry would have looked beyond a charge of treason to investigate its cause; he would have listened to a plea for justice. But now, the king appeared determined to ignore his youngest son's intrigues.

'You could hang for this,' Marshal said grimly.

'They'll have to take Kilkenny first.'

'So?' Marshal snapped sarcastically. 'How long would that give you? A month? Two months? Through the summer, if you are fortunate. And then you will hang. You can't defend your lady's rights from a rope's end.'

Ranulf's leathery face hardened into a stubborn mask. 'It's no concern of yours.'

Marshal expelled a hiss of frustration. His head was pounding now. 'Why didn't Lady Isabelle find an intermediary to bring her case before His Majesty?'

'We're not fools, Marshal! She tried! She sent her priest to beg the intercession of the Bishop of Llandaff, but John intercepted him. Probably the man is dead.'

Marshal nodded grimly. From what he had heard, John was ruthless enough to eliminate the priest and clever enough to get away with it. If so, he was prepared to go to any lengths to hide his manoeuvring in Ireland from the king.

'We sent a messenger north to the Lord of Meath,' Ranulf said, 'but we can't be sure he'll get through. Nevertheless, Meath is bound to hear of this siege if we hold out long enough. He and Earl Richard were friends; he'll care enough to find out what's happening here.'

'Even if he does,' Marshal responded, 'what makes you think the king will take your side? You are committing treason, old man. That's the tack John will take. Do you believe the king will tolerate rebellion?'

'I received Kilkenny from the king,' Ranulf grated, 'and John never bothered to secure my homage. *De jure*, he is not my liege lord, so my resistance cannot be considered treason.'

Marshal said nothing. Ranulf did not need Marshal to tell him that the argument was parchment thin. And Ranulf undoubtedly had no friends at court; there would be no one to advocate on his behalf.

'There is no alternative,' Ranulf said stiffly, responding to Marshal's grim expression.

But there *was* an alternative, Marshal knew.

He turned away, resisting the impulse to become involved. It was *not* his concern, and the last thing he wanted was to make an enemy of John. Pehaps he could have ignored the instincts of a lifetime and let is pass. Perhaps. But as he stared into the fire, he saw Eustace astride the roan, shielding him with his sword as the last of his blood poured down his side and splattered in the dust. The debt was there, not to be denied.

'There is another way,' Marshal said at last. 'You could negotiate an honourable surrender with Meiler and come out of Kilkenny with me. End your resistance now, before it's too late. I have the ear of the king, Ranulf. I was father in chivalry to his son, and he will listen to me. I can promise that your lady's case will be heard.'

Marshal thought he saw hope flare briefly in Ranulf's eyes, but the moment passed, and the old knight's gaze was again flint hard and unreadable.

'That's a generous offer,' Ranulf said finally.

'Accept it, Ranulf. Accept it in payment for the debt I owe your son.'

Ranulf did not respond at once. Thoughtfully, he scratched his wiry grey beard. 'An honourable surrender may no longer be possible,' he said slowly. 'Not if Meiler believes he has the upper hand.'

'You have nothing to lose by trying. Let me negotiate with him as an arbiter. He can take this castle eventually, but he knows the cost.'

'There are complications . . .'

'What complications?' Marshal demanded impatiently. 'Your mistress would not want you to make a hopeless stand when there is an alternative. Anyway, you cannot consult her. John must be determined to keep this quiet; he'll be holding her in isolation.'

'That's the complication,' Ranulf said with a thin, humourless smile. 'John is not holding her.'

Marshal's eyebrows rose in surprise. 'Where is she?'

Ranulf pointed a blunt forefinger towards the ceiling. 'Sleeping above us. Lady Isabelle bribed her way out of Pembroke Castle, crossed to Ireland and slipped in here five nights ago.'

6

Marshal woke with a start from a wine-drugged sleep, jolted into consciousness by the castle alarm. On the tower's parapet, the watchman was hammering on a sheet of copper, the blows sounding like thin, high-pitched thunderclaps. Marshal sat up too suddenly, and he groaned aloud as a wave of pain slammed against the inside of his skull. His queasy stomach contracted, and he gritted his teeth against the spasm, swallowing back the acid in his throat.

He took a deep breath and then another, waiting for the pain in his head to subside. He had slept in his robe on a pile of straw against one wall of the great hall, and while he slept someone, presumably Ranulf's squire, had set up a canvas screen to give him a measure of privacy. Marshal's two baggage chests were placed nearby. His shield rested against the wall, and his sword and armour lay on a cloth on the floor.

The screen shielded him from the sunlight streaming into the hall through the arrow-slits, but it was the wine that had kept him from waking at first light. He guessed that it was at least an hour after dawn. From beyond the screen he heard men who had come off watch at dawn cursing sleepily as they gathered their weapons and stumbled out of the hall, leaving him alone.

Mercifully, the tower watchman ceased his hammering, and Marshal sighed with relief. He tried to discern what was happening from the shouts drifting faintly in from the court-yard. The orders were in Welsh, of which he understood little, but he detected no sense of urgency. An attack might be imminent, but it was not yet under way. Probably an over-anxious tower watchman, Marshal thought sourly.

He eased himself into a kneeling position to offer his morning prayer. He was sure there would be no Mass to hear in the chapel, for Ranulf was not the type to suffer a priest in a castle under siege. Marshal's view of religion was practical, and his prayer was short and to the point. 'Please, oh Lord,' he murmured, 'if I must fight today, take away the ache in my head.'

One of Ranulf's mastiffs came over and licked his ear. Marshal irritably pushed the dog away. He hastily added a routine devotional to round out his prayer; then he got to his feet.

At that moment, Ranulf's squire burst into the hall. 'Alarm, sire!' he cried breathlessly, running towards him.

'Softly, lad, softly,' Marshal said, closing his eyes and massaging his forehead.

'I'm sorry, sire.'

'What's amiss out there?' Marshal asked, his eyes still closed.

'Meiler's army is advancing through the forest, sire. Sir Ranulf and Lady Isabelle are on the forward palisade and ask that you join them at your convenience.'

Marshal nodded and opened his eyes. The sunlight from the arrow-slits diffused in the hall's smoky grey haze, but even that dim light seemed too bright. 'Was that the entire message?'

'Aye, sire – I mean, no,' the boy stammered, reddening. 'Lady Isabelle asked me to convey her apology that she was unavailable to greet you on your arrival.'

'Never forget the details of a message, lad – even the courtesies.'

'Aye, sire.'

'And never run if you don't have to. It sets a bad example for your men. Let them do the running.'

'Aye, sire,' the squire repeated, chagrined.

'What do they call you?'

'Jean d'Erly, sire.'

Marshal did not recognize the family name, but that was not surprising. If Ranulf held a fief of his own from the House of Pembroke, it would be small, and he would not have a baron's son as squire.

Marshal appraised the boy. It did not matter that this was

Ranulf's squire; the boy aspired to knighthood, and it was the duty of every knight to evaluate and guide the young men who might one day join their fellowship.

Jean d'Erly was tall and straight, with thick black hair that contrasted with his fair, clear skin. He was fit and alert, and Marshal noted he was excited, not frightened, by the alarm. That was a good sign. Eagerness for combat was an essential quality that could not be instilled.

'All right, Jean. How long before Meiler has his troops in position?'

'Their encampment is half a league off, sire. Half an hour, perhaps a little longer.'

'There is time then, whatever your enemies have in mind. Are you free to attend me?'

'Aye, sire. I'll bring a washbasin for you and whatever you require.'

'I'm not hungry, but I have a devil's thirst. Is your well clear?'

'Aye, but . . .'

'Is it, or isn't it?'

'Aye, sire, but do you want to drink water?'

'Yes,' Marshal said, ignoring his astonishment. 'And some beer, as well. Water to kill the thirst and beer to settle my stomach.'

'My pardon, sire, but you look as if your head aches.'

'What of it?' Marshal said in irritation.

'I could bring you a dead man's tooth to hold.'

Marshal smiled and shook his head. 'That remedy has never worked on me.'

He turned and walked towards the latrine chamber, built into the thick stone wall at the rear of the hall.

'Mind the splinters in the seat,' the boy called after him, but Marshal did not need the warning. He had discovered the dangers of the latrine's wooden seat the night before.

Marshal slowly climbed the stone staircase which spiralled up through the tower's wall to the parapet, his chain mail clinking softly in time to his measured steps. His headache was subsiding, but he had to rest at intervals to keep it under control. Before he went out to meet Ranulf and the mistress of Kilkenny, he wanted to gauge the situation for himself.

He squinted against the sunlight as he emerged on to the parapet. The storm had passed in the early hours of the morning, pushed aside by the first warm auguries of spring. To the north, broken rain clouds hugged the horizon, but overhead the sky was clear. The red-and-gold Pembroke banner flying from the peak of the tower's conical wooden roof flapped lazily in the soft southerly breeze. The clear air was a relief after the dank atmosphere of the tower.

The young watchman standing on the catwalk encircling the base of the roof touched his cap and said something in Welsh which Marshal didn't understand. Marshal acknowledged him in English. Like the others of Ranulf's garrison, the watchman carried the Welsh longbow, and he had the barrelled chest and muscular arms to draw it.

Ranulf must have anticipated the possibility of a siege, Marshal thought, to have recruited so many longbowmen for his small garrison. Tactically, it was a shrewd move that maximized defensive power with a minimum of mouths to feed, but Marshal was not impressed. Sound tactics could not make up for a suicidal strategy.

He stepped to the edge of the stone parapet and looked out over the spreading forest below. In the distance, a long column of men and carts crawled towards the castle along a narrow track from Meiler's encampment. The men and horses were largely screened from view by the overhanging treetops, but they did not have the look of an assault force ready to storm the castle.

As Marshal expected, it had been a false alarm. Ranulf had said that Meiler was building a trebuchet, and the warlord would certainly wait for his catapult. The castle's forward stockade wall cut across an open slope dropping steeply down to the forest line. In front of the wall was a wide dry moat screened by sharpened stakes and piles of brambles. As long as the stockade was intact, Ranulf's longbowmen would have no difficulty stopping a daylight attack.

Without an engineer to build a catapult, Meiler might have tried to destroy the defences with fire arrows, either directed against the stockade itself or into the cluster of wooden buildings within. Only the keep was of stone. Abutting the tower was a wooden chapel and the kitchen and bake house. Other wooden structures were built alongside the stockade walls adjacent to the cliffs: a smithy and stable, a granary and, on the opposite side of the courtyard, a long wooden building that served in peacetime as barracks.

Ranulf had guarded against the threat of fire by covering the roofs of the wooden buildings with hides to retard ignition. Scattered through the compound were barrels of water to fight a blaze before it could spread.

Ranulf's garrison was well provisioned. A cacophony of barnyard noises drifted up from the courtyard. Chickens and geese, some wandering free, but most locked in rows of stacked cages, cackled and honked, and from the barrack hall came the lowing of cattle herded in from pens outside the stockade. The granary was overflowing, and Marshal assumed that the storeroom on the ground floor of the keep was filled to capacity.

But frontier castles like Kilkenny had been built to hold rebellious Irishmen at bay, not to withstand Norman siege engines – particularly a trebuchet. Once Meiler hauled the catapult into place at the bottom of the slope, he could bombard the antiquated stockade above him with boulders or with firebombs and destroy the wooden wall in a single day.

The defenders' retreat to the keep was already prepared. Narrow bridges extended from the near walls of the stockade to a wooden platform halfway up the tower, from which an outer wooden staircase rose to the parapet. Men on the ground retreating to the tower from the courtyard would raise the drawbridge after them, and those coming across from the wall would cut the ropes securing the bridges to the tower. Yet once the garrison was forced into the keep, surrender was only a matter of time.

And now, it appeared, Meiler was moving to prevent Lady Isabelle's escape. Two knights and half a dozen mounted *serjants* emerged from the forest, followed by skirmishers on foot, carrying slings and Irish battle-axes. Behind them came workmen with picks and shovels. Ox-carts trundled in their midst, piled high with poles and tent canvas. Meiler was preparing to dig in.

Several carts, Marshal noted, were loaded with fire-hardened stakes, which would be driven into the ground in a defensive line to protect the tents against a sortie from the castle. This was an unnecessary precaution, and it indicated that Meiler overestimated the strength of Ranulf's garrison. Perhaps that would make it easier for Marshal to negotiate a surrender.

Marshal sighed and gingerly rubbed his eyes. His head still ached, and he felt sluggish from lack of sleep. God help me if my head doesn't clear soon, he thought. I'll need my wits about me today.

He grimaced as part of him rebelled against his entanglement in the affair. Meiler was just the first obstacle. He had promised to present Lady Isabelle's case before the king, but he could not promise success. If he failed, Ranulf most certainly, and perhaps his lady as well, would pay the price. It was a responsibility he did not want.

Yet even as he chafed under its burden, he knew that he had no choice. It was not just that he owed a debt to Eustace. Ranulf was defending his lady's rights. Marshal could not turn away from that and still call himself a knight. Some knights could, when it suited them, ignore their sacred oath to defend the right, but not Marshal.

He saw Isabelle de Clare standing beside Ranulf on the forward wall. Meiler fitz Henry was not the only unknown quantity he would have to deal with. The girl certainly had courage, but John must have distanced her from her late father's advisors, as almost any other course of action would have been preferable to the one she had chosen.

The sunlight glinted on her copper tresses, and Marshal groaned inwardly. A young woman could be unpredictable enough, but a redhead . . . He sighed and turned to leave the parapet; it was time to meet the mistress of Kilkenny.

Isabelle stood next to Ranulf on the stockade's fighting platform, looking towards the forest, pretending to watch the approach of Meiler's siege column, but from the corner of her eye she was studying Ranulf. Please, my faithful old friend, don't fail me now, she prayed silently.

'False alarm,' Ranulf said. 'Meiler's not fool enough to attack now without the trebuchet. He must be preparing to dig in and seal off your escape, milady. John doesn't intend to let you slip away from him a second time.'

'I wish you had woken me last night,' Isabelle said tensely.

'I thought it best to let you sleep, milady.'

'I'm no longer a child, Ranulf!'

'I know that, milady. I only thought . . .' His voice trailed off in a grunt of resignation. He didn't understand her irritation and was in no mood to try to fathom a woman's preoccupation with irrelevancies.

Isabelle caught herself gnawing on her lower lip and stopped. More than Ranulf's obedience, she needed his confidence; but the stranger who had slipped into Kilkenny the previous night had managed to rekindle the old man's doubts. If only she had been present when Ranulf had talked with William Marshal.

Apparently, they had talked through the night, blithely settling her fate between them, as men were so quick to do. Ranulf had come to her at first light to tell her of Marshal's presence and his offer. Caught off-guard, she had played for time, not giving Ranulf a direct answer. But she had no intention of surrendering.

Isabelle shivered imperceptibly. John had driven her to this desperate gamble, and no one could persuade her to submit voluntarily to his custody again – not Ranulf, and certainly not the meddlesome William Marshal. But how could she refuse Marshal's offer without some plausible reason and still retain Ranulf's trust?

Marshal had already won Ranulf's confidence; the old knight spoke of him in a way he had once reserved for her father. She had seen how quickly bonds could form between warriors, and Marshal was more than a famous knight. If half of what she had heard as a girl were true, there were few knights who could equal him on the battlefield. That would weigh heavily with Ranulf, even if it meant little to her.

She knew nothing of Marshal's character, only the legends that had grown up around him, and she had no faith in legends. Marshal was a stranger. How could she blindly entrust her fate to him?

'Where is your William Marshal?' Isabelle asked testily. 'Jean said he was up and about, which was half an hour past.'

'Probably up on the parapet, milady,' Ranulf said, studying the lead elements of Meiler's column just emerging from the forest. 'Evaluating the situation from the highest vantage-point. That's what I'd do.'

Isabelle turned and looked up at the tower in time to glimpse a figure in chain mail turn away and disappear from view. 'You were right, Ranulf, but he's gone now. Come,' she said peremptorily, 'it's time I met our famous guest.'

After calling to the men not on watch to stand down, Ranulf said to Isabelle, 'I'll have to tell the tower watchmen not to sound the alarm by day without an order from me.'

It was an indirect acknowledgment that she was still committed to holding Kilkenny, but Isabelle knew Ranulf did not accept her coolness to Marshal's proposal. He could not understand without an explanation – an explanation she dared not give.

Ranulf preceded her down the ladder to the courtyard. The ground was still muddy, and he offered her his arm as she stepped off the ladder on to the narrow walkway of planks laid out for her. As she walked towards the keep with Ranulf trudging beside her through the mud, the old knight murmured, 'Try to look a little more cheerful, Rusty. The man *is* on our side, y'know.'

Isabelle saw Marshal emerge from the entrance to the keep, and she slowed her pace so that he would have time to come down to their level before she reached the steps to the drawbridge. She did so automatically, without *hauteur*, out of consideration for a guest. Because of her rank, if they met while he was on the steps above her, Marshal might feel awkward.

He was a big man, as she had expected, but as he strode across the drawbridge and came down the steps to the courtyard, he moved with surprising grace. He also was not vain, for the burnished steel of his chain mail was not lacquered, and the white surcoat over his armour was without embroidery.

'Lady Isabelle,' Ranulf said as Marshal approached, 'may I present Sir William Marshal, formerly companion to the Templars and now returning to His Majesty's service.'

The unaccustomed formality in Ranulf's voice struck Isabelle as comically out of character.

She smiled politely and stepped forward to grasp Marshal's hands in welcome. Ranulf had told her that Marshal's wrist was broken, and she noticed the splint poking out from his mailed sleeve.

'You are most welcome, Sir William,' she said, looking up at him.

'I thank you, Lady Isabelle,' Marshal replied, bowing with just the right degree of deference. But as he straightened up, Isabelle was sure she saw a suppressed wince of pain, and noticed his eyes were bloodshot. So the great knight has his weaknesses, she thought wryly. With Ranulf as a drinking companion, he had been overmatched.

'And I thank you, Sir William,' she said, 'for travelling so far to bring solace to Ranulf, my faithful knight. I deeply regret that I could not receive you properly last night.'

Marshal smiled. 'Believe me, I am grateful enough that last night's welcome did not include a crossbow bolt.'

Isabelle was surprised that his smile revealed no missing teeth. Few knights who rode the tournament circuit professionally could boast a full set. Despite his scruffy stubble, his face made a good impression – intelligent and forceful. He had brown hair receding from a high forehead and a broken nose, which Isabelle decided was to his advantage, for it saved him from being too handsome. His thick, projecting eyebrows, prominent cheekbones and strong jaw would have given him a fierce appearance, had it not been for his disarming smile.

Marshal was appraising her as well, and Isabelle found his direct gaze strangely disconcerting. He had held her hands a trifle longer than politeness demanded. He has the courtier's touch, she thought, suddenly recalling the rumours she had heard as a girl. There had been talk linking him to Prince Henry's young wife, Marguerite of France. Isabelle felt a flash of annoyance which she did not understand.

She turned to Ranulf and said lightly, 'It appears we are not in danger of attack at the moment, so you gentlemen can shed your armour. We will dine in the open, I think, and a touch of festivity would not be amiss. We'll forget the rationing today and eat a proper meal in Sir William's honour.'

'Yes, milady,' Ranulf said without hesitation.

She was surprised he did not object, but only momentarily. Meiler's trebuchet would be completed long before they exhausted their livestock, and once they were driven into the tower, only the provisions they could hold in the keep would be of use.

'Meanwhile,' Isabelle said, 'I will have a bath prepared for you, Sir William, and you can . . .'

'I hope the need for a bath is not too obvious,' Marshal interrupted with a smile.

'No, of course not,' Isabelle said quickly, then flushed. That she should be flustered by Marshal's harmless joke surprised and annoyed her, which only made her cheeks burn more hotly.

Marshal gave no sign he noticed. 'A bath would be most welcome, Lady Isabelle,' he said easily. 'And then, perhaps, we could talk. Ranulf has explained the situation, and I – well, if I can, I would like to be of service to you. At your discretion, of course.'

Isabelle was not reassured by the proviso. Was he really prepared to defer to her judgment, or was he simply approaching her carefully, as one might handle a difficult child? She saw now that Ranulf's trust in Marshal was due to more than an affinity between warriors. There was a self-assurance to the man, unmarred by arrogance. In other circumstances, he would have inspired her confidence.

'I would, of course, value your counsel, Sir William,' she said in a deliberately neutral tone. 'And we appreciate your offer of help. When you have refreshed yourself, Ranulf and I will wait for you in my chamber.'

She saw a flicker of surprise as Marshal registered her reserve. Once again, he was appraising her. But although his look was probing, it was not detached; there was genuine concern in his eyes. She had suspected Marshal's offer of help to be, at least in part, a gratification of his conceit – the *noblesse oblige* of a hero of the lists. But she could detect neither condescension nor self-importance in the man. Marshal was not at all what she had expected.

Marshal shifted on the stool in the wooden bath tub that had been prepared for him behind his screen in the great hall and closed his eyes. Lady Isabelle had sent her lady-in-waiting to wash his hair, and now that the woman had departed, he could relax. He never felt at ease when women attended him in his bath, but it was an idiosyncracy he never revealed.

Without decent Saracen soap his body would only be partly cleansed, but the steaming water eased the stiffness in his muscles and took away the last of his headache. He felt human again.

He slid further down in the water so he could soak the stubble on his jaw. He shaved as infrequently as possible, and he could have let his whiskers grow for another few days; but he had seen the girl's eyes focus on the stubble, and he wanted to make himself more presentable. It was a matter of courtesy, he told himself, due her as a lady of high degree.

He would be more persuasive if he made a favourable impression, and now he knew that persuasion would be necessary. Lady Isabelle was clearly not ready to accept his proposal. Why? he wondered. He understood her reluctance to trust a stranger, but Ranulf must have explained that her continued defiance was likely to end in disaster.

Marshal picked up the dagger he had brought from Palestine and began to scrape his jaw. The blade was blue Damascus steel with a keener edge than any European shaving knife, yet shaving was a painful ritual.

It was ironic, he thought, that the very richness of Isabelle de Clare's inheritance should hold her hostage in the social limbo of an unmarried heiress. If she were free to choose, she could have her pick of eligible bachelors, not to mention the barons who would willingly put aside their wives to take her hand. With the lands she could bring to a marriage, she would be desirable even if she had been an ugly girl.

And this, Isabelle de Clare certainly was not. Her broad forehead and generous mouth did not conform to the courtly standards of beauty, nor did her freckles and turned-up nose, but Marshal preferred the open vivacity of her features and manner to the pouting, narrow-faced blonde ornaments of the French courts.

He smiled wryly, admitting his immediate attraction to her, but he had long since learned to suppress such feelings towards high-born women beyond his reach. Despite his fame, Marshal's prowess had gained him no fiefs of his own. He was still a landless knight. Other men could walk the line between flirtation and indiscretion, but he knew from bitter experience that he could not.

Marshal ascended the spiral staircase to the chamber above the great hall, taking the stone steps two at a time. The bath had refreshed him, and he felt energetic and purposeful. The reluctance and concern gnawing at him earlier had vanished with his headache. He was sure that he and Ranulf could persuade Isabelle to surrender Kilkenny, and he was reasonably confident he could plead her case successfully before the king. She was defying her lawful guardian, but Prince John's misuse of his trust was too flagrant to be overlooked.

His optimism evaporated as he reached the level of the second floor and heard Ranulf's gravelly voice explode in anger. The words were muffled by the thick oak door to Lady Isabelle's chamber, but Marshal understood them well enough: 'Why won't you listen to reason, milady?'

Marshal heard no response, and he knocked on the door. Isabelle called for him to enter, and Marshal walked in. The girl was sitting on the bed, rigidly erect, looking very small and vulnerable in the empty, stone-walled chamber, but there was nothing timid about her demeanour. Her green eyes were hard and uncompromising. Ranulf stood nearby, hands clasped behind him, and though his tone had been angry, there was only confusion and concern in his eyes.

'Perhaps I've come at an inopportune moment,' Marshal said.

The girl shook her head. 'No, Sir William. It was your proposal we were discussing.'

Isabelle's voice was controlled, but Marshal caught an undertone of accusation that took him by surprise.

'It was only a proposal for you to consider, Lady Isabelle,' Marshal said.

'A proposal to surrender,' Isabelle said coolly.

'With honour, and with a safe conduct for you and your men. It is true that you would almost certainly be required to return to Prince John's custody, but I would proceed immediately to the royal court to present your grievances to the king. As I understand it, you are without an advocate and are hoping for the intercession of Lord Meath.'

'That is correct, Sir William.'

'But you cannot be sure your messenger got through to Meath – or of Meath's response. I know that you hope the news of this siege will eventually reach him, but would you not prefer to exchange a possibility for a certainty? I stand ready to present your case, and I . . .'

'Why?' Isabelle interrupted.

Marshal saw that the abrupt question had slipped out before the girl had considered it, and her eyes flickered as she regretted it an instant later; but Marshal would not let it pass. The implication nettled him. 'Because you have been wronged, Lady Isabelle. That is reason enough for any knight who remembers his oath.'

Isabelle took a deep breath and nodded. 'I apologize, Sir William,' she said as gracefully as she could manage. 'The question was unworthy.'

Marshal cursed silently, feeling he was bungling the situation. For some reason, the girl felt on the defensive, and he was only making things worse.

'Lady Isabelle, I have no intention of interfering in this affair against your wishes.'

Her tongue flicked out to moisten her lips, and she glanced at Ranulf uncertainly. She was obviously afraid of losing his support, but she was even more afraid of something else. What?

'I can assure you, Lady Isabelle,' Marshal said, 'that neither Prince John nor anyone else in the realm can prevent me from reaching the king. I have safe conduct from His Majesty and a written order commanding my presence at court. You can be sure your case will be presented, and I suggest that I can serve your interests better than could Lord Meath. The king would be suspicious of any case brought against his son by a baron with a power base in Ireland; he would be bound to look upon it as a challenge to John's authority as Lord of Ireland. I firmly believe that my proposal offers you the best chance for justice.'

Ranulf nodded in agreement and looked to Isabelle. For a moment, there was silence, broken by a rhythmic thumping from above as the watchman on the parapet idly tapped his pike on the scaffolding. Isabelle's expression had not changed; it was clear she still resisted the idea. Her fingers plucked restlessly at the folds of her robe. Why was she resisting? What was she afraid of?

'I take your point, Sir William,' Isabelle said at last. She took a breath and added, 'And I would welcome your intercession on my behalf – with heartfelt thanks – for I believe His Majesty would listen to you. But could you not go now, leaving us to hold Kilkenny? Why must we surrender?'

'Rusty, you know very well why!' Ranulf burst out in frustration.

To Marshal it was a measure of the old knight's concern that he had slipped and addressed her familiarly in front of a stranger.

'You would be damaging your own position, Lady Isabelle,' Marshal said. 'Prince John's misuse of his guardianship is against all custom. But to hold Kilkenny in defiance of his order is rebellion, and that places you outside the law.'

Again Marshal saw uncertainty in the girl's eyes. It was clear she understood their argument, yet something still prevented her from assenting. She compressed her lips and shook her head.

'If you feel you cannot represent us while we still hold Kilkenny, Sir William,' she said, 'you may withdraw your offer of advocacy, but I have no intention of surrendering.'

Ranulf expelled his breath in exasperation. 'I am your liege man, milady,' he rasped, 'and I owe you counsel as well as service. I am bound to say that your decision is irrational. In fact, it's stubborn and reckless! Pride must have its limits!'

Isabelle stiffened as if in anger, but there was a hint of desperation in her eyes. She blinked rapidly, and Marshal saw she was holding back tears. Ranulf was wrong, he realized. The girl was neither reckless or foolish, and pride was not the reason for her stubbornness. Isabelle de Clare was frightened.

'You may withdraw, sirs,' she said hoarsely, turning away.

'As you wish, milady,' Ranulf said curtly. He bowed stiffly and strode from the chamber.

Marshal followed him to the door, but then he stopped and closed it, remaining in the chamber.

'I would like to be alone, Sir William,' Isabelle said, her face still averted.

'You *are* alone, Lady Isabelle,' Marshal said quietly. 'That is the problem. What is it that you won't tell Ranulf?'

She looked up at him and shook her head quickly. Her face was very white, and in that instant Marshal guessed the truth.

7

‘God's truth,' Marshal breathed. ‘It's John you're afraid of!'

Isabelle's eyes widened in alarm, and she stood up, stretching out her arm towards him. ‘No, you must not think that!'

But it was there, plain in her eyes. Marshal would have had to be blind not to see it. A wave of revulsion swept over him, followed an instant later by a rush of white-hot anger. No wonder she did not dare tell Ranulf. If the old knight found out, he would track John down and kill him with his own hands, or die trying.

‘What happened?' Marshal demanded, his pulse hammering at his temples.

‘You are wrong, Sir William!'

With an effort of will, Marshal mastered his anger. The last thing he wanted was to strip the girl of her dignity. Slowly, he shook his head. ‘I'm not wrong, and if I am to be of service to you, I should know the truth.'

Isabelle swallowed hard and shook her head, unwilling to speak. Several seconds passed before she finally yielded. ‘Ranulf must never know,' she said, her voice barely above a whisper. ‘If he found out . . .'

‘I will say nothing, Lady Isabelle, on my honour.'

‘It was not as terrible as you may think,' she said, taking a deep breath. ‘He didn't – he didn't succeed. It was late at night, and I was alone with him. He was furious that I refused to sign a letter instructing Ranulf to surrender Kilkenny, and he was drunk – very drunk. He told me that he had stopped my priest from carrying my petition to the king, and he hinted that he had Father Bertrand killed . . .'

Isabelle broke off and bit her lip uncertainly. ‘Now, I think he may have just wanted to frighten me. Would he dare kill a priest, Sir William?'

'I don't know,' Marshal said hoarsely.

'Still, I refused to sign, and when I tried to leave him, he – he attacked me.'

Marshal felt the blood draining from his cheeks. He was no innocent, and he knew of barons who had taken advantage of their wards; but that did nothing to quell his anger and disgust.

Isabelle looked through Marshal as if seeing it all again in her mind. Her words came in a flurry. 'He was so drunk that I managed to kick free of him. I hurt him – hurt him badly. And while he was helpless, I took his head and banged it against the floor.'

She looked up at Marshal, her eyes blinking rapidly, and then stepped back and wearily dropped to the bed. 'That was all. He lost consciousness and it was over.'

'And you told no one?'

'No. Not even Mattie. I didn't want to . . .'

Marshal nodded, finding it difficult to speak, imagining the girl's terror and what it must have cost her to keep the secret locked inside her, lest someone seek to avenge her.

Isabelle suddenly compressed her lips and shook her head. 'I should not have fled Pembroke. John was so drunk he may not even recall what happened.'

'Lady Isabelle, I . . .'

'In truth, I've blundered! You're right, Sir William. Of course I'll agree to an honourable surrender. If John had not been drunk, he would never . . .'

'No!' Marshal burst out, horrified that the girl was blaming herself. 'You will not be returned to John. Not as long as I live to prevent it.'

Despite Meiler's siege line, it should be possible to bring the girl out of Kilkenny by night, but there was another possibility that Marshal preferred. Rage burned like a hot iron in his innards, and the urge to strike back at John was more than a desire, it was a need. John was out of reach, but Meiler fitz Henry was not – and he was John's man.

Isabelle was looking at Marshal strangely, and he tried to regain his composure. He was not adept at masking his feelings, and his thoughts were ugly. 'If you permit,' he said stiffly, still fighting to control his anger, 'I'll leave you now to speak with Ranulf.'

'But don't you think . . .'

'I think we can find a way to keep you out of John's hands, Lady Isabelle, and secure your safety and rights. John may be Lord of Ireland, but Henry is king.'

'But what will you tell Ranulf?'

'I'll have to let him believe his mistress is simply too stubborn to listen to reason,' he said, forcing a smile.

'It will not be hard to convince him,' Isabelle said bleakly.

'Just as well. It took great courage not to tell him, Lady Isabelle, the kind of courage that would make any knight proud to serve you.'

Marshal meant what he said, and Isabelle knew it. Her cheeks reddened under his gaze, and she looked away.

'When we have developed a plan,' he said, 'we will submit it for your consideration.'

Isabelle shook her head and rose from the bed. 'I give my consent now to whatever you and Ranulf decide – on one condition: you must consider the risk to yourselves.'

'Neither one of us is reckless,' he responded.

Isabelle smiled tentatively. 'I hope that's true, Sir William.' She stepped towards him and took his hands. Her fingers were feverishly hot. 'Trusting that it is,' she said huskily, looking up at him, 'I place myself under your protection, and gratefully do so.'

This time it was Marshal who flushed.

By the time Marshal found Ranulf in the tower's cellar storeroom beneath the great hall, he was confident that he had calmed down enough to fool Ranulf. Marshal did not like deceiving him, but Isabelle was right; Ranulf could not be told.

A single torch burned on the wall beside the stairwell, soot curling upward from its oily flame. It barely illuminated the dungeon's recesses, so Marshal had to wait until his eyes adapted to the gloom. The musky odour of rats' nests hung in the air.

With the exception of the torture chamber, the cellar was undivided. Wine casks and beer barrels lined one wall, and small barrels containing cheeses were stacked against another. Additional stores for the siege were distributed haphazardly throughout the room, and Ranulf was opening barrels at random to check for spoilage. There were supplementary stocks of salted fish in brine, smoked and salted meat, barrels of flour, and raw grain to feed the fowl that would be brought into the keep at the last minute.

Checking the provisions was the responsibility of the steward, but Marshal guessed that Ranulf had sent away his steward, as well as the castle's priest. Ranulf resealed the cask he had opened and came over to Marshal. The end of a cherry twig protruded from the corner of his mouth.

He shifted the chewing-stick to the other side of his mouth and asked, 'Did she change her mind?'

Marshal shook his head. 'She won't surrender to Meiler.'

'Christ's blood!'

'My sentiments, precisely,' Marshal said with feigned exasperation.

Ranulf grunted sourly. 'Then you'd best leave tonight. Unless you want to try to slip through Meiler's siege line, we'll lower you down to the river by rope. Then we'll use the same hoist to lower the skiff we have on hand for just this situation. You can row downriver all the way to Waterford. I only wish Lady Isabelle would accompany you.'

'She won't,' Marshal said. 'Not as long as there's a chance of being intercepted. If Meiler takes her hostage, you'd be forced to surrender, and she doesn't want to see you hang. As long as she remains here, she can hope to bargain for your life if surrender becomes inevitable.'

'That leaves us with little choice. We'll just have to hold out here as long as we can and hope that you can persuade the king to intervene.'

'I don't like the idea of leaving her here.'

'God's teeth, man!' Ranulf growled. 'You just told me she won't go with you.'

'I know,' Marshal replied coolly, 'but we may have another option.'

Ranulf bit off the end of his stick and spat out the piece of pulp. 'I'm listening.'

'Last night, you told me that Meiler has been challenging you to single combat. Will he come again today?'

Ranulf frowned in puzzlement, and then his eyes narrowed and he shook his head sharply. 'Put it from your mind.'

'Will he come?'

'Listen to me, Marshal. You're the best man with sword and lance I've ever seen – but not with only one arm.'

'*Will he come?*'

'You don't know Meiler! He's tough, and he's good. Too good. He might even be able to teach you a trick or two.'

Marshal said nothing, by his silence forcing Ranulf to answer him.

'Yes, damn his eyes, he'll come! He's having too much fun baiting me to stop now. But you . . .'

'When?' Marshal cut in impatiently.

'Near *terce*; I think it's his way of developing an appetite for dinner.'

'Does he come armed?'

Ranulf shook his head. 'He did the first day, but not after that. You'd have plenty of time to pray.'

'I prayed this morning,' Marshal replied with a smile.

Ranulf spat out another piece of wood. 'Excellent,' he said sarcastically. 'You won't mind if I say a prayer or two for us. If you fall, we fall with you.'

'Then don't take the chance,' Marshal said. 'But if I defeat Meiler today, we can bring your lady out of here without the risk of pursuit.'

Ranulf eyed the splint on Marshal's wrist. '*If* you can beat him,' he said pointedly.

'I think I can.'

'With that arm? It will never take the strain, Marshal. Even if you manage a pass or two with lances, what happens when Meiler closes with you? He uses a mace, not a sword, and he's as strong as an ox. He'll batter down your shield arm and then go to work on your skull.'

'Who said I'd let him close with me?'

'Unseat Meiler? No one ever has.'

'He's never fought me.'

Ranulf laughed – an explosive, coughing bark. 'I see modesty is not one of your virtues.'

Marshal didn't smile.

The old knight bit through his chewing-stick again, then threw it away. He looked at Marshal thoughtfully.

'Well?' Marshal asked. 'What shall it be?'

'You tempt me. I would give my right arm to see that scurvy bastard humbled. But can you do it?'

'Shall we find out?'

Ranulf drew breath, then expelled it in a long hiss. 'All right,' he said finally. 'Let's wager all.'

The discordant fanfare of three unskilled heralds announced Meiler's appearance before Kilkenny Castle, and accompanied by his knights and standard-bearer, he started up the hill.

All morning his men had laboured to establish a new encampment stretching three hundred paces along the edge of the forest, blocking the approach to the castle, but now all work stopped. The men of Meiller's small army watched his progress up the hill, grateful for the opportunity to rest and hoping for entertainment.

'Trumpets, no less,' Ranulf remarked drily to Isabelle, who stood beside him on the forward wall.

'Will he take the bait?' Isabelle asked, unsure of the answer she wanted to hear. She was amazed that her voice sounded so calm.

'He'll take it, all right.'

'But won't he be suspicious when we accept his challenge?'

'I doubt it. He'll think we're desperate.'

All the garrison, including cooks and varlets, lined the forward wall, drawn by the rumours they had heard, and Ranulf was content to allow the breach of discipline. Seeing the number of men on the wall, Meiler reined in short of where he usually threw down his challenge. But he did not hesitate long. He spurred his mount and continued up the slope.

Isabelle surreptitiously brushed her damp palms against her silk *bliaut*. She was glad she would have to shout to Meiler, for it would help to mask her anxiety. Now, dismayed by what she had set in motion, she wished she had never fled Pembroke.

If Marshal's wrist failed him, as Ranulf had warned her it might, Meiler would surely kill him. Kilkenny would fall, and Ranulf would be the next to die. And all she had to fear, she thought bitterly, was a return to John's custody.

John was a drunk and a lecher, not Satan himself. She wanted to be worthy of her father, but where was her courage when she had rejected Marshal's original plan? John was vindictive enough to punish her, but he could not go too far once Marshal presented her appeal to the king.

Fear, not pride, had prompted her refusal. How could the groping of a drunken weakling have frightened her so? Once she had told Marshal what had happened, she saw it in a different light, as simply a loathsome incident. John would not dare try again; there were limits even to a prince's power.

Yet the effect on Marshal had been just the opposite. His emotions had been as plain as words on parchment. She had seen his initial shock, followed by fury.

When he returned to tell her that he intended to answer Meiler's challenge, she begged him to consider that Meiler would certainly demand a fight to the death. Again, she had seen the ominous glint of anger in his eye. He hoped for nothing less.

For the first time in her life, she glimpsed the power, however unwitting, that a woman could have over a man's emotions. It was as if she had pushed a boulder down a hill and could not stop it.

Meiler shouted up to the castle, 'I call upon you to yield to your lawful lord's command, Lady Isabelle, and surrender Kilkenny to me!'

Isabelle stepped forward, prepared to answer, but then hesitated, seized by the desire to halt the rush of events before men died because of her misjudgment. She could still ask for a parley, could still return to Marshal's original plan – now, before it was too late.

Ranulf gripped her arm, seeing her hesitation but not understanding it.

'Answer him, milady,' he pressed.

But it *was* too late. The time for second thoughts had passed.

Isabelle drew a breath and lifted her head. 'I answer you as I have before, Sir Meiler,' she shouted. 'The king placed Kilkenny in Sir Ranulf's hands, and only the king can relieve him of that duty.'

'Then let him defend that claim before God!' Meiler cried. 'I challenge him one last time to decide the issue in single combat. Sir Ranulf! Do you find sufficient courage today, or will you continue to hide behind your wall?'

Ranulf smiled and released Isabelle's arm. 'Dangle the bait, milady,' he said, and Isabelle nodded.

'It is I who deny you entry to Kilkenny,' she shouted, 'not Sir Ranulf. Dare you meet a champion of my own choosing?'

Meiler's response was immediate. 'If he be a knight, Lady Isabelle. But I believe Sir Ranulf is the only knight among your company, and I will not dishonour my lance with the blood of a *serjant*.'

Isabelle cupped her hands to her mouth to be sure her challenge reached Meiler's troops at the foot of the hill. 'My champion is a true knight, Sir Meiler, as you will discover to your sorrow if you have the courage to meet him. Unlike Sir Ranulf, his hair is not grey!'

Meiler's horse reared as the burly warlord angrily jerked on the reins, and Ranulf chuckled. 'That should do it,' he muttered gleefully.

Isabelle glanced at him in astonishment. This was no game. Had he forgotten Marshal's injury?

'I will meet your champion, Lady Isabelle,' Meiler yelled, 'and gladly – if he exists.'

'So he thinks we're bluffing, does he?' Ranulf grinned. 'Well, we have a surprise for him.'

It *was* a game to them, Isabelle thought, a deadly game that these men loved to play. She swallowed to relieve the dryness in her throat and continued as Ranulf had instructed her. 'My champion will meet you one hour from now,' she cried, 'on the level below this slope. He offers you three passes with the lance, to be followed by combat with sword, axe or mace. Single combat with only squires in attendance. To the victor, Kilkenny Castle.'

'Agreed, Lady Isabelle! As I will be hostage to the outcome, I could by right demand a hostage of you. But I will settle for your word of honour that Kilkenny will be surrendered to me *unconditionally* when I defeat this nameless champion.'

'He means to hang you, Ranulf,' Isabelle said anxiously.

'Aye,' Ranulf said. 'Agree, milady.'

'I do so promise, Sir Meiler,' Isabelle called. 'Upon my honour and the honour of my father.'

'And you, Sir Ranulf? Do you pledge your word as well?'

Ranulf's face darkened at this fresh insult. 'I give my word,' he shouted hoarsely, 'though a knight who understood honour would not demand my separate assurance. Now I will make a demand of my own. Let your own knights swear before God to honour the outcome of this combat, and let their oaths be heralded before your troops!'

'It will be done,' Meiler shouted back and laughed. 'I am glad you refused to meet me yourself, Ranulf. I prefer to see you dangle from a rope.'

Marshal prepared himself for battle in the courtyard, beneath the roof of an open shed attached to the stable. He preferred the light and the scent of hay and manure to the gloom of the great hall, with its dank odour of charred firewood. Isabelle and Ranulf had retired to the keep, and the men and boys of the garrison were avoiding the area around the stable. The long trestle-tables set up for a dinner in the open stood unused; the cooks had served a hasty meal, which everyone had eaten individually or in scattered groups.

A heavy, uneasy silence had descended on the castle, and the buzzing of flies around the stable's manure pile seemed unnaturally loud. The waiting would be hard for Ranulf's garrison, Marshal knew; their fate had been placed in the hands of a knight they did not know. A knight with an injured arm. Marshal examined the splint on his wrist. Jean d'Erly had reinforced it and added padding beneath new bindings. All that could be done to protect the wrist had been done, but would it be enough?

Marshal dismissed the thought. He had made his decision. He might have tried to slip out of Kilkenny with the girl, as Ranulf had suggested, but there was the danger of pursuit if Meiler guessed that Isabelle had escaped. The shipping out of Waterford was irregular, and it might take days to obtain passage out of the port. To leave her behind, under siege, seemed no less dangerous.

Marshal had rationalized his decision, but he had not really tried to weigh the risks against each other. In truth, he was driven by anger. He wanted to defeat Meiler fitz Henry with cold steel.

He had stripped to his linen shirt and breeches, and

although the sun was strong, the air beneath the shed roof was cool. That suited him; he would be sweating soon enough. He knelt on a low mound of straw, crossed himself and began a litany, going through the motions of prayer, but his mind remained focused on the coming duel, envisioning Meiler's attack.

A man who used a mace enjoyed battering an opponent. If, as Ranulf said, Meiler had never been unhorsed, he would be good with the lance; but he would be satisfied to break lances in a stalemate, looking forward to the moment when he could close with his enemy and hammer him down.

If it came to that, Marshal could try to fight him on his right hand, sword-to-mace, but Meiler would soon notice the splint and force combat shield-to-shield. No, he could not allow Meiler to close with him, and he could not rely on conventional tactics. If he could not unseat Meiler on the first or second pass, he would have to try the French shift.

As skilled as Marshal was, he had only used the dangerous manoeuvre once in combat, and that was years ago. He was still as strong as he had been then, but he was not so sure of his speed. The timing had to be perfect . . .

Jean d'Erly emerged from the stable and looked at Marshal expectantly, bright-eyed with excitement. Marshal rose and casually brushed the straw clinging to the knees of his breeches. His show of calm was a bit of theatre for the boy's benefit; Jean was excited enough for both of them.

'Your horse is saddled, sire.'

'Bring him out,' Marshal said, 'and I'll have a look at him.'

Jean brought out Marshal's charger and tethered him to a shed post. Marshal walked over and patted the chestnut stallion's head. 'Not a pretty beast, is he, Jean? Too thick a neck and the skull of a dray.'

'His age concerns me, sire,' the boy said hesitantly.

Marshal nodded. 'That's why I was able to buy him cheaply in Waterford. For the long term you'd be right to be concerned, but this old devil will last for a pass or two, and he responds well to knee commands. He knows all the moves, and that's what I need today.'

'What's his name, sire?'

Marshal shrugged. 'I don't know. He's just a horse, lad –

a tool, and an expendable one. Don't make a pet of your charger. Someday he may have to die for you.'

Marshal checked the chestnut's shoes, then tested the saddle girth. He still used his unpainted Templar saddle with a simple saddle blanket. The rig was unimpressive, but it was strong and reliable. Jean had done his work well, and Marshal nodded approvingly. 'He hasn't been watered recently, has he?'

'No, sire, not since early this morning. Are you sure you don't want caparisons?'

Marshal shook his head. 'You know there's no point. They won't stop a lance, even if Meiler is fool enough to attack the horse instead of me.'

'I know, sire, but . . .'

Marshal smiled. 'You'd like to see some pageantry.'

Jean blushed, and pushed back a shock of black hair that immediately fell across his brow again.

'That's all right, lad, I understand. But this is not a tournament, and we're not putting on a show for the ladies in the *loges*. If Meiler is unimpressed by my appearance, so much the better. Have you checked my lances?'

Jean nodded. 'The grain is solid, sire, though one is slightly warped.'

'Badly enough to make a difference?' Marshal asked, knowing the answer.

'I don't think so.'

'Good. I'm glad you're coming out with me, Jean.'

'Thank you, sire,' Jean beamed. 'It's a great honour for me.'

'Let's hope you think so when it's all over,' Marshal said with a wry smile. 'Has Sir Ranulf provided you with helmet and hauberk?'

'Aye, sire. I have everything in the stable. I wasn't sure . . .'

'Well, bring it out here. It's nearly time.'

Grinning, the squire dashed into the stable. Not every knight permitted his squire to appear beside him armed, but Marshal found this conceit idiotic. In his opinion, only a fool required another man to ride into hostile territory unarmed.

The squire's excitement brought a wan smile to Marshal's lips as he recalled how it had been for him when he was young – his impatience to prove himself in battle and the early thrill of combat. He remembered the joy of those wild, rough-and-tumble years, but the joy of combat for its own sake had slipped away with his youth. Now there was only controlled tension, calculation and the grim determination to get the job finished. When the fighting began, excitement would come with the rush of adrenalin, but it would be reflexive, born of the instinct to survive.

Jean carried out his armour, shield and sword, placed the equipment beside Marshal's in the straw, then helped him dress for battle. First the chain-mail leggings were pulled up over the baggy breeches and fastened to a cord round the waist. Next came the thickly padded, quilted tunic, followed by the hauberk. After the boy had laced the mailed sleeves and coif to the hauberk, Marshal slipped his lightweight white Templar surcoat over the armour, and Jean knelt to attach Marshal's plain steel spurs.

Jean quickly put on his own armour; Marshal helped him with the laces. He set the squire's open-faced, conical helmet on the boy's head and rapped it sharply with his knuckles. 'Tie that down well. You don't want it flying off at the first blow.'

Marshal picked up his sword, buckled it around his waist and slipped on a pair of thin leather gloves. He had roughened the palm of the right-hand glove and smeared it with pine pitch. He would not be wearing chain-mail gauntlets; for what he had in mind, a sure grip on the lance was essential.

'You will not carry your shield, Jean,' Marshal ordered, 'and you will tie your sword to the back of your saddle. You haven't been knighted, and I want those men out there to know it. You're not to become involved in the fight, no matter what happens. If Meiler's squire comes to his master's aid, let me handle him. You are to fight only if *you* are attacked, which is not likely. Meiler's knights have sworn to stay clear, and I don't want you giving them an excuse to break their oaths. Is that understood?'

'Aye, sire.'

'Don't forget! Now bring your mount.'

Marshal's charger was standing patiently, but as Marshal mounted him, the ageing stallion came to life. Marshal looped the reins about the saddle pommel and touched his spurs to the horse's flanks. The chestnut responded instantly, and Marshal cantered him around the compound, shifting him left and right with knee commands alone.

Several onlookers had appeared to watch the performance, and Marshal was sure his preparations had been discreetly observed all along. As he rode back to the stable and reined in, Jean whistled appreciatively, and Marshal nodded.

'He'll do, won't he? Let me have my helmet and shield.'

Jean handed up Marshal's shield and then the helmet, which Marshal set before him on the pommel. As the squire placed Marshal's lances in canvas slings attached to his own saddle, Marshal glanced critically at the palfrey the boy would be riding. The bay gelding was smaller and less powerful than a warhorse, but looked swift enough to carry Jean to safety.

Across the courtyard the door to the keep opened, and Ranulf and Isabelle walked out over the drawbridge.

'Mount up, Jean,' Marshal said, feeling his stomach muscles tighten.

He turned his charger and rode towards the keep, followed a moment later by Jean. As they crossed the courtyard, Marshal's warhorse began to prance. 'One of us welcomes this, at least,' he muttered with a wry smile.

Ranulf and Isabelle had done what they could to demonstrate their confidence, and despite Marshal's renewed tension, he was affected by the gesture. They were both dressed as if for an appearance at court. The old knight was resplendent in red and yellow: he wore a silk, saffron tunic, short scarlet boots and a scarlet cloak edged with ermine. Around his neck he sported a heavy gold ceremonial chain, and he had even combed his thinning hair and tough, wiry beard.

It had become the fashion in tournaments for a knight to wear his chosen lady's colours, but Isabelle had taken this homage upon herself. She was dressed entirely in blue and white, Marshal's colours. Over a white pelisse whose tightly fitting sleeves extended to the wrist, she wore a filmy, sky-blue *bliaut*. The blue gown flowed behind her in a long train, and its wide, trailing sleeves billowed in the soft breeze. Her cape was white, and on her head she had placed a simple crown of intertwined silk cords of blue and white.

But she, not her attire, captured Marshal as he reined in beside the drawbridge. He was no stranger to elegance, nor to youthful beauty. What struck him was the absence of self-conceit in Isabelle's manner. Like Ranulf, she had dressed with care only to do Marshal honour, and the concern he saw in her eyes as she tried to smile convincingly was not for her own safety.

'May God give you strength, Sir William,' she said in her low, husky voice. 'I have said a prayer for your victory.'

'Thank you, Lady Isabelle,' he answered formally, but then, on impulse, he lightened his tone. 'That makes two of us,' he smiled.

'God's blood, every man in the garrison has been praying!' Ranulf exclaimed in mock-despair.

Isabelle tried to stifle the laugh the two men surprised out of her, and it emerged as a giggle. She recovered her dignity, but Marshal was glad to see that her eyes were no longer grave. The jesting wasn't bravado; it was simply a way to release some of the tension.

Isabelle was holding a long blue scarf, and now she bent down and gave it to Marshal. 'Ranulf said you asked for a scarf of mine.'

Marshal wrapped it round his left wrist. 'Meiler will assume I'm wearing a token of yours, Lady Isabelle, and it may prevent him from noticing the splint.'

'But I do have a token for you, Sir William,' Isabelle said, and from the voluminous sleeve of her *bliaut* she withdrew a pair of spurs of red gold. 'These were my father's. I have kept them with me ever since he died. I know he would want you to have them.'

From the corner of his eye Marshal saw Ranulf smirk, but ignored him. 'I'd be honoured, Lady Isabelle.'

A fanfare sounded below the castle, and the watchman on the parapet shouted that Meiler was making his appearance.

'Better go,' Ranulf growled impatiently.

'There's no need to dismount, Sir William,' Isabelle said quickly, running lightly down the steps to the ground. 'It will only take me a moment to put these on for you.'

'No,' Marshal said in embarrassment. 'Jean can . . .'

But she was already at his side, unfastening his spur.

Ranulf was grinning broadly, displaying a set of chipped, yellowed teeth. Marshal glared at the old knight, but Ranulf's grin only widened. 'My true knight,' Ranulf mouthed silently, and his belly shook with suppressed laughter.

8

'Raise the portcullis and open the gate,' shouted Ranulf from the platform roof of the timber gatehouse.

Marshal lowered his helmet over his head and lashed it down as Ranulf's men winched up the heavy iron grate blocking the passage through the gatehouse to the outer doors. His nostrils twitched at the enveloping stench of the sweat-stained helmet-liner. He slipped his left arm through the straps of the shield, and Jean, mounted beside him and carrying his banner, handed him a lance.

Two of Ranulf's men ran into the passage, unbarred the great double doors of the main gate and swung them open. Marshal touched his spurs to his charger's flanks and rode forward, followed by Jean. As Marshal passed beneath the murder-hole in the roof of the passage, Ranulf shouted down a final farewell: 'Try not to break your other wrist!'

Marshal's answering grin, hidden by his helmet, was fleeting. As he rode out through the gate, his eyes locked on to the figure of Meiler fitz Henry waiting for him below, and he barely registered the sharp, clear notes of the garrison's trumpeter saluting him from the parapet.

Meiler and his squire waited at the southern end of a grassy flat lying between the foot of the slope and the stakes of Meiler's siege line. The field was one hundred paces long and no more than thirty wide, bounded on one end by the castle's outlying corral and cattle-pen, and on the other by a large garden, walled by thick hedges.

Meiler was offering no excuse for Isabelle's champion to deny him combat; he had withdrawn his troops from the area adjacent to the impromptu battlefield. They were clustered at the far ends of their encampment, close to the forest line, and screened from access to the field by knights and *serjants*. In the centre of the field, Meiler had stationed a mounted herald.

As Marshal eased his prancing steed down the slope, the incoherent crowd noise washing up to him from Meiler's troops became a rhythmic chant: 'Mei—ler. Mei—ler. Mei—ler.' If Kilkenny's men were cheering as well, Marshal could not hear them over the bellowing of the siege army.

Marshal and Jean rode to the northern end of the field and turned to face Meiler, and the crowd's chant broke into a roar of jeers and catcalls. Marshal glanced at Jean. The boy's dark eyebrows were drawn together in anger. That's right, Marshal thought, stay angry. Keep a cool head, but stay angry.

Meiler's herald was riding towards them, but Marshal looked past him to where Meiler waited astride a magnificent jet stallion. His saddle was draped with yellow and black silks, and he wore a yellow surcoat over black-painted armour. Ranulf had said he was as strong as an ox, and he looked it. The burly warlord radiated arrogance.

The sight of Marshal's banner instead of the triangular pennant of an ordinary knight must have surprised him, but Meiler was apparently unconcerned. Even at a hundred paces, Marshal could see his opponent's broad grin. He wore the old Norman helmet, with nothing but a steel nasal to protect his face. It was easier to fight in than the helmet Marshal wore, and showed Meiler's contempt for the additional protection of a steel cylinder.

Good. Meiler was a man accustomed to victory and confident that he could hammer down anyone daring to ride against him, and Marshal was relying on that confidence. A man who relied on overpowering strength could succumb to finesse.

The herald drew up before Marshal. He was a sallow-faced youth with a short, thin beard. Meiler had given him a bright-red robe, but his tunic was soiled and greasy, and the smell of him drifted in through the eye-slit of Marshal's helmet.

The herald addressed Marshal. 'My lord, Sir Meiler would have your name announced – unless you prefer to die anonymously,' he sneered.

'I meet him in the name of Lady Isabelle de Clare,' Marshal replied, loudly enough to carry over the continuing roar of the onlookers. 'That will suffice.'

The herald nodded curtly and rode back to the centre of the field. He took the trumpet slung from his saddle and blew a single long blast to quiet the crowd. 'Be it known,' he cried hoarsely, 'that Sir Meiler fitz Henry has graciously agreed to meet the champion of Lady Isabelle de Clare in single combat, so that God may vindicate his right to custody of Kilkenny Castle. Three passes of the lance will be followed by combat with hand weapons of choice. This combat shall be to the death. No man shall intervene on behalf of either combatant, and all men present are bound by the outcome. In assurance of this, Lady Isabelle de Clare and Sir Ranulf de Barre have so sworn, as have the knights of Sir Meiler's banner. At the next sounding of this trumpet, the combat shall commence!'

The herald's final words were nearly lost in the renewed roar from Meiler's army, and Marshal grimaced in anticipation. As the herald rode off the field, Marshal shifted his shield higher on his shoulder and tightened his grip on his lance. His attention was riveted on Meiler, and he did not hear Jean d'Erly's shout of encouragement. The herald reached the edge of the field, turned his mount and lifted his trumpet.

Marshal took a deep breath, then another, as his pulse quickened and his lungs demanded oxygen, and he let the anger that had been simmering inside him boil up. Across the field, Meiler's shield rose and his lance swung down. The roar of the troops clustered behind the siege line swelled abruptly as Meiler dug in his spurs an instant before the herald's trumpet blast, and his stallion surged into a gallop.

For a full two seconds, Marshal held his own mount in check, feigning hesitancy, letting Meiler come, knowing that he could give his own horse a shorter run and still meet Meiler at full speed. The warlord was charging him in standard fashion, bent low, with his shield at the optimum angle. Unless Marshal's aim was perfect, his lance would glance off harmlessly.

Now! Marshal dug in his own spurs, and the old stallion lunged to the attack. The horse knew what was expected, and

Marshal let him run straight out, his concentration focused on the exact spot where he would have to strike Meiler's shield. He watched for a last-moment shift in its angle, and the alteration came a split-second before impact. Marshal shifted his aim a fraction to the left to compensate. He had adjusted his own shield to minimise the shock to his wrist, and he did not alter its slant. Let Meiler think he was an amateur.

The aim of both knights was true, and their lances struck simultaneously, rocking both men back in their saddles with bone-jarring force an instant before the ashwood shafts snapped with a thunderous crack. Marshal's shield slammed back against his splint, and tears spurted into his eyes. He cried out in pain as the chargers drove past each other, the sound of his agony lost in the animal roar of Meiler's men yelling for blood.

Gritting his teeth against the stabbing pain in his wrist, Marshal dropped the splintered haft of his lance, took the reins in his right hand and slowed his mount, turning the horse in front of Meiler's squire, who was staring at him with wide eyes.

'What ails thee, lad?' Marshal yelled hoarsely. 'Did you think your master would unseat me on the first pass?'

At the far end of the field, Meiler had also made his turn, and they cantered past each other, twenty paces apart. Meiler was no longer grinning, but Marshal saw he was unhurt. The roar of the onlookers continued unabated.

'Give me the warped lance,' Marshal shouted to Jean as he drew up and turned to face Meiler for the second pass.

'How's your wrist, sire?' Jean cried, handing Marshal the lance. 'Christ's thorns! He's coming at you!'

Meiler had seized a fresh lance as he turned, and now he was charging back down the field. Marshal lowered his lance and galloped to meet him, bracing himself for a second shock to his pain-torn wrist. The gap between the charging horses closed with lightning speed, and this time the steeds met almost head-on. As the lances struck the opposing shields, driving the riders back in their saddles, the force of impact actually slowed their mounts' momentum before the lances splintered.

An involuntary shriek of pain was wrenched from Marshal's throat, and for an instant he was afraid he would faint. The roar of the crowd rose to an incredible level when Meiler's men saw Marshal pitch forward in his saddle as the two chargers swept by each other. Tears blurred Marshal's vision. He grasped the reins in his right hand and blindly wheeled his charger about, unwilling to allow Meiler to get a start on him on the last pass. It would have to be the French shift now, and he needed a full run.

Marshal was gasping with pain as he reined in and picked up the third lance – pain that knifed up from his wrist through his entire arm. He had known he could not withstand the battering of Meiler's mace, but hadn't reckoned with the agony that assailed him now, crowding out thought and all other sensation.

Grinding his teeth, he seized the lance, and with an effort of will, took an extra second to find just the right point to grip it. He was unaware that he was groaning and oblivious to the sudden shock in Jean d'Erly's eyes. Meiler was taking his lance now, turning his horse – more slowly this time.

Ignore the pain! Concentrate! Marshal willed himself.

Across the field, Meiler's lance swung down into attack position, and his stallion lunged forward.

'He's hurt!' Ranulf said tightly as he watched Marshal turn and ride back to pick up the third lance. 'I warned him about his wrist!'

Isabelle didn't trust herself to speak. Her throat had contracted, choking off her involuntary cry when she saw Marshal reel after the second pass, and the ferocity in the roar of anticipation from Meiler's army chilled her. The horde of Irish auxiliaries jostling one another behind the screen of Meiler's knights seethed with blood lust.

Ranulf was gripping the pointed ends of the stockade pilings with his gnarled fists. If his hands had been at his sides, Isabelle would not have been able to resist the urge to slip her hand into his, as she'd done so often as a child. She felt as helpless as a child, and that magnified her fear. Below on the field, churned and muddied by the chargers' hooves, a man was fighting for his life, and she could do nothing but watch!

Ranulf, no less impotent, clenched his teeth in desperate frustration, making the cords in his neck stand out, and Isabelle could see his pulse throbbing. He had seemed confident until the second pass, believing in Marshal – perhaps because he had to – but now he stood rigid, feet planted wide, gripping the pilings as if he meant to tear them from the earth.

'Marshal, you've got to do it this time,' Ranulf growled through gritted teeth. 'You've got to finish him now.'

Isabelle's anxiety flared into anger. 'How?' she burst out. 'What is he supposed to do?' Marshal and Ranulf had been so determined to play their bloody game, and now they were going to pay for it with their lives. Yet part of her anger was directed at herself. She should have stopped them! She could have, but she had not had the will.

Ranulf tore his gaze from the field below and looked at Isabelle. 'I don't know what he'll do,' he said hoarsely, shaking his head. 'But he must have something in reserve. He knew what he had to face, and still he was determined to fight. He must have *something*!'

'But he's hurt, Ranulf! You saw it, and they know it, too. Listen to those animals screaming down there!'

The old knight had no time to answer. Marshal and Meiler fitz Henry had couched their lances and spurred their horses into the final charge. The two stallions raced towards each other along the dark track of churned-up sod which marked the line of the first two passes; the pounding of hooves were drowned in the unremitting roar from the siege line.

Isabelle gasped. Marshal had been charging Meiler almost head-to-head, as he had on the second pass, but as the galloping steeds closed to the centre of the field, Marshal veered to the right, as if he had suddenly lost his nerve. Instantly, Meiler turned his mount to intercept him, the warlord's lance poised to strike at a fatal angle.

As Meiler moved left to cut Marshal off, Ranulf gave a wild shout of exultation: he realized what Marshal intended. What happened next occurred in the space of three heart-beats, and Isabelle was never to be sure how much she actually saw and how much her imagination filled in later to bring clarity to the blur of action.

Marshal's stallion abruptly swerved back to the left, and

Meiler found himself bearing down on the wrong side of his enemy, unprotected by his shield and too late to alter course. With blinding speed Marshal swung his lance across to the right-hand side of his body, relying only on the strength of his right arm to absorb the impact when the lance struck. As the two horses flashed by each other, Marshal's lance-tip caught Meiler squarely in the chest and swept him from the saddle.

The roar of Meiler's army died instantly, and the metallic crash as Meiler hit the ground carried clearly up to the castle. For a moment, there was stunned silence, and then pandemonium broke out along the stockade wall. Ranulf was yelling incoherently at the top of his lungs, as were his men, waving their arms, slapping one another on the back and literally jumping for joy. But Isabelle felt hot tears streaming down her cheeks, and they were not tears of joy.

The weeks of strain and moments of raw fear had taken their toll, and Marshal's sudden victory released a torrent of delayed anger, as if a dam had broken inside her. Her pent-up hatred of John and of the man who lay helpless on the field below swept her away, and now it was she who wanted blood.

Meiler lay on his back with the breath knocked out of him. First one leg twitched, then the other, and he feebly raised an arm, grasping in thin air for something to pull himself up with. In those seconds of shocked silence among Meiler's company, no one rushed to his aid. Meiler's squire sat unmoving on his horse, as did his knights. It had happened too quickly for the onlookers to absorb before it was too late to intervene. Marshal had already turned and was bearing down on Meiler with his lance.

Meiler, still partially stunned, lay helpless, with no means of defending himself. His stallion had galloped off the field with the warlord's mace still slung from the saddle pommel, and his shield and lance lay six paces away. For a moment, Isabelle thought that Marshal would drive his lance into his prostrate enemy, and she clenched her fists in fierce anticipation. She felt no pity for the man who had sought to terrorize them all, who would have gladly killed Marshal and executed Ranulf. She wanted him to die.

But, abruptly, Marshal reined in his mount. Meiler lifted

his head and managed to raise himself on to his elbows, staring up at Marshal, who advanced on him deliberately and pinned him to the ground with the point of his lance. The cheering from the castle died away, and in the sudden hush the men on both sides awaited Marshal's decision.

'Kill him!' Isabelle hissed. 'Kill him!'

Ranulf turned and stared at her. 'No, milady, he won't,' Ranulf said. 'If he meant to, Meiler would already be dead.'

'Do you yield, Sir Meiler?' Marshal demanded loudly, his powerful baritone breaking the tense silence.

'Aye!' Meiler cried hoarsely, and a sound like a collective sigh drifted up from the soldiery, followed by a low, incoherent muttering – whether of relief or discontent, it was impossible to say.

Isabelle shuddered as her rage spent itself, and slowly the tension drained out of her, leaving her with a slack, empty feeling of anticlimax. Marshal said something to Meiler and backed away his horse. The warlord got unsteadily to his feet, removed his helmet and turned to face his troops.

'I hereby surrender my claim to Kilkenny,' he called out bitterly, 'until such time as the matter is brought before His Majesty, the king. My chamberlain shall pay off all enlisted auxiliaries at once, and all knights, *serjants*, officers of my household and men in my service shall retire without delay and return home.'

Meiler turned back to Marshal, and Marshal spoke to him again. Isabelle saw Meiler shake his head vehemently, and she heard his growl of protest. But Marshal raised his lance, and the warlord immediately nodded in assent.

'My squire and I,' he announced, 'shall remain in Kilkenny as the "guest"' – Meiler spat out the word – 'of Lady Isabelle de Clare, to ensure the proper execution of my orders.'

'Marshal, you devil!' Ranulf chortled. 'What a malicious sense of humour you have!'

Grinning, he turned to Isabelle, and suddenly she found herself smiling in return. They had won! She took a deep, shuddering breath of relief. The future was still uncertain, but for the moment, at least, she was free.

'Rusty,' Ranulf said, shaking his head. 'I had no idea you were so bloodthirsty.'

Isabelle laughed, intoxicated by the relief flooding through her.

'Just be glad Marshal had a cooler head than you,' Ranulf said seriously. 'I wouldn't have minded seeing Meiler skewered, but it's better for you he lives. Killing him would not have helped your case at court.'

Isabelle looked down at Marshal, still astonished that he had spared Meiler, who would cheerfully have killed him if their positions had been reversed. Perhaps Marshal was level-headed enough to choose the politically wise course, but she had seen the anger burning in his eyes and found it difficult to understand how it could be checked so quickly.

Meiler's lieutenants were already shouting orders to their men, organizing the retreat, and Jean d'Erly and Meiler's squire had ridden over to join Marshal and his captive. One of Meiler's knights led out the warlord's charger and handed the reins to Marshal, who gestured for Meiler to mount.

As Marshal started up the slope with Meiler in tow, Kilkenny's garrison roared its approval. Ranulf shouted up to the herald on the parapet, 'When Sir William comes through our gate, Tom, I want the longest, loudest fanfare you've ever blown!' The man grinned and waved in acknowledgment.

'I didn't think he could do it,' Isabelle said huskily. 'I thought . . .'

'So did I,' Ranulf grated. 'And I knew what he could do. I hoped he had a surprise for Meiler, but the French shift . . .' Ranulf shook his head in wonderment. 'That's something you hear about but never see, and now that I've seen it, I still don't believe it. If Marshal's charger had reacted an instant too late, Meiler would have run him down. And to swing the lance to the offhand side and strike the target in one motion . . . God's blood! The impact should have wrenched the lance from his hand.'

The afternoon sun was in Isabelle's eyes, and she raised her hand to shield them from the glare. Marshal's exhaustion and pain were evident in the way he sat his horse. He was leaning back heavily against the high cantle of his saddle, his right hand gripping the reins of Meiler's mount, which he had looped around the lance resting on his stirrup. He held his own reins slackly in his left hand, the splint resting on the pommel, and his left shoulder sagged. Isabelle wished she could see his face, but it was still hidden by his helmet.

Meiler's face was fixed in a fierce scowl. Behind him rode his dazed squire, who stared blankly ahead. Bringing up the rear was Jean d'Erly, grinning from ear to ear. As the party approached the gate, Jean spurred his mount forward and drew up alongside Marshal. 'Open the gate!' Jean cried triumphantly. 'Open for Sir William Marshal and Lady Isabelle's "guest"!'

'God's legs!' Ranulf laughed. 'That cub's never going to be the same!'

Nor am I, old friend, Isabelle thought. Nor am I.

As Marshal rode into the courtyard and Ranulf's men swarmed down from the wall to surround their triumphant champion, the sharp, clear blast of the herald's trumpet cut through their cheers. Ranulf was tone-deaf, and he could not appreciate the trumpeter's inspired virtuosity as the young man's fanfare climbed the scale, but it was as loud as a single horn could be, and that was enough to satisfy the old knight.

Ranulf looked up at the parapet, and the veteran *serjant*, Black Fulk, made a sign to him. Certain now that at least the tower watch would be maintained, Ranulf ushered Isabelle down from the gatehouse roof and led her through the throng to Marshal. Jean d'Erly had swung down from the saddle and rushed to assist Marshal dismount. Goaded by Jean's example, Meiler's own squire belatedly did the same for his master. Jean unlashed Marshal's helmet and lifted it off as Ranulf and Isabelle joined them.

Marshal's face was haggard, and his attempt at a smile to Isabelle was more a grimace as he cradled his broken wrist in his right arm. As Isabelle looked up at him, she realized she had no words to express what she was feeling. Gratitude, relief, admiration – the words were totally inadequate.

'Thank you, Sir William,' she said simply, hoping he would understand. 'Thank you for all of us.'

'Here, here!' Ranulf cried, provoking a fresh outburst of cheering from the men pressing in around them.

Isabelle, still unable to find the right words, thought to convey something of the depth of her feelings with her eyes, but Marshal glanced away, looking towards Meiler, who stood with his squire, surrounded by hostile stares.

Isabelle stiffened and approached the warlord, and the men around him fell silent.

A look of resignation had replaced Meiler's scowl. 'I am your prisoner, Lady Isabelle,' he said tonelessly.

She ignored the silence pressing in on them and looked into Meiler's eyes for a long moment without speaking. A residue of the hatred that had gripped her on the wall stirred deep inside her, and she glanced at the spot where Marshal's lance had gashed Meiler's chain mail. The lance-tip must have penetrated to some extent on impact, for the rent was stained crimson by blood that had seeped through the armour.

If she, and not Marshal, had held the lance pinning her enemy to the ground, she believed she would have driven it home. As she met Meiler's eyes again, a faint, ironic smile of understanding played across his lips. He knew what she was thinking.

'Not my prisoner, Sir Meiler,' Isabelle said icily. 'I prefer the word chosen by my champion. Consider yourself my guest. That has a far more pleasant ring.'

'As you wish, Your Ladyship,' Meiler responded drily.

'Yes,' she agreed. 'As I wish. But do not think I mock you, Sir Meiler. You will be confined to the dungeon at night, but by day you will have the freedom of the castle.'

If Meiler was relieved that he would not be left to rot in the dungeon, he was too proud to show it.

'Tomorrow we will celebrate our victory,' Isabelle added. 'Unless you cannot stomach a feast in honour of the knight who defeated you, I would be pleased to have you attend.'

'I can accept food under any circumstances, Lady Isabelle,' Meiler answered calmly. 'And I remind you that custody of this castle is still undecided. Prince John may not be content to share my defeat.'

9

The night of Marshal's victory, Isabelle went to bed far later than usual. Only reluctantly had she left the great hall, where the men were already celebrating in advance of the feast to be held the following day. The singing, gambling and drinking still continued when exhaustion finally forced her to retire.

Marshal had wanted her to leave Kilkenny immediately, but in the end yielded to her insistence that one day's delay would make no difference, and Ranulf had reluctantly concurred. Suppressing a yawn, Isabelle entered her chamber, preceded by Matilda, who carried a candle lantern to light their way. The odour of woodsmoke and the sound of raucous laughter drifted up the stairwell and followed them into the chamber.

Matilda removed one of the lantern's translucent horn windows to light the all-night candle by the bed. As the candle-flame flared, suffusing the chamber with a soft yellow glow, Isabelle went to the trestle-table holding her toilet articles and sat down heavily on the canvas seat of the folding stool. Despite her fatigue, she wondered if she would be able to sleep. Her body was alive with nervous energy.

'How much did you win, Mattie?' she asked as Matilda came over to loosen her hair.

Matilda opened her fist and proudly displayed a handful of silver pennies. 'The odds were two-to-one against you, milady,' Matilda said and hiccuped. 'You should have seen poor Fulk's face when he had to pay up,' she added, her tongue tripping over the words.

Isabelle smiled. She had never seen Matilda tipsy before. This had been a rare day in all respects. 'You were luckier than you know,' she said, stifling another yawn. 'Sir William very nearly finished me when he brought out his bishop at the end.'

'He never had a chance, milady, and you know it. You are a murderous chess-player. Winning Fulk's money was child's play.'

'I thought you considered wagering a sin,' Isabelle said, still smiling.

'Certainly not,' Matilda sniffed, stepping behind her mistress and untying the ribbons on Isabelle's braids. She seemed to be having difficulty manipulating her fingers. 'The priests don't approve, but they hate anything that's amusing. At worst, it's indiscreet for a woman to gamble.' Matilda giggled. 'And you, milady, were being discreet enough for both of us.'

'What are you suggesting?'

'Nothing, milady,' Matilda said innocently, but as she unbraided Isabelle's hair, Isabelle sensed that Matilda was grinning.

'All right, Mattie,' Isabelle said impatiently. 'Speak your mind.'

'I only thought that when Sir William offered you a game of chess, you might have invited him to play the game up here – away from all the noise. But no, you were the very soul of discretion.'

'Noise has never disturbed my game,' Isabelle said, deliberately missing the point, but she felt her cheeks flush. It was not difficult to guess what Matilda meant, and she wondered how many others had the same thought. Did Marshal?

'Of course you were right, milady. Very proper,' Matilda said, patting Isabelle's shoulder. 'And I suppose your game might actually have suffered. Up here, alone with him, it might have been even more difficult to concentrate.'

'Don't be impertinent!'

'I know it would have been difficult for me,' Matilda sighed, ignoring the rebuke. Then she chuckled. 'I wouldn't have protested washing more than his hair this morning, if he weren't so shy. Yes, I do believe I could become accustomed to that chore. I think . . .'

'I'm tired, Mattie,' Isabelle interrupted. 'I'm going to retire now.'

'Not before I've brushed your hair, milady,' Matilda said, preventing her from rising. 'One hundred strokes a night, makes tresses shine bright.'

'And ladies who've been drinking, talk without thinking,' Isabelle responded tartly. She wouldn't admit it, but Matilda was embarrassing her.

As a girl, Isabelle had always confided in Matilda. Neither the king nor Prince John had bothered to see to it that Isabelle was raised in the customary manner for a young lady of her rank, and she had grown up on her family estates surrounded by men and boys, with Matilda as her only intimate female companion. Matilda had been part mother and part older sister to Isabelle, and it was Matilda to whom Isabelle turned for solace and advice in the first years of her sexual awakening, entrusting to her the joys and sorrows of her adolescent infatuations with a handsome squire or the occasional silver-tongued trouvère.

But this was different. Isabelle was no longer a girl, and Matilda, however tipsy, was speaking to her woman-to-woman about Marshal. It was a new experience for Isabelle, and it made her uncomfortable. Marshal had been at the centre of her thoughts all evening, to the exclusion of everything else, and the feelings he aroused in her were bewildering.

Her youthful yearnings had not altered her straightforward view of men, and the strength of her attraction to Marshal took her by surprise. His gallant courage and skill on the battlefield were dazzling, but it was the sound of his voice, deep, resonant and surprisingly gentle, that lingered now in her mind – his voice and his infectious smile. She had been able to talk with him as if they were old friends, and it seemed incredible that only that morning he had been a stranger.

Matilda began to brush Isabelle's hair. 'I've seen Sir William before, milady,' she said.

'Yes, you told me.'

'At the queen's court in Poitiers. I saw him myself only once or twice, but I heard all the gossip. He was thinner then, more boyish, of course. All the ladies were in love with him.'

'Don't talk nonsense, Mattie.'

'But that was the fashion then, milady. And still is, I imagine,' Matilda added wistfully. 'The French courts are civilized, and they permit a lady to enjoy the attentions of her true knight – within bounds, of course.'

'Of course,' Isabelle smiled.

Matilda still pined for the days she had spent at Eleanor's court. That had been before the queen had made the mistake of supporting her son, Prince Henry, in his first abortive revolt against his father. The king and his son had been reconciled, but Eleanor had been banished to England under house arrest, ending for ever her reign as queen of the most fashionable Court of Love in France.

Matilda had wiled away many a rainy afternoon telling Isabelle of those Courts of Love, where Eleanor, together with her daughter from her first marriage to King Louis of France, Marie of Champagne, and her daughter-in-law, Marguerite of France, wife of Prince Henry, would rule on questions of principle and adjudicate disputes of love brought anonymously before the court. The heroes of the tournaments and ladies of high degree would listen attentively to the amatory wisdom of these three high-priestesses of Courtly Love.

Could true love exist in marriage?

Judgment: Possibly, but love and marriage were basically incompatible.

Could a lady's true knight breach his sacred silence to come to his lady's defence if he heard her charms disparaged?

Judgment: Not without incurring the lady's displeasure, but she should forgive him eventually.

Even as a girl, Isabelle had thought it all childish, an excuse for posturing and gossip.

'There were all sorts of rumour about Sir William in those days,' Matilda said admiringly. 'And some in later years, as well.'

'Yes,' Isabelle said drily. 'I suppose there were.'

'Of course, the rumours may have been the result of wishful thinking, milady. Marshal was never the flirtatious type, and I doubt that the ladies I knew received his attentions – not even the queen. And if anyone could have claimed Marshal as her true knight, Eleanor could.'

'Why do you say that?' Isabelle asked, unable to curb her curiosity.

'Because there was a bond between them, milady, going back to a time just after Sir William was knighted. He was only modestly equipped at the time, as he had no independent means, and his uncle, Patrick, Earl of Salisbury, took him into his household.

'The Lusignans were in rebellion at the time, and Earl Patrick crossed to France with the king to help him put down the revolt. Knowing that the Lusignans were no match for him, the king allowed Eleanor to come with him. Having occupied Lusignan Castle, the king left Eleanor there under Earl Patrick's protection while he continued in pursuit of the rebels. Unknown to anyone, a war party under Guy de Lusignan slipped past the king at night and made for the castle, in the hope of capturing the queen.

'They tried to ambush her while she was riding outside the castle with her escort, but they were sighted some distance away. Earl Patrick sent Eleanor and the rest of the escort fleeing back to the castle, but he and Marshal stood their ground to delay the raiders. Neither of them was fully armed, and only Marshal was wearing a hauberk.

'The Earl was trying to mount his charger when he was killed by a lance-thrust in the back, and Marshal barely had time to seize a pike and place his back against a hedgerow. Crying challenges to keep the knights from pursuing Eleanor, he fought them on foot, with neither shield nor helmet, cutting down their horses one after another. They say he fought like a boar cornered by dogs.

'He wounded or killed fifteen men before one of Lusignan's knights came up behind the hedge and drove a lance into Marshal's thigh. Guy de Lusignan was furious that his knights had turned aside to fight Marshal, allowing Eleanor to escape, and had Marshal thrown on a horse and carried off for ransom. Had he known that Marshal was a landless knight, he probably would have killed him on the spot. When they discovered their mistake, the Lusignans continued to hold Marshal, but they left him to tend his own wound, not caring whether he lived or died.

'But Eleanor cared. His allegiance had been to his uncle,

not Eleanor, and after the earl fell, Marshal could have surrendered with honour. Yet he fought on.

'Eleanor ransomed him and kept him with her until his wound healed. Then she equipped him with the finest arms and horses that gold could buy, giving him his start in tournament. Once he established a reputation, it was through Eleanor's influence that he became Prince Henry's tutor in chivalry.

'But that was years ago, milady. He may have been the queen's knight once,' Matilda said with wine-enhanced pride, 'but now he is yours.'

'You're being ridiculous, Mattie, and that's enough brushing,' Isabelle said dismissively and stood up.

'Am I?' Mattie persisted as she helped Isabelle undress. 'Marshal risked his life for you today, and whether you acknowledge it or not, there is a bond between you. You chose him as your champion, milady, and he served you magnificently. He *is* your true knight, and you must reward him.'

'I know better than you how much I owe him,' Isabelle said sharply, slipping into bed. 'But you do him a disservice by implying that he expects a reward – a reward you know very well I am powerless to give. I am not Eleanor of Aquitaine.'

'I was not referring to gifts of land or gold,' Matilda said coyly.

'Then what?' Isabelle asked, instantly regretting the question.

Matilda smiled knowingly. 'You must have seen the way he looked at you this evening. Your chastity is reserved for your future husband, milady, but your love – that is something you should give to the man of your choice.'

At that Isabelle groaned and turned on her side, pulling the coverlet over her head. 'Go to bed, Mattie!'

Marshal stopped trying to reconstruct the sequence of moves that had led to his defeat. Now that the game was over, he could no longer summon the energy to concentrate. He rubbed his eyes tiredly and gathered up the discarded chesspieces scattered among the remains of supper.

'You don't like losing, do you, Marshal?' Ranulf said, belching alcohol fumes.

'Not particularly,' Marshal said, giving Ranulf the answer he expected. Actually, Marshal did not mind losing to a better player, and the girl was good – very good.

Ranulf sat beside Marshal at the head table on the raised dais at the lord's end of the great hall, facing the long trestle-table for the garrison's men, which ran lengthwise down the centre of the hall. Ranulf was sprawled in the canopied ceremonial seat Isabelle had vacated, a wine cup grasped none too securely in his hand.

Marshal stretched out his legs and leaned back in his chair, easing the stiffness in his body. He was no longer as resilient as he had been at twenty, and he would have to sleep soon. Yet he wanted to stay awake a while longer. With fatigue clouding his mind like an opiate, he felt no compulsion to think ahead; for the moment, at least, he could savour the satisfaction of his small victory and the pleasure he found in Isabelle de Clare's company.

Tomorrow, he knew, sore muscles and stiff joints would remind him that time was working against him. His strength, speed and endurance would not last for ever. He might not have many more years to win something enduring for himself by his sword. And in the cold light of morning, when reality reasserted itself, he would have to forget the smiling green eyes and flame-red hair of a girl for ever beyond his reach.

Ranulf reached over and clapped Marshal on the shoulder. 'Cheer up, my friend. At least you didn't lose any money.'

'I never wager on my own game,' Marshal said absently, as a cold sense of loneliness descended on him suddenly – a loneliness that had attacked him at odd moments throughout his adult life, always when he least expected it.

He had always had friends, but there were times when that was not enough, when he missed the deeper ties of family and home, the sense of belonging somewhere and to someone.

'I hope you didn't mind my wagering on Her Ladyship,' Ranulf said, jingling the coins in his purse, 'but I've seen her play.'

'That's all right,' Marshal said, raising his voice to carry over a sudden swell in the noise level.

A few of Ranulf's men were slumped over their table,

overcome by wine, but most of them were clustered in a sweating pack at the table's far end, throwing dice. The hall resounded with the yelling of the onlookers, the triumphant cries of the winners and the groans and curses of the losers.

'Poor old Fulk,' Ranulf laughed, gesturing at the *serjant* who, Marshal knew, had helped Isabelle escape from Pembroke. 'He never learns; he has no head for gaming.'

Fulk was a dark, slack-jawed giant, with long, powerful, almost simian arms. From the puzzled scowl on his face, it was clear the dice were running against him, and his jaw muscles worked furiously.

'What is he chewing on?' Marshal asked.

'A chunk of rawhide. Half the time he forgets and swallows it. But he isn't as half-witted as he looks.'

Marshal shook his head. 'I hope not.'

'He's a tough campaigner,' Ranulf said with drunken affection. 'We were together when the earl took Waterford. God's blood, that was eighteen years ago!'

Marshal could see that Fulk could be a formidable enemy, and he understood why Isabelle had relied on him. His type was to be found in many baronial households – unimaginative, but unswervingly loyal. His devotion to the late earl had clearly been transferred to Isabelle, for when she was near, Fulk's watchful, protective gaze never strayed from her for long.

'I'm telling you, Marshal,' Ranulf said, hiccupping and belching simultaneously, 'those were the days! The land was here, just waiting for men with courage to take it and the will to hold it. The Danes never tried to push inland from the seaports they settled; they were content to let the wild Irish tribes war among themselves. Until we brought in civilization, the people here were living like savages. With no law worth the mention, and no idea of what to do with the land. They still reckon their wealth in cattle, and left on their own, they'd only clear the forest for pasture-land.

'Then, of course, the king made *his* move,' Ranulf grumbled. 'He came over with an army, including a siege train, to be sure the earl and the other Marcher lords did homage to him for the lands *we'd* taken – the land we'd won with our own sweat and blood.'

Marshal smiled. 'That's civilization for you.'

Ranulf grunted, drained his cup and set it down on the table with a bang. 'The king skimmed the cream. He took Wexford, Waterford and Dublin into his own hand, along with a third of the territory Earl Richard claimed as his.'

'Your earl could not have done too badly,' Marshal said without much sympathy. 'Henry never pressed a man too hard.'

'Oh, His Majesty gave something in return,' Ranulf said sourly. 'The lands in Wales he'd seized from Earl Richard years before, on the pretext that the earl's father had supported King Stephen in the civil war.'

'Leaving Richard de Clare the wealthiest baron in the realm,' Marshal said pointedly. 'That's not so hard.'

'It wouldn't have been, if the king had not given Ireland to John. When John came over two years ago with an entourage of youthful courtiers to receive homage from the Irish chieftains, he nearly provoked a rebellion. The chieftains came to his court in Dublin to do him honour, and John and his pimply-faced court mocked them. Christ's blood, some of his courtiers even tugged on the chieftains' long beards. And now he has Normans pitted against one another. His agents are all over. I'm telling you, Marshal, John must have been weaned on intrigue.'

Ranulf looked up sharply as a snarling dogfight erupted over a bone tossed to one of his mastiffs. 'Tom!' he yelled. 'Throw some water on those damned dogs before they tear each other apart!'

Marshal yawned and rubbed his eyes.

'You look weary,' Ranulf said. 'You can sleep in my chamber in the barracks hall. We've moved out the livestock and cleaned up the place, but the stench is still there.'

'I prefer that to the smoke in here,' Marshal said, suppressing another yawn. 'And that latrine is foul. When was the last time the pit was cleaned out?'

'What do you care? You're leaving soon.'

'I wish it were tomorrow,' Marshal said with concern. 'John may have wanted to keep this quiet up to now, but once he learns what's happened here, he'll go straight to the king to protect himself. I want to get to the king first.'

'One day won't make any difference,' Ranulf said easily.

'Meiler's henchmen will return home as they were told, and they won't have the wit to send word to John.'

Marshal nodded, but still he wanted to be on his way with Isabelle. Neither she nor Ranulf would be safe from John's wrath unless he could persuade the king to intervene; and now that Meiler had been taken care of, this last obstacle loomed larger in his mind. He had to get to Henry first.

'If I were John,' he said, 'I'd have alerted my customs agents to watch for Lady Isabelle to make sure she remains trapped in Ireland.'

'It's a possibility,' Ranulf agreed. 'We'll have to disguise her.'

Ranulf's tone was casual, making Marshal uneasy. He sensed that both Ranulf and Isabelle, impressed by his victory over Meiler, had too much confidence in him.

'Did you have any trouble with bandits on the way up from Waterford?' Ranulf asked.

'Nothing I couldn't deal with, but I didn't have a lady with me.'

'I'll give you Fulk, Jean and five others. What are you going to do when you reach England?'

'If I knew where the king would be, I would take Lady Isabelle straight to him; but I don't want to wander around the countryside with her. I'll take her to the queen. Eleanor has no great love for her youngest son, and she'll welcome a new face. Neither John nor the king should complain, for, once Lady Isabelle joins the queen, she'll be under royal control. She won't be able to bribe her way past the guards watching Eleanor the way she did in Pembroke.'

'She'll have to leave Matilda behind for the time being,' Ranulf said. 'Smuggling one woman aboard ship will be difficult enough. But she'll want to bring Fulk; he's something of a talisman to her. Besides,' he added with a crooked grin, 'I wouldn't want to be the one to deal with Fulk if we tried taking her out of here without him.'

Marshal nodded.

Ranulf cleared his throat tentatively. 'You could use a squire, couldn't you?'

Marshal looked at him in surprise. 'Are you offering me Jean?'

'If you'll take him. He's a good lad, quick and eager.'

'What about you?'

Ranulf grimaced. 'I won't find a lad as good as Jean, but we both know he'll be better off. With you, his future is assured.'

'Have you mentioned this to him?'

Ranulf shook his head. 'I didn't want to raise his hopes.'

'All right, if you're sure about this, I'll take him.'

'I am sure. I hate the thought of training a new squire, but I'm sure. One more thing. How long do you want me to hold Meiler?'

'It's your decision. A few weeks should be sufficient. Even if he breaks his word and musters another siege force, that will take time. By then, you should have received word of the king's decision, and that will settle things – one way or the other.'

Ranulf turned and placed his hand heavily on Marshal's shoulder. 'Listen, my friend, however it goes, we owe you much.' He refilled his wine cup. 'Now, if you're not going to take more of this wine, you might as well retire. The lady of the castle will have you up early tomorrow for some hawking.'

'What!'

'I don't think there's any risk. My scouts tracked Meiler's knights far enough to be sure they're marching north.'

'And what if they double back?'

'They won't. None of them has that much imagination, but if you're concerned, you'll have to explain it to Her Ladyship. I'm going to have my own hands full tomorrow. My wife will be coming back from St Canice Abbey. I tell you, Marshal, I thank God Meiler didn't burn down our manor. If my wife had to move in here with me, life would not be worth living.'

10

Marshal reined in his horse, and Isabelle halted beside him. 'Don't look so concerned, Sir William,' she said. 'Meiler's men will not return.'

Marshal nodded absently, studying the lay of the land. They were riding along the east bank of the river half a league south of the castle, following a narrow strip of dry ground between the marshland bordering the river and the virgin pine forest on their left. It was just after dawn. Fog shrouded the river's glassy surface and rose in ghostly fingers from the marsh.

The early-morning stillness, the mist in the half-light and the great fir trees of the limitless, primeval forest created a scene of enchantment and mystery, but Isabelle could see that the effect was lost on Marshal. He sat stiffly erect in the saddle, listening, his restless eyes probing the dark forest.

He had not wanted her to venture outside the castle, and now she wished she had not insisted. The hunting party had the air of a war patrol. Fulk and Ranulf's marshal were riding fifty paces ahead, and Jean trailed at the same distance. They were fully armed, and Marshal's armour lacked only the enveloping steel helmet. Two young Welsh riders kept pace on the left flank, threading their way through the trees thirty paces inside the forest.

Despite these precautions, Marshal had not relaxed for a moment, and Isabelle felt a pang of guilt. She was sure Ranulf was right and that Meiler's men would not have doubled back, but Marshal was not so certain. Now she regretted forcing him to go against his own better judgment. Hawking was her passion, and she had not immediately appreciated the depth of his concern.

'Let's ring up your bird, Lady Isabelle,' Marshal said, managing a smile, but there was a hint of impatience in his tone.

For a moment, Isabelle considered giving up the hunt, but the falcon she carried on her gloved hand was stirring with infectious anticipation. Now that they had come this far, surely one flight could do no harm.

Eagerly, Isabelle unhooked the short tether binding the bird to her wrist, and the falcon spread its wings. She removed its hood, and the hawk lifted its head, its fierce eyes flashing. Isabelle's heart beat faster. Her falcon was a magnificent peregrine she had trained herself, and part of the reason she had been so anxious to hunt this morning was to show off her hawk to Marshal.

She stroked the falcon affectionately. 'I think she bears a distinct resemblance to you, Sir William,' she said impulsively. 'The same colouring, the same . . .'

'Beak?' Marshal interjected with a smile.

Isabelle laughed self-consciously. 'Well, I wouldn't have put it that way,' she said with a sidelong glance at him.

Marshal did have a hawk-like profile, but now she was flustered, thinking the remark revealed how aware of him she was. When she had risen at first light, she had been torn between her desire to see him as soon as possible and her wish to take the time to make herself attractive. Matilda's suggestive chatter the night before had embarrassed her, but she had woken with secret excitement and anticipation. Did he sense the intensity of feeling he aroused in her? A part of her wanted him to know, and the other part quailed at the thought. What would he think if he knew? How could she possibly compare with the sophisticated women he must have known at court?

'All right, Isolt, catch us a nice fat heron!' she cried, launching the hawk.

Isolt's powerful wings dug sharply into the air, and the falcon climbed in a swift spiral, its wings beating rapidly, the tiny bells attached to its legs tinkling in the stillness. Isabelle smiled with pleasure as the hawk spread its wings and tail-feathers to catch an updraught, and she felt the familiar exhilaration as the bird spiralled higher and higher, riding the air current, until it was only a speck against the sky.

This was the thrill of hawking for her: watching the hawk she had trained soar into the sky, an extension of herself, her spirit carried aloft on its wings.

'Fulk!' she shouted excitedly, waving in the direction of the river, and Fulk turned his horse and rode out into the marsh to flush the game.

Isabelle spurred her horse and called over her shoulder, 'Come on, Sir William! And try to stop frowning!'

In moments, she came abreast of Fulk, whose horse was splashing through the marsh at the river's edge, and she had to slow down. Ranulf's marshal had kept ahead of her, maintaining his point position, and as Marshal caught up with her she saw him turn to check that Jean was following at the correct distance.

Again she felt guilty, but then a pair of herons hidden in the mist-shrouded marshreeds were startled into flight.

'There!' Isabelle cried, digging in her spurs.

The herons rose above the marsh and flew downriver, with Isabelle in full chase. She overtook the point rider and raced ahead of him.

'Take care, Lady Isabelle! Slow down!' she heard Marshal cry, his horse pounding over the treacherous terrain in pursuit.

Abruptly, the hawk dropped into view, streaking down on the unsuspecting herons. The falcon dropped a wing, veered and then plummeted, wings folded, towards its prey. At the final instant, the falcon's talons shot forward, and it struck the trailing heron with a sound like the punch of a fist. The stunned heron dropped like a stone into the marsh, and the falcon swooped down to deliver the *coup de grâce* with its lethal beak.

Isabelle swung her horse into the marsh, riding towards the spot where the falcon had disappeared in the reeds, closing in on the tinkling bells. Fulk and Marshal rode up, and Fulk dismounted to retrieve the heron.

'Take care!' Isabelle said, her cheeks flushed with the excitement of the chase. 'Don't frighten her.'

Fulk gently lifted the dead heron out of the water, the falcon still jealously hanging on. Isabelle whistled softly to the hawk and coaxed it back on to her glove. She tethered it, slipped on the hood and fed it bits of fresh pigeon meat.

'It's a fine kill, milady,' Fulk said approvingly, tying the heron to his saddle and remounting.

'Let's try further downriver!' Isabelle said happily. 'We'll bag another for the feast.'

Marshal shook his head. 'We've come too far from the castle already, Your Ladyship.'

Still caught up in the excitement of the hunt, Isabelle started to protest, but she checked herself as she noted Marshal's concern. She glanced back at the castle, nearly out of sight beyond a bend in the river, and was surprised by how far they had come.

'You're right, Sir William,' she agreed. 'One heron is enough,' and she turned her mare upriver.

Marshal began to relax as soon as they started back. He trusted Ranulf's judgment enough to know that an ambush was unlikely, and now that they were returning, his anxiety ebbed away. But he was not at peace with himself.

He should have insisted that Isabelle remain within Kilkenny's walls. An hour's sport was not worth the risk, no matter how slight. Yet he had found himself unable to resist the anticipation in the girl's eyes when she had appeared before sunrise in the great hall with her hawk.

It was a small warning, but a warning nevertheless. He would have to keep a tighter rein on his attraction to Isabelle de Clare. If he allowed his feelings to warp his judgment, things could end badly for both of them.

He smiled self-derisively to himself. It had not been as easy to ignore her charms as he had thought, for she was unlike other women of her station. She had a distinctive beauty of which she seemed strangely unaware, and her manner melded a man's directness with a natural femininity that was unmarred by affectation.

Marshal was not just drawn to her as a man to a beautiful young woman; he *liked* this courageous, unaffected girl, and that made him wary. It would be too easy to be captivated by Isabelle de Clare, he thought; and perhaps because he wished it were otherwise, Marshal failed to realize that he already was.

They were still half a league from the castle when the two young Welshmen suddenly burst upon them from the forest.

Marshal drew his sword instantly. One of the boys babbled excitedly to Isabelle, but Marshal didn't understand a word. He only knew the boys were frightened.

'What's he saying, Lady Isabelle?' Marshal cut in as the other men converged on them, reining in and drawing their swords. His voice was controlled, but inwardly he cursed himself for allowing Isabelle to leave the castle.

'Goblins!' Isabelle responded, her face going white.

'What?'

'Goblins,' she repeated. 'The forests here are supposed to be full of them!'

'That's right, sire,' Jean confirmed loudly, and Marshal shot him an angry glance. Now all the men, including Fulk, were eyeing the forest nervously.

'But what exactly did they *see*, Lady Isabelle?' Marshal said impatiently. He was tempted to order a dash for the castle walls, but if this was an ambush, they might ride straight into it.

'They didn't see anything,' Isabelle said anxiously. 'They just heard noises – strange noises.'

'What sort of noises? Men on foot? Horses?'

'Neither. They are sure there are goblins in there, Sir William. Goblins hate the sun, but the forest is so dark . . .'

'It's an ambush I'm worried about,' Marshal said, turning to Fulk. The *serjant* could be relied on to protect Isabelle with his life if necessary. 'I'm going into the forest,' he said. 'Count to thirty, then move out. Keep your weapons at the ready and hold the pace to a trot so I can stay ahead of you on the flank. If men are lying in wait up ahead, I want to flush them out.'

Marshal was uneasy about leaving Isabelle's side, but the fear of goblins he saw in the boys' eyes forced him to take the flank.

He turned his horse and moved into the forest, its darkness closing over him. The scent of pine was heavy in the air. There was no undergrowth, and the soft tread of his horse's hooves on the thick carpet of fir needles barely disturbed the silence. He rode in as far as he could without losing sight of the light at the forest edge and turned to ride parallel to the river bank.

The gaps between the massive, primeval trees were wide

and the riding was easy, but Marshal suppressed the temptation to press forward too quickly. He eased his left arm out of the sling he was wearing and slipped it through his shield straps, wishing now that he had his helmet.

As his horse trotted forward, Marshal's eyes restlessly scanned a wide arc, and he strained to pick up any strange sounds. At regular intervals he looked upward, for he had known knights who had died because they forgot that men could climb trees.

He started as a squirrel chattered at him from a branch directly above his head, and he deliberately eased his grip on his sword. There was no reason to be jumpy. Without undergrowth for cover, he would see an ambusher as soon as the man spotted him. How much time had passed? One minute? Two? He picked up the pace, anxious to stay ahead of Fulk.

The sound that had frightened the boys must have been fairly close to them or Marshal would have heard it too. He rode for another fifty paces and then reined in to listen. Nothing. Behind him and to his left he heard the snort of a horse. The others were catching up with him. Marshal was about to move on when he heard something else – off to the right. A dry slither, followed by a strange, whistling sigh. There was a pause, and then the sound came again.

Marshal cocked his head, waited, and got another bearing on the noise. He turned towards it and moved deeper into the forest. The sound had an eerie quality that he could not place, but goblins? Marshal had no idea what sounds a demon might make. Maybe the boys knew something he didn't? The Welsh reputedly knew more about such things.

Marshal crossed himself for good measure, but he kept going, following the sound ever deeper into the forest gloom. Slither – sigh. Slither – sigh. Goose-pimples rose on his arms as his imagination worked on him.

Slither – sigh. He was close now, very close. He should see it any moment. Marshal caught a flicker of movement ahead and gently reined in, willing his horse to remain still.

The next sigh Marshal heard was his own, and it was an involuntary sigh of relief. The 'goblin' was an emaciated hunchback dressed in a filthy patchwork of black woollen rags, dragging the carcass of a freshly killed doe across the needle-carpeted forest floor.

The man's head was swathed in a greasy tangle of hair and beard. It was impossible to judge his age, but he was clearly nearing exhaustion. He was an asthmatic, and the whistling sigh Marshal had heard was just the first and loudest of the man's gasps for air every time he dragged the carcass another few feet.

Bent over as the man was, too exhausted to raise his head, he didn't see Marshal watching him. A leather sling hung from a cord about his waist, and Marshal assumed he had killed the doe with a stone to the head. It must have been an incredibly lucky shot, Marshal thought grimly – bad luck for the deer, and worse luck for the man. The man was obviously not a professional poacher, or he would use a more effective weapon, and he had to be desperate to risk killing a deer so close to the castle.

Forest game was reserved for the lord, and the penalty for taking it was death without appeal. The man had killed one of Isabelle's deer, and for that he would have to die.

He was dragging the deer deeper into the forest. Perhaps he was a charcoal burner with a family to feed. Perhaps they were starving, but that would not matter to a court. Maybe he was ignorant of Norman law, but that mattered even less.

Marshal swallowed back the bitter taste that rose in his throat. It made no difference that he was not in Isabelle's service; he was sworn to enforce the law wherever he might be, and he had caught the man red-handed. The only mercy he could show would be to kill the wretch now, sparing him the mental torment of a trial and certain execution. Marshal was less than thirty paces away, and he could attack and kill him before the man realized what was happening.

The man seized the deer's forelegs to drag the doe another few paces, and Marshal drew his sword. He had no choice. Here, alone, with no one to know, he was all the more honour-bound to do the right . . .

The wretch was dragging the carcass out of sight, and Marshal still had not moved. Now he could no longer see him, but he could hear the man, hidden by the trees, wheezing for breath. As he listened to the receding sounds, Marshal, sword poised, realized that he was not going to attack. His duty was absolutely clear to him, but he could not bring himself to do it.

With a grimace of self-disgust, he sheathed his sword, turned his horse and rode back towards the river.

The victory feast was held outdoors in the courtyard before the keep. The banquet tables, covered in white cloth, were arranged in a T-formation on a wide, green carpet of freshly cut rushes. Isabelle's canopied chair was centrally placed at the head table, and her guests were seated at varying distances from her, according to rank. Knights and ladies were served at Isabelle's table, while everyone else sat at a long row of tables forming the spine of the T, with the priest and castle officers sitting nearest the top.

Despite the best efforts of Ranulf's wife, the feast did not begin on time. The bells of St Canice Abbey had long since rung *sexte* when the herald finally sounded the call to the feast in the early afternoon. The knights, ladies, officers and soldiers converged on the tables, waited impatiently for the end of the priest's long-winded blessing and then sat down to gorge themselves.

It was difficult to believe that only the day before the castle had been under siege, stripped of non-essential personnel, the courtyard filled with the stench and barnyard noises of livestock and cluttered with the paraphernalia of war. The return to a peacetime footing had already begun on the afternoon of Marshal's victory. Word that the siege was over quickly spread, and Ranulf's steward and butler returned to organize the small army of retainers streaming back to the castle.

Ranulf's wife, Madame de Barre, escorted by Ranulf's priest and the chamberlain, returned from the abbey while the hawking party was hunting downriver, and she immediately plunged into the confusion of cleaning operations and preparations for the feast. The steward resented her intrusion into his domain, but she enforced her demands with an iron will. She was a tiny sparrow of a woman, who looked like a nun in her simple gown and wimple, but she used her tongue like a whip.

Unsatisfied with the steward's initial efforts, Madame de Barre ordered a second cleaning of the barracks and the keep's chambers, the removal of the manure piles from the courtyard and the raking of every inch of ground. Next, she had the excess stocks of grain carted down to the town for distribution. There was not enough to compensate for the losses to Meiler's scavengers, but the example was intended to prompt St Canice's tight-fisted abbot to open his own ample storehouses.

All this was accomplished in the frenetic swirl of activity around the bakery and kitchen, where varlets and cookhouse assistants toiled under the demanding supervision of the steward, who, in turn, was driven by the lash of Madame de Barre's tongue. Prodigious quantities of fresh meat and poultry sent up from the castle slaughterhouse were dressed and cleaned and variously stewed, baked and roasted. The domestic fare was augmented by the game and fish brought in during the morning by the castle's huntsmen and the local fishermen.

Having tasted the butler's souring wines, Madame de Barre sent to the abbey for several cartloads of wine, and a variety of spiced and honeyed wines were prepared, gallons at a time. For cruder palates, barrels of beer were stacked outside in readiness.

She had intended to cut down the walkways suspended between the stockade fighting platform and the tower, but when Ranulf refused, she ordered varlets to drape them with brightly coloured bunting she miraculously conjured up, probably from her own manor, from which she also drew additional cutlery, cups, platters and table linen.

The whirlwind transformation of the castle's appearance and the spur-of-the-moment feast were an impressive feat, but Marshal was in no mood to enjoy the festivities. Preoccupied by the incident in the forest, he would have preferred to miss the celebration. He believed in the rule of law, and he despised those who did not. In his own mind, he shared the poacher's guilt. By letting the man go, he had abetted a capital crime, and his conscience gave him no peace.

'More wine, sire?' Jean d'Erly asked.

Marshal turned to look up at his new squire and frowned. 'If it pleases the *lady*,' he said pointedly.

Jean cleared his throat in embarrassment. 'Would you care

for more wine, milady?' he asked Matilda, seated to Marshal's left and sharing the cup with him.

Matilda smiled up at Jean and nodded. As the squire poured from the pitcher, he was clearly aware of Marshal's scrutiny, and he took care not to spill a drop.

Jean moved away to serve the others at the head table, and Matilda whispered, 'Don't be too severe, Sir William. The lad is trying hard.'

'He has to learn, Lady Matilda,' Marshal said, raising his cup with both hands and extending it to her. Matilda's rank did not entitle her to be addressed as Lady Matilda, but it was permissible to bend the rule, and Marshal knew she appreciated the gesture.

'I'm sure he's thrilled to be your squire,' Matilda said. 'I know I would be. The royal courts are nothing if not exciting.'

Matilda chattered on, as she had throughout the banquet, and Marshal, half listening, nodded at appropriate intervals, grateful that he was not required to add to the conversation.

He had taken something from nearly every dish brought to the tables by the parade of varlets streaming back and forth from the kitchen. The courses followed one another in a staggering array: stag, beef, mutton, trout, eels, rabbit, duck, heron, pork pies, chicken pies, custards and pastries, nuts, dried fruits and honey bread.

He ate mechanically, without real appetite, and although he normally enjoyed music, he barely registered the surprising skill of the local flute- and harp-players performing off to one side. He had, however, noted Isabelle's performance. Although she was seated on Marshal's right, they exchanged few words, for she was fully occupied with entertaining her 'guest', Meiler fitz Henry.

Throughout the banquet she engaged her enemy in courteous conversation, plying him with questions about his exploits. She overcame his initial, surly reserve and actually managed to draw him out. Now she was asking the warlord about his family, and Meiler was responding. Marshal considered it a bravura performance, for he had seen the hatred flickering in her eyes when she had accepted Meiler's surrender.

Meiler must have seen it, too, which made it even more surprising that she could persuade him now to put aside their enmity for the sake of courtesy. There was still something of the coltish, volatile girl in Isabelle de Clare, but she could, when it suited, display the manners and wit of a great lady.

'Ranulf!' Madame de Barre snapped, her sharp voice knifing through the drunken clamour rising from the soldiers' table. 'Control your men!'

Marshal smiled and looked over to Ranulf at the far end of the table. Isabelle had placed Madame de Barre between Ranulf and Meiler, but from the dogged look on the old knight's face, Marshal guessed that he would have preferred the company of his enemy.

The pikemen and archers were becoming unruly, hurling chunks of meat and bread across the table at each other, and Ranulf decided on the simple expedient of ending the feast. He caught Isabelle's eye, and she nodded.

'Father!' Ranulf yelled to the priest. 'Let's have the benediction.'

The priest rose to his feet unsteadily and, forgetting his linen napkin, wiped his greasy fingers on his cowl. He was a thin young man, and the wine had affected him. He began to speak, but his words were lost in the drunken shouts and laughter from the far end of the tables. He was about to raise his voice when he was struck by a wave of nausea. Covering his mouth, he hurriedly made the sign of the cross and rushed away.

Isabelle laughed, shook her head and rose from the table, bringing the banquet to an unceremonious end.

'Fulk!' Ranulf shouted. 'I don't want those men to go to sleep now, or too many will be unable to stand watch. Organize a stone-throw and wrestling, and set up some archery butts on the forward slope. I'll put up five sous prize money for the winner of each contest.'

Isabelle turned to Marshal and looked up at him with a smile. 'Are you going to participate in the stone-throw, Sir William? It only takes one arm.'

'I think I'd prefer a quiet stroll, Lady Isabelle,' he said, returning her smile and noting that Matilda had moved away as soon as Isabelle turned to him.

'We could walk down to the garden,' Isabelle said. 'If you don't mind company.'

'Of course not.'

Looking at her, Marshal wondered why he had never considered freckles attractive on a girl. The thought was only fleeting, for from the corner of his eye he saw Meiler fitz Henry, who had managed to drift away, making for the courtyard stable. The stockade gate was open, and the two guards manning the gatehouse looked none too alert.

Marshal excused himself and went over to Ranulf, who was staring, glassy-eyed, at his wife, clearly not listening to what she was saying. He had not yet adjusted to the renewal of marital bliss, and had been using wine as a palliative.

'I think your hawk is about to fly the coop,' Marshal said, gesturing towards Meiler.

Ranulf gaped for a moment, and then his eyes snapped back into focus. Cursing, he yelled to the men supposed to be guarding the warlord.

I I

'I'm suprised you didn't put on your hauberk, Sir William,' Isabelle teased as they walked down the long slope towards the castle's garden. Jean, mounted on his gelding, trailed them at a discreet distance. He carried Marshal's sword and shield and was leading two horses for Isabelle and Marshal. 'Are you always this cautious?'

'Always,' Marshal said, nodding in response to a black-clad old man who bowed to him and Isabelle as he passed.

The townsfolk who had shared in the feast at rude tables set out in front of the gate were streaming back down the hill, many of them staggering from a surfeit of beer. Bread, beef and mutton had been their fare, with beer instead of wine, but for many it was the first time their bellies had been full since the previous year's harvest. The poor who were too old, sick or crippled to make the short journey up to the castle would receive the remains collected from the tables.

'The people here are certainly partial to black,' Marshal remarked.

Every man, woman and child he had seen was dressed from head to foot in crude black woollens. The men's costumes were curious. Instead of hooded mantles, they wore tightly fitted patchwork caps attached to short, knee-length capes, and their hose and breeches were all one piece. But what struck him most was the lack of any colour but black.

'They don't dye their clothes black,' Isabelle said with a smile. 'It's the wool. They raise only black sheep here.'

Marshal shook his head. 'Ranulf was right when he said this territory is backward. You need trade here. If I were . . .'

'If you were what?' Isabelle prompted. 'A lord in Ireland?'

'I suppose that's what I was thinking,' he admitted. 'I

would do what your father probably meant to do if he'd lived – construct inland ports along the rivers, build up some river traffic and use trade instead of arms to bring calm to the region.'

'I'm not sure that was in his mind,' Isabelle mused. 'I think he was an adventurer at heart. At least that's the way Ranulf talks about him.'

'A man can tire of adventure, Lady Isabelle. It's a young man's game.'

'And do you feel old, Sir William?' she asked with a sidelong glance.

Marshal smiled. 'Sometimes.'

'Have you no land of your own?'

'None. I was a fourth son. My father was King Stephen's marshal and saved his lands by switching sides in the civil war, but his holdings were modest. When he died there was too little to share out. I knew from the start that I'd have to make my own way.'

'You'll receive a grant from the king,' Isabelle said confidently. 'After all, what knight banneret in his service has not? All it takes to make you a baron,' she said, snapping her fingers, 'is a word from the king.'

'That's right,' Marshal laughed. 'That's all it takes.'

They were approaching the entrance to the garden, which was situated on a knoll beside the river and surrounded by a high, thick hedge.

'From what I hear,' Isabelle said lightly, 'the king has stored up a rich supply of marriageable heiresses. Who knows, he might even give you my lands.'

With that, she slipped through the arched gateway in the hedge and disappeared into the garden, sparing Marshal the necessity of a reply. Marshal looked back at his squire, who had halted halfway up the slope to keep watch. Jean waved to assure Marshal he was alert.

The late-afternoon sun was behind Marshal, and the low angle of its rays illuminated the castle's whitewashed keep, casting it in sharp relief against the horizon. Once again, Marshal was gripped by a sense of having been here before and a haunting uneasiness. He was sure that somewhere, long ago, he must have been in just such a castle and looked at it at the same time of day from a similar angle . . .

Unaccountably he shivered, and he turned away and entered the garden. It was surprisingly large and elaborate for a frontier castle and designed for pleasure as well as utility. The largest area was reserved for vegetables, herbs and spices, but there were small groves of fruit trees and also extensive beds of flowers, some beginning to bloom.

Isabelle had vanished, and Marshal grimaced. To his right was a maze, its hedge-walls grown to the same thickness and height as the hedge surrounding the entire garden. She must have gone into it, and he would have to follow. Claustrophobia was not a word in his language; he only knew that he detested garden mazes.

The path between its hedge-walls was little wider than Marshal's shoulders. At first curving in a wide arc, the track then turned sharply in the reverse direction. As Marshal strode along, it twisted and turned, endlessly doubling back on itself, with multiple side-exits, most of which eventually led to a dead-end.

Despite the open sky above, Marshal felt the walls closing in on him as he went deeper into the maze, and he walked more quickly, anxious to reach the centre. But the design was too clever for him and he became disoriented. As he found himself in the same cul-de-sac for the third time, cold beads of sweat began to dot his forehead.

The walls seemed to be squeezing out the air he was trying to breathe, and he could barely resist the urge to smash his way straight through them. Marshal closed his eyes to fight down his rising panic. That was what it was, he knew. Panic. But why? He wasn't trapped in the damned garden maze. He wasn't trapped!

'It's a fine maze, isn't it?'

Marshal opened his eyes. 'Yes, Your Ladyship,' he said, feeling sweat running down over his ribs.

'Follow me,' Isabelle said, taking his hand. 'I'll show you the way. There's a turning further on that looks like a dead-end. That's what fooled you,' Isabelle laughed. 'You certainly don't have much patience. I heard you barging around in here like an angry bull. My father loved mazes. He ordered them planted almost everywhere he built a stronghold.'

The maze ended at a gate opening into a long hedge-walled corridor leading directly out of the garden. Isabelle opened the gate, and Marshal followed her out to a rock ledge overlooking the river. The sun still shone on the rolling forest beyond, tingeing the green with orange. The river below lay in shadow, its dark, mirror surface occasionally broken by the splash of a fish.

Isabelle spread out her robe and sat down, clasping her arms about her knees, and Marshal sat down beside her. From the direction of the castle came isolated shouts of Ranulf's archers on the slope, but the sounds were muted and only emphasized the peaceful stillness hanging over the river.

For a long while they said nothing, and Marshal wondered what Isabelle was thinking as she looked out over the forest. Was she thinking about him? He smiled inwardly. He had been with the Templars too long. Finding himself alone with a beautiful woman after so many years was like swallowing brandywine on an empty stomach.

When Isabelle finally spoke, she caught Marshal off-guard. 'What did you see in the forest this morning?' she asked.

'Why do you think I saw anything at all, Lady Isabelle?' he responded lamely.

Isabelle turned towards him, smiled and shook her head. 'Dissembling is not one of your talents, Sir William.'

'I didn't see any goblins.'

'But something was out there. When you caught up with us, you acted – I don't know – differently.'

Marshal remained silent. He knew that his evasion aroused her curiosity even more, but he did not want to lie to her, and had no wish to discuss the incident in the forest. He would wrestle with his own conscience alone.

'You don't want to tell me, do you?' Isabelle said.

'No, Lady Isabelle,' he replied, more bluntly than he intended. But she did not appear to take offence, and to Marshal's surprise, she did not press him. Instead, she changed the subject.

'Ranulf told me you're worried John may have alerted his customs agents at Waterford to watch for me,' she said. 'He suggested I disguise myself as your manservant until we reach England. With the right clothes, I think I could pass for a boy.'

'I think that's a good idea. It may take a little practice,

though – acting like a servant, I mean. Your voice is all right, but we'll have to dirty your face. You're too pretty to be a boy.'

Isabelle bowed. 'Thank you, sire.'

'Of course, the freckles will help,' Marshal said without thinking. 'Most women cover them with powder.'

'Do you think I should?' Isabelle asked quickly.

'No – no, of course not, Lady Isabelle! That's not what I meant,' Marshal said in confusion.

Isabelle smiled slightly and nodded, but Marshal was sure the damage had been done, and he silently cursed his clumsiness. He liked those freckles of hers.

'And what will you call me in front of strangers?' she asked.

'What about Rusty?'

'How did you know that?' Isabelle laughed.

'I heard Ranulf use it.'

'You did? When? Oh, it doesn't matter. Rusty it will be,' she said with pleasure. 'I've always preferred my nickname, anyway.'

'Well, you'll have to change back when we reach England,' Marshal said. 'I don't think you'd care for the rough comfort of wayside inns, and if we're to make use of castles along the route to Winchester, we don't want to deal with the complication of a disguise. We'll just say that the queen has invited you to visit her. The lack of an entourage for a lady of your station will seem odd, but we should be able to invent a plausible excuse.'

'What is the queen like?' she asked.

Marshal thought for a moment. 'Regal. Eleanor of Aquitaine is a woman fit to rule the kingdom and for ever disappointed that she could not.'

'Is she bitter?'

'No, I don't think so. Eleanor is too much of a realist to be bitter. I haven't seen her in more than six years, but I doubt she has changed very much.'

'Are you sure she'll consent to my staying with her?'

'That's the one thing I *am* sure of,' he said firmly. 'She'll welcome your company, Lady Isabelle. Some of her ladies-in-waiting are even older than she is. Young ladies don't care to share imprisonment, even with a queen. She'll welcome you, and she will keep you safe from John.'

'You're not going to tell her about that!' Isabelle said in alarm.

'One of us should. That is the main reason for bringing you to her.'

'But I'd feel so – uncomfortable if she knew.'

Marshal smiled and shook his head. 'If you think she would be shocked, you're wrong. We're speaking of a woman who has borne the children of two kings and has had more than her share of consorts. Eleanor is a woman of the world, and she knows her sons.'

Isabelle nodded, but she was clearly still troubled by the idea of telling a queen that her son was a lecher and would-be rapist.

'You know the queen well, don't you?' Isabelle said.

'Well enough, but within limits. A queen does not confide in a landless knight.'

'But Mattie said . . .'

'Yes?' Marshal prompted with a smile. 'What stories has she been telling you?'

'She said that – well, she said there was a bond between you.'

Marshal laughed. 'She flatters me. Ladies-in-waiting don't always sift the wheat from the chaff when they pick up their gossip.'

Marshal leaned back on his elbows and stretched out his legs. 'What else did she say about me?' he asked.

Isabelle unconsciously bit her lower lip, and Marshal grinned. 'Is it that bad?'

'No,' she said, looking away from him. 'Mattie told me that all the ladies in Eleanor's court were in love with you.'

'Well, *that's* certainly true,' Marshal said with a straight face. 'Of course, I was younger and handsomer then.'

'As a matter of fact,' Isabelle said airily, 'that's exactly what Mattie said – that you were better-looking then.'

They were drifting into flirtation, and it made Marshal uneasy. The more he tried to resist his growing attraction to Isabelle, the stronger its pull became.

He was too experienced and objective to be flattered or surprised that Isabelle might feel drawn to him. He had appeared out of nowhere to rescue her from a siege, and he had defeated her enemy before her eyes. That alone was enough to turn a girl's head, though Marshal himself discounted its significance.

He had known too many women who, when they looked at him, saw the legend, not the man – a legend which trouvères had embellished out of all proportion to reality. How could he expect Isabelle to appreciate what he knew: that behind the mystique of knightly combat there was simply sweat and muscle, experience and timing?

For Isabelle, a flirtation might be a harmless diversion, but not for him. It would be too easy to fall in love with her. Marshal had made that kind of mistake once before, and once was enough for a lifetime.

'Is Marguerite of France very beautiful?' Isabelle asked abruptly, startling Marshal. It was as if she had read his mind.

'Yes,' he said after a moment. 'Very.'

High above the river an eagle appeared, sweeping in a majestic arc across the sky, and Isabelle tilted back her head to watch it. 'I'd like to have an eagle of my own one day,' she said. 'I know they're supposed to be flown only by kings, but that's not law, is it?'

Marshal shook his head. 'It's only custom,' he said, guessing that this was not the question she wanted answered. Matilda might have told her about Marguerite, or she could have heard the rumour elsewhere; the scandal had dogged him for years.

But Isabelle did not ask, and there was a long silence between them before Marshal decided to break it. 'You were asking about Marguerite of France,' he said.

Isabelle shook her head, and her tongue flicked out to moisten her lips. 'I'm sorry,' she apologized. 'It's nothing to do with me.'

Marshal smiled slightly. 'Do you know that no one has ever asked me about it, directly?'

Isabelle looked at Marshal in surprise. 'But I thought you went before the king himself.'

'Oh, I heard the rumours, and I brought them out in the open when the prince and his father held Christmas Court together. That was six years ago,' he said. He remembered it all quite clearly, but now it seemed surprisingly remote, as if it had happened in another life. 'I demanded the right to face my accusers in judicial combat, but no one came forward.'

'That doesn't surprise me,' she said with a wry smile.

'The point is, Lady Isabelle, that no one ever put the question to me.'

'But I – I have no right to ask.'

'Yes, you do,' Marshal said quietly, 'because I want you to know. There was nothing improper between myself and Marguerite of France.'

Isabelle looked gravely at him. 'But were you in love with her?' she asked huskily.

'Marguerite was the future Queen of England and the wife of my liege lord. I had no right to be in love with her.'

'Even as – as her true knight?'

Marshal grimaced. 'I don't think you believe in that sort of nonsense any more than I do.'

Isabelle dropped her eyes. 'No, I suppose not.' Then she looked up at him through lowered lashes and said, 'But either you were in love with her or you weren't. What does "right" have to do with it?'

She held his gaze, and he knew it was time to put a stop to what was happening. They faced a long journey together, and it would be difficult enough without additional complications.

'Right has everything to do with it,' he said. 'Love is for those who can become man and wife. For others, it can lead only to bitterness.'

Isabelle's eyes flickered, but she did not look away, and Marshal felt she had not understood what he meant to say. 'Lady Isabelle, outside the garden you joked that the king might give me your hand in marriage. But that could never happen. You are quite beyond my reach.'

She blushed and turned away. 'I never meant to imply . . . And I was asking about Marguerite of France just now, Sir William, certainly not about myself.'

Seeing her reaction, Marshal suddenly felt like a fool, and this time it was he who flushed. He had misread her completely. His sense that she was attracted to him had been nothing but his own imagination and conceit. She might be grateful to him, but that was all.

Marshal's own embarrassment was nothing compared to his chagrin at having embarrassed and perhaps insulted Isabelle, and he tried to make amends.

'Please accept my apologies,' he said quickly. 'I didn't mean to imply anything on your part. I – well, I suppose I was voicing my own feelings – that I wished I were a baron who could hope, through the king's favour, to win your hand. But I am not such a baron and never will be.'

Isabelle, still not looking at him, sighed theatrically. 'And I thank you for those pretty words, Sir William. If I understand you correctly, you are saying that you might love me if that were possible, but, unfortunately, it's not. You *do* have the courtier's touch.'

Marshal was relieved that Isabelle had the kindness and wit to let him off the hook gracefully – dismissing his words as courtly flattery. Or perhaps she believed that's what they'd been? She had no way of knowing how far she'd thrown him off-balance; he could hardly believe it himself.

Yet his relief was mixed with a disappointment far deeper than he would have thought possible, and he knew that what he had said to her was true. He *did* wish she were not beyond his reach.

Isabelle had turned towards him, and now she moved on to her knees, so that she was kneeling beside him. She looked into his eyes and smiled – very slowly. 'Or is it possible,' she said in her low, husky voice, 'that you were not speaking as a courtier – that you really meant what you said?'

Marshal swallowed, and he felt his pulse begin to race. He knew he should ignore the feeling sweeping over him – that he should deflect the question with a smile and a clever reply. But like a man seized by dizziness on a precipice, he stepped off the edge.

'Milady,' he said hoarsely. 'If it would do any good, I'd ride into hell itself to win your hand.'

Isabelle looked at him in silence for a moment longer. Then she placed her hands lightly on his shoulders, leaned forward and kissed him softly. The touch of her lips lingered long after she had risen and left him sitting alone on the ledge.

12

Isabelle glanced anxiously at the Danish guards blocking the approach to the ship in which Marshal had secured passage. The Danes were posted at the shore end of a stone jetty thrusting out into Waterford Bay. No shore watch had been evident when Isabelle had landed at Waterford only ten days before, and the guards' presence now was ominous. It was more than likely that they were on the lookout for her, as Marshal had feared.

Marshal had not allowed Isabelle to leave her room at the inn where they had spent the night until the last possible moment. Fulk and Jean had stowed most of Marshal's and their own gear aboard ship and then brought Isabelle from the inn.

Dressed as a manservant, she had led the packhorse carrying the last of their luggage down to the waterfront. Her hair was hidden beneath a skullcap, and her cheeks were smudged with soot. She had thought she could pass for a boy easily enough, but now that the moment was at hand, she was no longer sure.

Isabelle swallowed back her anxiety, determined not to lose her nerve. Marshal, she knew, had been on edge from the moment they had entered the port city, but he gave no sign of nervousness now as he chatted amiably with the Norman officer in charge of the guard detail.

'Ready, milady?' Jean asked in a stage-whisper, and Isabelle nodded.

A manservant would be expected to shoulder a share of the luggage, and Fulk lifted an iron-bound oak chest and lowered it on to Isabelle's back, waiting until she had a firm grip before releasing it. Although they had nearly emptied the chest for her benefit, its bulk was almost too much for her.

'Are you all right, milady?' Jean whispered worriedly.

'Yes,' Isabelle hissed through gritted teeth, 'but let's go quickly!'

Jean and Fulk swung the last of the luggage on to their shoulders and signalled the boy from the inn to take the packhorse. Their ship was too small to accommodate their horses, and they would buy fresh mounts in England. With Isabelle trudging between Jean and Fulk, they went down the rock slope to the jetty.

As they approached the guards, Isabelle heard Marshal begin a ribald story to divert the officer's attention, but the raw-boned, blond guardsmen understood too little French to be distracted. Bent under her load, Isabelle could see only the ground in front of her, but she sensed the Danes' eyes on her, and suddenly her disguise seemed hopelessly transparent.

Her heart pounded wildly as she passed through their midst, and at any moment she expected one of them to reach out and snare her. The chest's iron bindings were biting into her shoulders, but she dared not shift the burden for fear of losing her grip and dropping the empty chest at the guards' feet.

But no one tried to stop her, and as she followed Jean out on to the spray-washed jetty, she breathed a constricted sigh of relief. If the guards had not seen through her disguise, it was unlikely that the sailors and dockworkers on the jetty would take any notice of the slight-figured boy struggling under the weight of his master's chest.

Isabelle's relief was short-lived. Behind her, she heard Marshal following them out to the ship, and he was beginning another off-colour story. Apparently, the Norman officer had decided to see Marshal off.

Already her arms and shoulders were beginning to ache. She wished she could put down the chest for a moment, but with the Norman so close behind her, she couldn't risk calling attention to herself. Fortunately, their ship was the nearest of those moored beside the jetty, and she willed herself to make it to the ship without resting.

The early-morning sun still lit the bay, but the wind was

stiffening and dark clouds were building on the landward horizon. A storm was coming, and had Isabelle not been preoccupied with the present danger, she would have quailed at the prospect of crossing the Irish Sea in the tiny cargo vessel awaiting them. It was hardly more than a Viking ship in design.

Yet Marshal had had no choice. The ship's master was the only captain in port at the moment who was willing to accept a bribe to bypass the ports in South Wales under John's control and make the longer run to England.

Jean had heard Marshal's voice, too, and he quickened his pace, anxious to stay well ahead of the customs agent. Breathing hard, Isabelle struggled to keep up.

'Watch your step, milady,' Jean said as they finally reached the gangplank. He spoke softly to be sure he was not overheard by the sailors standing nearby, who were prepared to cast off as soon as their passengers came aboard.

Isabelle looked anxiously at the treacherously narrow gangplank, which was rising and falling in response to the rocking of the ship on the swell. There was no guard-rope.

Jean quickly negotiated the swaying gangplank and stepped aboard, and now it was Isabelle's turn. For an instant, she couldn't move. Even without the chest's weight precariously balanced on her back, she would have hesitated. Fulk was close behind her, and with a pang she realized that he was moving to assist her – automatically, without considering how it would look.

Quickly, she stepped on to the plank and staggered up the incline, praying that she would not lose her balance and topple into the water. She would have made it without incident, but just as she reached the ship's gunwale, the gangplank dipped suddenly and the chest slipped sideways.

She lurched forward and tripped. Jean's arm shot out to steady her, but he was too late. She pitched headlong on to the deck, the chest crashing on to the planking beside her amid a burst of raucous laughter from the crew. She had landed face-down, and as she lay on the deck, grimacing in pain, she found herself staring at the hairy toes of a sailor.

'Hurt, are you, laddie?' she heard him say as he moved to help her. Too late, she realized the danger as he slipped his hands under her chest to lift her.

'What the devil!' he burst out, recoiling with surprise. Then he laughed coarsely and hauled Isabelle to her feet. 'Boys, lookee here!' he yelled. 'We've a girl aboard!' And before Isabelle could resist, he plucked the cap from her head, freeing her braids.

Isabelle looked in fright towards the Norman officer beside Marshal on the jetty, and she saw his expression change as he noted the colour of her hair. They *were* on the lookout for her.

Marshal saw it, too. 'Fulk! Jean!' he cried, throwing back his cloak and drawing his sword. The Norman froze, his expression a mixture of anger and dismay.

Fulk, at the top of the gangplank, tossed the chest he was carrying on to the deck, unslung his longbow and nocked an arrow with incredible speed. He drew the bow and held it drawn, the muscles in his gorilla-like arms and shoulders bulging under his tunic, the shaft trained on the Norman officer.

'If you or your men try to stop us,' Marshal growled to the officer, 'you'll be the first to die.'

The Danes at the end of the jetty, drawn by the commotion, were running towards the ship, and the white-faced officer bellowed for them to halt. Jean had drawn a dagger and was covering Fulk's back. The startled sailors on board had been slow to react, but as Marshal came running up the gangplank, sword in hand, some of them produced knives and others scurried in search of whatever weapon came to hand.

Isabelle's momentary shock fell away as she saw the danger. If the captain and crew turned against them, they were lost. 'We're not pirates!' she cried, pulling free of the sailor who had lifted her from the deck. The captain stood on the steering platform in the stern. 'Captain!' she called peremptorily, running towards him, 'I am Lady Isabelle de Clare, and I order you to cast off at once!'

Her title and commanding tone had the desired effect. The sailors in her path did not hinder her, and the captain, confusion evident in his weatherbeaten face, gave her time to reach him.

'Captain,' she said, seizing his hand and pressing a fistful of silver coins into his leathery palm. 'Please cast off.'

Isabelle saw him unobtrusively heft the silver in his hand,

gauging its worth, and as Marshal, scything the air with his sword to force the sailors back, came running aft, the captain let him approach.

Marshal leapt up on to the steering platform and flashed a grin at Isabelle as he spotted the money in the captain's hand. 'You need hesitate no longer, Captain,' he said softly, thrusting his sword under the captain's chin. 'Your incentive is in your hand, and your excuse before the law is in mine. The customs agent can see that you are at my mercy.'

The captain gave Marshal a sly wink and cupped his hand to his mouth. 'Linesmen, cast off,' he shouted. 'Oarsmen, to your stations.'

Then he turned to look at the glowering officer on the jetty and shrugged in a show of helplessness. The sailors on the jetty slipped the moorings, scampered aboard and pulled in the gangplank. Fulk still stood at the gunwale, his bow drawn, holding the Norman and his men at bay.

'Mind your helm,' the captain snapped to the gaping seaman manning the steering oar. 'Steer for the harbour mouth.'

As the oarsmen pulled the ship away from the jetty, Fulk finally let his bow slacken, but the Norman officer waited until the ship had moved well out of bowshot before shouting after them: 'I know your name, Sir William Marshal, and it won't be long before Prince John knows it, too, you bastard!'

The wind was blowing off the land, and the captain ordered the oars shipped and the sail raised. Minutes later, the ship was running before the wind towards the open sea.

Marshal had sheathed his sword and was talking with the captain, who was in a jovial mood. The silver Isabelle had added to the exorbitant sum Marshal had already paid gave him more than enough reason to be happy – happy and content to remain ignorant of the circumstances surrounding his passengers' bizarre flight from Waterford.

Isabelle stood at the port rail, watching Waterford's walled city recede into the distance. The ancient, needle-like Viking tower, rising like a stone spire above the town, gradually lost definition as its grey outline merged with the cloud-mass which was gathering behind it.

Her spirits were flying too high to be affected by the threatening weather. Overhead the sun still shone, and she relished the salt-laden wind on her cheeks. They had beaten John at Kilkenny, and now they had beaten him again. Lifted by exhilaration, she felt as if she, not the ship, were sailing on the wind.

The captain left the steering platform to go forward, and Marshal came over to stand beside her. 'You did well, Lady Isabelle,' he said quietly, his voice inaudible to the steersman through the singing of the wind in the rigging and the crash of the sea against the hull.

'Thank you, Sir William,' she replied, smiling up at him, amused that he continued to address her formally.

This was the first time they had been alone, even for a moment, since she had left him in the garden at Kilkenny, and he had maintained a discreet distance during the ride to Waterford – presumably out of the desire to preserve her reputation.

Marshal was looking at her with concern. 'It's not over yet, Lady Isabelle,' he said. 'Once John learns of your escape and knows you're in my company, he's bound to realize that I will present your case before the king. My guess is that he will try to reach the king before me, and if he does . . . Well, I've heard that His Majesty dotes on him.'

Isabelle nodded, managing to assume an appropriately solemn expression, for she did not want to worry him more by appearing foolishly unconcerned. Yet she *was* unconcerned, and she wished she could reach out and smooth away his frown. She wished she could convince him, as she herself was convinced, that it would be all right.

She could not escape the feeling that all of this had been meant to happen. Marshal's journey from the Holy Land had taken the better part of a year, yet he had appeared unbidden at Kilkenny at precisely the right moment. A few days earlier, and she would not have been there; a few days later, and he would have been denied entry by Meiler's siege line. Could that be anything but God's hand at work?

And how could her feelings for him have grown so quickly if they had not been predestined to meet? Alone with him in the garden at Kilkenny, she had flirted shamelessly, feeling the giddy, tumultuous excitement of an adolescent infatuation. But underneath had been an attraction far deeper and enduring than she had imagined possible, and it had grown stronger with each passing day.

She could no longer recall with clarity her first impression of Marshal, and looking at him now, it seemed as if she had known him all her life. His features, the sound of his voice, his gestures – they no longer registered individually. They had become an indissoluble part of the man as a whole – a man she knew she loved as she could no other – a man God *must* have given her to love.

What had she to fear from John or anyone? What God hath joined together, she repeated to herself.

Marshal steadied her as the ship's bow suddenly lifted on the first heavy swell of the open sea. Isabelle's stomach lurched in response, and she tightened her grip on the rail.

'You'd better go forward, Your Ladyship,' Marshal said. 'You'll be more comfortable near the mast.'

Isabelle frowned and looked at him questioningly, wondering why he persisted in his formality. She was about to ask, when a second wave hit the bow and the stern dropped precipitously. The question was blotted from her mind as the deck beneath her rose again with sickening speed and her stomach heaved.

Isabelle's euphoria did not survive the storm that chased their boat across the Irish Sea, a storm that terrified her and prostrated her with seasickness. As she lay hour after hour, retching on the deck, soaked with spray and the wash of waves cascading over the gunwales, she was certain that the groaning mast would snap and the ship would founder. Her relief when they finally reached port was immeasurable.

Yet, for Isabelle, the sea voyage was only the beginning of a miserable journey. Marshal, driven by his determination to keep ahead of John, turned the long ride eastward from the coast into a forced march. She would have cheerfully endured the fatigue and the wind and rain that beset them day after day across England, had it not been for the way Marshal treated her.

He was invariably courteous – too courteous. Day after day, he used a screen of formality to keep a discreet distance between them. It was as if he were trying to pretend that those moments in the garden at Kilkenny had never happened. In vain, she waited for him to acknowledge with words, or even a look, what had passed between them – what she had thought had passed between them.

As desperately as she wanted an explanation, her pride prevented her from asking, and she began to respond to his insufferable courtesy with a mask of cold indifference, hiding the ache she felt inside. If Marshal wanted to forget Kilkenny, she was determined not to let him see how much it hurt her . . .

They were approaching Winchester at last, and Isabelle gazed bleakly through the driving rain at the painted battlements of the castle in which Eleanor was held. The blue-tinted whitewash on the castle walls and towers and the crimson paint on the towers' conical roofs silently proclaimed Eleanor's presence; blue and red were the queen's favourite colours.

Thirty paces ahead, Marshal turned in his saddle and called back to Jean d'Erly, who was riding beside Isabelle – riding where Marshal should have been. The taciturn Fulk brought up the rear, his longbow carefully wrapped in oiled cloth to protect it from the rain.

'I'll have to go ahead to announce your coming, Lady Isabelle,' Jean said apologetically. 'Be of good cheer, Your Ladyship,' he added, his dark, serious eyes wide with concern. 'You'll be warm and dry soon, and you'll feel better then.'

'Jean!' Marshal called again, and the squire spurred his horse forward.

As Jean rode on towards the castle, Marshal turned back to accompany Isabelle, his face shrouded by the hood of his rain cloak. 'We're almost there,' he said needlessly, turning his horse to ride beside her.

'So I see,' she replied, fighting back tears.

The love which she had come to regard as a blessing of destiny had turned out to be no more than a pitiful, girlish illusion. In the garden that day, he had simply thought to entertain her with the games of court, not realizing that she might take his words seriously. What a fool she had been!

'Let me hold that for you,' Marshal said, reaching for the

pole supporting the small, tent-like canopy shielding Isabelle from the rain.

'Don't trouble yourself, Sir William,' she said stiffly.

'Rusty, I . . .'

'*Lady Isabelle*, if you please, Sir William. That's the way you prefer things to be, isn't it?'

'No,' Marshal said softly. 'It's the way things are.'

Isabelle shook her head and looked away, determined not to weep. Despite everything, she still wanted to be near him; and had it been possible, she would have prolonged their miserable journey. And he knows this, she thought. It's not just the threat of John that's driving him; he wants to get away from me.

'Rusty – I've behaved like a fool,' Marshal said suddenly.

'You flatter yourself,' Isabelle responded icily. Now, at the last moment, he apparently wanted to give her an explanation, but she no longer wanted to hear it.

The dirt road they were following ran across a stretch of low-lying pasture land before it wound past a cluster of tenant farms on higher ground and up a long slope directly to the castle gate. Three heavily loaded ox-drawn carts trundled towards them, straddling the narrow road, and the villeins driving the carts started to move off into the soggy ditch in deference to the lady and her knight.

'Please make way for them, Sir William,' Isabelle said, turning her horse off to the side and reining in. 'If we force them into the mud, they will never get out again.'

The villeins did not understand French, but they appreciated the gesture. 'God bless you, milady,' said the man hunched on his perch on the lead cart, giving Isabelle and Marshal a toothless grin as he went by. 'And you, sire.'

The rain had streaked the villeins' dirt-smeared faces, and Isabelle felt the urge to tell them to lift their heads and give the rain a chance to wash them clean. She commanded enough English to do it, but she knew the men would only think she was trying to torment them.

'I wanted to – I wanted to talk to you,' Marshal said to her, 'but I couldn't find the right words.'

'In all this time?' she responded. 'You can stop looking for those words, Sir William. I found them myself.'

'I should never have said what I did that last afternoon in Kilkenny,' Marshal continued lamely.

'Oh, so you *do* remember that,' Isabelle said, urging her mare back on to the roadway. She had intended her response to be cold and firm, but the voice she heard was very small. Marshal was only confirming what she had already guessed. Why should his words cut her so? 'I've been wondering when you would find the courage to withdraw what you said,' she added.

'Withdraw it?' Marshal said with a surprise that should have been obvious. 'I can't . . .'

But Isabelle, no longer able to suppress her tears, was not listening. She dug in her spurs and cantered ahead. The wind caught her rain canopy, twisting the pole from her hand, and it fell by the wayside. She wanted to reach the castle and get it over and done with – once and for all.

She heard hoofbeats pounding up behind her, but before she could urge her mount into a gallop, Marshal caught up with her and seized the bridle.

'Listen to me, Rusty!' Marshal pleaded. '*Listen*, for God's sake! I can't withdraw my words, because they were true. I said that I wished I were a highborn baron who could hope to marry you, and I meant it. But in the garden that day, you only listened to the first part of what I said and not the rest, and I made the mistake of letting it pass. I am *not* that baron and never will be.'

'How convenient for you,' Isabelle shot back, not daring to believe him, no matter how much she wanted to.

'Don't you understand?' Marshal demanded. 'There is no future for us together, no matter what I might want. Yours will be a political marriage. I could love you, Isabelle de Clare, but that's irrelevant. *Irrelevant*!'

Isabelle's hood had fallen back on her shoulders, and she blinked against the rain blowing into her face. Marshal was staring at her fiercely, and the intensity she saw in his eyes finally made her believe him.

'Do you understand me now?' Marshal demanded, and Isabelle nodded, unable to speak, smiling and crying at the same time.

'When will I see you again?' she asked.

'I don't know,' he said gruffly, taking the reins of her horse to lead it. 'But by that time, Your Ladyship, you will probably be married to the next Earl of Pembroke and have assumed your rightful place beside him as countess.'

As Marshal led Isabelle up to the curtain walls of Eleanor's castle prison, heralds atop the gatehouse announced their approach. Jean d'Erly was waiting with the castle's first squire to greet them at the gate and escort them through the bailey to the inner court of the castle's shell keep.

Rain pelted Isabelle's face as she looked up at the battlements and the men-at-arms staring down at them in curiosity, and she was aware of the contrast between the cool rainwater and the hot tears streaming down her cheeks. She was crying silently, and she made no attempt to hold back her tears.

They were not tears of sadness. She was sure now that he loved her, and for the moment that was all that mattered.

I3

The queen chose to receive Marshal in one of the chambers she occupied in the southwest tower of the keep; to his surprise, he found no one in attendance. Perhaps because of the rain, or more probably because of Eleanor's advancing age, a fire blazed in the chamber's hearth, making the room uncomfortably warm.

As Marshal approached, Eleanor did him the honour of rising from her high-backed chair to greet him. Marshal knelt before her, and she grasped both his hands and bade him rise. She lifted her face to him, and he dutifully kissed her on both cheeks.

'Welcome home, Will,' she said, smiling up at him.

'Thank you, Your Majesty,' Marshal said, grateful for the affectionate reception.

He had always liked Eleanor, and she had favoured him with her friendship. He had been away for many years, and he was relieved to find that neither age nor a decade of imprisonment had greatly changed her. The queen he had known would not turn Isabelle away.

'You've injured your arm,' she said. 'Is it serious?'

'No, Your Majesty.'

'Good. I trust Grenville provided you with all you require in the way of comfort and refreshment.'

'Yes, Your Majesty.'

Eleanor nodded. 'He's a conscientious soul, and I'm afraid he does not enjoy the role of jailer.'

Still smiling, Eleanor stepped back and gave Marshal a measuring look. 'You've changed a lot,' she observed. 'It is not just age. The last time we saw each other you still had a devil-may-care air about you. Did the Holy Land take that away, along with your beard?'

'It's been at least six years, Your Majesty. Those were different times.'

Eleanor smiled wryly. 'Less serious, you mean – in the service of a carefree prince.'

'I did not mean . . .'

'Don't apologize. We both know that my oldest son was a disciple of Pan, not Mars. But on reflection, you were changing even then – growing more serious. I believe the king saw it, too. That's why he allowed you to rejoin my son five years ago, during that pitiful second attempt at a revolt. Henry must have known you would dampen it. You were the only one who did not intend to take advantage of the boy.'

'You haven't changed, Your Majesty,' Marshal said with a smile.

'Gallant as ever, Sir William.'

Marshal shook his head. 'The beauty lingers, Your Majesty,' he said truthfully. Age had made her slimmer, taking the voluptuousness from her oval face, and her once-raven hair, covered by a wimple, was doubtless grey by now. But she was still a handsome woman. She had been a black-eyed beauty, and her dark eyes still retained much of their youthful sparkle.

Seeing her again brought back memories, and for the first time Marshal truly felt that he had returned home. But it would not be as easy to resume his life as it might have been. First, he would have to deal with John's threat to Isabelle, and then – then he would have to try to forget her.

Marshal cursed himself for having made their final journey together a misery for both of them. Why had he tried to evade the issue, to pretend that nothing needed to be said? Why had he waited until the very last moment to speak to her?

Eleanor took Marshal's hand and led him to a windowseat built into a wide-angled recess in the wall. They seated themselves on red silk cushions and leaned back against the upholstered wood panelling covering the stone. Both the richness of Eleanor's clothing and the furnishings of her chambers testified to the king's desire to maintain her in comfort and dignity.

The ceiling and walls were fully panelled and decorated with murals and silk tapestries. The floor was strewn with fresh rushes and spring flowers, but beneath the rushes the floor was elaborately tiled. Although the decor was little different from that found in a chamber occupied by any lady of title, the craftsmanship in the tapestries and woodcarving was rare, and the windows of Eleanor's chamber were sealed with stained glass – the first Marshal had seen in a private dwelling.

Eleanor read his thoughts. 'My husband keeps me comfortable,' she said. 'Sometimes I think he may even feel a little guilty. And speaking of the king, does he know you are here?'

'No, Your Majesty.'

'He will soon enough. He keeps a close watch on me.'

'And you on him, Your Majesty?'

Eleanor laughed. 'I *am* glad you're back, Will. I truly am.'

'Thank you, Your Majesty. It's good to be home.'

'Were you with the Templars?' Eleanor asked, eyeing Marshal's white robe and tunic.

'I rode with them, Your Majesty.'

'Thank God you didn't join the order. What a loss that would have been to the ladies of the realm. And, speaking of ladies, I'm curious to know why my son's ward is in your company. If you've eloped with the girl, there is nothing I can do to help you.'

'It's not anything like that, Your Majesty,' Marshal said quickly.

Too quickly, he realized. Eleanor was too subtle to raise an eyebrow, or respond overtly in any way, but Marshal was sure she had observed his overreaction to her remark and had already arrived at her own interpretation.

Simply and succinctly, he described the sequence of events that had brought him to her.

The queen's sigh when Marshal finished was genuine. 'I always thought I would love my youngest son best,' she said, 'but John was such a *nasty* child. I'm afraid manhood has not improved him . . .'

Eleanor's voice took on a harder edge. 'It's unfortunate that his father doesn't see the boy's defects. Remember that when you see the king, Will. And keep to the issue of the girl's property rights. That John tried to rape his own ward will carry little weight with Henry; my husband would be the last man in the kingdom to recoil at that.'

Marshal did not take Eleanor's warning seriously, for he had a higher regard for Henry's moral judgment than Eleanor; but he had already decided not to risk accusing John of a crime that could not be proved.

'May Lady Isabelle remain here with you?' he asked.

'Of course. You knew that, or you wouldn't have brought her here. She can stay as long as the king permits – assuming, of course, that I don't find her insufferable.' Eleanor smiled. 'Will I?'

'No, Your Majesty,' he answered, returning her smile. For the time being, at least, Isabelle had found a safe haven.

Marshal was beginning to perspire, and he unconsciously wiped his brow with the back of his hand. Now that he had accomplished what he had come for, he wanted to be on his way again. He had to reach the king before John.

'Do you find it warm in here?' Eleanor asked.

'A little, Your Majesty.'

'Then take off your robe. There's no need for formality between us after all these years. And I have some advice for you. Give that robe away. The king will not want to be reminded of the Templars.'

'Oh?' Marshal said, removing his robe and draping it over his arm. Until this moment, Isabelle had dominated his thoughts, but now he forcibly cleared his mind. He did not understand Eleanor's last remark, but the queen was not given to idle comments, and he recognized the change in her tone. She wanted to talk politics, and Marshal knew it would be wise to listen.

Despite the isolation the king had imposed on her, Eleanor of Aquitaine continued to spin her webs, which, fragile though they were, continually threatened to entangle her husband.

'You have heard about the Saladin tithe, haven't you, Will?'

'Yes, Your Majesty. Even the churchmen are howling in protest.'

The Saladin tithe was the special tax the king had levied to support a Crusade to save Jerusalem. The fall of Jerusalem had galvanized Western Europe and had induced Henry and young Philip of France to declare a truce in their long-smouldering border war. Jointly, the two monarchs had taken the cross.

'Clever of the king to agree to the Crusade, don't you think?' Eleanor said. 'I doubt he ever intended to go himself. Richard was to go in his place.'

So that was why Henry had supported the Crusade so generously, Marshal thought. Two birds with one stone. Not only would Henry be rid of Philip for a while, but he would also obtain a respite from Richard. And it would cost only money.

'Unfortunately,' Eleanor continued with evident satisfaction, 'His Majesty has been entrapped by his own proverbial efficiency. Last month, word came that Philip has broken the Truce of God. The French are ravaging Berry and have taken Chateauroux, and Henry has no money to fight a war with Philip. He has already given the proceeds of the Saladin tithe to the Templars, and they won't return it.'

'Why did Philip attack?' Marshal asked.

'Does the pretext really matter?'

'I suppose not, Your Majesty.'

The provinces of Berry and the Norman Vexin had been the focus of a desultory border war between Henry and the young King of France ever since Philip had ascended the throne. It was not simply a territorial dispute; the roots of the conflict lay in the thirty-year power struggle between the Plantagenets and the Capets.

Philip's father, Louis VII, had maintained a semblance of authority by playing off his vassals against one another, but with the ascendancy of Henry of Anjou, the power balance had shifted inexorably to the English king.

Louis had been forced to look beyond his own lifetime for a restoration of Capetian power, and he sought that restoration through marriages of state. He had arranged the marriage of his daughter, Marguerite, to Prince Henry, the designated heir to the English throne; and he had betrothed his infant daughter, Alais, to Richard, whom Eleanor had made heir to Aquitaine. The marriage and betrothal were potentially rich prizes for the Capets, and in return for his agreement, Henry had exacted a stiff price.

As Marguerite's dowry, Henry had received control of the

Norman Vexin, a key border territory that had long been disputed by the Dukes of Normandy and the Capetian kings. Henry had also taken immediate custody of the child, Alais, and her dowry, the province of Berry.

Mercifully for Louis, he did not live to see the collapse of his grand design. When Prince Henry died in 1183, Marguerite had returned to Paris – without her dowry. Philip had only recently inherited the throne of France, and when Henry refused to part with the Vexin, Philip could do no more than complain.

Philip had been equally unsuccessful in the matter of Richard's marriage. Richard was now presumptive heir to the crown of England, and his marriage to Alais could still salvage something of Louis's dream. Philip demanded that the long-promised marriage take place at last, but Henry, wary of Richard and unwilling to see him allied by marriage to Philip, procrastinated endlessly.

Henry continued to hold the Vexin, the province of Berry and Alais herself, and the Capets had nothing in return. For five bitter years, Philip had chafed with frustration, and now, it appeared, he had run out of patience. By breaking the Truce of God, he had incurred the wrath of the church – a grave situation for any monarch – and Marshal took this to mean that Philip now felt strong enough to win back in war what his father had lost through diplomacy.

'The king will not have an easy time with Philip,' Eleanor said. 'Philip is twenty-three now – a man, not a boy – and he's far more determined than his father to recoup the losses the Capets have suffered at our hands. This may be much more than a border skirmish this time, Will, and the king no longer has the money to fight a prolonged war. The Saladin tithe emptied his coffers.'

'The king doesn't need mercenaries if his vassals on the Continent remain loyal,' Marshal responded.

'*If*,' Eleanor said with heavy emphasis. 'A number of barons across the Channel are looking for fresh leadership.'

Marshal raised his eyebrows. 'Looking to Richard?' he asked, and Eleanor nodded.

It was no secret that Eleanor hoped Richard would one day humble the king. But the queen was not in the habit of voicing her hopes and dreams, and Marshal felt she wanted something from him. What?

'Will, are you absolutely determined to enter the king's service?' she asked abruptly.

'That was my promise to him, Your Majesty,' he said, startled by the question.

'In return for what?'

'Nothing, Your Majesty,' Marshal replied, certain that Eleanor already knew.

'Precisely,' Eleanor said. 'Not even a promise of his own – or so I've heard. You've been away for years, Will. Even the king could not hold it against you if you changed your mind. You've always been loyal to the Plantagenets, despite the opportunities you might have had elsewhere on the Continent – even in Paris. I wouldn't want to see you change that loyalty, but there is more than one Plantagenet in the realm.'

Suddenly Marshal realized what Eleanor was hinting at, and it stunned him. She was asking him to desert the king and join Richard, in anticipation of his revolt. He had thought she knew him better than that.

'Will,' Eleanor reached out and gripped Marshal's arm. 'What I'm suggesting is for your *own* good. Do you believe me?'

'Yes, Your Majesty,' he answered, but he was stretching the truth.

'You know as well as I do that Richard will be the next King of England,' Eleanor said. 'whether or not my husband formally recognizes him as heir.'

'That may be true, Your Majesty,' Marshal replied, finding it difficult to match Eleanor's calm. 'But the king is unlikely to relinquish the crown while he lives.'

'If it's left up to him,' she responded. 'As I said before, this time he may find Philip more than a match for him on the battlefield.'

'Surely you're not suggesting, Your Majesty, that Richard might side with Philip against the king,' Marshal said, but he knew this was precisely what she was suggesting.

'I don't know everything that's in my son's mind,' Eleanor replied, and that, at least, Marshal believed. They supported each other, but Richard was his own man. 'But I know,' she continued, 'that the king will lose Richard if he does not soon declare him his heir. If my husband drives Richard away, he will be making a fatal mistake.'

'You're suggesting I choose the stronger side,' Marshal said woodenly.

Eleanor nodded. 'For your own good, Will. For your own good.'

But Marshal was not as certain of the outcome of a civil war as the queen appeared to be. Henry of Anjou had confounded his enemies for a third of a century, and, ageing or not, he was still a king to be reckoned with.

At worst, Marshal would have assessed the odds against Henry as even, but he was not gambling on the outcome. Marshal had pledged his word to the king that he would return to his service, and that he would do. It was not just a matter of promise; to Marshal, treason was an anathema.

Eleanor had been watching him, and now she shook her head. 'A man can have too many scruples, Will. If you never bend, life can break you.'

'I don't break easily, Your Majesty,' Marshal said, and there was a hint of coldness in his tone. Why, he wondered, was Eleanor so anxious to have him defect to Richard? One knight more or less could not possibly make a difference.

'Your father knew when it was time to change sides,' Eleanor said quietly. 'I thought you might have learned from his example.'

The remark caught Marshal off-guard, and he felt a flash of anger. 'I did, Your Majesty,' he responded stonily. 'I learned some things I'll never forget.'

Marshal's tone was clear enough, but if the queen took offence, she did not show it. 'Well,' she said smoothly, lifting a gloved hand to indicate she intended to rise. 'I think we've exhausted the subject. The king is probably still in London,' she said as Marshal assisted her to her feet. 'At Bermondsey Manor. But you know how he is. If you want to catch him there, you had better leave soon.'

'With your permission, Your Majesty, I'll leave immediately.'

'Immediately?' Eleanor said, arching her eyebrows. 'Without presenting your lady to me? And surely you intend to bid her farewell.'

'We've said our farewells, Your Majesty, but of course I should present . . .'

Eleanor cut him off with a gesture. 'That's not necessary, and perhaps it is best for you to go at once.' She paused and held Marshal's eyes for a long moment. 'I do wish you only good fortune, Will. I hope you know that.'

'Thank you, Your Majesty.'

'And where did Grenville lodge the lady?'

'In the tower on the north wall of the keep, directly across from this one, Your Majesty.'

Eleanor nodded. 'That will do for the moment, I suppose. Grenville has been dallying over the renovation of the apartments in the *palais*. I think he feels more secure with me confined here. The poor man has not grasped the simple fact that the *palais* is inside the keep, the keep is inside the castle and the castle is inside England. Ah well, it always takes me at least six months to train a new jailer.'

'If Your Majesty permits . . .' Marshal said, bowing and starting to retreat.

'You may kiss me goodbye,' Eleanor commanded. 'And, Will – do it properly this time,' she added, lifting her face to him and closing her eyes. Marshal kissed her lightly on the lips.

Eleanor smiled and sighed wistfully. 'I was still beautiful when we first met, wasn't I?'

'I thought so, Your Majesty,' he said truthfully.

Eleanor shook her head. 'What a pity I was always so chaste with you. Looking back, I don't understand why.'

'Farewell, Your Majesty,' Marshal said, bowing low.

'*Au revoir*, Will. And when you see my husband, give him my love.'

For the third time in the last hour, Isabelle moved to the window overlooking the bailey as she heard the sharp clatter of horses coming out through the gate to the keep. The castle's great outer courtyard abutted the western wall of the town, and Isabelle's window offered a panorama of Winchester, with the Conqueror's palace and the cathedral rising above a tightly packed jumble of burgher's houses and shops, but Isabelle's eyes were fixed on the two horsemen riding out across the courtyard's muddy cobblestones.

The rain had driven most of the chickens, dogs and pigs to shelter, but the bailey teemed with people. The castle walls enclosed a village in miniature: the chapel, barracks for the lower-ranked castle servants, kitchens, bakery, armoury, smithy, carpentry shop, stables, hawkhouse, livestock pens and storehouses. The servants were unloading carts from the town and surrounding farms and continually crossing the courtyard as they plodded through their chores.

As Marshal appeared, followed by Jean leading their packhorse and Marshal's charger, a path through the confusion opened before them, and the knight and his squire picked up a retinue of half-naked urchins who had been playing by the courtyard fountain. Marshal rode directly for the main gate, but Isabelle refused to believe that he would leave without looking back.

She was sure she understood him now. The legendary William Marshal was afraid of something, after all – afraid of losing his heart to a woman he could not have. He thought to sever the tie before it grew too strong – to cut it quickly, once and for all.

Isabelle knew how powerless she was to control her future – the king, inevitably, would choose her husband – but that simply did not matter now. She loved Marshal, and she wanted his love in return. The future would have to take care of itself.

Marshal was approaching the outer gate now, and the guards were saluting him; in a moment, he would be gone. Isabelle held her breath, willing him to turn and look back. He had to look back; he *had* to. The gateway was clear, and Marshal touched his spurs to his horse, but at the very last moment he reined in and turned, looking up towards the tower where he knew Isabelle might be. He raised his arm high over his head and waved once. Then he was gone.

Isabelle smiled a slow, secret smile. He had not found it easy to cut the bond between them, after all; and if it was in her power to prevent it, he never would.

'How does it feel to be rescued by the most famous knight in the realm?' came a woman's voice from behind, startling Isabelle.

She turned to see a tall, slim, oval-faced woman standing on the threshold of the chamber. The purple, ermine-trimmed robe the woman wore declared her rank, but, even without it, Isabelle would have known she was facing Eleanor of Aquitaine. 'Regal' had been Marshal's word for her, and it was apt.

'Your Majesty,' Isabelle said, sinking to her knees.

'Get up, child,' Eleanor said, coming into the chamber. 'A curtsey will do in future. It appears we will be seeing a lot of each other.'

'Yes, Your Majesty,' Isabelle said.

'You *are* beautiful,' Eleanor remarked with a measuring look. 'And there's just enough of the devil in your eyes to tempt a man. I can't say I blame my son.'

Isabelle felt her cheeks redden.

'Do I shock you?' Eleanor said innocently.

'Not nearly as much as Prince John did, Your Majesty,' Isabelle responded coolly. Eleanor laughed.

'*Touché*. Now I know we'll be compatible. From what Marshal told me, I didn't think you were the timid type, but I prefer to see for myself.'

The statement did not seem to require a response.

'You are fortunate to have Sir William as your advocate, Isabelle. I'm sure you were impressed with his battle prowess, but in this case his sword alone could win you nothing. The king has no patience with ladies who undermine his policy. I can testify to that.'

'I am only seeking to secure my rights, Your Majesty, nothing else.'

'What you seek and what you do are two different things. The king made my son Lord of Ireland to prove his princely qualities and enhance his standing among the barons. His Majesty will not be sympathetic to a charge of malfeasance against John, apart from the accusation of attempted rape. That's why I said you are fortunate. Marshal will not make it easy for the king to decide against you.'

'I'm not sure I understand, Your Majesty.'

'It's a matter of Marshal's unusual character. He has two exceptional traits, which can be viewed as virtues or flaws, depending on your point of view. The relevant one in this case is his obsession with justice and the law. If you kill his friend and are within the law, you have nothing to fear from him; but if you murder his enemy in violation of the man's feudal rights, Marshal will hold it against you. Odd, don't you think?

'The king knows that Marshal will never serve him if he flouts the law, and he wants to take Marshal into his mesne. My husband wants Marshal on his side, Isabelle, and that may be your strongest card. I only hope, when the time comes, that our knight can champion his own cause as effectively.'

'Your Majesty?'

'It's not important,' Eleanor said dismissively. 'I'm sure you're not interested in the musings of an old woman.'

'Oh, but I . . .'

Isabelle broke off as she saw the momentary flicker of acknowledgment in Eleanor's dark eyes, as if an unspoken question had been answered.

Eleanor smiled. 'Yes, I suppose you *are* interested – at least as far as Marshal is concerned.'

Isabelle saw no point in denying it, but she was puzzled by Eleanor's apparent interest in her feelings. Why should the queen care what she felt towards William Marshal?

'I am thinking of the second of the odd traits I spoke of,' Eleanor continued. 'His loyalty. I'm afraid he carries it to extremes. Stormy times are coming, and a man should be prepared for sudden shifts in the wind; but Marshal, left to his own devices, will probably hold to his chosen course no matter what. Even strong ships can founder that way.'

Eleanor waited a moment, but when Isabelle did not respond, she said, 'We have Marshal in common, you and I; he once risked his life for me, too, you know. The time may come when we have to work together to help our stubborn champion – assuming, of course,' she added briskly, 'that His Majesty does decide to take you under his wing. Prince John is clever. For your sake, I hope Marshal reaches the king before he does.'

14

Prince John's eyes narrowed as William Marshal appeared in the garden of Bermondsey Manor and started up the gravel path to the arbor where the king, flanked by John and the Lord Chancellor, awaited him. John had been seventeen when Marshal left for the Holy Land, and he remembered Marshal well, but the towering figure striding up the path was even more imposing than John recalled, the broken-nosed, hawk-like visage even fiercer.

But John was unimpressed. Marshal's sword arm would avail him nothing here. This would be a battle of wits, and it was a battle John had already won. He smiled inwardly as he saw Marshal recognize him. That's right, you meddling cur, I got here first, he thought.

John was certain that his version of the Kilkenny affair would shield him from any charges the girl might make through Marshal; and having protected himself, he was concerned only with revenge. He had been careful not to attack the king's favourite knight directly, dismissing Marshal's role as unwitting, overzealous meddling; Henry was annoyed with Marshal, not genuinely angry. But that was enough for John's purposes. He knew Marshal and what motivated him; he knew how to get his revenge.

The king started to rise to greet Marshal, caught himself and remained seated, his eyebrows drawing together in a deliberate frown. 'So, you've come back to us at last, Marshal,' he said, his voice grating with the hoarseness of age.

As Marshal went to one knee before Henry, John could see that he was taken aback by the change in the king, for Henry had aged far beyond his years.

When Marshal had left for the Holy Land, the king had

still been robust and muscular. Now he was obese, his skinny legs appearing almost atrophied in relation to his swollen torso, and his once-reddish-brown hair and beard were completely grey. The sagging flesh of his florid face was etched with strain and disappointment. Only Henry's grey eyes were the same – still alert and probing.

'I returned as soon as my pilgrimage on behalf of your late son was completed, sire,' Marshal said.

'But not without a detour to Ireland,' Henry replied irritably, gesturing for Marshal to rise.

As Marshal stood up he glanced at John, and John caught a flash of anger – perhaps even hatred – in his deepset eyes. John returned the look with a sly half-smile. So the girl *had* told Marshal everything. Good; without that, revenge might not have been possible.

'Christ's wounds, Marshal!' Henry growled. 'I thought you'd outgrown your recklessness.'

'I did what I thought best to secure Lady Isabelle's safety, sire. Her castle at Kilkenny was under siege, and she was in jeopardy.'

Marshal was handling himself well, John noted with ironic detachment; he spoke as firmly as possible without sounding impertinent. It was a fine line to walk.

'That's the usual result of rebellion,' Henry responded sarcastically.

'Rebellion, sire?' Marshal said. 'Lady Isabelle has taken refuge with the queen at Winchester, which places her entirely in your power. That is the act of a supplicant, not a rebel.'

'Rebellion against *me*,' John interjected coldly, 'not against the crown of England. I am her lawful guardian and Lord of Ireland, and she has openly defied me.'

Marshal looked at John and raised an eyebrow. 'And you would elevate a girl's defiance to rebellion, sire?'

The chancellor chuckled softly, and John glanced sharply at his half-brother. Geoffry Plantagenet, Bishop of Lincoln and Royal Chancellor, was a thin, ascetic-looking man in his mid-thirties, with dark, wiry hair lying close to his scalp. He bore no resemblance to Henry, but he was the king's bastard son.

Geoffry owed his position to his keen mind and utter

devotion to his father; and John was always careful in his presence, for the chancellor was the king's most trusted advisor. But John would remember that short, derisive chuckle, as he remembered similar slights in the past, and one day there would be a reckoning . . .

The king was not amused by Marshal's jibe. 'There is no humour in this affair,' he snapped.

'I agree, sire,' Marshal said. 'Lady Isabelle fled Pembroke Castle because – rightly or wrongly – she believed it was the only way to bring her complaints before your court. I appear before you now, sire, not only to offer my allegiance and service to you, but to plead on her behalf. You know me well enough to trust that I would not do so lightly, and I know my king well enough to have confidence in his sense of justice.'

It was a good speech, John acknowledged, as he saw the king's expression soften.

'You were the best of my son's knights, Marshal,' the king said, smiling for the first time, 'and perhaps the very best we have. I have long awaited your return, but I would not ask you to serve a king you thought unjust. I will hear you now.'

Marshal glanced at John, expecting him to try to block a hearing of Isabelle de Clare's complaints, but John remained silent. Say what you will, Sir William. It will do you no good, he thought.

Succinctly and dispassionately, Marshal related how he had come to Kilkenny and why he had intervened on the girl's behalf. Ranulf de Barre must have briefed him well, John reflected, for Marshal was able to list the castles and lands in Leinster that John had already ceded to willing barons.

But to John's surprise, Marshal made no mention of the girl's last night in Pembroke, and John's estimate of Marshal's intelligence rose a notch. Just as John had been loath to attack Marshal directly, Marshal was not ready to accuse the prince without irrefutable proof.

'I therefore request, sire,' Marshal said in conclusion, 'that you take custody of Lady Isabelle and her lands and exonerate Sir Ranulf of any charge of treason. Sir Ranulf has never sworn allegiance to Prince John, and he received Kilkenny

Castle from your own hand. He was therefore within his rights in refusing to surrender it.'

'I agree that Sir Ranulf was *de jure* within his rights,' Henry said, 'and I will not call him to account this time. But he must proffer his allegiance to Prince John as Lord of Ireland at once.'

'Yes, sire,' Marshal said, his relief evident in his voice, and John felt a smile tugging at his lips.

Marshal thought he had won.

'As for the girl,' the king continued, and John wet his lips in anticipation, 'she is unhappy with the way her guardian has administered her lands. That's all her "plea" amounts to.'

'But, sire!' Marshal burst out, shocked at the king's dismissive tone. 'You mustn't . . .'

Henry peremptorily raised his hand, cutting Marshal off. 'Her mistaken belief that my son has violated his trust is nothing more than a misunderstanding of his motives – a misunderstanding which Prince John has already explained to me to my satisfaction.'

John could barely resist grinning openly as Marshal's face darkened with anger, and again Marshal started to protest.

'It may interest you to know, Sir William,' Henry said sharply, overriding Marshal, 'that Prince John did *not* authorize Meiler fitz Henry's siege of Kilkenny. In fact, as soon as he learned of the siege, he sent a written order for Meiler to withdraw at once. In future, you would do well to take the wild imaginings of a distraught, headstrong girl less seriously.'

'But, sire, there can be no justification for the parcelling-out of Lady Isabelle's lands!'

'You're exaggerating, Marshal,' Henry snapped. 'Even – *even* – if it were true that the barons who have taken custody of Lady Isabelle's castles in Leinster mistakenly believe that they have title to the surrounding lands – and Prince John assures me that this is not so – they would be disabused of that notion when the time came for her to marry. She will marry when I see fit, and when that time comes, her entire inheritance will pass into her husband's control. I see no reason to burden myself with her custody at this time.'

No longer able to resist, John smiled, but he contrived to

make it a smile of amused tolerance rather than of triumph. But triumph was what he felt, for he knew that he had read Marshal correctly. He could see the dismay and worry in Marshal's face as he realized that the de Clare girl would now be returned to her former guardian.

John could not afford to proceed too harshly against her – at least not immediately – but neither the girl nor Marshal could be sure of his restraint. Neither would know when or how he might choose to exact revenge, and that in itself – the never-ending fear and uncertainty – would be the sweetest revenge of all. To a man like Marshal, it would be a torment . . .

Abruptly, the chancellor spoke up, shattering John's complacency.

'Sire,' Geoffry said, 'taking custody of Lady Isabelle would hardly be a burden. In fact, it would be highly advantageous. The income from her estates is considerable, and we are facing the prospect of war with nearly empty coffers. Surely the Royal Treasury has greater need of funds than Prince John.'

John ground his teeth as he saw the king's expression suddenly turn thoughtful. Marshal was looking gratefully at the chancellor, who was staring into middle-distance, as if totally detached. You cur, John wanted to snarl, certain that Geoffry had intentionally taken Marshal's side. Money was a powerful argument, and John could see that Geoffry's remark was having its effect.

'Sire!' John implored, grasping his father's shoulder. 'Don't debase my authority. Lady Isabelle *must* be returned to my custody, if only for appearances. She has defied me openly, and if you take custody of her now, it will be seen as a rebuke to me.'

The king looked up at John, and John held his eyes, calling on his father's affection and demanding his support. As Henry started to nod in assent, John knew he had retrieved the situation.

'Sire,' Marshal said quickly, 'I would be the last to ask you to debase Prince John's authority. If he feels that Lady Isabelle should be returned to his custody against her will – if he insists on calling her defiance rebellion against his authority – then let the matter be settled in his own court, according to law and custom.'

John looked at Marshal in astonishment, taken aback by his sudden capitulation. Why was he yielding? Was he simply seeking a delay? John's lip curled. If so, it made no difference. Marshal had blundered, and John had no intention of letting him take back his hasty words.

'I will agree to present the case in my own court, sire,' John said. 'For that is where it belongs.'

The king was frowning, and he shot John a warning glance; but John ignored it, assuming that Henry simply did not relish deferring to a lesser court.

'Are you sure?' Henry asked.

'Yes, sire,' John said firmly. 'I accept Sir William's proposal.'

Marshal's expression had become uncharacteristically impassive, and John suddenly sensed a hidden trap.

'You *are* sure?' the king asked, watching John coolly, and John recognized the look; Henry was testing him, intentionally loosening the reins and giving him his head. But what trap could there be? In his own court, he would have his way.

'I'm sure, sire.'

'Very well,' Henry said. 'So be it.' Then he looked up at Marshal, and John thought he detected a glint of wry amusement in his father's eyes. 'I don't suppose, Sir William, that you intend to withdraw as Lady Isabelle's advocate.'

'No, sire,' Marshal replied evenly. 'I will appear in Prince John's court on her behalf – as her judicial champion. And I will demand trial by combat.'

John's stomach muscles knotted, and he felt the colour drain from his face as the trap sprang shut on him. How could he have overlooked it! Marshal had found a way to bring his sword arm into play, after all, and John had given him the opening. There was no one in John's court – not even his own champion – who would stand a chance against Marshal.

'Furthermore, sire,' Marshal said coldly, fixing John with an icy stare, 'I would feel compelled to speak out more fully in Lady Isabelle's defence than I have up to now, and I would be prepared to prove *any* counter-charge I might make before God in judicial combat.'

John swallowed hard. With Marshal as the girl's champion, a charge of attempted rape would go unanswered, and John would stand convicted in his own court – a blot on his character and dignity he simply could not tolerate . . .

The look of pure hatred John shot Marshal was so fleeting that only Marshal caught it. An instant later, John smiled disarmingly and spread his hands in a gesture of royal beneficence, and it was this swift change of expression that made Marshal realize just how dangerous the young prince was.

'Sire,' John said, 'Sir William is a true and gallant knight, but I fear he misreads my purpose. I could not countenance what I perceived as Lady Isabelle's defiance of my authority, but now that she, through Sir William, has agreed to accept judgment in my court, there is no need for a trial. I am completely satisfied.

'As the Lord Chancellor has quite properly pointed out, you have far greater need of the income from Lady Isabelle's estates than I. With Philip of France threatening war, I can do no less than to surrender the wardship to you, sire.'

The king settled back with a sigh and smiled warmly. 'Well spoken, my son,' he said with satisfaction. 'Well spoken, indeed.'

'Thank you, sire,' John said smoothly.

Still smiling, the king looked at Marshal and Geoffry in turn, as if to say: You see, gentlemen, the boy is learning. Marshal couldn't understand the king's affection for the weasely prince, but John's hold on him was undeniable.

Cold trickles of nervous sweat still rolled down over Marshal's ribs. John had very nearly won, and he would have if the chancellor had not intervened at the crucial moment, driving a wedge between John and his father's own interests. Henry had known at once that Marshal would demand trial by combat; he had seen the trap, but had let John walk into it.

Glancing at the chancellor, Marshal saw some of his own relief mirrored in Geoffry's eyes. Why? Why should Geoffry have cared enough to intervene? But the question was washed away on the tide of relief sweeping over him. Isabelle was finally safe; that was all that mattered.

The king looked up at Marshal. 'Now that this business is

settled,' he said drily, 'I trust there are no further impediments to your accepting service with me?'

'No, sire,' Marshal affirmed. 'I'll serve you, and serve you gladly.'

Grunting with the effort, Henry rose from the stone bench on which he was seated and gripped Marshal's shoulder. 'God's legs, it's good to have you back, Marshal. Just seeing you again reminds me of happier days.'

'Thank you, sire.'

Out of the corner of his eye, Marshal saw John smiling benignly, and he knew that he had made an enemy for life.

'As of this moment,' the king said, 'you are captain of my household knights, but I'll demand far more of you than that title implies. You will attend all baronial councils, and I expect you to speak your mind.'

'I will do as you ask, sire,' Marshal said diffidently, 'but surely your barons will resent the intrusion . . .'

'Of a landless knight?'

'Yes, sire.'

'Perhaps,' Henry said, 'if they're fools. But in any event, the question is moot. While you were in Prince Henry's service, you could receive no grants from me, and my son had no lands of his own to give. Yet in serving my son, you served me, and your reward is long overdue.'

The king sat down again and gestured to the chancellor. Geoffry smiled broadly and nodded.

'Sir William,' he said formally, 'in recognition of your service to the royal family and in anticipation of future service to the crown, the king has awarded you title to the land of Cartmel in Lancashire. The income from Cartmel is modest, thirty pounds a year, and would be insufficient to maintain you and the knights who will follow your banner.

'Therefore, His Majesty appoints you guardian of the heiress, Helwis of Lancaster. You will henceforth enjoy the income from her estates, and, if you choose, you have the king's permission to marry the lady and become the seigneur of her lands.'

Caught completely by surprise, Marshal was unable to think of an appropriately elaborate reply. 'Thank you, sire,' he said. 'I didn't expect . . .'

'We can see that, Marshal,' Henry said with a grin, 'but

I'm not known for my largesse. These grants are not gifts; they're compensation, and you won't find your service with me a sinecure.'

'I didn't expect it to be, sire,' Marshal said distractedly, struggling to adjust to the abrupt change in his fortunes. At a stroke he was no longer a landless knight, and Henry had opened for him the way to the baronage.

Isabelle's words came back to him: 'All it takes is a word from the king.'

Henry and the chancellor were smiling at him, and Marshal tried to appear as pleased as he knew he should be. He now possessed what he had desired for so long: land of his own and the king's permission to marry a lady of title; but instead of pleasure, he felt only aching regret. The lady would not be Isabelle de Clare.

What was the matter with him? He'd known from the start that Isabelle de Clare was hopelessly beyond his reach, and because of that he had made their final journey together a misery. Why couldn't he face it now? Forcibly, Marshal turned his thoughts back to the present – back to reality.

'I've heard, sire,' he said, 'that Baudouin de Bethune and Hugh de Harlincourt joined your mesne some time ago. With your permission, I'd like to ask them to follow my own banner.'

'Of course. You three made a formidable team in the old days, and I wouldn't have it any other way. Besides,' Henry added, 'I'd prefer them to drain your purse instead of mine.'

Abruptly, the king's smile vanished. 'They're both in France now,' he said grimly. 'I sent them to accompany the Earl of Essex to Paris. I assume you've heard that Philip has invaded Berry and taken Chateauroux?'

'Yes, sire, but not the reason for it.'

'Reason!' Henry snorted. 'Excuse is the word – an excuse to stab me in the back. I sent Essex to Paris to demand an explanation, and the answer reached me two days ago. It seems the Count of Toulouse made the mistake of picking a quarrel with Richard, and Richard responded in predictable fashion by taking several of Toulouse's castles. Toulouse apparently complained to Philip, and Philip used the appeal as a pretext for his raid into Berry.'

'But, sire,' Geoffry said quickly, 'Toulouse is a vassal of the French crown, so Philip would be bound to support him.'

'Then he should have moved against Richard, not the king,' John snapped. 'He knows full well that Richard acted on his own.'

'Precisely,' Henry concurred. 'It's simply an excuse to break the Truce of God. He probably heard that our treasury is drained and thinks he can get away with it. Damn the Templars! They know Philip has double-crossed me, and they won't give me back a penny. Not one damned penny!'

'Philip may still withdraw of his own accord, sire,' Geoffry said, 'once you make it clear to him that Richard acted on his own.'

'Oh, I'll give him a chance to withdraw,' Henry growled. 'The question is, what if he stays in Chateauroux?' Henry looked at Marshal and said, 'My council met yesterday. Their advice was to drive Philip out of Berry by force.'

Marshal was inclined to agree, but the contrasting attitudes of John and the chancellor made him hesitate. He had as much reason to trust the chancellor's judgement as he had to suspect John's: while John was clearly spoiling for war, Geoffry just as clearly wanted to avoid it.

But Marshal was sure that King Philip would only become obdurate if Henry showed restraint, interpreting that restraint as weakness.

'I agree with your council, sire,' Marshal said. 'Philip must be driven out.'

'But if we go to war, sire,' Geoffry protested, 'it will strain our remaining resources beyond the limit. We can't pay our mercenaries for more than a few months in the field.'

'All the more reason to attack Philip at once and strike hard, sire,' Marshal said. 'To convince him *and* your own barons in France that you're as strong as ever. Give Philip a quick, sharp jab that will take the wind out of him.'

Henry compressed his lips and nodded in satisfaction. 'Exactly. I've already sent out orders to muster Welsh archers at Portsea, and we should be able to cross the Channel by the end of the month.'

'But let's not strike without giving Philip a clear warning, sire,' Geoffry said urgently. 'We must send another embassy to Paris and . . .'

'Another one!' John cut in. 'God's blood, there's been enough talk already. It's time for cold steel!'

'And can we look forward to your leading the troops, sire?' Geoffry said sarcastically to John.

'Enough!' Henry barked. 'I already told you, Geoffry, that I'd give Philip a chance to withdraw on his own. I'll send the Archbishop of Rouen to Paris – to remind Philip just whose side the church is on. But I'm not going to ask Philip to withdraw; I'm going to *tell* him. I will give him an ultimatum: either he withdraws immediately, or, by God, I'll renounce my allegiance to the crown of France.'

Startled, Marshal glanced at the chancellor, wondering if this was what Geoffry had been afraid of. If Henry renounced his nominal allegiance to Philip, the war that followed would be no mere border skirmish. It would be prolonged and costly. Again, Marshal noted the contrast between Geoffry and John. The king's threat of an ultimatum had brought a glint of satisfaction to John's black eyes.

'That's an extreme measure, sire,' Marshal said worriedly.

'Extreme or not,' Henry grated, 'it's what I'll do. If Philip won't deal fairly with his vassal, the Duke of Normandy, we'll see how he likes war with his peer, the King of England!'

Shortly thereafter, the king dismissed Marshal, and as Marshal left the garden, John allowed his smiling mask to slip from his face. If Marshal thought he could humiliate him and get away with it, he would soon learn otherwise. Marshal's small victory would only cost him more dearly in the end; John would see to that.

'You made the right decision concerning Richard de Clare's daughter, sire,' Geoffry said, meeting John's eyes with a challenging look. 'We need a man like Marshal as never before.'

John stared coldly at his half-brother. Now he knew why Geoffry had intervened: the chancellor had feared that the king might lose Marshal.

'What would you think of sending him with the archbishop to Paris, Geoffry?' Henry asked. 'He was with my son at the Paris court years ago, and he knows Philip.'

'That's a good idea,' the chancellor agreed readily. 'The

archbishop is a fine speaker, but I'm not sure he listens well. We want to be certain sure of Philip's response.'

'I'm more concerned that the archbishop might try to soften the ultimatum,' Henry said. 'I can rely on Marshal not to mince words.'

The chancellor frowned and shifted restlessly.

'What ails you, Geoffry?' Henry asked in annoyance.

'Are you really determined to go so far as to renounce your allegiance to Philip, sire?'

'You know I am.'

'It's certain to make Philip think carefully, sire, but if he refuses to give way, we will face a long and costly war.'

'So be it,' Henry growled. 'We may have no funds for mercenaries, but neither does Philip. Our baronial forces are more than a match for his, and I'm tired of his incessant snapping at my heels. I mean to put an end to it once and for all.'

Geoffry cleared his throat. 'Sire, we can match Philip, only for as long as the barons across the Channel continue to support you.'

Henry's eyes narrowed. 'What exactly are you worried about – Richard?'

'We cannot ignore the fact that Philip has been courting him, sire. That's probably the reason Philip was so careful not to attack his lands.'

'Richard is my *son*,' Henry said sharply, 'and he knows better than to desert me.'

'But *does* he, sire?' Geoffry said, seizing on the opening. 'You could make sure of that by declaring him to be your heir and allowing him to marry Alais. You would cut the ground from under Philip.'

'No! By making Richard Philip's brother-in-law, I would create the very alliance you're warning me against.'

'And if you don't, sire, you risk driving Richard into Philip's arms.'

The king's face hardened, and he got to his feet and began to pace. His knee had been smashed years before by a horse's kick, and he limped badly.

'I won't force Alais to marry Richard,' Henry said with an involuntary grimace of distaste. 'I couldn't do that to the girl.'

John smiled inwardly. Unlike Geoffry, he had no doubt that Henry could prevail against both Philip and Richard. If Richard did rebel, he would be defeated, and the king would not forgive him as he had his eldest son so many years ago.

'She's not a girl, sire,' Geoffry protested. 'She's twenty-seven years old.'

'Damn it, Geoffry, I won't do it! Alais deserves better than to be forced into a marriage with a man who prefers boys to women.'

'God's blood!' John interjected. 'For years it's been Richard who has refused to marry her.'

'But he's changed his tune, sire,' Geoffry said desperately. 'And I'm sure it's because of the rumours.'

'What rumours?' Henry demanded. 'That I've taken Alais as my mistress?' He paused to draw a breath. Even the brief exertion of his pacing had winded him. 'If Richard believes that, he should be even less willing to marry her.'

'Not if he thought you intended to marry her yourself, have children by her and disinherit him.'

'That's nonsense!' Henry snorted. 'Is that the latest slander from Paris?'

'I'm afraid so, sire.'

'Richard's not stupid enough to believe that,' Henry said flatly.

But he might be, John gloated silently; Richard just might be that stupid.

'If you won't give him Alais, sire,' Geoffry persisted, 'you should at least declare him your heir and require your barons to do him homage as the future King of England.'

'I'll not make *that* mistake again!' Henry burst out, and John had to suppress a smile of satisfaction. 'I did that for young Henry, and he thanked me by trying to take my crown.'

Breathing heavily, Henry returned to the bench and sat down, staring out across the Thames at the White Tower, whose massive, whitewashed walls gleamed in the afternoon sun. The river swarmed with galley barges. He saw, too, the single-masted merchant ships with their square, brightly coloured sails, bringing cargo to London's teeming wharves.

The Tower of London was the Conqueror's monument, but the burgeoning city itself was a tribute to Henry, for it mirrored the economic growth his thirty-year reign had given England. The city's tightly packed shops and houses seemed to be jostling one another for space, straining at the confines of London's high walls. London was congested and filthy, its narrow streets darkened by overhanging second storeys and thronged with noisy crowds, but it pulsated with the excitement and profit that drew travellers from all over Britain.

'I built an empire,' Henry said, half to himself. 'I was strong enough to build it, and I'm still strong enough to hold it. I'll let *no one* take my crown.'

Two nights later, John sat alone in his unlit chamber at Bermondsey Manor, awaiting his chamberlain, Roger Poole. Moonlight streamed in through an open window. He did not fear darkness as did so many men of his time; he was a creature of the night. Without the distraction of the light and sounds of day, he found it easier to think, to plan – to dream.

Never before had his dreams seemed closer to reality. War with Philip was coming soon – was perhaps only weeks away – and Richard, John was sure, was about to make the greatest mistake of his life. Henry would crush both Philip and Richard, leaving John the undisputed heir to an even stronger kingdom.

Events were moving inexorably in his favour, proving his mother wrong. It was he, not Richard, who was destined to be king. The thought of Eleanor's coming disappointment added to John's anticipation, for the knowledge that she did not love him was like a running sore. He longed to wound her in return.

Poole's knock on the chamber door came just as the sand in John's hourglass ran out. Punctuality was a sign of subservience that Poole unfailingly observed.

'Come!' John called, and Poole entered, raising the lantern he carried.

'Do you mind if I light a candle, sire?'

'If you must,' John said, and Poole walked to the all-night candle standing beside the canopied bed and lit it with his lantern.

'I have seen to it that your household is prepared to follow you to France whenever you wish, sire. I understand that His

Majesty will be assembling his army at Alençon. Will you be joining him there?'

'No. I will be travelling to Prince Richard's court at Poitiers. It is vital that he support my father in the coming conflict, and I intend to do my best to encourage my brother to do his duty.'

'Of course, sire,' Poole said with a perfectly straight face. 'As to the other matter – concerning William Marshal. I thought that might be the reason for your summons, and I have a suggestion for you to consider.'

John's breathing quickened; he was sure that Poole was about to give him the means for revenge. He had not forgotten Isabelle de Clare, and one day there would have to be a reckoning with her, but first he would deal with the insufferably arrogant William Marshal.

'I would have thought it would take more time,' John said, 'to find the right man.'

'An infinite amount of time, sire – for what you originally planned.'

John frowned. 'What do you mean? Have you found a man or not?'

'Sire, you asked me to find a replacement for your court champion – a knight who could surely defeat Marshal in single combat – but that request was unrealistic. There are few knights in England or in France who might successfully challenge him, and each one is a baron of substance. A king might prevail on such a knight to act as his champion, but you, sire, are not yet a king.'

John held back his rising anger. Poole had never failed him yet, and he could not deny the truth of what he said.

'Well?' John demanded impatiently.

'A combat challenge is out of the question, sire, and Marshal is also beyond your reach politically. He has the king's favour, and there is no doubt that he will serve His Majesty faithfully and with distinction. But this knight has wronged you, sire – grievously – and he should be made to pay. There is one, and only one, way to strike back at him.'

John gazed stonily at the mild-looking man before him. Poole, he realized, was suggesting an assassin.

'I have a man who should suit your purpose, sire,' Poole said. 'He is a knight, not a cut-throat who might betray you for the sake of a greater reward. His name came to my attention when he recently applied for service with the king. But now that Marshal is captain of the king's household knights, his employment would be quite impossible. As I understand it, there is no love lost between them. If you should choose to take this knight into your own service, sire, I could see to it that he be apprised of the wrong Marshal has done you and of the rewards to be expected for redressing that injury – by whatever means, however drastic. From what I have heard, he would require very little encouragement.'

'*Discreetly* apprised,' John said coldly. 'Discretion would be absolutely essential.'

'Of course, sire.'

It was not what John had desired; he had wanted Marshal humbled on the field of battle for all to see. But what Poole was suggesting was far better than nothing, and vengeance could not always be perfect. John hesitated only long enough to assess the risk to him if something went wrong, but he could see no danger at all.

'What is this knight's name?' John said, making up his mind.

'Gerard de Ridefort, sire. Formerly Grand Master of the Templars.'

Familiaris Regis

15

Gisors, France, August 1188

Marshal surveyed the enemy camp from a vantage-point high on the slope of the fortress hill overlooking the River Epte. Above him, the great tower keep of Gisors Castle jutted against a hazy sky. The keep was surrounded by a massive curtain wall, and encircling the gleaming, whitewashed stone fortress was an outer palisade of wood, which encompassed sufficient area to accommodate the bulk of King Henry's army should it be forced into retreat.

Philip had responded to Henry's ultimatum by requesting one last parley at Gisors, on the border between the Norman Vexin and Philip's royal domain, and Henry had agreed. But both kings were prepared for war if the conference failed, and their armies now faced each other across the Epte.

Henry's forces were dispersed among thick shade groves on the Norman side, but Philip's army was encamped in an expanse of open, dusty fields, and his troops sweltered in the oppressive August heat. The day was barely two hours old, and already men were sweating, even in the shade. The torpid, humid air lay on the land like a steamy blanket, and the horizon was washed out in a grey haze.

Far below the castle, near the riverbank, a great elm spread its limbs over the English king and his entourage. The elm was the time-honoured site for meetings between French kings and the Dukes of Normandy, and there Henry sat serenely in its cool shadow, sipping English ale, awaiting the appearance of his liege lord, Philip of France.

Henry believed that Philip's request for a parley meant that the young French king would back down rather than precipitate an all-out war, but Marshal was not so sure. In Paris, Philip had not even blinked when the Archbishop of Rouen had delivered Henry's ultimatum. Marshal could not escape the feeling that Philip was coming to Gisors not to accede to Henry's demands, but to present demands of his own.

Baudouin de Bethune and Hugh de Harlincourt, Marshal's old comrades-in-arms, had come up the hill with him to scout the French camp. They were among the knights of Prince Henry's mesne who had joined the king's household following the prince's death, and they had eagerly transferred to Marshal's banner. He was glad to have them at his side again.

Marshal turned to Bethune. 'How many do you count, Bo?'

'About three thousand foot and four hundred cavalry,' Bethune said.

'I make it about the same,' Harlincourt agreed.

The two knights were a study in contrast. Bethune was a tall, slim man with blue, mischievous eyes and tightly curled blond hair. Harlincourt was shorter and chunky, with dark, straight hair and bulbous cheeks, and his brown eyes always looked serious, even when he smiled. What the two knights shared was a lust for combat and the skill to win.

Marshal turned and glanced back at Jean d'Erly, who waited a short distance away with the other two squires. 'Jean,' Marshal called, 'How strong is the enemy?'

'Three thousand, three hundred and twenty-two pikemen, sire. Two hundred and sixty-five *serjants*, and one hundred and seventy-one knights.'

'Impudent pup,' Marshal growled under his breath, but he could not quite suppress a smile. Jean had trained hard, and Marshal's stern discipline had not dampened his spirits.

'Go easy on the boy, Will,' Bethune grinned. 'At least he's awake enough to tease you. As I recall, your reputation as a squire was for sleeping and eating.'

'However you look at it,' Harlincourt said seriously, 'we are outnumbered. It's just as well we have the castle to support us.'

'Is this in earnest?' Bethune asked. 'Or are they just bluffing down there?'

'His Majesty isn't bluffing,' Marshal said grimly and rubbed his gritty eyes. The humid heat had robbed him of sleep and given him a throbbing sinus headache.

'Good,' Bethune said with satisfaction. 'God knows, Hugh and I need combat. I tell you, Will, there were times in the last five years when I wished I'd taken the cross myself.'

'You wouldn't have liked it,' Marshal said. 'Two few eligible women.'

'Well, there's that I suppose,' Bethune said doubtfully, 'but, by God, it's been dull! You'd think the Old Man would have let us enter a tournament once in a while, just so we could keep an edge.'

'Amen to that,' Harlincourt concurred.

Marshal smiled and shook his head. 'You look sharp enough to me,' he said, eyeing Bethune's gilded armour and flaming-red surcoat. Baudouin de Bethune had always been the most ostentatious knight in Prince Henry's mesne.

Marshal had found his friends surprisingly unchanged, as if he alone had aged. Bethune, of course, with his smooth, apple-cheeked face would probably look boyish for ever; and Harlincourt had looked middle-aged at sixteen. But it was not simply a matter of appearance. These two still thirsted for glory – in war or in the occasionally deadly mock-warfare of the tournament – and to some extent Marshal envied them this passion that he could recall but no longer feel.

The old excitement was no longer there; yet as Marshal looked out at the enemy, he found himself hoping that the war – if war it was to be – would begin here at Gisors. It would release the tension that had been building in him for weeks as his responsibilities had grown, and it would absorb him mind and body, helping him to close the small chapter of his life that he had not yet put behind him.

Isabelle was safe, her inheritance secure. He had fulfilled his promise to her, and it was high time he forgot the copper-coloured hair and smiling, innocently seductive eyes of a girl he could not have. Those images belonged to the past, were as ephemeral as a desert mirage. Soon, he hoped, they would begin to fade.

'There will be action soon enough, gentlemen,' Marshal said, 'but I want discipline from our knights. And that means you two, as well. Anyone who can't resist charging into the enemy on his own will find himself riding with our *serjants*. We will attack in units and withdraw in units.'

Bethune looked at Harlincourt and winked. 'I'm afraid the Templars made an old maid of him, Hugh.'

Marshal turned sharply on Bethune, and the knight held up his hand and laughed. 'Don't worry, Will, we'll do it your way.'

Harlincourt pointed towards a distant party of horsemen riding along the riverbank. 'Look,' he said. 'The lion stirs.'

Marshal nodded. The powerful, tawny-haired knight riding in the lead was immediately identifiable, even without the crimson banner emblazoned with three golden lions which his standard bearer carried. Richard had arrived late the previous evening, having marched up from Poitiers at the head of one hundred cavalry and eight hundred foot, and he had brought Prince John with him. For the time being, at least, Henry was supported by both his sons.

Marshal squinted up at the sun, estimating its angle. 'We have another hour yet before Philip comes across,' he said. 'I think we should go down and renew our acquaintance with the Count of Poitou. He's the unknown factor in this game.'

Marshal watched Richard's stately progress along the riverbank as the prince returned from his inspection of the opposing lines. His palfrey, a white gelding, was as impressive as most warhorses and was draped in crimson silks. Richard periodically lifted his arm in regal acknowledgement of the scattered cheers of the soldiers he passed, and Marshal noted that the cheering came from both sides of the river. Whatever else Richard might be, he was a born leader of men.

At one hundred paces, Richard caught sight of Marshal's blue-and-white banner, which Jean d'Erly carried, and he spurred his mount into a canter, followed immediately by his entourage. As Richard rode up he was grinning.

'Welcome home, Will!' he cried heartily, reaching out to grasp Marshal's hand. 'Bethune. Harlincourt. Good to see you. So, the old team is taking the field again. It's about time!'

'Thank you, sire,' Marshal said.

'God's leg, Marshal, what's it been? Five years? You're

looking healthy enough. I'll wager Saladin is glad to have seen the last of you.'

'You're looking fit yourself, sire,' Marshal said. Richard, at thirty, appeared to be at the peak of his strength and assurance.

Richard laughed and slapped his belly. 'I've been putting on some weight lately, but if this little quarrel with the Franks develops into something, campaigning will slim me down soon enough.'

Richard was heavier than Marshal remembered him, but there was muscle beneath the fat. He was a taller, handsomer version of the king, with the same ruddy complexion but with tawny, rather than reddish, hair. His powerful arms were exceptionally long, giving him a three-inch advantage in reach over men of equal stature, and he had the skill to make use of it.

Richard was every inch a warrior, powerful and recklessly brave, but there was a disturbing softness to his round face, particularly in the eyes and in the lines of his mouth; and in contrast to his father, who invariably looked dishevelled, Richard's appearance was a shade too neat. His carefully combed hair and beard were too precisely trimmed, and he was fastidious about the fabric and cut of his cloaks and surcoats.

Richard's eyes became serious. 'What went amiss out there, Marshal? At Hattin, I mean.'

Marshal shook his head. 'I wasn't there, sire.'

'Thank God you weren't,' Richard said. 'We lost too many good men in that disaster. But you must have some idea, and I need to know.' Richard pointed to the green cross embroidered on the shoulder of his yellow surcoat. 'Jerusalem has to be saved, and I'll be going out there soon. The reports of the battle have been sketchy, but you must have formed an opinion. I asked Ridefort – thought I'd get the story from the source – but the fellow wouldn't talk about it.'

'Gerard de Ridefort, sire?' Marshal said in astonishment, not believing he had heard correctly. 'The Grand Master?'

'The former Grand Master,' Richard said. 'Didn't you know he'd returned? My brother took him into his mesne two months ago.'

Speechless, Marshal shook his head, forgetting the courtesy due Richard's rank; again he tasted his hatred of Ridefort.

Richard looked at him curiously. 'Ridefort is a Lusignan by blood, isn't he?' he said, shaking his head. 'God's legs, Marshal, twenty years is a long time to hold a grudge.'

Marshal's expression hardened. 'You asked my opinion on the Battle of Hattin, sire,' he said coldly. 'Well, I'll tell you. There are only two inviolable rules of warfare with the Saracens: never let your heavy cavalry advance too far ahead of your infantry, and never forsake your water supply.

'Saladin refused to cross the desert separating his army from ours, and King Guy and the Grand Master did not have the wit to wait for him. Instead, they marched out to meet him across three leagues of waterless hell. With the Turks harassing them, it might as well have been a hundred. Once our men left Suffariya Wells, they never stood a chance.'

Richard looked speculatively at Marshal and then nodded, but Marshal wondered if the prince accepted his verdict. Saladin had beheaded the four hundred Templars and Hospitalers he had captured at Hattin, but spared the lives of Guy de Lusignan and Gerard de Ridefort, presumably in recognition of their bravery.

Apparently, the Templars had not been as charitable. Marshal doubted that Ridefort would have left the order voluntarily – not at the cost of the power he had wielded. So he was John's man now. They were a good match, Marshal thought grimly.

'What about the Saracens' weapons?' Richard asked. 'Is it true their steel is superior to ours?'

'It is true, sire,' Marshal said, still distracted by the surge of bitter memories. He slipped the dagger he carried from its sheath and handed it to Richard. 'Their blades are stronger and hold a keener edge.'

Richard examined the blue-hued blade, its polished surface covered with an intricate tracery of spidery lines, the hallmark of Damascus steel. He tested the edge with his thumb and whistled appreciatively. 'Did you take this from a dead Saracen?'

'No, sire. I bought it at a bazaar.'

Richard hefted the dagger and held it to the sun, so that

the blade flashed. He grinned. 'I fancy this, Marshal. Would you care to make me a present of it?'

'I'm afraid not, sire,' Marshal said firmly, running his hand over his jaw. 'It's my only decent shaving blade.'

Richard looked surprised, and then he scowled petulantly. He made no move to return the knife until Marshal held out his hand.

'You'll get your own in Palestine, sire,' Marshal said.

Richard, who was used to being given whatever happened to catch his eye, irritably slapped the knife into Marshal's outstretched palm. 'If and when we finally do mount our Crusade,' he muttered.

Marshal gestured towards the French camp across the river. 'Over there is the man who stands in the way,' he said. 'While your father was draining his treasury to support a fresh Crusade, Philip was making plans of a different sort.'

Richard's face darkened. 'I know, and I don't understand it. I was sure Philip would . . .' His voice trailed off and he shook his head. 'The Capets have always been a slippery lot. We'll just have to teach Philip a lesson he won't forget.'

'My thought, exactly,' Marshal said, satisfied that he had managed to score a point off Philip. But he was under no illusions. Richard's holy zeal could be all too easily quenched by his ambition to be king.

The time set for the conference was at hand. The trumpeting of heralds from across the Epte signalled King Philip's approach. The barons, knights and bishops waiting under the elm with Henry stirred in expectation and relief. Most of them had been standing for the past three hours while the king, comfortably seated on a cushioned throne, had held court.

Henry was in an expansive mood; he had argued religion and philosophy with his bishops, battle tactics with his mercenary captains, and had engaged all and sundry in discussions ranging from horse-breeding and crop rotation to the proper medicine for a moulting hawk. It was reminiscent of the young King Henry whose court, so observers had complained, had been a place where school was held every day.

Flanking the king were Richard and John, seated in their

own ceremonial chairs, with their retinue interspersed among the nobles attending Henry. Each entourage mirrored the character of its master. Richard's men were battle-hardened knights. John's young retainers were creatures of the court who aped the prince's foppish tastes. Richly attired in the latest fashion, they had soft hands and softer minds, and their smiles and high-pitched laughter always came on cue.

Watching Richard and John, Marshal was struck by the perversity of physical inheritance, which in the princes' case had produced flawed caricatures of their parents. Richard, who resembled his father, had Henry's strength and boldness, but neither his intelligence nor political ability. John had his mother's black hair, black eyes and oval face, but the dynamism in her features was washed out in his visage, mirroring his indolent personality; and, in John, Eleanor's craftiness had emerged as sneaky malevolence.

The king looked towards Marshal who was standing with Bethune and Harlincourt behind the barons in the front rank. He caught the knight's eye and winked.

'The Old Man's in a good mood,' whispered Bethune.

'But for how long?' Marshal said softly.

Henry certainly had the advantage over Philip in terms of appearances. The Crusader's cross was conspicuous on the breast of his surcoat, and the bishops surrounding him proclaimed the church's support of the English king. In this particular quarrel, Henry had the moral justification. Rome's call for a Crusade to save Jerusalem was the principal reason Richard now sat beside his father in common cause against the violator of the Truce of God.

But Henry himself had proved that the church's support was no substitute for military and political strength. Philip's father, Louis of France, had tried in vain to gain advantage in his protracted struggle with Henry by supporting Thomas à Becket's cause, but Henry had prevailed in spite of the church's opposition, even weathering the storm loosed by Becket's martydom.

Marshal sensed that now the tables had been turned. It was the young French king who was bold enough to scoff at the church's condemnation, and Henry was the ageing monarch who, feeling his power slipping away, grasped at bishops' skirts for support.

'What the devil did you do to Prince John?' Bethune muttered under his breath.

John, whose black eyes rarely left his father's face in his fawning attention to the king, had caught Henry's wink and was looking at Marshal. As Marshal glanced towards him, John's sly, sensuous lips twitched into a half-smile that failed to touch his eyes, and he bestowed a regal nod.

'I cost him the revenue of a rich wardship,' Marshal answered without moving his lips.

'You'll have to tell us about it sometime,' Bethune said. 'He looks as if he could kill you.'

But Marshal wasn't listening, for he had caught a glimpse of Gerard de Ridefort standing behind John in the outermost rank of knights. Ridefort was staring at him, and as their eyes met, Marshal could almost feel Ridefort's hatred beating against him in waves.

Abruptly, Ridefort was blocked from view as the crowd shifted in response to the appearance of Philip on the opposite bank of the Epte. All eyes turned towards the river, and at a signal from Henry, his heralds trotted their horses towards the river to form a line of trumpeters to salute Philip. The French horses splashed across the ford, the spray sparkling in the sunlight, and as Philip reached the near bank, thirty Norman trumpets blared in fanfare.

Mounted on a prancing, snow-white charger, the King of France rode up towards the elm, followed by a retinue of knights in silvered and gilded armour; their surcoats and silk saddlecloths blazed with the colours of the rainbow. Philip came unarmed, dressed entirely in white and gold. His surcoat and lightweight cape were of white silk, trimmed with ermine and richly embroidered with gold thread. His boots gleamed with gilt lacquer, a rope of gold thread girded his waist, and on his head he wore the gold crown of France.

Henry, who had been slouching, straightened up. His own crown had been resting in his lap, and now he placed it on his head and picked up his sceptre. In so doing, he made it clear that he was meeting Philip as the King of England, not as Philip's vassal, the Duke of Normandy.

As Philip rode into the shade beneath the elm and reined in, Henry did not rise. The packed gathering waited tensely to see how Philip would respond, for no chair had been provided for the French king. To stand while Henry remained on his throne was unthinkable; yet if Philip seated himself on the ground, he would have to look up to the English king.

Philip was only twenty-three, but he had been King of France for eight years; he could not be flustered. He solved the dilemma neatly by not dismounting, forcing Henry to look up at him. It was a trivial point, but everyone knew Philip had won the first round in the contest of wills.

'Good morning, Henry,' Philip said with a relaxed smile, breaking the brief silence that followed the conclusion of the trumpet fanfare. 'It's a shame we have to meet with our armies at our backs – all these thousands forced to sweat in this accursed heat.'

Philip was a slight young man with light-brown hair and high colour in his cheeks. He carried himself with a graceful elegance that contrasted sharply with the rough-cut manner and appearance of his ageing antagonist. As Philip looked over at Richard and smiled warmly, it occurred to Marshal that Philip might be particularly appealing to a man of Richard's blurred sexual proclivities.

'Do you find this amusing?' Henry snapped. 'Jerusalem is in mortal danger – or had you forgotten? We both took the cross at this very spot only seven months ago, and I kept my faith. But while I was making every effort to prepare for the Crusade, you were raiding into Berry, attacking my lands without provocation.'

'You've already had my answer on that,' Philip replied calmly. 'As for the Crusade, I am as ready for it as you are.'

'Then prove it!' Henry barked. 'Give up Chateauroux and retire at once from Berry.'

A fine trickle of sweat started down from Philip's right temple, and he delicately wiped it away with his little finger. 'And why should I withdraw?' he said with the same unflappable calm. 'They are my lands, after all.'

'Your lands!' Henry thundered. 'Berry has been ours for twenty-five years – given freely by your father as Alais's dowry.'

'Twenty-five years,' Philip said, drawing out the words with heavy emphasis, and he exchanged a long look with Richard. 'My father ceded Berry to you as dowry for a *marriage*, Henry, not for an empty promise.'

'She will be married at the proper time,' Henry said. 'I will keep my pledge, but I will not be rushed.'

'Rushed!' Philip exclaimed. 'My sister has languished in your custody for *twenty-five years*. What, pray tell, are you waiting for? Why, sir, won't you marry her to Richard?' Philip paused and looked again at Richard. 'We *all* wonder why?'

'I repeat,' Henry said stubbornly. 'I will keep my pledge.'

For the first time, Philip elected to show impatience, and he compressed his lips. 'Will you now? As you kept your pledge with regard to the Vexin, I suppose. You promised my father that the Vexin would be returned to Marguerite if her husband died. Instead, she sits a widow in Paris with a paltry yearly pension.'

'A pension you accepted five years ago,' Henry shot back.

'I was a boy then, and easily fooled. I am a boy no longer.'

'Fooled?' Henry burst out. 'The Vexin has been Norman from the time of the first duke, as you very well know. And *I* was a boy when your father forced me to cede him the Vexin in return for recognition of my ancestral rights in Normandy and Anjou. When he gave the Vexin as Marguerite's dowry, he was simply returning what was rightfully ours.'

Philip sighed theatrically and shook his head. 'Yes, you always have a ready excuse to explain your broken promises.'

'Enough!' Henry said peremptorily. 'I did not agree to meet with you to discuss this. We swore to put aside our differences for the sake of Jerusalem. It was a holy oath, which I have kept and you have broken. I charge you now, Philip of France, to declare before this assembly that you will withdraw from Berry to restore peace between us, so that we may work together to save Jerusalem.'

Philip looked down at Henry and nodded slowly, and for a moment he had the assembly believing he was about to yield. 'I will withdraw from Berry,' he said, and paused for effect, 'if you will announce – here and now – the date on which my sister, Alais, shall wed your son, Richard.'

'By God, sir, you try my patience,' Henry thundered, shifting angrily in his seat.

Philip stared down at him, unmoved. 'And you try mine, but if there is a reason why Alais and Richard should not at long last be married, perhaps you'd care to share it.'

'That's my business!'

'No, sir, it is not yours alone. It concerns both our houses – and certainly your son, Richard.'

'I ask you again,' Henry said, breathing heavily. 'Will you withdraw from Berry?'

Philip smiled slightly. 'No.'

In the heavy silence that followed Philip's refusal, Marshal heard Bethune sucking air through his teeth.

'Damned back tooth's gone rotten,' Bethune whispered. 'Can you see any swelling, Will?'

Marshal shook his head. 'Don't worry,' he said under his breath. 'The way things are going, there will soon be a few thousand Franks over there anxious to knock it out for you.'

Slowly, the King of England rose from his throne. 'Is that your last word, Philip?'

'For now,' Philip replied flippantly.

Henry's face darkened. 'Then I, Henry, Duke of Normandy, Count of Anjou and Maine, hereby renounce my allegiance to you, Philip of France, and I will henceforth defend my lands on this side of the sea as my own.'

'Then you have given up your right to those lands,' Philip replied coolly, 'and I take them back into my own hand.'

Henry laughed bitterly. 'You can try.'

'Yes,' Philip said. 'I certainly will.'

16

Philip launched his war against Henry with a joke.

Following the break-up of the parley, the French and Norman armies remained in place all day, in apparent stalemate; the Franks had superior numbers, and the Normans had Gisors Castle. But an hour after sunset, Marshal was abruptly summoned to a council in Henry's command tent at the foot of the fortress hill.

The king sprawled in his chair, flanked by Richard and John. He breathed heavily in the muggy air, which was thickened even further by the incense burning in and around the tent to hold mosquitoes at bay. Moths fluttered about the two candles illuminating the tent's interior, and the light flickered each time a moth immolated itself in one of the flames.

'Now that we're all here,' Henry said irritably as Marshal entered, 'we can get started.'

To Marshal's surprise, only the chancellor and William, Earl of Essex, were with the king and his sons. Essex, ten years older than Marshal but still in his prime, was the leading member of Henry's baronial council. Apparently, Henry had not wished to convene a full war council, and Marshal's inclusion in this select group was sobering proof of the trust Henry placed in him.

'It appears, gentlemen,' the king said, his deep voice rumbling with suppressed anger, 'that war amuses the King of France. I have just received a message from him, challenging me to settle our differences with champions. He proposes to decide control of Berry and the Vexin by the outcome of a combat between two knights from each side.'

'But that's an interesting idea, sire,' Essex said enthusiastically. 'It would save . . .'

'Please allow me to finish,' Henry snapped, mopping his fleshy face with a sodden kerchief. 'Philip offers as his own champions the Counts of Clermont and Flanders, but he proposes that they fight William fitz Ralph and William de la Mare.'

Richard burst out laughing, and John started to join in until he noticed that the king was not smiling. It was obvious that Philip was simply tweaking the tail of the Plantagenet leopard. Although the Counts of Flanders and Clermont were two of France's leading duellists, fitz Ralph, the Seneschal of Normandy, was sixty-five years old, and de la Mare was notoriously imcompetent with sword and lance.

'It's only a joke, sire,' said John, still trying to suppress a grin.

'I *know* it's a joke, and I see it's infantile enough to amuse you!'

John's grin vanished instantly. 'Simply ignore it then, sire,' he said quickly, trying to reingratiate himself. 'His proposal is not worthy of a response.'

Richard shrugged nonchalantly and nodded in agreement.

'We certainly can't accept, sire,' Essex said, obviously puzzled by Henry's annoyance, 'as Philip knows full well. If the joke amuses him, so be it. Let it pass, sire.'

If anyone but John had made the suggestion to ignore Philip's jest, Marshal would probably have accepted it along with the others; but the very sight of John disgusted him, and he distrusted anything he said. It was also clear that Henry wanted something more. If he had been content to let the joke pass, he would not have called for advice. In contrast to Richard, who appeared amused by Philip's flippancy, Henry was angry and frustrated.

Marshal found the contrast ominous. Richard's partiality towards the young French king was all too manifest in the detached amusement with which he viewed his father's discomfiture, and Henry's impotent anger smacked of weakness. The concern Marshal saw in the chancellor's expression confirmed his feeling that the wrong tone was being set.

'So, you would let Philip amuse himself at the expense of your king's dignity?' Henry said angrily.

'What do you suggest, sire?' Essex asked calmly.

'I've asked for *your* counsel, gentlemen!' Henry snapped, plucking restlessly at the folds of his tunic, which stuck in places to his bulky, sweating torso. 'And I'm still waiting for it.'

For several seconds there was an awkward silence, and no one ventured a suggestion. When Marshal saw that no one was going to speak, he made up his mind.

'I disagree with Prince John, sire,' he said. 'We should not let Philip's joke pass – and not merely because it affronts your dignity. His jest is an affront to every Christian in Europe, and it should not be ignored.' Marshal paused and looked directly at Richard. 'Philip has chosen to war against the king he swore to join with in Crusade, and now he laughs about it. Jerusalem is in the hands of Saladin, and Philip sits across the river making jokes. It's intolerable!'

'Just what do you propose?' John said churlishly. 'We can't accept the challenge, and refusing it would make us look foolish.'

Marshal felt his lip begin to curl, and he could not quite control the reflex. 'Prince John is wrong, sire,' Marshal said. 'We *can* accept the challenge – and impale Philip on his own barb. He has issued a public challenge, and he has named *his* champions. But it is not his right to name ours. As the challenged party, sire, you are free to name your own champions. I suggest you accept the French king's challenge and pick knights who will win. Then we'll see who finally laughs.'

'God's teeth, Marshal, you're the man for me!' Henry exclaimed happily, slamming a fist into his palm. 'That's exactly what we'll do!'

Essex slapped Marshal on the back, and everyone, save John, grinned with approval.

'Well, Marshal,' the king said, 'who should be our champions?'

'The choice is yours, sire, but Essex and I should make as good a pair as any.'

'Christ's blood!' Richard cried, his face flushing with sudden anger. 'You can't leave me out of this! I'm a match for any knight in France, including you, Marshal, and, by God, I stand ready to prove it – here and now, if you wish!'

'More than a match,' John added, his voice rising in pretended outrage. 'Marshal, you insult my brother!'

'Silence!' the king barked, and John wilted.

But Richard remained tense, his hand on his sword hilt.

'I meant no insult, Prince Richard,' Marshal said easily. 'Your participation would be quite impossible. We cannot risk the heir to the throne in a duel when there are others who can serve as well. As far as your skill and courage are concerned, they are as well known – as your temper.'

Richard blinked and then smiled self-consciously. He waved his hand in a gesture of dismissal. 'Sorry, Marshal. My mistake,' he said, his anger gone as quickly as it had come.

Marshal had deliberately referred to him as the heir to the throne, and he hoped Richard had noted Henry's acquiescence. John, taking his cue from Henry's and Richard's smiles, nodded solemnly, as if he, too, were satisfied.

But Marshal had had his fill of John's sniping. He looked at John and said drily, 'Of course, I see no reason why the second in line to the throne should be denied the honour of championing the king's cause. Perhaps you would care to take my place on the team, Prince John?'

At that, even Henry joined in the ensuing laughter. Still chuckling, he heaved himself to his feet and threw off his cloak, which a servant hastened to retrieve. Henry patted John good-naturedly on the shoulder and then limped to his cot. With the servant's help, he removed his tunic and sat down heavily, the cot's frame creaking in protest. The servant knelt before him and stripped off his boots and stockings. Clad only in his sweat-stained linen shirt and breeches, Henry lay back with a sigh.

'Well, that's that,' he said, contented. 'Marshal, you will see to it that Philip receives our answer tomorrow morning. And now, gentlemen, off with you. My guess is that the fur will start to fly tomorrow, so we'd best retire.'

Geoffry, the last to leave the king, caught up with Marshal not far from Marshal's tent.

'A moment, please, Sir William,' Geoffry said. 'I'll be returning to England tomorrow, and I wanted to speak with you before I left. I'd like to remain with the king, but His Majesty wants me to try to raise more money.'

'I wish you good fortune,' Marshal said. 'We'll need every penny you can find.'

'How do you think we will fare?' Geoffry asked.

'Against Philip?'

'Yes.'

A full moon flooded the countryside with ghostly light, illuminating the chancellor's pale, narrow face, but his eyes remained in shadow. Marshal did not need to see them to feel the tension he knew Geoffry kept bottled up inside. Alone among Henry's sons, Geoffry, the bastard, clearly loved his father.

'Philip is no match for us at this point,' Marshal said, 'and he must know it. That's what concerns me.'

'Precisely,' Geoffry hissed. 'It's Richard he counting on. That's why he asked for the damned parley – to harp on Alais in front of Richard. You've heard the rumours, I'm sure.'

'About the king and Alais?'

'Yes.'

'Are they true?'

'The king has no intention of marrying her and disinheriting Richard. That much I'd swear to. But it's what Richard believes that matters.'

'I assume you've tried to persuade His Majesty publicly to declare Richard his heir.'

'Of course,' Geoffry said in exasperation. 'The king is as determined as ever, but he's losing his objectivity. He's becoming increasingly inflexible. Unfortunately, Richard doesn't understand that. He sees the king's grey hair but fails to realize that the king is ageing in other ways as well. Richard looks for a rational explanation of the king's refusal to acknowledge his rights where there is none, and sooner or later he may come to believe the rumours.'

Marshal made no comment, for there was nothing to say. If Geoffry, the closest of Henry's advisors, could not persuade the king to placate Richard, no one could. Marshal was struck less by what Geoffry had told him than by his sense that the chancellor was desperate for someone to talk to. It confirmed what he had come to suspect in the short time he had been with the king: Henry was losing the support of his barons.

'Is there any chance at all of finding enough money to hold our mercenaries through next year?' Marshal asked. With a mercenary army, Henry could hold his own, even if Richard defected.

'None whatsoever,' Geoffry said.

Marshal had known what his answer would be, but still he had to suppress a sigh of frustration. 'Well, then,' he said, 'we'll just have to draw enough blood in the next month or two to make Philip reconsider this war he's so eager for. If we strike hard enough, we should be able to win enough time to replenish the treasury.'

'If Richard remains in the fold.'

'Yes,' Marshal said grimly. '*If.*'

They both understood the implications. A war with Philip could not seriously endanger the king, even if he should be defeated. At most, he risked losing prestige and territory. But if Richard turned against him, it would mean civil war, and no one could say how that might end.

'Well, I'm glad of one thing,' the chancellor said, impulsively gripping Marshal's arm. 'I'm glad you're with us.'

'I know,' Marshal responded drily.

The chancellor laughed softly. 'Is it that obvious?'

'It's in the air. Quite a few rats seem to be leaving the ship.'

For a long moment, the chancellor was silent; then he said, 'Any regrets, Will?'

Marshal shrugged. 'Not if we win.'

Geoffry smiled and shook his head. 'You'd like to be that cynical, wouldn't you? I've got bad news for you, Marshal: you never will be.'

After Geoffry left him, Marshal remained where he was, collecting his thoughts, but as he stood alone in the moonlight, something made him look towards a nearby grove of trees. Perhaps he'd caught the sound of movement; but he could not be sure, and the darkness in the wood was impenetrable. Yet he sensed he was no longer alone – that someone was watching him.

For a moment, he was tempted to investigate, but then he

shrugged off the feeling, certain that it was his imagination, and went to his tent.

The following day was even more oppressive than the first. Not even the hint of a breeze stirred the thick, humid air, and by mid-morning even the shade offered no respite. A French attack was not expected, but the Franks were too close to ignore, and Marshal had ordered his knights to don their hauberks despite the heat.

'What's happening?' Hugh de Harlincourt asked as Marshal approached the cluster of tents housing the king's mesne. Harlincourt was lounging in the shade, his body propped against a tree trunk.

'The king's acceptance of Philip's challenge has been delivered, and Essex and I are going down to the river to await a response.'

Harlincourt laughed. 'I didn't think the Old Man had a romantic bone in him!'

Marshal shrugged. 'Nothing will come of it, Hugh, but now that we've pushed the joke back down Philip's throat, I'll enjoy watching him choke on it. Essex said . . .'

Marshal broke off as a howl of pain burst from inside Bethune's tent. 'What in hell is that?' he asked as the howling continued.

'Bethune,' Harlincourt sneered. 'What a baby! When he saw the size of the tongs the surgeon brought with him to pull that tooth of his, he nearly fainted.'

Abruptly, the howling stopped, and Marshal smiled. 'Sounds like he just did. Where did my squire disappear to?'

'Can't you hear them?' Harlincourt said, gesturing in the direction of a wood from which came the sound of youthful hooting and cheering. 'He's practising with the other squires. In this heat, no less. Oh, for the eagerness of youth!'

'What's happening with the challenge?' Bethune called, emerging from his tent. He was holding his jaw and spitting blood.

'You tell him,' Marshal said to Harlincourt and went off to fetch Jean d'Erly.

In a clearing in the wood, ten squires from the king's mesne were tilting at a quintain. They had attached an old shield to a wooden beam that pivoted on a post driven into the ground. One after the other, they charged the shield with blunted lances, endeavouring to strike the small target circle painted in the centre of the shield.

Marshal was pleasantly surprised that the squires had summoned the energy for practice in spite of the debilitating heat, but his approval evaporated as he came near enough to see that they were not wearing their armour. The squires had stripped to their linen shirts and breeches.

He was furious. The other squires might do as they pleased, but Jean was *his* squire and was bound by *his* rules. And his cardinal rule was to wear armour whenever an enemy was near.

As it happened, Jean was about to take his turn at the quintain, and Marshal let him make his run. Reflecting on it later, Marshal knew he should have called Jean over at once. The delay only allowed his anger to build.

Jean couched his lance and made his run at full gallop, riding with the skill and ease of a natural horseman. The squire preceding him had missed the target altogether, but Jean's lance struck the shield dead in the circle's centre, sending the pivot arm spinning. At any other time, Marshal would have applauded the performance, but not now.

Jean grinned and raised his lance in triumph as he turned his palfrey and acknowledged the cheers of his fellow squires.

'That's three in a row, you lucky dog!' yelled Harlincourt's squire.

'Jean!' Marshal barked, startling the group, and Jean immediately rode across to him and dismounted. He guessed that Marshal had seen his run, and he was smiling broadly; but as he noted Marshal's expression, his smile vanished.

'Carry on,' Marshal called to the others. He knew his rising anger was excessive, but he was in no mood for restraint. 'Not a bad run,' he said tightly. 'You've got the touch, Jean.'

'Thank you, sire,' Jean said uncertainly. His black hair was slick with sweat and plastered against his scalp, save for the recalcitrant shock that was for ever falling across his forehead. 'I was fortunate.'

'I think not.'

'Is something wrong, sire?'

Marshal compressed his lips, took the reins of Jean's horse

and swung up into the saddle. 'Let's go,' he said curtly, gesturing for Jean to precede him.

Jean looked up at Marshal in confusion and then turned and walked ahead of him through the wood towards the mesne's tents. As soon as they were out of sight of the clearing, Marshal drew his sword. At the sound, Jean spun around apprehensively.

'We're going to play a little war game, lad,' Marshal said. 'Just the two of us. Think of me as one of those French knights across the river.'

'I – I don't understand . . .'

Marshal smiled thinly. 'It's simple. I'm going to attack you, and you are going to defend yourself – with that lance you're carrying. Of course, it won't do you much good. Too bad you're not wearing your iron.'

Jean's eyes widened as he realized his mistake. 'I'm sorry, sire, but it was so hot I thought – we all thought . . .'

Marshal raised his sword and spurred forward. Jean stumbled backward with a startled cry and brought up his lance to parry the blow he could not quite believe was coming. Marshal's sword flashed down, its tip so close to Jean's nose that the boy felt the swish of the blade's passage; it snapped his lance-shaft like a twig.

'Sire! What are . . .'

'I think you'd better make a run for it,' Marshal replied brusquely, raising his sword again. Jean turned and ran.

Marshal hesitated for a moment, then coldly pursued the boy through the wood. He caught up with him as they came in sight of the tents, and again his blade flashed down. He struck Jean across the shoulderblades with the flat of his sword, knocking the boy headlong on to the ground. It was a careful blow that drew no blood, but Marshal knew Jean would feel the welt it raised all day.

Marshal reined in and turned to face Jean, who struggled, panting, to his feet. 'None of the other squires was wearing a hauberk, sire,' Jean cried, fighting back tears of anger and humiliation. 'Surely in this heat . . .'

'I don't care about the other squires!' Marshal snarled. 'You're *my* squire, and you'll do as you're told while you're in my service. Do you understand that?'

Jean swallowed hard. 'Aye, sire.'

'As for the heat, we're all sweating like pigs, but what of it? Do you think the enemy attacks only when it's convenient? The enemy is right across that river, and if I'd been a Frank, you wouldn't be feeling any pain now. You'd be dead!'

'Will!' Bethune called from fifty paces off. 'You having a problem?' Bethune and Harlincourt had watched the scene and were looking curiously in their direction. No other knights or squires were near, and the servants moving around the tents pretended not to notice.

Marshal expelled his breath in a hiss, sheathed his sword, dismounted and handed the reins to Jean. 'Where's your hauberk?'

'At the corral, sire, with the other squires' armour,' Jean said huskily, and Marshal felt a pang of guilt, wishing he'd not let his anger carry him away. The last thing he wanted was to break the boy's spirit.

'All right, saddle my charger and get your hauberk on. The Earl of Essex and I are going down to the river to answer a challenge. I'll explain on the way. We will be meeting the Counts of Flanders and Clermont, and you should take a good look at them. They are two of the best knights in France.'

Ordinarily, Jean would have questioned Marshal excitedly, but now he showed no interest and refused to meet Marshal's eyes. 'Shall I lay on your new silks?' he asked stiffly.

Marshal nodded. 'Yes. This time we *are* putting on a show.'

Jean cursed as he bent over and struggled into his hauberk, wincing at each fresh stab of pain from his bruised back. Marshal's stallion, which Jean had draped in new blue-and-white silks that trailed to the ground, restlessly pulled at its tether nearby. Normally, Jean would have prepared his master's charger with anticipation and a sense of pride, but now he felt demeaned and surly. His throat was parched, and the odious stench of the corral's manure pile filled his nostrils.

He jumped as he felt hands grasp his hauberk and help him pull it down over his shoulders. 'Thank you,' he said, straightening up with a sigh, and turned, expecting to see one of the other squires. Instead, he looked up into Bethune's mischievous blue eyes.

'It doesn't hurt too much, does it, lad?' Bethune asked.

'No, sire. I suppose not.'

Bethune grinned and spat a clot of blood on to the dusty ground. 'It can't hurt as bad as my jaw does right now. Christ's thorns, I don't think I'll be able to chew for a week. Come to think of it, that may not be too bad. I'll just go on a diet of wine and beer.'

Jean smiled uncertainly, wondering why Bethune had sought him out.

'You think Sir William was too hard on you, don't you?' Bethune said quietly.

'Your squire isn't wearing his hauberk, sire,' Jean challenged. 'Do you mean to beat him?'

'Maybe I should,' Bethune said. 'I'm sure he'd appreciate your reminding me.'

Jean swallowed and dropped his eyes. 'I'm not always this dim-witted, sire.'

'I know,' Bethune said. 'If you were, I wouldn't have bothered speaking to you. But I wanted you to understand why Sir William did what he did.'

'I wasn't wearing my hauberk. That's why.'

'But do you know why he didn't just scold you – why he rode you down and humiliated you?'

'No, sire, I don't.'

'Because he likes you, Jean, and because he knows you're going to make a fine knight one day – a fighting knight.'

Jean shook his head.

'It's true, lad, believe me. You've seen that mess of scar tissue on Sir William's thigh. Well, he got that in a skirmish when he was only twenty-one. The party he was with was ambushed by the Lusignans, and his uncle was killed – speared in the back, trying to mount his horse. Sir William loved that man, who was like a father to him. The point is, Jean, that his uncle died because he wasn't wearing his hauberk. They were in hostile territory, but they weren't expecting trouble. It was hot, that day, very hot – just like it is today.'

Marshal and the Earl of Essex sat astride their silk-draped chargers at the riverbank, waiting in the blaze of the noonday sun for a response to the message they had sent across to the King of France. Their coifs were pushed back and their squires held their helmets, but they were fully armed. All around them was an unnatural quiet as the Norman knights and soldiers, in the shade, and the Franks, sweltering in the sun on the opposite bank, watched and waited with them.

Essex eased himself in the saddle and looked across at Jean d'Erly. 'The last time your master and I fought side by side, he wasn't much older than you are now. A cocky pup, he was; but after that fight I had to give him a talking-to. I'll wager he's never told you about it.'

'No, sire,' Jean said, smiling.

Marshal glanced at Jean, surprised that the boy had recovered his spirits so quickly.

'He fought bravely enough, but he forgot the first rule of knightly combat. He has passed that on to you, hasn't he?'

'I'm not sure, sire.'

Marshal grinned. 'Make sure of your booty,' he said, remembering.

'That's right,' Essex said sternly. 'Make sure of your booty. Sir William must have put at least three knights out of action in that skirmish, but he didn't take the time to capture a single one of them. He didn't even seize a horse. Battles aren't worth winning if you don't come away with a profit. Ransom, horses, equipment, in that order.'

'That fight was at Driencourt,' Marshal said. 'What? Twenty years ago?'

'Damn near,' Essex agreed. 'And we were up against Flanders that day. Never did get a run at him myself. Now, maybe I will.'

'Not a chance, sire,' Marshal said, wiping the sweat out of his eyes. 'Philip won't accept the challenge.'

Essex shook his head regretfully. 'Probably not. It's too bad, because it's the civilized way to settle things,' he said, lifting a skin of diluted wine to his lips. 'How long do you plan to sit out here in the sun, Marshal? We could just as easily wait in the shade.'

'The men on both sides know what's afoot, sire. Let them witness Philip's withdrawal. That's the only amusement we're going to have from this charade.'

Essex grunted noncommittally, but then he raised his hand to shade his eyes and smiled with satisfaction. 'Here comes our answer. No banners, but I believe that's Flanders – and Clermont, too.'

'Banners or not, everyone will know who they are soon enough,' Marshal said with relish. 'I'll wager Philip isn't laughing anymore.'

The two French counts, tall, powerfully built men with the unmistakeable look of seasoned warriors, rode up to their side of the ford. Leaving their squires on the bank, they crossed to the river's midpoint and reined in. It was clear they wanted to avoid a shouted conversation, and as neither Marshal nor Essex intended to embarrass the counts personally, they rode out to meet them.

'Essex, Marshal, good day to you,' said the Count of Flanders casually.

Flanders was about the same age as Marshal, and at the height of his power and renown. Some years back he had flirted with rebellion, but now he was Philip's principal war counsellor. Despite a pockmarked face and thinning hair, he was a handsome man, with a grace and dignity that matched his king's; but beneath the courtly manner and carriage was a hard edge. He was as tough as he was courteous and intelligent.

'I understand that you'd like to challenge us,' Flanders said.

'No, sire,' Essex responded. 'We are acting on behalf of the king. His Majesty has accepted King Philip's proposal of a combat between champions, and Marshal and I are his choices. King Philip, I understand, has chosen you.'

'Surely you realize that His Majesty was only jesting,' said the Count of Clermont with an uncomfortable smile.

'No, sire,' Essex replied, keeping his face perfectly straight. 'His Majesty received a challenge and has accepted it. That's where the matter stands, as far as we are concerned.'

'Pressing the point, are you, Essex?' the Count of Flanders said with a good-natured grin.

Essex shrugged and returned the grin.

'Well,' Flanders said, 'if you two were looking forward to a fight, I'm sorry to disappoint you. His Majesty has withdrawn the challenge.'

'That's unfortunate,' Essex said. 'It might have proved interesting.'

'Interesting, perhaps,' Flanders said, 'but I for one am not fool enough to meet Marshal in single combat, no matter what my king might have said. I can't speak for Clermont, but I'm getting too old for that kind of risk.'

The Count of Clermont laughed softly. 'You can speak for me. I might try you, Essex, but with Marshal present . . . I must say, Marshal, you were tough enough before, but you've come back from the Holy Land looking even more dangerous.'

'Thank you, sire,' Marshal said with a smile. 'If that was intended as a compliment.'

'A fact, Sir William. A fact.'

'Than King Philip's refusal to go through with the challenge is final?' Marshal asked.

'Definitely,' the Count of Flanders replied. 'To quote His Majesty: this damned joke has gone far enough.'

'Well,' Marshal said drily, 'let us not forget that it was a joke which he began.'

'Quite,' the Count of Flanders said curtly. 'Now, unless you have further business to discuss, we'll bid you adieu. Another few minutes in this sun and I'll be tempted to jump into the water, armour and all.'

As Marshal and Essex returned to their side of the river, someone in the Norman ranks called out to them. 'Has Philip withdrawn his challenge?'

'Yes!' Marshal shouted back, and, as if on signal, a horde of foot soldiers poured out of the woods and ran down to the river, hooting and yelling like madmen. Within minutes, three hundred men had lined the riverbank and taken up a rhythmic chant: 'Cowards! Cowards! Cowards!'

Essex shook his head. 'Those poor devils baking in the sun over there must be fed up. They're in no mood to take abuse for long. Philip probably doesn't intend to attack, but my guess is, there'll be trouble before the day it out.'

Marshal smiled and nodded. 'I wouldn't be surprised.'

I7

Marshal was asleep and dreaming when the French attacked in the middle of the afternoon.

He lay in the shade of a tree, his head pillowed on one of its roots. In his dream, he was riding in the midst of a party of solemn knights, one of whom led his horse. The horse was huge, and Marshal's feet could not reach the stirrups. He had to hold the saddle pommel with both hands to keep his balance.

He was frightened of the grim, towering knights surrounding him and unaccountably helpless. But although he read danger in the knights' stony faces, he did not know its origin. He kept asking where they were taking him, but no one answered. They just rode on at a funeral pace, ignoring him and avoiding one another's eyes. On a hill in the distance, silhouetted against the sky, was a stone tower keep surrounded by a wooden palisade . . .

'Wake up, sire!' Jean d'Erly cried, shaking Marshal's shoulder. 'They're coming across the river!'

Marshal's eyes shot open, and he was on his feet before his mind cleared. Jean slipped Marshal's sword belt about his waist, and Marshal buckled it as he strode to his charger, tethered nearby. Fifteen knights of King Henry's mesne were already mounting up. Everyone had expected an attack.

As the dregs of sleep drained away, Marshal found himself grinning, relieved to be free of the nightmare and looking forward to action. After the slow build-up of tension, waiting for the war he had known was coming, combat would be a release.

From the direction of the river, screened from view by the woods, came the blare of trumpets and the rising roar of yelling men rushing into battle. As yet, it sounded as if only a few hundred were engaging, but the noise was swelling minute by minute.

Marshal swung up into the saddle, and Jean handed him his shield, mailed gloves and helmet. Marshal pulled the mail coif up over his head and tightened the laces; but he did not put on his helmet, and his knights followed his example.

Hugh de Harlincourt, who had been keeping watch by the river, galloped up on his palfrey. 'Infantry's coming across at the main ford at our centre,' he reported, dropping from his saddle and mounting the charger his squire held for him. 'A hundred or so Franks started across on their own, and our archers cut them down in the river. Our captains are pulling the Welsh back now, and the French are pouring across, engaging our pikemen.'

'What about the deep ford downriver?' Marshal asked.

Harlincourt shook his head. 'So far they're crossing only at the centre. This isn't a planned attack, Will. Some of the Franks tired of our men's insults and decided to silence them. But Philip will have to throw in reinforcements at once, or lose a large part of his army. The Welsh are back at the edge of the trees, screened by our infantry, and using the French coming across the river for target practice.'

At that moment, Bethune, who had been at his post at the king's command tent, rode up. His blue eyes were frosty with anger. 'Christ's blood, Will! The king is ordering a general retreat. The right flank is to fall back to the town walls; the left and centre are to retreat to the fortress. Philip is moving cavalry forward now, and Richard is leading out his knights to cover the retreat in the centre.'

'It's the right move,' Marshal said sharply, raising his voice so all could hear him. 'If the French are stupid enough to attack fortified positions, we'll wipe them out, and if we don't retreat, we play into their hands; they outnumber us three to two. Bethune, Harlincourt, Clifford, Quency and Preux, stay with me. The rest of you, fall back to the fortress with the king.'

Marshal's directive was instantly greeted with cries of protest from the knights he had not named.

'That's my order!' he barked. 'Now get your squires

moving! You've got time, so don't leave any equipment or pack-animals behind.'

An orderly retreat in the event of a French attack had been planned from the beginning. The bulk of the Norman army's stores were inside the fortress, with additional supplies in the walled town. The soldiers emerging from the woods and moving up the steep slope towards Gisors Castle were bringing their wagons and pack-animals with them. The withdrawal was proceeding quickly and smoothly, and the roar of men fighting and dying was still confined to the immediate battle zone in the army's centre, between the river and the shade groves.

Bethune mounted his charger and hastily armed himself. A grin had replaced his angry look as soon as Marshal had given his orders, and Harlincourt's normally serious eyes were bright with anticipation.

'All right, let's get down to the river,' Marshal said calmly, spurring his horse forward. 'Hugh, carry the banner.'

Harlincourt took Marshal's banner from Jean d'Erly and grinned at the disappointed knights being left behind. 'Better luck next time, lads!'

But the grins of the five knights following Marshal faded as he led them diagonally through the woods, downriver and away from the battle. They had to ride slowly at first, threading their way through the masses of infantry streaming back from the river towards the town walls.

'Where, in Christ's name, are you taking us, Will?' Bethune complained. 'The battle's over there. Listen, there goes Richard!'

They all heard the concerted yell – 'Lionheart!' – rise above the frenzy of battle cries as Richard led his knights in a charge somewhere far to their left, but Marshal's response was to veer farther downriver.

'I've got a feeling,' Marshal responded. 'I'm heading for that deep ford. If I'm wrong, we can still cut back upriver.'

As the press of infantry retreating past them lessened, Marshal moved the pace up to a trot, his own excitement building. He felt healthier and stronger than he had in months, and it was good to be riding into a fight with his comrades again. For the first time in many years, he felt some of the old, joyous anticipation.

Through the trees ahead, he saw the sparkling flash of the river and the light of the open fields beyond. As they neared the edge of the wood fifty paces from the water, he held up his hand and reined in. Across the river, the masses of Philip's infantry and cavalry swirled in apparent confusion, but Marshal saw at once that the captains were marshalling their units and keeping them under control.

Philip had already thrown sufficient forces across the river to support the contingents that had made the initial, unplanned thrust, but he clearly had no intention of pressing the attack. He was holding back the bulk of his army.

The woods cut off Marshal's view of the restricted battle raging upriver, in the vicinity of the Elm of Gisors, but they were close enough to hear individual cries for help and shouted orders above the bedlam of yelling, screaming, and clashing steel. Countless bodies and parts of bodies were floating lazily downriver, amid wooden shields and broken pike-shafts. The gently flowing water was streaked with blood.

Marshal and his knights viewed the ghastly flotsam with indifference. To them, dead foot soldiers were simply the refuse of battle.

'Just what are we doing here?' Bethune demanded impatiently. 'We're missing all the action!'

'Not for long,' Marshal said, pointing towards a detachment of knights emerging from the milling throngs of men and horses on the far side of the river.

Harlincourt shaded his eyes and squinted. 'That's Flanders in the lead. They're coming directly towards us!'

'I knew it!' Marshal said, vindicated. 'The fox is up to his old tricks. They're going to cross here and attack Richard's flank.'

Bethune grinned. 'You're right. That's the same trick he used at the tournament at Lagni.'

The Count of Flanders, one of France's leading patrons of chivalry, espoused a highly practical view of tournaments. He and his team habitually remained aloof from the battle until most of the combatants had exhausted themselves. Then he would charge with his knights into a flank and win an easy victory.

'Clermont isn't with him,' Marshal said, 'but it appears

he's brought along Clermont's knights. Twenty men to our six. Is that enough action for you, Bo?'

'It'll do, Will. It'll do.'

'All right, gentlemen, we'll attack with lances as they're coming out of the water and make a stand with swords on the bank. That ford is narrow, and they won't be able to spread out. Lace your helmets!'

Grinning, the knights lowered their helmets over their heads, lashed them down, slipped on their mail gauntlets and took lances from their squires.

'Just like old times,' Harlincourt said happily, his voice muffled and metallic behind the helmet.

Flanders had reached the opposite bank, and his knights were probing the river's depth with their lances to be sure of the ford's location. Flanders raised his hand and started across. The knights rode two abreast, the leaders continually sounding the bottom. The river current was barely perceptible, but the ford was so deep that the water rose above the riders' stirrups.

'Any deeper and they'd be swimming,' Bethune said.

'If the fight takes us into the water,' Marshal cautioned, 'try to stay upriver of the ford. Spread out now. We'll go out abreast in a single echelon on my order.'

Marshal tensely watched the knights' approach, waiting for just the right moment to attack. When Flanders and the knight riding beside him were ten paces from the near bank, Marshal raised his hand and lifted his shield into position.

'Now!' he shouted, digging in his spurs.

Marshal and his five companions burst from the woods in line, their stallions surging into a gallop. In unison, their lances swung down into attack position, and Marshal's knights honoured him with their battle cry, shouting his name in a single, blood-curdling yell. 'Mar – shal!'

The French knights saw the Normans pounding towards them and frantically spurred their mounts forward, but Marshal had timed the charge perfectly. The Count of Flanders and the knight beside him reached the bank when the Normans were still forty paces away, and Flanders had only seconds to make a choice. He made the wrong one.

Marshal's lips drew back from his clenched teeth in a triumphant grin as he saw Flanders rein in. Instead of instantly counter-charging, Flanders waited for the knights coming up immediately behind him to form a line of six against six. Too late, their lances swung down and their spurs dug into their chargers' flanks. As the French started forward, Marshal and his men crashed into them at full gallop, sweeping four of the six from their saddles as if they were quintain targets.

The instant Marshal's lance drove his opponent from the saddle, he swung the lance-tip to the offhand side as his charger's momentum carried him down the embankment, and he buried his lance in the chest of the next horse in line. The rider flung himself from the saddle only to be trampled under the water by Bethune's charger.

'Out of the water!' Marshal bellowed, drawing his sword. 'Hold the bank!'

But Marshal's own horse had carried him too far into the river, and he was instantly surrounded by the French knights surging forward in a packed mass and pressing in around him. He swung viciously at a Frenchman on his right; he caught the knight with a backhand blow across the side of the helmet, denting the steel plate and sending the man reeling. It was Marshal's last decisive sword stroke.

Blades struck at him from all directions at once, caroming off his shield and ringing on his helmet with deafening clangs. In the midst of the plunging, thrashing horses, Marshal could not manoeuvre for position.

He finally managed to wheel his horse about, and as his charger turned back towards the bank he glimpsed his knights holding their position, their swords flashing down on the French and beating them back into the river. Marshal winced as a sword blow from behind rang off his helmet and bit into his shoulder armour. Before he could react, two more jarring blows struck his helmet, and suddenly he couldn't see.

The first blow had severed the leather thong tying down his helmet, and now it had twisted around on his head. Another vicious stroke caught him in the side of the head, denting his helmet and knocking it further askew. Blindly, he swept his sword left and right, sometimes striking a shield and sometimes scything air, but the jarring blows to his head kept coming, numbing his mind.

Worse, with the helmet's breathing-hole out of position, he was sucking in his own exhalations. He was suffocating.

'To Marshal! To Marshal!' came a cry from the riverbank, and a moment later Marshal heard Bethune yelling at him somewhere close by. 'Get out of here, Will!'

'Go!' he heard Harlincourt thunder at him above the shouts and clanging of steel on steel.

But Marshal was completely disoriented now, and although the sword blows had abated, he could not guide his horse.

'Give me your reins, sire!' yelled Jean d'Erly, close on Marshal's right hand, and the reins were torn from his grasp. Suddenly, he pitched forward as his stallion unaccountably foundered under him. The saddle rolled, throwing him into the river. It happened too quickly for him to feel fear, but he knew he would sink like a stone.

Just as the water closed over his head, a hand seized the back of his mail coif and lifted him to the surface.

'I've got you, sire,' he heard Jean cry, and he was dragged, coughing and choking, through the water to the riverbank, like a puppy by the scruff of the neck. Dimly, he heard Flanders bellowing to his knights to retreat.

Marshal stood with the king and Richard on the parapet of Gisors Castle's gatehouse, looking out across the Epte. It was a half-hour past sunset, and clouds darkened the sky. Heat-lightning flickered silently on the horizon.

'Wind's picking up,' Richard said. 'Looks like this storm will clear the air.'

'Why the devil did he chop down the elm?' the king asked morosely. 'What was the point of that?'

Far below them, barely visible in the fading light, lay the fallen Elm of Gisors. Enraged and frustrated by the Normans' retreat, French foot soldiers had attacked the only target left to them – the giant tree. They had hacked it down with battle-axes. From a distance, it was the only visible sign that the short, sharp engagement had taken place. The French had retired, carrying away their dead and wounded, and the Normans, reoccupying their encampment, had buried their own dead. The men who had fallen in the river had been washed downstream.

'I doubt that Philip ordered it done, sire,' Marshal said, finding it difficult to speak clearly. His lips were split, and the right side of his jaw was bruised and swollen from the battering his face had received in the fight at the river. 'His men were just taking out their frustration. They suffered heavy losses coming across, and they accomplished nothing. We took one or two hundred casualties, and I estimate they lost twice that number.'

Leaning on his elbows against the parapet wall, Henry nodded woodenly and continued to stare out at the elm, as if reading an evil omen in its fall. Again, Marshal was struck by the contrast between Henry and his son. Richard was relaxed and good-humoured in the wake of the initial, inconclusive clash with Philip, but Henry seemed depressed and drained. And there was no good reason for his morose lethargy.

'Our spies report that Philip will begin pulling back his troops as soon as darkness falls,' Marshal prompted. 'He'll undoubtedly start releasing his levies over the next few days; the grape harvest is due.'

'He must not relish stalemate any more than I do,' Henry said sourly, and Marshal suppressed a frown of impatience.

Until now, the king had seemed determined to teach his young opponent a lesson. Now, suddenly, he seemed to lack the will to follow it up. But the king who had deliberately challenged Philip to war was the king Marshal had known, and Marshal was sure that the old fire was still there inside that bloated, tired body. It was up to Marshal to fan the flames into life again.

Marshal waited for Richard to point out the obvious, but the Count of Poitou remained silent.

'If Philip disbands his army, sire,' Marshal said, 'we don't have to settle for stalemate.'

Henry looked up, and Marshal saw a glint of interest in his eyes.

'You know the French, sire,' Marshal continued. 'They campaign from spring until the harvest, and then retire from the field. Neither Philip nor his father ever relied on mercenaries as heavily as we do, and my guess is that it won't occur to Philip that we're not bound by the same rules. We can fight until the money runs out, and I suggest we do that. Let

Philip see us disband our forces, but issue secret orders for our men to reassemble next week – farther south. If we raid in force across the Epte, we'll catch Philip off-guard – and do him a lot more damage than he did you by chopping down that tree.'

Henry straightened up and slapped the parapet stone with the flat of his hand. 'Sounds good,' he said firmly. 'What do you think?' he asked Richard, but the question was only a matter of form.

'It's a good plan,' Richard said, 'and we can make it even worse for Philip if I slip down to Poitiers and then cut into Berry towards Chateauroux. I think we can afford to split our forces.'

The king nodded in agreement, and Marshal could think of no way to object, because the tactic was sound. Yet he did not like the idea. So far, Richard had fully supported his father against Philip, adopting the view that it was Philip who stood in the way of a fresh Crusade, but Marshal wondered how long his loyalty would last once he was no longer physically in Henry's camp.

The wind was gusting heavily now, ruffling their hair, and Henry, his optimism and energy renewed, took a deep breath and grinned up into the black sky. The lightning flashes were coming closer, accompanied by the rumble of thunder.

'We'd better get off this parapet,' he said jovially. 'I'd hate to have lightning do Philip's work for him. Let's go down to the great hall and speak to the barons. If they're not already too drunk to listen, they may be interested in hearing what we have in store for the King of France.

Because of the storm, the king, his older barons and the few bishops who remained behind after the break-up of the parley sheltered in Gisors Castle for the night; but Richard, the fighting barons and Marshal weathered the storm in the encampment with their men. John and his entourage stayed in the castle.

Marshal was surprised to find his tent empty when he returned; Gilbert, his manservant, should have been waiting to attend him. The rain trench around the tent was overflowing, and the rushes on the floor squished underfoot, but either Jean or Gilbert had safely stowed his oak chest and armour on improvised platforms of brushwood.

The torrential rain had soaked Marshal to the skin, and he stripped down immediately, towelling himself vigorously to remove what sweat and grime he could. Soon, he hoped, he would have a chance to bathe; he itched, and he was sure he smelled like a goat.

Wearily, he dropped naked on to his cot and pulled a sheet over himself. As he was reaching to put out the candle lantern hanging above him, Jean pulled aside the tent flap and came in, dripping wet. He was out of breath and panting.

'What have you been doing?' Marshal said, propping himself up on his elbows.

Jean's boots and breeches were caked with mud, and there was blood on the sleeves of his tunic.

'I sent Gilbert to try to find the carcass of your horse, sire,' he said excitedly, 'and he found it just before dark. It washed up on our side of the river half a league downstream.'

'Why? What did you want with it?'

'It didn't make sense to me, sire – your mount dying under you like that. I was almost certain it hadn't been wounded in the fight, and I was right,' he said triumphantly, holding out his hand and displaying his find. 'Your horse wasn't killed by a French knight; it was brought down by this, sire. I dug it out of the carcass.'

'Where was the wound?' Marshal said, staring at the steel crossbow bolt in Jean's hand.

'In the chest, sire,' Jean said angrily. 'The bolt was discharged from our side of the river. One of our men must have tried to hit an enemy knight. It's a disgrace, sire, and the blackguard nearly killed you!'

Marshal considered the implications of the steel bolt gleaming evilly in the lantern light, and he felt a tingle in his spine as he reached a chillingly different conclusion.

'I'm in your debt, lad,' Marshal said. 'You saved my life today.'

Embarrassed, Jean looked away and shifted restlessly on his feet.

Marshal smiled crookedly with the undamaged side of his mouth. 'You did well, but I don't want you to take that kind of risk again.'

'I know a squire is supposed to stay out of a fight between knights, sire,' Jean said quickly. 'I didn't draw my sword.'

'That might not make any difference in the heat of battle. You have to stay clear. There are some knights who would cut you down like a foot soldier.'

'I understand, sire.'

'Good,' Marshal said, wishing more than ever that he had not punished Jean that morning. 'How's your back?'

'It hurts like the devil, sire,' Jean said with a straight face, and Marshal laughed, certain now that the lad had taken it in his stride.

'Then you'd better get some rest. You can sleep on your stomach.'

'May I ask you a question first?'

'What is it?'

'You told me that the Counts of Flanders and Clermont are two of France's foremost knights, and I heard Sir Hugh and some of the other knights talking late this afternoon. They said Flanders and Clermont were afraid to fight you.'

'Just talk, Jean. Just talk. It was Philip's decision,' Marshal said, playing down the incident. He demanded respect and obedience from his squires, but he tried to discourage the hero-worship so many squires were prone to. A squire would be a knight one day, and no knight, Marshal believed, should stand in another's shadow.

'I also heard Sir Hugh say that Prince Richard challenged you this morning – at the Barons' Council.'

Marshal frowned. 'That's how rumours start,' he said. 'He did nothing of the kind.'

'But if he had, sire,' Jean persisted, 'could you win against him?'

'I don't know,' Marshal said truthfully. 'Maybe. But I hope I never have to find out. Now get out of here and let me get some sleep.'

Jean extinguished the lantern, plunging the tent into darkness, but as he turned to leave, he said confidently, 'You would win, sire, I *know* you would.'

As Marshal lay back on his cot, listening to the crash of thunder and the rattle of raindrops on the tent, it was not Richard he was thinking about.

'Ridefort,' he said into the darkness.

There had been no crossbowmen in the wood where they had waited to ambush Flanders; there had been no infantry at all. Jean had assumed the bolt had not been meant for Marshal, but he had not been present at the parley. Jean had not seen the look in Gerard de Ridefort's eyes.

18

Isabelle stifled a yawn as Master Edmond Orri, the most acclaimed troubadour of Aquitaine, launched into the final stanza of the romance of Tristan and Isolde. Edmond, a renowned poet and singer, was also an accomplished actor, and he gave life to the dialogues woven into the tragedy's narrative. But his rendition of the epic in prose, verse and song was three hours long, and Isabelle ached to rise from her cushioned bench and relieve the stiffness in her back.

The queen had commanded the performance to celebrate the redecoration of Winchester Castle's *palais*, and it was held in the great feast hall before the queen, the Bishop of Winchester and a large gathering of lesser knights and noblewomen. The pillared hall with its high arches and vaulted, frescoed ceiling swallowed up sound, but Edmond's rich, powerful voice filled the air. He was a tall, blond, dynamic man who appeared no less larger-than-life than the heroic figures depicted on the bright new tapestries covering the walls.

As Edmond sang the tragic last lines of his tale of ill-fated love, Isabelle saw that many of the ladies were silently weeping. She started to yawn again, but caught herself as Edmond's piercing blue eyes sought her out – as they had repeatedly during his performance.

At supper the previous evening, Eleanor had seated Isabelle next to the troubadour, and he had danced with her more often than with any other lady present, provoking jealous looks from the neglected women and smiles of detached amusement from the queen.

Isabelle had been flattered, and although the air of professionalism in Edmond's attentions had not escaped her, she had found them a welcome diversion. For a time after she had come to Winchester, the restricted life she led as the queen's lady-in-waiting had been a comfort; but as she became accustomed to her new-found security and past terrors receded from her mind, she began to chafe with boredom.

And with boredom came melancholy. Four months had passed since she had watched Marshal ride out of Winchester Castle. She had thought then that the future would take care of itself; but as the empty weeks had stretched into months and she received no message from him, she had begun to fear that Marshal's own resignation to their separation might be self-fulfilling.

She longed to find a way to take her destiny into her own hands, but she was as powerless and isolated as the queen – even more isolated, for the devious Eleanor had her private sources of information. Isabelle did not even know precisely where Marshal was, or how he fared.

The queen herself was a daily reminder of the king's ultimate power over their lives. Isabelle had always known that she could marry only at the king's pleasure; but knowing and feeling were very different, and now Isabelle felt her helplessness.

At last Edmond's song ended, and as the final note died away, the audience burst into applause and stood for a prolonged ovation. Isabelle's smile of relief was indistinguishable from the others' smiles of pleasure, but it vanished abruptly as the cheers turned to cries for an encore.

Edmond bowed to Eleanor and smilingly shook his head, spreading his hands in an apologetic gesture of fatigue, with which Isabelle heartily concurred.

'That was extraordinary, Master Edmond,' said the queen as the applause subsided, 'but surely you would not let us down from the heights so abruptly. Vespers is not far off, and I know you are tired, but could you not favour us with one last, short piece?'

'Your Majesty,' Edmond replied, brushing his yellow hair from his damp forehead, 'I thank you for your kind reception of my art, but I *am* tired, as I know you will understand, and my throat is parched.'

'But that is easily remedied,' Eleanor said briskly, snapping her fingers. A servant hurried forward and thrust a wine cup into Edmond's hand.

The troubadour drank deeply, then bowed to the queen's request. 'A short piece, then, Your Majesty. I could recite a rather witty *tenso* for you and your gracious company. It poses and answers the question: should a lady display her affection by asking her true knight to go abroad and win renown, or should she simply ask him to love her always in his heart?'

The queen frowned and shook her head. 'I think we would prefer a song, Master Edmond – a little chanson.'

'Ah,' Edmond said thoughtfully, and then he looked deliberately at Isabelle for what seemed an embarrassingly long time. 'Perhaps you might care to hear a song I recently composed myself. I've had the melody for sometime, but it was not until last night, shortly before I retired, that I settled on the lyrics in their final form.'

'By all means,' Eleanor said. 'What is it called?'

'I have not yet given it a title, Your Majesty,' Edmond said, taking the harp from his young accompanist. The boy rose, and Edmond seated himself on the accompanist's bench and strummed the harp strings, adjusting the silver frets until the tuning was to his satisfaction.

'First, the melody,' he said, and as the audience settled into hushed silence, he closed his eyes and began to play a slow, haunting melody that drifted softly through the hall. When he had played the song through, he opened his eyes, nodded dreamily to himself and began to sing, harmonizing with chords on the harp.

> Fair to me are the scents of spring
> When April rains new flowers bring
> And in warming skies larks above me soar
> To fill the world with song once more.

As the troubadour came to the chanson's refrain, he turned and again looked directly at Isabelle as he sang.

> Then my thoughts turn to you, my love
> The memories borne on the wings of a dove
> Your emerald eyes and fiery hair
> Have caught me in enchantment so fair.

The allusion to Isabelle's eyes and hair was made all the more obvious by Edmond's steady gaze, and she flushed as heads began to turn her way.

'He's written the song for *you*, milady!' Matilda whispered excitedly, and Isabelle seized her arm to silence her.

Matilda, who had rejoined Isabelle the month before, was thrilled that Isabelle had caught Edmond's eye the previous evening, and she had driven Isabelle to distraction before the afternoon performance by demanding repeated changes in Isabelle's costume.

Matilda despised Norman trouvères as effeminate wastrels, but apparently she held no such prejudice when it came to a southern troubadour favoured by the queen. The *bliaut* she finally settled on for Isabelle was a present from the queen – a gown of bright-green silk embroidered in gold, with extravagant sleeves that trailed to the floor.

Edmond sang on.

> In summer's sun I take my ease,
> Forsaking all that does not please
> When fields are graced with a mantle green
> And woodshade grants me rest serene.

> Then my thoughts turn to you, my love
> The memories borne on the wings of a dove
> Your emerald eyes and fiery hair
> Have caught me in enchantment so fair.

There was no need for Edmond to make it any clearer that he had completed the lyrics with Isabelle in mind; and as he continued to sing, she, not the singer, became the focus of the audience's smiling attention.

> When autumn paints the forests all
> I hear the rustle of each leaf's fall
> And hark to the cry of geese in flight
> Foretelling the coming of winter's night.

When Edmond came again to the refrain, his accompanist, and then several of the knights in the audience, joined in, all of them looking at Isabelle. Determined not to give way to her embarrassment, she raised her eyes to the troubadour and returned his smile. Edmond sang the last verse to her as if she were the only person in the hall.

> I dread not winter's drifts of snow
> Nor icy blast of the winds that blow
> For a blazing hearth will warm me well
> And on the past there's time to dwell.

Every man in the hall who could sing joined in the final refrain, and as the song ended, the audience's applause was as much for Isabelle as for the song itself. Edmond seemed genuinely pleased with the reaction.

'Now that your chanson has taken its final form, Master Edmond,' said the queen when the applause abated, 'you must give it a title.'

Edmond smiled and nodded. 'I was thinking of calling it "Seasons of Love", Your Majesty, but now another title occurs to me, in honour of the fair lady who inspired the final lyrics.' He paused and looked again at Isabelle. 'I shall call my little song "Green sleeves".'

Isabelle managed to slip away from the gathering soon after and went out alone to the deserted castle garden outside the eastern curtain wall. Now that the weather was turning cold, she knew she could find privacy in the garden in the late hours of the day, and for her it was still pleasant. The flowers were gone, but the trees had not yet lost their foliage, and the low-angled rays of the setting sun brightened the yellowing autumn leaves to a fiery orange.

Isabelle thought she could never walk into a garden again without being immediately reminded of Marshal – seeing in her mind's eye his disarming smile and recalling his deep, reassuring voice. She smiled slightly, wondering if she alone saw him as a thoughtful, gentle man. Or did others, too, look beyond the strength and daring of the legendary William Marshal?

To Ranulf, Marshal was the quintessential knight, a man's man, hard and true. To Matilda, he was the dashing, romantic hero in shining armour. And to Eleanor? How did he appear to her?

Isabelle heard the crunch of footsteps on the gravel path behind her and turned. The queen had entered the garden and was coming towards her. Eleanor was alone, but two of her ever-present guards had stationed themselves at the garden entrance.

'I thought I might find you out here,' Eleanor said as Isabelle walked back towards her. 'I'm afraid Master Edmond was disappointed when you made your exit so quickly. I told him that the excitement of the honour he'd bestowed on you had probably left you feeling faint.'

'Thank you, Your Majesty. I didn't intend to offend him,' Isabelle said, wondering why Eleanor had sought her out. The queen was not given to quiet walks in the garden.

Eleanor handed Isabelle her cane and took Isabelle's arm for support as they started up the path towards the garden's fountain. The queen's arthritis was the principal sign of her advancing age, and Isabelle guessed that she endured considerable pain to disguise it. At a glance, Eleanor could pass for a woman fifteen years younger, and although she walked slowly, her bearing was as erect and commanding as ever.

'Edmond's attention doesn't distress you, I hope,' Eleanor said.

'Not in the least, Your Majesty,' Isabelle answered easily. 'I'm flattered.'

'But you don't take it seriously, I gather.'

'Should I, Your Majesty?'

Eleanor laughed. 'I suppose not. He's a professional heart-breaker. And he's persistent. He made me promise to seat you beside him at supper again tonight.'

Isabelle suspected that Edmond was more to Eleanor than an entertaining troubadour. His home was in Poitiers, and he was said to be a favourite of Richard, who was a troubadour in his own right. Eleanor's communications were strictly censored and her visitors screened, and it had occurred to Isabelle that Edmond might carry information of greater import than a troubadour's usual repertoire of titillating gossip.

Eleanor had never volunteered any news of the war that was not common knowledge, and she had hardly mentioned Marshal to Isabelle since the day Isabelle arrived. But without knowing precisely why, Isabelle sensed this might be the time to ask, and she wanted to know what was happening in France.

'Has Master Edmond brought news of the war, Your Majesty?' she asked.

Eleanor smiled knowingly. 'Is it news of the war you want – or news of Sir William?'

'I *would* like to know how he fares, Your Majesty.'

'Well, Edmond has brought news,' Eleanor said. 'As a matter of fact, that's why I came out to talk with you. According to Edmond, the king does have Philip on the defensive at the moment, as we've been told, and I gather that Marshal has become a leading figure in the Royal Councils. Apparently, Prince Richard considers him the driving force behind His Majesty's recent successes.'

Isabelle smiled with unabashed pleasure and pride. 'That is good news, Your Majesty. But I must say, it doesn't surprise me. I only hope . . .'

Eleanor raised an eyebrow as Isabelle broke off. 'Yes?'

'Well, Your Majesty,' Isabelle said, hesitating, but she could see no harm in saying what was uppermost in her mind. 'I was about to say that I hope His Majesty will reward Sir William appropriately.'

'You needn't worry,' Eleanor replied breezily. 'As a matter of fact, the king has already rewarded him – by giving him custody of the heiress, Helwis of Lancaster, and permission to marry the lady.'

Isabelle's smile froze, and she felt as if a hand had suddenly closed on her heart. Eleanor's eyes were on her, and she struggled to master her shock. 'That's excellent, Your Majesty,' she heard herself say. 'It's no more than he deserves.'

Why was she shocked? She herself had told Marshal that the king had a surfeit of heiresses at his disposal, and Marshal could hardly have refused the king's gift. Why did she feel betrayed? Why the sudden rush of panic? Helwis might be his ward, but he did not have to marry her.

'He hasn't married her yet,' Eleanor said with that same knowing smile, as if reading Isabelle's thoughts. 'Besides, my dear,' she added solicitously, 'love and marriage rarely go together in this world.'

Isabelle was off-balance, but still she detected a look of cool appraisal behind the apparent sympathy in Eleanor's coal-black eyes. Eleanor, she realized with a flash of anger, had wanted to observe her reaction to the news.

'Just what is it you want of me, Your Majesty?'

Eleanor smiled sardonically. 'I see you share at least one trait with our Sir William. You prefer the direct approach.'

'Yes, Your Majesty, I do.'

'Well, that's not easy to become accustomed to, Isabelle. Believe me, royalty sees very little of it.'

They had reached the fountain, and the queen seated herself on a bench nearby. Isabelle remained standing.

'Actually, my dear,' Eleanor said, pulling her robe more tightly around her shoulders, 'it's not a question of what I want of you, but of what you want for yourself.'

'And what is that, Your Majesty?'

Eleanor smiled. 'I suspect you want a great deal, Isabelle – a *great* deal. What a pity you're so rich a marriage prize; that complicates matters considerably. Of course, as long as Sir William does not marry, I suppose there's hope. He will undoubtedly continue to rise in the king's esteem – perhaps even high enough to win the gift of lands as rich as yours. But if I were in your position, I would not be content with hope alone.'

Isabelle's pulse quickened. Whatever Eleanor wanted, it had to do with Marshal.

'I'm hardly content, Your Majesty,' she said.

'But are you willing to do what may be necessary to secure your hopes?'

'Yes, Your Majesty,' Isabelle said firmly, 'if that's possible.'

'Then you must understand the current political situation, for politics, not love, is the way of this world. When my husband was in his prime, he was a rock – impervious to the storms swirling about him – but age is crumbling that rock. He has Philip on the defensive now, but Philip has time on his side. Our barons in France know that Henry is losing his grip, and they are questioning his leadership.'

'You sound as if you wish it weren't so, Your Majesty,' Isabelle said impulsively.

Eleanor glanced up at the battlements of her castle prison, silhouetted against the crimson sky. 'I've wished for many things in my life, but I've had to settle for reality. Henry, for all his faults, was a great king. Perhaps if I'd been fifteen or twenty years younger when we married . . .'

Eleanor broke off and shook her head. 'We're discussing your hopes for happiness, not my regrets. As I said, the king is slipping. He is challenged by Philip and losing the support of his barons. And, most dangerous of all, he is driving away the son who could save his empire. I do not think Richard will tolerate his father's abuse much longer.'

'Do you mean there will be civil war, Your Majesty?'

'It may come.'

Isabelle might have suspected that the queen was only guessing, had it not been for the strange ambivalence in Eleanor's tone – a mixture of anticipation and aching regret. Something more than rumour was in the wind – something that Edmond had conveyed to her.

'If there is a war between the king on one side, and Philip and Richard on the other,' Eleanor continued, 'I have little doubt that my son will prevail. The men who side with Richard will be assured of their reward, Isabelle, but those who oppose him . . . Well, they will go down with the king.

'I told you that loyalty is a virtue that Marshal is likely to carry to extremes, and I also told you that one day we might have to work together to save him from himself. Sir William is a stubborn man, but I think he just might listen to you.'

Isabelle swallowed to relieve the sudden dryness in her throat. 'Are you suggesting, Your Majesty,' she said huskily, 'that I try to persuade Sir William to desert the king for Prince Richard's banner?'

' "Desert" is not the word I would choose,' Eleanor replied. 'It is not desertion to bow to the inevitable, and you could make him see that. Sometimes, I think we women are the only realists. Men fight for glory, honour and power; it remains to us to fight for life and happiness.'

Isabelle had no doubt that Eleanor was intent on manipulating her, and she was wary of this woman, who was so adept at intrigue. But if there was the slightest chance for her to take her destiny into her own hands, she intended to seize it.

'Even if I could influence Sir William, Your Majesty,' she said, 'it's hardly likely that I will see him in the near future.

And urging him to treason is not something I would attempt in a letter.'

'It is not treason to support the legitimate heir to the throne against a failing king who seeks to deny his eldest son his lawful rights,' Eleanor responded, 'but I agree that you could not persuade Sir William with penned words. I believe you *will* see him again in the near future. In fact, I'd wager money on it. But in any event, I am speaking only of possibilities. Perhaps there will be no break between my son and the king, after all, but it is a possibility for which we all should be prepared.'

More than a possibility, Isabelle thought. She doubted that it was a coincidence that Eleanor had chosen this moment to probe her reactions.

'Then speaking of *possibilities*, Your Majesty,' Isabelle said, 'why should Sir William expect to find favour with Prince Richard? From what I've heard, Richard the Lionheart is his own war counsellor, and he can certainly lead his own army.'

'The king of England – whoever he may be – will always have need of knights of Marshal's calibre,' Eleanor replied. 'But beyond that, if there is war between Richard and his father, William Marshal is the one man who might hinder Richard's victory.'

'A single knight, Your Majesty?' Isabelle said sceptically.

'Yes, Isabelle, this particular knight. That is what I believe, and as far as you are concerned, it is my belief that counts. My son still values my opinion, and I would know what reward to suggest be bestowed on Marshal once Richard is king. I do not ask you to persuade Sir William on your own – only to support Richard in his own efforts to bring Marshal to his side when the time comes.'

So there it was, Isabelle thought, her heart hammering – a clear proposition: win Marshal for Richard's cause, and receive in return what she desired more than anything.

Now she understood the queen's interest in her relationship with Marshal; it must have occurred to Eleanor at once that she might use her to entice Marshal into Richard's camp. The queen was presenting herself as her friend – and perhaps she even thought of herself in that light – yet she had baited her hook with cold-blooded care.

But manipulation was a game two could play, and Isabelle

felt a stir of excitement as the germ of an idea took root. Perhaps Eleanor was right and she should try to persuade Marshal to desert the king, but she had no intention of trusting to Eleanor's judgment and promises alone.

'I'll – I'll think about it, Your Majesty,' Isabelle said, feigning uncertainty.

'If civil war comes,' Eleanor said, trying to sink the hook still deeper, 'and Marshal finds himself on the losing side, your hopes will die with Henry's cause. I am offering you the salvation of those hopes.'

It had not needed to be said, Isabelle thought; there was no need to hammer home the point, and Eleanor should have known that. Isabelle realized to her surprise that the queen was overanxious, and her hopes rose. The queen might indeed be giving her the chance to act on her own behalf – but not necessarily in the way Eleanor envisioned.

Isabelle knew there was a risk that Eleanor might see through her, but she was determined to discover which of them was the fisherman and which was the fish.

'Your Majesty, I . . .' Isabelle began in a deliberately halting voice, the callow girl caught on the horns of a dilemma. 'What you suggest frightens me. If I try to sway Sir William against his own conscience, I could lose him. I would have to be sure – absolutely sure – that our hopes would be realized once Richard became king.'

Eleanor smiled and touched her reassuringly. 'You have my word, my dear.'

'But, still . . .' Isabelle said, and as her voice trailed off, she blinked rapidly in an expression of helpless confusion.

'What would it take to reassure you?' Eleanor asked. 'I could write to Richard – today, if you wish – and send the letter with Edmond. And, of course, I'd let you read it first.'

'But I couldn't ask that, Your Majesty,' Isabelle protested. 'And I certainly didn't mean to imply . . .'

'Hush, child,' Eleanor interrupted benignly. 'I can understand your concern, believe me. I shall have the letter for you to read tonight.'

Isabelle remained silent, looking down at the ground and deliberately biting her lower lip.

'Is something still worrying you?' Eleanor said, a note of impatience creeping into her voice.

'I want to be certain that Prince Richard receives the letter, Your Majesty.'

'Of course he will receive it. Edmond is completely reliable.'

'But what if he should be detained and searched. *Someone* might guess that he is acting as your courier; it would not take much imagination.'

Eleanor smiled thinly. 'Perhaps, but if you want this letter sent, you'll have to take the chance. And I would certainly take care to couch it in terms that would safeguard Sir William, as well as myself.'

'I would prefer, Your Majesty,' Isabelle said softly, 'if the letter were conveyed by my own man, Fulk le Brun. He is absolutely faithful, and unconnected with you, Your Majesty.'

Isabelle held her breath as Eleanor hesitated with instinctive caution.

'The brute they call Black Fulk?' Eleanor asked. 'The *serjant* who acts as if he were your guard dog?'

'Yes, Your Majesty.'

Eleanor hesitated a moment, then slowly nodded. 'All right, if that's what you want. To say that the man is loyal to you is an understatement.' Eleanor rose and took Isabelle's arm. 'So, my dear,' she said, 'we have a bargain.'

'I'm not sure I understand, milady,' Fulk said in his slow, hoarse voice.

'It's not necessary for you to understand why,' Isabelle said patiently. 'Only that you do exactly as I ask.'

Isabelle had found it difficult to mask her excitement during the long supper that evening, and Master Edmond's inability to hold her attention had clearly frustrated the troubadour, who was accustomed to easy conquests. Isabelle had been plagued by the nagging fear that Eleanor might change her mind, and she had been on edge until the moment the queen placed the promised letter in her hand.

On Isabelle's return from Eleanor's apartments in the *palais*, she had immediately dismissed Matilda and summoned Fulk to her bedchamber. Once in possession of Eleanor's letter, her excitement had given way to a calmer sense of anticipation and confidence. For the first time in months, she did not feel helpless.

'You are to deliver this letter to Prince Richard, who is campaigning against the French in Berry,' Isabelle repeated to Fulk, who towered over her, his great arms hanging slackly at his sides. 'But first you must go to the Lord Chancellor in London and offer to show it to him for a price of twenty sous. You must play the part of a treacherous scoundrel, Fulk. Can you do that?'

'If I must, milady,' he said glumly. 'If that's what you wish.'

'It is,' she said firmly. 'Under no circumstances is the chancellor to know that I sent you to him.'

'Yes, milady. I will leave at once.'

'That's not necessary. I don't want you to risk travelling at night.'

Fulk laughed. 'There's no risk, milady. I never have trouble with bandits.'

'All right,' Isabelle said, believing him. Rationally, there was no need for haste, but Isabelle was anxious to set her plan in motion.

Eleanor would have her believe that the king was finished and that the future lay with Richard. Time would tell if she was right, but Isabelle preferred to sow her seeds in two fields at once. If Eleanor and Richard placed so high a value on Marshal's service, the king could value it no less. And Henry was still king – still the arbiter of Isabelle's and Marshal's fates.

She was convinced that Marshal would never ask Henry or Richard to bid for his loyalty; but she was not bound by his rules, and Eleanor had just given her the means to set the price.

'The letter, if you please,' the chancellor said, not bothering to hide his distaste for the dark, hulking *serjant* standing before him. This Fulk le Brun might be a Norman, but he had the look of a Welsh native. He had the same unnatural strength in his chest, shoulders and arms that came from regular use of the longbow, he wore the same dark, crude clothing and his black hair and beard were just as shaggy.

He even had the bright, white teeth of the Welsh, who made a fetish of tooth-polishing.

But it was not simply the man's appearance that put Geoffry off. Though he found them indispensable, Geoffry hated traitors.

'Twenty sous, Your Lordship,' Fulk muttered as he handed over the letter.

'Yes, yes,' Geoffry snapped. 'You'll get your money when you return tomorrow for the letter. I'll have to have it resealed. You're dismissed.'

'Aye, Your Lordship.'

Geoffry breathed a sigh of relief as Fulk departed. Why, he wondered, had Eleanor entrusted a letter to such a ruffian? Was she going senile? He sipped from a goblet of mulled wine, but it did little to relieve the ache in his throat. He felt a fever coming on, and although a brazier glowed nearby, he shivered with the fever's chill. So much for warding off the body's ills, he reflected sourly.

In response to the nagging of his mistress, Geoffry had allowed his barber to bleed him only the week before, and that had done nothing to prevent this feverish cold. Now, no doubt, she would insist that he be bled yet again. Thank God he didn't have to marry the woman. That, at least, was one advantage to his role as Bishop of Lincoln. He would have preferred a small barony for his income, but the king had insisted on a bishopric.

Geoffry examined the wax seal in which the cord binding the letter was embedded. It was intricately worked, but the artisans of the London mint could produce a forgery readily enough. He took a knife from his belt, cut the cord and carefully unfolded the letter.

He felt a tingle of anticipation as he saw that Eleanor had written the letter herself. It was written in the *langue d'oc* of Aquitaine. If she had dictated the letter to a clerk, the man would have automatically translated her words into Latin. This letter was obviously intended for Richard's eyes only. He read.

My dear Richard,

We have recently been entertained by Maître

Edmond Orri, and as you may imagine, he provided considerable relief from the *ennui* of my existence. He also provided me with a detailed account of the parley at Gisors and of the subsequent warfare. I can understand your desire to support the king in his effort to re-establish the Truce of God, so that you might fulfil your holy obligation to the cross. It appears, however, that this war may not end quickly. A border conflict could drag on for years, draining resources that could otherwise be employed to support afresh Crusade.

You no doubt feel a filial as well as a feudal obligation to your lord and father, the king, and that is as it should be. A prince, however, must also honour his obligation to his own destiny and to the lands and peoples he will one day surely rule. You deserve to have unambiguous title to the throne of England, and I am confident that if you show yourself firm in your resolve, the king will grant you this.

Geoffry smiled thinly. Eleanor was confident all right – confident that Henry would continue to refuse to take this step. She was clearly pressing for rebellion, but this was nothing new; and the letter was too carefully worded to prove a charge of treason. Geoffry quickly scanned the rest of the letter, which continued in the same vein. As he read the last lines, his smile vanished.

On another subject entirely, I would like to mention that I have a new companion, the young heiress of Pembroke, Isabelle de Clare. She is a charming, beautiful girl, and I cannot help but wish her every happiness. I have reason to believe that she and Sir William Marshal are truly drawn to each other, and you know that Sir William also stands very high in my regard.

You are, of course, aware of Sir William's value to the king as counsellor and captain, and I am

confident that if, in the course of time, the King of
England should favour him with this lady's hand,
Sir William would be boundlessly grateful.

Perhaps, when you've reflected on the matter, you
may think of a way to help bring this about.

'Oh, neatly done, Eleanor,' Geoffry said aloud.

Disguised as a plea for Richard to intercede on Marshal's
behalf, it was an open invitation to suborn Marshal at an
appropriate time with Richard's own promise to give him
Isabelle de Clare. Geoffry frowned thoughtfully as he refolded
the letter.

It came as no surprise that Eleanor would like to see
Marshal defect to Richard; it would gall her to see the knight
she had patronized serving the king against her son. But the
reward she proposed to offer Marshal was enormous. The
Pembroke inheritance would place him in the very first rank
of the English baronage.

Would Richard place that high a value on Marshal's
service? If he decided to rebel against the king, he just might
– if only to avoid conflict with Marshal. Eleanor's suggestion
was as much an assessment of Henry's failing leadership as it
was a tribute to Marshal's skills, and this, more than the rest
of the letter, was what worried the chancellor. The perception
of weakness was taking hold and spreading like a contagion
that could prove fatal.

And if Richard offered the bait, would Marshal take it?
The chancellor smiled wryly. He should have realized there
was more behind Marshal's concern for Isabelle de Clare
than the simple desire for justice. In a way, Geoffry was
relieved to discover that Marshal had his own secrets, for the
chancellor distrusted too much simplicity in a man.

Eleanor thought Marshal might be vulnerable, and Geoffry
had every reason to respect her judgment; but, in this case,
he thought she was indulging in wishful thinking. Marshal
was the one man the chancellor was sure would never desert
the king.

Yet Geoffry was too careful to ignore the threat entirely –
not when there was a simple remedy. What Richard could
only promise, Henry could deliver. If the situation should

warrant it, Geoffry would suggest just such a remedy to the king.

In the meantime, it would be wise to remove Isabelle de Clare from Eleanor's influence. The queen did not leave stones unturned, and if she could work on Marshal through the girl, she would. An inexperienced young girl was sure to be putty in the queen's hands.

19

'The Old Man's worried,' Hugh de Harlincourt said quietly to Marshal.

A biting November wind blew across the open meadow of yellowed grass in which the king and his entourage waited for Philip of France. Thick grey clouds scudded low overhead. Henry's servants had set up a tent and lit a brazier inside, but the king disdained the warmth it offered and remained on his horse. Muffled in his hooded, fur-lined robe, Henry stared bleakly out across the stream defining the frontier between Normandy and Perche. With him waited Prince John, the Bishops of Le Mans, Lisieux and Angers, and forty barons and knights, their banners billowing and snapping in the wind.

'He has a right to be concerned,' Marshal replied grimly. 'Where the devil is Richard?'

At Philip's request, Richard had arranged a parley between the kings, and Marshal had allowed himself to hope that Philip intended to sue for peace. Having disbanded his levies following the conference at Gisors, Philip had been unable to stop Marshal's repeated raids up and down the French territorial border. Philip had lost no land, but every raid brought fresh pressure to make peace. And in Berry, Richard's army was threatening to retake Chateauroux.

But Richard had been expected for the past thirty-six hours, and as the time for the parley approached, Henry had become progressively remote and introspective. Richard should have arrived well in advance of the meeting, and his unexplained absence was ominous.

Much depended on the outcome of this conference, for Henry's funds were exhausted and he had been forced to release his Welsh archers. If fighting resumed in the spring, the king would not have his mercenaries to rely on. Marshal extracted a handful of cloves from the pouch on his belt and popped some into his mouth to have something to chew on to quell his nervousness.

'You're going to ruin your stomach with those,' Bethune said.

'You should try cloves, Bo,' Marshal said, managing a smile. 'They sweeten your breath. That might improve your fortunes with the ladies.'

'What do you know about *l'amour*, Will? You've been living like a monk. That's your problem; you're as nervous as a cat.'

Marshal *was* on edge, and not simply because of Richard. John had gone south with Richard after Gisors, but he had recently returned to the king. Marshal had not forgotten the incident on the River Epte, and now that Gerard de Ridefort was in their camp again, he was wary of another ambush.

He had said nothing to his friends, for he had no proof; not even Ridefort deserved to die for a crime he had not committed. And he would die if Bethune or Harlincourt found out. They would force a fight with Ridefort and let God decide his guilt or innocence.

'Speaking of women,' Harlincourt said, 'when are you going to marry your *demoiselle*?'

'Marry her?' Marshal said in surprise. 'She's only fourteen years old.'

'So?' Harlincourt said, leaning closer to Marshal and lowering his voice to a stage-whisper. 'Right now, all you've got is the king's promise, and the way things are going . . . Take possession of the lady and her lands, Will, while you have the chance.'

'I'll think about it,' Marshal said, more curtly than he'd intended. He had already thought about it – often. He knew as well as Harlincourt that it was the safest thing to do.

Harlincourt had noted the unnecessary sharpness in Marshal's tone, and Marshal saw him wink at Bethune.

'You wouldn't be aiming a little higher, would you?' Bethune said slyly to Marshal.

'What?' Marshal said, caught completely off-guard.

Bethune pointed at Marshal's feet. 'You've never told us

how you came by those gold spurs, Will. You'll have to tell us some time; I'll wager it would make an interesting story.'

Marshal heard a sound like a stifled sneeze, and he turned and saw Harlincourt doubling over in silent laughter. Marshal compressed his lips and looked back at Jean d'Erly, but the boy was talking with another squire and did not notice. Now, both Bethune and Harlincourt were shaking with suppressed laughter.

Bethune, holding his ribs with one hand, reached out and grasped Marshal's arm. 'Don't blame Jean,' he gasped through spasms of hilarity. 'We pried it out of him.'

'*What* did you pry out of him?' Marshal said stiffly, feeling his cheeks redden.

'Not much,' Harlincourt laughed. 'Just how you got those spurs. Of course, we wondered why you didn't tell us about it yourself, and we could only guess before. But, judging from the look on your face, I'd say we hit the mark.'

'It looks that way,' Bethune agreed, grinning wickedly. 'It's good to know you're in one piece, Will. For a while, we were afraid the Templars might have deprived you of certain vital parts.'

Harlincourt shook his head. 'Maybe we shouldn't leap to conclusions, Bo. The lady may be entirely incidental to her lands; after all, she is a *very* rich heiress.'

'Be honest, Will,' Bethune said good-naturedly. 'Are you delaying marriage to Helwis in the hope of something better?'

Marshal was spared having to reply by the sudden appearance of a cluster of banners coming over a rise in the road beyond the bridge, drawing everyone's attention – everyone's but Marshal's. He was still trying to answer Bethune's question for himself.

Despite the turmoil of the intervening months, he had not succeeded in getting Isabelle de Clare out of his mind; memories of her refused to fade. Countless times he had felt the urge to write to her, but resisted it, telling himself that maintaining contact would only prolong the pain. They each had their own destinies to follow now, and to wish for more was pointless. But was Bethune right? Deep inside, was he hoping for the impossible?

'Christ's thorns!' Harlincourt breathed.

Marshal's eyes snapped back into focus, and as he saw the

banners clearly for the first time, his stomach muscles tightened. He looked towards the king and saw Henry staring in shock at the scarlet banner with three golden lions streaming in the wind beside the banner of the King of France.

King Henry's knights waited in tense silence as Richard, moving out in advance of Philip's party, cantered his horse over the bridge spanning the stream, cut across the meadow and dismounted before his father. Richard bent his knee, and Henry climbed stiffly down from his own horse to greet his son. There was a general creaking of leather and the clink of steel as his entourage dismounted with him.

'Good day, sire,' Richard said airily, his voice carrying to everyone despite the wind. Henry stretched out his arms, and Richard dutifully stepped forward and kissed the king's cheek. 'Good day, brother,' Richard said, turning to John and exchanging kisses.

The king's followers remained absolutely silent, ignoring Philip's approach as they stared at the Count of Poitou.

'We find you in strange company,' Henry said hoarsely, scrutinizing his son with narrowed eyes. 'Why?'

'There's no mystery to it, sire,' Richard said in the same light tone. 'We found oursleves on the same road, and to ignore King Philip's presence would have been discourteous.'

The king clearly distrusted Richard's easy explanation, for he flushed angrily. Yet in the face of Richard's bland pose, his dignity required that he accept it. In any event, there was no time for questions; Philip and his knights had crossed the bridge and were riding into the meadow.

Unlike the conference at Gisors, neither king was in a mood for posturing. Like Henry, the King of France wore no crown and was wrapped in a rich but utilitarian robe. Philip and his entourage dismounted, and Henry limped towards them. Flanked by their respective bishops, the kings met at the centre of a great circle formed by the attending knights.

John stood beside his father, but Richard took up a position to one side, between the two kings, literally standing with a foot in each camp. Richard's show of neutrality might have passed as mere formality, since he had arranged the parley, but, given his arrival in Philip's company, Marshal was sure the prince's stance was significant.

Marshal cursed silently. Philip had suffered losses in the field, but if he had managed to suborn Richard, the autumn's victories would be meaningless.

Henry must have had the same fear, but he gave no sign of it. Despite the pain in his knee, he stood with his feet firmly planted, his spine stiff and his shoulders back. Cloaked in his great robe, his torso appeared massive rather than obese, and as he looked down on his slight-figured rival, his expression was that of a conqueror.

Philip had requested the parley, so, after greetings had been exchanged, he spoke first. 'I am glad we could meet once again,' he said, with neither deference nor arrogance. He abandoned the haughty, ironic amusement he had used to provoke Henry at Gisors. 'This is a war neither of us wants, and I prefer to think that it was the summer heat that caused our tempers to get out of hand at our previous meeting.'

'I am ready to make peace at once,' Henry rumbled, 'if the terms are reasonable. Our object,' he said, looking at Richard in a deliberate gesture of inclusiveness, 'is to get on with the Crusade.'

Richard nodded; but he did not return his father's look, and there was a worrying aloofness in his expression. Richard was obviously watching and waiting – not as his father's ally, but as an onlooker determined to safeguard his own interests. John, in contrast, stood as close as physically possible to Henry, aping every nuance of his father's expression and carriage.

'I have a simple proposal to end our conflict,' Philip said, 'and I think it's fair. In effect, I propose that we accept the territorial status quo. I will allow Prince Richard to retain the castles he has seized from the Count of Toulouse, and I will remain in Berry. If you will then renew your allegiance to me as your liege lord in France, we can proceed immediately to the task of freeing Jerusalem from the Infidel.'

Henry looked towards Richard, this time for support, but again Richard avoided his eyes. Henry's face darkened. The proposal was impossible for the king to accept; it would amount to a victory for Philip.

'Is this a *serious* proposition?' Henry said angrily. 'Berry is mine – given me by your father.'

Philip coldly returned Henry's glare. 'It is not yours. Berry was given as Alais's dowry and belongs to the husband to whom she was betrothed.'

The young king paused and delicately dabbed at his nose with his kerchief.

'Since you won't accept the status quo,' he said, 'I will make you a proposal to end our conflict once and for all. My father gave you the Vexin as dowry for Marguerite, with the clear understanding that it be returned to her in the event of Prince Henry's death. You have not returned it. My father gave you Berry as dowry for Alais, and you have not married her to Richard. Return the Vexin to me, and marry Alais to Rich—'

'Enough!' Henry broke in furiously, hammering the air with his fist. 'We've been over this too many times before! It seems we freeze out here for nothing. You don't want an honourable peace, you want my surrender!'

Philip did not respond immediately. Assuming a look of patient tolerance, he let the silence stretch out.

'I offered you the status quo,' he said at last, 'which certainly is a logical compromise and would address only one of the wrongs we have suffered. For the sake of the Crusade, I was willing to leave the question of the Vexin in abeyance. Since you refused that, I am suggesting a just basis for an enduring peace. Let Alais marry Richard so that Berry passes into his hands – but remains within your house – and return the Vexin to poor Marguerite. That will end our dispute, and we can march on Jerusalem with glad hearts.'

'No!' Henry barked, and he looked angrily at Richard. 'Have you nothing to say?' he challenged.

'It seems, sire,' Richard replied insolently, 'that you've said it all.'

'Clifford!' Marshal hissed as he saw one of his knights reach reflexively for his sword. The knights of Richard's and Henry's mesnes were eyeing one another with undisguised hostility, for it was clear that Philip had managed to drive a wedge between Richard and his father.

Henry ignored the rising tension around him. His eyes left Richard and returned to Philip, studying his opponent in silence. As he began to stroke his beard thoughtfully, Marshal tensed, for he recognized the gesture. Henry was about to gamble.

'Your first proposal settled the question of Berry to your satisfaction,' Henry said to Philip. 'Your second proposal squeezed me even harder, but I assume that was simply shrewd bargaining on your part. Now hear my proposal. It conforms completely with the spirit of your first position.

'You wanted to settle the question of Berry. Very well. I promised King Louis to marry Alais to a Prince of England, and I am prepared to do that. Will you make peace with me now, in return for Alais's marriage to my son John?'

'God's teeth!' Bethune said to Marshal under cover of the wave of muttering and excited whispers that swept through the onlookers. 'Look at Richard's face!'

Marshal did not need to look to know Richard's reaction to Henry's surprise offer. Marshal was watching Philip, and he knew at once that Henry had overplayed his hand. He had fatally misjudged his young opponent, and there was a glint of triumph in Philip's eyes.

Henry had failed to appreciate that he was no longer dealing with a boy who might be content to accept a cheap and easy means of achieving one of his father's cherished aims. Philip wanted more than a marriage alliance; he wanted to strengthen Richard and emasculate the English king.

The Count of Flanders, who was standing behind Philip, caught Marshal's eye and shook his head gravely. In many ways, Marshal and Flanders were counterparts in their relationship to their respective kings, and if Marshal had any doubts that Philip intended to press his war with Henry to the finish, Flanders's look banished them.

Philip sighed theatrically. 'I thought you had a higher opinion of me,' he said to Henry. 'Do you really believe I would turn my back on my loyal vassal, Prince Richard, who, unlike you, has not revoked his allegiance to the crown of France? Alais was betrothed to Richard, and if Berry passes from my hands, it must go to him and no one else.'

'Is that your final word?' Henry grated, unconsciously pulling his robe more tightly about him, as if suddenly feeling the chill wind sweeping across the meadow.

'No, it is not,' Philip said coldly. 'I see now that I must

include in my terms some protection for the Count of Poitou. There will be no peace between us, Henry, until you return the Vexin to Marguerite, marry Alais to Richard and declare him to be the rightful heir to the throne of England, requiring all English barons to do homage to him as their . . .'

'God's legs, I'll hear no more!' Henry exploded, balling his fists in fury. 'Each time you open your mouth, you increase your demands. You presume to seek the preferment of one of my sons, but you have no right to meddle in the affairs of England. I will not be blackmailed!'

'And what do you say to me, sire?' Richard burst out, his face contorted as much in anguish as in anger. 'I must – once and for all – know where I stand with you. Give *me* your assurance that I am to be your heir!'

But Henry just stared at his son in stony silence, his expression set in the closed, stubborn look of a very old man.

Richard's face paled, and he shook his head. 'For years – *years*, sire – I have refused to believe what I see now with my own eyes,' he said in a hushed, unnatural voice. 'But it *is* true. You would deny me my inheritance!'

Still looking at his father, Richard unbuckled his sword, slowly, as if hoping his father would stop him with a word. Then he turned and approached Philip, his footsteps crunching in the dried grass. He dropped to his knees before the French king, laid his sword at Philip's feet, clasped his hands and raised them to Philip.

In that moment, Marshal realized the extent to which Henry had played into Philip's hands. On the ride to the conference, the King of France must have offered Richard the ultimate bribe – immediate title to Henry's Continental domains.

'Sire,' Richard said in a loud, clear voice. 'Reserving the allegiance I owe my father, I hereby offer my homage to you, Philip of France, and do swear my fealty for those lands which you may choose to grant me as my lord.'

'Traitor!' someone in the ranks of Henry's followers growled, and in an instant the rattle of swords being drawn swept around the circle of knights.

Marshal leapt forward. 'Hold!' be barked, raising his hand. 'By God, I'll kill the first man on either side to break the peace!' No one doubted his threat, and one after another, swords were slipped back into their sheaths.

Both Philip and Richard ignored the disturbance, and Henry, his face white with shock, stood as if frozen to the spot. Philip folded Richard's clasped hands in his own and said into the silence, 'Richard, Count of Poitou, in return for the service you offer me, I grant you title to the lands of Normandy, Maine, Anjou and Touraine and offer you my protection. Arise, Richard, Duke of Normandy and Count of Aquitaine, Maine, Anjou and Tourraine.'

As Richard got to his feet, Henry spun on his heel and stalked across the meadow to his horse, followed immediately by his entourage. The king climbed into the saddle and wheeled his horse about. Without waiting for all of his followers to mount, he galloped away.

'Do your latrines need cleaning, Maurice, or has the stench of treachery followed us all the way up here?' Henry rasped.

Maurice fitz Patrick, the fleshy, good-natured baron in whose castle the king had quartered himself and his entourage, cleared this throat. 'The latrines, sire. I offer my apologies.'

Fitz Patrick was taking the invasion of his castle in his stride, though a royal visit could be as devastating to the baronial stores as a plague of locusts. The sudden demands of hospitality on a royal scale had thrown his household officers and the ladies of the castle into a frenzy, but he remained above it all. 'Perhaps you would care to adjourn your council to the *palais*, sire,' he suggested.

'No,' Henry said with a heavy sigh, stretching out his lame leg. 'This will do. The stink of shit sets the right tone for this meeting.'

Henry had summoned his household knights, barons and bishops to a council in the seldom-used great hall of the castle's tower keep. The king sat on the dais in the baron's canopied chair, with John seated beside him. John was uncharacteristically silent, and his black eyes roved distractedly over the forty or so men standing in a semicircle before the dais.

The knights still wore their fur-lined cloaks, for the fire in the great hearth had not yet relieved the chill in the dank hall. Torches burned on the walls to supplement the grey, late-afternoon light entering through the arrow-slits in the gallery overhead.

It was clear that the baroness cared nothing for this hall. The wall hangings were frayed and musty, and dust covered the polished stone eyes of the moth-eaten hunting trophies which stared balefully down from the walls. The hall now served principally as an arsenal, and it was lined with long racks of gleaming pikes and varnished lances.

The shock of Richard's sudden defection still affected the knights who had witnessed it, but the king had already recovered. He seemed to be accepting Richard's desertion fatalistically, almost as if he had expected it all along.

Marshal couldn't understand it. For months, Henry had insisted that his son would remain faithful, and now he behaved as if the betrayal were simply one more trial to be endured. Marshal hoped that this was a measure of Henry's resilience, and not a flight from reality.

The king shifted heavily in his chair. 'Well, gentlemen, we're still at war, and England's coffers are empty. We won't be able to afford mercenaries when we meet Philip in the spring. What is your advice?'

Immediately, the Seneschal of Normandy stepped forward. 'I suggest, sire,' fitz Ralph said, 'that we prepare to fight a defensive war. Let him invade if he chooses. We should reinforce the garrisons of the key fortresses in his path and content ourselves with fighting a series of purely defensive battles. We may lose some territory over the spring and summer, but we will gain time – time to replenish the English treasury. In the long run, sire, Philip cannot match your financial resources.'

Henry scowled and nodded at the same time, hating the idea of being on the defensive, but acknowledging that he had little choice.

'It won't be that easy, sire,' objected Stephen de Marcai, the Seneschal of Anjou. 'We may face a war on two fronts: Philip from the west and Richard from the south. We'll have to worry about our strongpoints all along the Loire, and we all know how quickly castles fall to Richard's siegecraft.'

'There is more to war than strongpoints and armies, sire!' the Bishop of Lisieux called out in his best pulpit baritone.

'Let us not forget that God is on our side in the coming struggle.'

'God?' Henry snorted derisively and cast his eyes heavenward. 'God gave me my sons – sons who will never give me peace!'

'Not all your sons are faithless, sire,' John said plaintively, plucking like a child at his father's sleeve.

'I know, John, I know,' Henry said, patting his son's arm distractedly, his mind still focused on the military problem.

Now, William, Earl of Essex, stepped forward and said, 'It is all very well to garrison castles in the south, sire, but we must be sure of the loyalty of the castellans. It's not Richard's siege tactics that worry me, but the possibility that the castles in the south will fall to him without a fight.'

'Sire,' fitz Ralph interjected, 'it is not clear to me that Prince Richard intends to oppose you actively. After all, when he swore fealty to Philip, he made a point of reserving the allegiance he owes you. It could be that he merely intends to sit out the war.'

'Wishful thinking,' the Seneschal of Anjou said bitterly. 'Does anyone here know where Richard is now? No? Well, I'll tell you. One of my own knights has friends in Richard's mesne, and he remained behind at the bridge to talk with them. Richard did not elect to remain in the vicinity. He has stolen away like a thief, and at this moment is riding south.'

An uncomfortable silence followed, but the king's reaction was not to be read in his face. It was set in the same stony expression with which he had viewed Richard's submission to Philip.

Fitz Ralph broke the silence. 'That still doesn't prove he intends to war against his own father.'

'Perhaps not,' the Seneschal of Anjou replied, 'but his abrupt departure is not the only bad news. According to the knights of Richard's mesne, Richard and Philip were on the road together for two days, and became so close that not even the bed separated them at night.'

Henry flushed and uttered an inarticulate oath. He seemed suddenly to have difficulty breathing, and the renewed silence in the hall was punctuated by the sighing rasp of the king's laboured inhalations.

Marshal had intended to stay out of the discussion, leaving

it to the barons who would have to shoulder the major burden of the defence of the Angevin domain; but the atmosphere had degenerated dangerously, and no one had pointed out the obvious.

'Sire,' Marshal called out, and stepped forward. 'It is vital that we know Prince Richard's intentions and not simply guess them. I suggest we discover the road he has taken and send a representative after him.'

'To what purpose?' Henry asked, taking another deep, ragged breath.

'To ask him to return and explain himself, sire – with your assurance of safe conduct. Prince Richard's homage to Philip was quite legal, since you previously revoked your allegiance to the French crown. In itself, it does not challenge your immediate authority. Your representative can assure him that he has nothing to fear from you if he remains neutral.'

'And if he refuses to return and explain?' Henry rasped.

'Then, sire, we'll have our answer: he intends to fight.'

'All right,' the king said, leaning back and rubbing his eyes wearily. 'That's a sensible suggestion. I'll send you, Marshal; Richard trusts and respects you as much as any man here. When can you leave?'

'As soon as we find which road the prince has taken, sire.'

John glared at his chamberlain and took another gulp of wine. He had already drunk too much and his head was spinning, but he had not succeeded in dulling his anxiety.

'What do you mean, you can't find him?' he snapped.

'Ridefort left the castle an hour ago, sire,' Poole said defensively.

'But I told you to bring him to me!'

'Yes, sire, but he was already gone by then.'

John blinked, trying to keep Poole's image in focus. Damn the wine! It had done him no good at all. The scene in the castle's great hall that afternoon had frightened him, and John was not used to being frightened. The pessimism, resignation and, in some instances, the submerged panic he had read in many of the barons' eyes came as a shattering revelation.

For months, the chancellor had warned of the danger Richard's defection would pose, but John had not believed him. Over-awed by his father, John had never doubted the king's ability to crush Richard, and he had eagerly awaited Richard's rebellion, sure that civil war would leave him undisputed heir to the thone. But in the council that afternoon, John had suddenly seen Henry as others saw him: a weary old man ineffectually reacting to events, not controlling them. For the first time, it occurred to John that Richard might actually win.

Holy Mother, if he were caught on the losing side . . .

'Why did Ridefort leave?' John demanded.

'I'm not sure, sire,' Poole said uncomfortably, not understanding John's black mood. 'But he rode out with the contingent of Flemish mercenaries you'll be releasing at the end of the week.'

'What!' John exploded, banging the goblet against the arm of his chair. 'In God's name, man, he must be after Marshal!'

John's stomach convulsed as a violent wave of nausea swept over him. Marshal's party would have to ride far and fast to catch up with Richard, so the knights would be only lightly armed – and travelling a deserted highway in the dead of night.

'But, sire, I thought . . .'

'You thought, you thought!' John shouted, spittle flying from his lips. 'Don't you understand? We *need* Marshal now!'

Poole blanched, and his evident confusion at his master's abrupt turn-around only made John angrier. Why couldn't Poole think for himself for once!

'Sire, we don't know for certain that Ridefort intends . . .'

'Don't be a fool!' John cut in, grinding his teeth in frustration. Everything had seemed to be moving his way, and now, suddenly, it was all going wrong. It was all going wrong!

'But, sire,' Poole said quickly, not understanding but anxious to calm John down, 'even if Ridefort has gone after Marshal, we shouldn't assume he'll succeed. Don't forget, sire, he's already failed once.'

It took a moment for his chamberlain's words to penetrate John's whirling thoughts, but as they registered, he drew a deep breath and slowly nodded, wanting to believe. Marshal must have had a substantial start, and Ridefort and his mercenaries would be weighed down by armour. Even if they had brought extra horses, they probably would not catch up with him. Yes, John told himself, Poole was right; Ridefort was a bungler.

'You think he'll fail again?' John said.

'It wouldn't surprise me, sire,' Poole replied, and John settled back in his chair with a faint sigh.

But in John's desire to grasp at any straw, he had not noticed the lack of conviction in his chamberlain's voice.

20

It was nearing midnight when Bethune's stirrup gave way. Marshal, Bethune and Harlincourt were riding side by side behind their squires, whose torches lit the highway they were following through league after league of unpopulated forest. Thick clouds blackened the sky, and beyond the reaches of the flickering torchlight the darkness was absolute.

Bethune cursed and reined in, and Marshal called a halt. 'What's the trouble?' Marshal asked irritably, his breath condensing in the cold night air.

'Stirrup leather's parted,' Bethune said, climbing stiffly down from the saddle as his squire rode back to help him. 'Robert will have it fixed quickly enough, Will,' he said with a yawn. 'No need for concern.'

'We're wasting our time, anyway,' Harlincourt said. 'Richard would not be riding south if he didn't intend to fight us.'

'We have to make sure,' Marshal replied curtly, unwilling to admit that Harlincourt was right. There might still be a chance of dissuading Richard from warring against his father, but Marshal knew it was remote.

He shifted restlessly in his saddle. The impenetrable darkness of the forest seemed to be pressing in on them, constricting the circle of torchlight. There were no reports of marauders on the roads, but bands of deserters were always a potential threat in wartime, and Marshal did not want to be taken by surprise. 'Andrew,' he said to Harlincourt's squire, 'ride on down the road a hundred paces and keep alert. Jean, ride back and cover the rear.'

'How far do you think we've come?' Bethune asked, taking a wineskin from his saddle.

'Not far enough,' Marshal said. 'We won't get much sleep tonight. It's still at least a four-hour ride to the Loire.'

Bethune took a long drink of wine, belched with satisfaction and passed the skin to Harlincourt, who had dismounted and was flexing his stiff leg muscles.

'What makes you so sure Richard is spending the night at Amboise?' Harlincourt asked.

'I'm not sure,' Marshal replied, easing himself in the saddle and suppressing a yawn of his own, 'but he had a six-hour start on us, and I don't believe he'll stop until he reaches the Loire.'

'Want some of this?' Harlincourt asked Marshal, offering Bethune's wine. 'It's better than that watered-down swill you carry. You're not in the desert anymore, you know.'

Marshal smiled and was reaching for the wineskin when they heard a short, sharp whistle from Jean.

'Mount up!' Marshal ordered.

'I haven't finished, sire,' Bethune's squire said.

'Forget it, lad,' Bethune said, leaping into the saddle and pulling his mail coif over his woollen cap.

Jean was riding hard towards them, and Harlincourt's squire, who had heard the warning whistle, was returning at a gallop.

'Riders coming up on us fast, sire,' Jean cried, as he hauled on his reins and his horse skidded to a stop beside Marshal. 'Half a league beyond the rise back there.'

'How many?'

'I'm not sure, sire, but too many for us.'

Marshal did not argue. They weren't equipped to stand their ground, and he wasn't looking for trouble. It was possible the approaching riders had seen Jean's torch, but the odds were against it.

'Swords or lances, Will?' Bethune asked.

'Swords,' Marshal said, 'but we're moving off the road. We'll have a look at them as they go by. Put out those torches.'

They were plunged into darkness as Bethune's squire extinguished the torches. Bending low over their saddles to avoid being struck by the tree-limbs they could not see, they moved blindly into the forest. Fifteen paces from the road,

Marshal reined in, and they turned their mounts and waited together in silence.

Minutes later, they heard the pounding of hooves on the hardpacked road-bed as the riders came over the rise. The pounding quickly swelled to a thunder of hoofbeats as twenty horsemen swept by, the light of their torches glinting on full suits of armour.

'Did you see their helmets?' Bethune said as the sound of the riders faded down the road. 'They're Flemish mercenaries.'

'Yes, but whose?' Harlincourt said. 'No standards, no banners.'

'And armed to the teeth,' Bethune observed. 'Whoever, or whatever, they're after, they're in the devil's hurry. With all the iron they're carrying, they'll kill those horses if they don't rest them soon.'

'What now, Will?' Harlincourt asked.

'We go on,' Marshal said, 'but we keep our eyes open. They are going to have to slow down or call a halt soon, and we don't want to stumble into them. There's no point in courting trouble.'

Three leagues farther on, Marshal ordered the torches extinguished as they spotted the lanterns of an isolated wayside inn, and they approached cautiously. The inn was built in a clearing close beside the road. Attached to the ramshackle, two-storey building were sheds and a large stable.

'Jean,' Marshal said softly, 'check the stable.'

The Flemish mercenaries had been pushing their mounts too hard to travel far, and if they had intended to halt, this was a logical place. Jean slipped from the saddle and ran lightly across the clearing, his shadowy form visible for only a moment before it merged with the darkness surrounding the sheds. Two minutes later, he was back.

'They must be here, sire,' he said in a stage-whisper. 'All the stalls are filled, and the horses are still wet.'

'The fools didn't have their mounts rubbed down?' Bethune said incredulously.

'The stable boys are asleep, sire. I could hear them snoring.'

'Mount up, Jean,' Marshal snapped impatiently. 'Whoever

they are, we can forget them now, and we still have a long way to go.'

'It doesn't make sense,' Harlincourt muttered. 'Why ride like the devil through the dead of night, only to finish here in the middle of nowhere?'

'Maybe they were chasing someone, sire,' Jean said, remounting, 'and couldn't catch up before their horses gave out.'

Marshal shrugged in the darkness and spurred his horse forward. The question was puzzling, but he had no answer and was too tired to wonder about it.

The great castle guarding the city of Amboise surmounted a steep hill overlooking the Loire and commanded a majestic view of the valley, but what little consideration Marshal gave the scenery was in terms of siege tactics. Amboise lay on Henry's eastern frontier and would be in the first line of defence against a French assault on Tours.

Bethune and Harlincourt rode in silence beside Marshal, blinking sleepily in the dim, early-morning light as they followed a line of ox-carts snaking up the face of the hill to the castle's main gate. From above came the rattle and squeal of the portcullis being raised, and the gate's iron-bound doors swung open to admit the crowd that had gathered in the cold, grey dawn.

Marshal arched his spine to relieve the stiffness in his back and tiredly rubbed his gritty eyes. The bleak, sunless day matched his mood, for the long night had sapped his energy and left him feeling empty and depressed. Chasing after Richard *was* futile; he was almost certainly beyond reach, whether or not they found him here at Amboise.

Harlincourt looked up at the castle and shook his head dolefully. 'Too fancy,' he said, eyeing the spotless, white-washed walls and gilded turret roofs. 'Will Montfort fight, or will he be too afraid of damaging his pretty castle?'

Marshal shrugged wearily. 'It's not our concern. The king knows his barons; he'll have to assess their loyalty and spirit.'

'I know Montfort,' Bethune said. 'He'll fight, all right – if he thinks he's on the winning side.'

Marshal had sent Jean ahead to announce their coming in the name of the king, and as they approached, trumpeters on the gatehouse parapet heralded their arrival. Marshal grimaced at the piercing fanfare, which, in his present condition, jarred him as it would a man with a hangover.

He recognized no one from Richard's entourage as they crossed the bailey, and he found himself hoping that Richard had pressed on in his flight south. Then he could sleep and for a time avoid confronting the increasingly grim prospects of the king and those who followed him.

But as they rode into the castle's inner courtyard, the portly lord of Amboise Castle emerged from his *palais* to greet them, and his dress proclaimed Richard's presence. Robert de Montfort was splendidly attired in what must have been his richest robe.

'Good morning, Sir William,' said the middle-aged baron, 'I am Robert de Montfort. It's a pleasure to meet you at last.'

'Good morning, Sir Robert,' Marshal said, his voice hoarse from lack of sleep. 'I believe you know Bethune. May I introduce Hugh de Harlincourt. We are seeking Prince Richard on behalf of the king, and we believe he may have passed this way.'

'You're fortunate, Sir William,' Montfort said with a smile that was too broad and failed to disguise his nervousness. 'Prince Richard is here now.' The castellan's smile slipped as he swallowed anxiously. 'He spent the night here, but I assure you that – well, I could hardly deny him entry could I?'

'And why should you wish to deny Prince Richard entry?' Marshal said sharply.

Montfort spread his hands in a gesture of helplessness. 'I had no reason, of course – but when I saw . . . I assure you, Sir William, I am steadfastly loyal to His Majesty, and I would never have . . .'

'Talk straight, Sir Robert!' Marshal snapped impatiently, but he already understood the message that the baron's anxiety conveyed. Bethune was giving Marshal a knowing look.

'Prince Richard was up all night,' Montfort said breathlessly. 'He summoned the monks of our local abbey and had them working until a few hours before dawn – copying letters. He sent out over two hundred letters, Sir William, and he's made no secret of their content. Richard has declared himself

Lord of the Angevin domains, allied himself with King Philip and is calling the barons of the region to his banner.'

'Christ's blood' Bethune groaned. 'Let's go home, Will.'

Marshal sighed wearily and shook his head. 'I want to talk to him,' he said, climbing stiffly down from the saddle.

'It's a waste of time,' Harlincourt said angrily. 'Richard has deserted us for the sake of his damned pride. What's the use of talk now?'

'Because I have to be absolutely sure of his position,' Marshal said, knowing it was pointless.

The final quenching of all hope weighed Marshal down even more than his fatigue, and his steps were leaden as he followed Montfort into the *palais*; but he had been charged by Henry to confront Richard, and he had to go through the motions.

Richard's squire ushered Marshal into the apartment Montfort had placed at Richard's disposal and closed the door, leaving Marshal alone with the Count of Poitou.

Richard slouched in a heavy chair beside the bed, a wine cup held slackly in his hand. He motioned Marshal to approach, and Marshal walked forward and briefly inclined his head.

'You look rotten, Marshal,' Richard said. 'You didn't get much sleep either, I take it.' Alcohol fumes drifted across to Marshal, mingling with the sour smell of Richard's body. The usually fastidious prince was still attired in the clothes he had worn the day before, and his cloak and surcoat were rumpled and travel-stained.

'His Majesty has sent me to ask you to return and explain yourself, sire,' Marshal said formally. 'When you did homage to the King of France, you reserved the allegiance you owe your father. His Majesty would like to know if that means you intend to remain neutral in our war with Philip.'

'Neutral!' Richard snorted. 'My father must be dreaming.' Richard's eyes were bloodshot and watery, but they burned with grim determination. Richard, after years of vacillation, had clearly made up his mind. 'I was blind, Marshal, but King Philip has opened my eyes. He is fighting this war on my behalf as much as his. *I* am now the lawful lord of the

Angevin domains, and I damned well intend to take them and hold them as my own.'

Marshal was running on nervous energy, and depression and fatigue had frayed his temper. He could see from Richard's appearance what it must have cost him to declare war on his father, but Marshal felt no sympathy. Richard might have felt himself driven to rebellion, but his action was more than treason; it was betrayal.

'You can try, sire,' Marshal said coldly.

'Why so harsh, Marshal?' Richard said. 'I would have expected otherwise. When my brother Henry felt compelled to fight for his rights against my father, you stood by him.'

'He was my lord, sire,' Marshal replied stiffly, 'and I served him as I was bound to do. But I counselled him to make peace – as you well know. You are playing into Philip's hands by this rebellion, sire. Only the Capets will profit from a war between you and your father.'

'I am not as weak as my brothers,' Richard snapped. 'And I'm no puppet – of Philip or of Henry.'

'No?' Marshal retorted. 'And I say we will cut each other up and Philip will pick up the pieces.'

Richard stretched out his legs and shook his head in condescending tolerance. 'Cut each other up? Open your eyes, Marshal. My father's castles will fall to me like ripe apples.'

Marshal compressed his lips, but did not reply. He could see there was no point in further argument, and he could not effectively dispute Richard's prediction. Every one of Henry's counsellors feared the possibility of wholesale defection.

Richard had been studying Marshal, and now he leaned forward and said earnestly, 'You know my destiny as well as I do, Marshal. I *will* be king, and I cannot believe you wish to fight me.'

'No, sire, but I . . .'

'Then listen to me and consider well what I say. You're as true a knight as I know, and nothing would give me greater pleasure than to have you at my side. You, more than most, must realize that my father cannot hope to prevail against both me and King Philip. Nor should he! Henry's time has come and gone. The future is with me, Marshal, and I'm inviting you to be a part of it.'

For a moment, Marshal was tempted. He no longer doubted that Henry was in decline; he had seen the ageing king's growing indecisiveness and his ever more frequent flights from reality. Henry had ceased to be a match for the two young men arrayed against him.

But as strong as the temptation was, it was only fleeting. By remaining with the king, Marshal might be sacrificing his future, but to betray his liege lord would cost him more. He had built his life on the feudal code of honour, and to deny it now would be to deny himself – what he was and what he hoped to be.

'I cannot serve you, sire,' Marshal said. 'Not while His Majesty lives. I have sworn my allegiance to him, and he has given me no cause to rescind it.'

'Bravely spoken,' Richard responded, 'but hardly realistic. Allegiance is not absolute, Marshal; it never has been. My father demonstrated that at Gisors, when he renounced the allegiance he owed Philip of France.'

'With cause, sire. With cause.'

'And do you not also have cause to reconsider your allegiance in the coming conflict?' Richard said insistently. 'My father has openly forfeited his legal claim to the lands for which we will fight. I – not Henry – am now Duke of Normandy and Count of Anjou, Maine and Touraine.'

'From Philip's point of view, perhaps, sire; not from mine.'

Richard scowled with the same petulant air he had displayed when Marshal refused him the Saracen dagger; but slowly his expression changed, and he gazed speculatively at Marshal.

'I admire loyalty,' Richard said, fingering his carefully trimmed beard. 'I really do. But loyalty should work both ways. You should ask yourself if my father has rewarded you in proportion to the value of your service.'

There was an uncharacteristic note of slyness in his tone that surprised Marshal, and he frowned. 'I am satisfied, sire.'

'Are you really? With that scrap of land in Cartmel and custody of Helwis of Lancaster?' Richard said disparagingly.

'I'm *satisfied*, sire,' Marshal repeated, taken aback by the realization that Richard was about to offer a bribe. Bribery had never been Richard's way.

'If I were king,' Richard said, 'I would consider a far

greater reward to be appropriate for a knight of your calibre. The hand of the heiress of Pembroke, for example.'

Richard's words caught Marshal like a fist in the stomach. Eleanor, he thought dimly, as the blood rushed to his head. It had to be Eleanor. She alone could have guessed that this offer was the one bribe he would find almost impossible to refuse.

And why can't you accept? a voice inside him cried. Richard *was* the future, and he was offering the prize that Marshal wanted more than anything else in life. Why could he not accept what logic and overwhelming desire demanded? Why could he not – just this once – break the bonds of honour?

'No, sire,' Marshal said hoarsely, the refusal torn from him. 'No,' he repeated, turning on his heel and walking blindly towards the door.

'Marshal!' Richard barked. 'I will not tolerate insolence!'

Marshal spun around, but with an effort of will he stifled the biting reply that flew to his lips. He was here as the king's representative, not as his own man.

'I apologize, sire,' he said stiffly, 'and request permission to withdraw. I regret that I cannot accept service with you. When our armies meet in the spring, you will find me with the king.'

The winter of 1188–89 was harsher than any in recent memory, but as Marshal rode through the south gate of Le Mans, he noted with some satisfaction that the heavy snowfall and sub-freezing temperatures had not slowed the work on the city's fortifications. Le Mans was the king's birthplace. Here he had established his winter court, and Le Mans was to be his headquarters when war broke out in the spring.

Returning from yet another fruitless peace conference arranged by the church, Marshal and Jean had covered ten leagues since dawn. The laboured exhalations of their weary horses steamed in the frosty air, but Marshal dug in his spurs and drove his tired palfrey up through the narrow, twisting streets towards the castle dominating the hilltop city.

Now that they were almost home, Marshal hungered for warmth. Jean's face was pinched and blue, and Marshal could no longer feel his toes, despite his fur-lined boots. The sun shone brightly in a clear sky, but it did nothing to relieve the bitter cold. As Marshal rode through the castle's courtyard towards the central tower, he acknowledged the welcoming cries of the knights he passed, but he was too anxious to get inside to stop and talk.

'Make sure the horses are properly cared for,' he said to Jean as he dismounted. 'Don't leave it to the varlets.'

'Of course, sire,' Jean said cheerfully, and it occurred to Marshal that he, too, had been able to withstand the cold when he was Jean's age. It was not a comforting thought.

Upon entering the vestibule at the entrance to the great hall, Marshal had to pause to allow his eyes to adjust to the gloom. For a few moments, he was blinded by the bright-green after-image from the glare of the sun on the snow outside.

'His Majesty has dismissed the morning court, Sir William,' said the young herald at the door, 'but he is still in the hall.'

'Good,' Marshal said, removing his gloves and warming his fingers with his breath. 'Announce me.'

The great hall was empty of courtiers, and servants were busily setting up the long trestle-tables for the midday meal. On the dais at the far end of the hall, Henry sat on his throne, attended by John and the Earl of Essex. A fire blazed in the hearth, and, in contrast to the cold outside, the hall seemed suffused with warmth.

'What news?' Henry called out with forced vigour as Marshal strode towards him.

'Bad news, sire,' Marshal responded with his customary bluntness. 'Prince Richard and King Philip flatly refused to listen to the arguments of the papal legate. As soon as they learned you were not coming, they cancelled the conference.'

'But they knew I couldn't . . .'

Henry's words were cut off by a deep, racking cough that shook him to the core. His forehead glistened with beads of sweat, and his ruddy cheeks were a shade too red. Fever again, Marshal thought grimly. The recurring fever had first struck Henry early in December. He would shake it off for a time, but never for very long.

'I assured them that you were too ill to attend, sire,' Marshal said, 'but Prince Richard refused to believe me. And when the legate protested, Prince Richard accused him of being in our pay.'

'He said *that* to the papal legate?' Henry said with a disbelieving shake of his head. 'That's it, then. War can't be avoided.'

'War was inevitable from the start, sire,' Essex said quietly. 'The conference would have been a waste of time in any event – unless you were willing to surrender to their demands.'

'Never!' Henry rasped. 'Not while I live.'

Marshal exchanged a look with Essex, and Henry caught it.

'I'll be well enough come spring,' he said sharply, 'and, sick or not, I can still do what's necessary. I put on a good show this morning, didn't I, Essex?'

'That you did, sire,' Essex said with a smile. 'I'm sure Evreux was impressed.'

One by one, Henry had been summoning his barons to court to reaffirm their loyalty, and despite his illness, the king delivered a virtuoso performance. The king these barons saw was resolute and confident, and Henry played upon their individual desires and fears with the consummate skill that had won him an empire.

Whether or not his barons would stand fast in the face of the enemy was still an open question, but the king had at least prevented the wave of open defections that his counsellors had feared. Paradoxically, the bouts of fever had seemed to stiffen his resolve, banishing the moodiness that had afflicted him in the autumn. Marshal did not believe it could last, but he strove to bolster that resolve.

'I see that the reinforcement of the city walls is proceeding apace, sire,' Marshal said, looking at John with a deliberate expression of approval.

Richard's rebellion had wrought a change in John that surprised everyone. His incessant fawning had given way to a more substantial support. In council, he no longer automatically deferred to his father in policy disputes. Instead, he listened to the arguments and exercised reasoned, independent judgment. John had shouldered what he could of the administrative burden, and had taken charge of the fortification of Le Mans. His notorious indolence appeared to be a thing of the past.

Marshal doubted he would ever overcome his antipathy towards John, but he accepted the prince's contribution for what it was worth.

Henry reached out and grasped John's shoulder affectionately. 'My son has done well,' the king said proudly. 'My *true* son. He'll see me through this struggle.'

'Thank you, sire,' John said.

One of Henry's mastiffs rose from the floor and came over, laying his great head on his master's lap, demanding attention.

'Jealous, are you, old boy?' Henry said, stroking the dog. Despite the news of the papal legate's failure, Henry now appeared relaxed and unaffected by it, but his eyes were too bright, and Marshal guessed that the fever was rising. He had seen the cycle before; Henry's spirits were highest just before the fever drove him to his sickbed.

'Well, Marshal, you did what you could,' the king said almost jovially, 'but it appears that the die is cast. Unless you wish to wait out the winter here, I see no reason why you cannot return to England to attend to your affairs. It won't be a pleasant journey at this time of year, but it will be your last opportunity for some time to come.'

'Thank you, sire,' Marshal said gratefully. 'I *would* like to make the acquaintance of my ward. I'm sure the Sheriff of Lancashire is taking good care of her, but I should see for myself.'

The journey would be hard and it was unnecessary, but Marshal was glad of the excuse to leave for a time. Now that negotiations with Philip and Richard had finally been broken off, there was nothing to do but wait.

The thought of seeing Isabelle again had darted into his mind at once, but he shied away from it. As hard as it would be to stay away, it would be harder still to see her. A visit to Winchester would be rubbing salt into the wound.

'Marshal, I want you . . .' Once again, the king was seized by a prolonged coughing fit that left him gasping for breath. 'Before you leave England,' he said at last, 'I want you to pay a visit to Lord Geoffry in London. He's anxious to return to court, and if he convinces you that he can accomplish nothing more where he is, he has my permission to come to Le Mans.'

'Yes, sire,' Marshal said with a smile. It was time Geoffry returned. Marshal was still wary of John, and with the exception of Essex, he had no great faith in the few barons wintering at Le Mans. Stephen de Marcai, Seneschal of Anjou, and William fitz Ralph, Seneschal of Normandy, were able counsellors, but their own responsibilities kept them from court for extended periods.

'And while you're in London, Marshal, there is someone else you should see,' Henry said enigmatically.

'Sire?'

Henry's eyes crinkled with secret amusement, and he did not respond immediately. Marshal glanced at Essex and then John, but it was clear they did not know what the king had in mind.

'It was Lord Geoffry's idea, actually,' Henry said, obviously enjoying Marshal's puzzlement, 'though I imagine I would have come to it on my own. I think you should look in on that ward you foisted on me, Lady Isabelle de Clare. At one point, as I recall, you were extraordinarily concerned for her welfare.'

'I have no reason to be concerned now, sire,' Marshal heard himself say above the sudden rushing in his ears as hope exploded inside him. Richard had offered him Isabelle's hand. Was the king about to . . .

Henry grinned. 'Well, you should be concerned, Marshal. When this war is over, I'll see to it that the lady becomes your responsibility. Essex, let me introduce your future peer, William Marshal – the next Earl of Pembroke.'

Essex, clearly surprised, exclaimed with pleasure and bounded forward to seize Marshal's hand, but Marshal barely heard Essex's enthusiastic congratulations as he belatedly registered the king's words: when this war is over . . .

'God's legs, Marshal!' the king laughed. 'You look green around the gills. Not afraid of marriage, are you?'

'No, sire,' Marshal said in confusion, his mind reeling in its abrupt swing from euphoria to crushing disappointment. The king had not given him Isabelle, after all – only his promise. And should Richard triumph, Henry's promise would be worthless, its fulfilment swept away on the winds of war.

21

London, January 1189

'Ouch!' Isabelle cried as she accidentally pricked her finger
with her sewing needle.

Matilda, seated on a high stool before a lectern, looked up
from the book she'd been reading aloud and said quickly,
'Don't get any blood on the silk, milady. Do you need a
kerchief?'

'No,' Isabelle said irritably, sucking her finger. 'But I'd
think you'd worry about me instead of this damned
embroidery.'

'If you would use a thimble, milady, it wouldn't happen.
And please stop cursing. You're getting into the habit.'

'Oh, what's the point?' Isabelle burst out in frustration,
tossing aside the silk *bliaut* on which she was embroidering
an elaborate floral design. 'I'm no good at this. Any seam-
stress could do it better and in half the time.'

'Embroidery is a skill any lady should command,' Matilda
said pedantically, as if that settled the matter, and she
resumed her reading of the *Song of Roland*. It was only one of
several lengthy *chansons de geste* contained in the thick, leather-
bound volume the queen had presented Isabelle as a parting
gift.

'That's enough reading for today, Mattie,' Isabelle sighed.
She was seated on her bed, and now she fell back on to the
mattress and groaned. 'Oh God, I'm bored.'

'Don't curse, mi—'

'I know, I *know*! But what do you expect after I've been
cooped up in this prison for nearly three months?'

'The White Tower is a stronghold, not a prison, milady,

and you're hardly a prisoner. I'll admit the surroundings here are not exactly cheerful, but the justiciar and Master Hubert have done their best to keep you entertained. You've been introduced to all the leading families in and around London, and you can go into the town whenever you wish.'

Isabelle grimaced. Matilda's complacency only irritated her more. Without the stimulation of a thriving court and its gossip, Matilda had quickly tired of their stay at Winchester. The mix of nobility and wealthy civil servants who had come to prominence through Henry's burgeoning administration was much more to her liking.

But Isabelle felt even more isolated in London than she had at Winchester, where the queen had been a conduit for news from France. The Royal Justiciar, Ranulf de Glanville, in whose charge she had been placed, and his secretary, Hubert Walter, showed no inclination to share what they knew with her; and the women with whom she came in contact cared little for what occurred beyond London and its environs, save for politically neutral social gossip from the European courts.

Isabelle suspected that Lady Glanville was as well-informed as her husband, but she was no more forthcoming than the justiciar himself. Isabelle did not think they were intent on keeping her in the dark. They simply did not want to talk about the news from France; and as the justiciar's fortunes were tied to the king's, Isabelle was forced to conclude that the tidings from across the Channel were ominous.

Yet all she knew for certain was that the king had established his court at Le Mans for the winter and that the war with Philip was expected to resume in the spring.

'Why do you suppose the king ordered me to take up residence here?' Isabelle asked, staring up at the canopy of her bed.

'I'm sure I don't know, milady,' Matilda said patiently. She had answered the same question in the same way countless times before.

The clatter of iron-shod hooves in the narrow courtyard far below drifted in through the chamber window, and out of idle curiosity Isabelle got up from the bed and went to the window. 'Let's go out for a ride, Mattie,' she said, moving aside the window-screen and peering out. The gentle, icy draught on her cheeks was a refreshing contrast to the smoky heat from the fireplace in the chamber, and she breathed deeply.

'It's too cold, milady,' Matilda protested. 'And come away from that window before you catch your death.'

'Oh, don't be a killjoy. We have a bright, clear day for once.'

In the courtyard below, a messenger dismounted and disappeared. Isabelle set the window-screen back in place and began to pace restlessly. To be sure she made her point, she started to whistle off-key.

'Oh, very well, milady,' Matilda said testily. 'I'll go down and arrange an escort. You'll have to wear your warmest robe; it's bitter outside.'

'We can watch the skaters on Mooresfield for a while, and then go on to Smithfield Fair to see if there are any new furs available.'

'There won't be many stalls open today, milady.'

'Of course there will; the sun's out.'

'And I don't know why you like to watch boys knock one another's brains out on the ice at Mooresfield,' Matilda said, but she did know.

When Mooresfield Marsh was frozen over, boys from the town raced across the ice on crude skates fashioned from horses' shinbones. They propelled themselves forward with the aid of an iron-shod pole, and invariably the skating degenerated into a mêlée of jousting as boys paired off at random, rocketed towards each other and, using the pole as a lance, tried to knock their opponent off his feet. Cracked skulls were not uncommon.

Isabelle liked to watch for the same reason she loved the horse-racing on Smithfield in the autumn: it was the closest she could come to participating herself. In fact, the only popular sport she did not like was bear-baiting.

'Off with you, Mattie!' Isabelle said impatiently, and Matilda left the chamber in resignation.

Matilda had not been gone five minutes, when she returned with a satisfied smile on her face. 'We're going out, milady,' she said excitedly, 'but for more civilized entertainment.'

Isabelle's face fell. 'What does that mean?'

'You've been invited to the Bishop of Lincoln's house. The chancellor has been in residence for some time now, and he's requested the pleasure of your company.'

'The chancellor?' Isabelle groaned. 'I don't even know him. What does he want with me?'

'Just what the invitation stated: "The pleasure of your company",' Matilda said, and then she giggled. 'He has a mistress, you know. Maybe we'll meet her.'

The Bishop of Lincoln's house was in a western suburb of London, on the opposite side of the city from the White Tower. The chancellor had provided Isabelle and Matilda with an escort of six mounted *serjants*, who were more than adequate to force a quick passage through London's crowded streets, and the party rode across the city, rather than around it.

The crisp, bright day had given way to a bleak, cloudy afternoon, and although the temperature was rising, the gusting, moisture-laden wind had a bite to it. Snow was in the offing. Despite the deteriorating weather, travellers continued to pour into the city, and people clamouring for admission, their entry fees clutched in their fists, thronged Newgate.

The crowd parted before the shouting *serjants*, who continued to clear the way as they rode out of the city on Watling Street. A few hundred paces from the massive Newgate gatehouse, the road dipped sharply down into a ravine cut by the small River of Wells, which flowed south into the Thames. Crossing the bridge, the horses' hoofbeats were all but lost in the steady rumble of millwheels and the rush of water through the millraces.

As they rode up out of the ravine on to Old Bourne Hill, Isabelle adjusted her scarf to shield her face from the icy wind sweeping up from the Thames. Although she disliked binding her neck and head in a wimple, which she considered best suited to nuns and elderly matrons, she wished she had worn one today.

Still, it was good to be out; and although she expected the polite conversation with the chancellor and his guests to bore her, she preferred a social afternoon to the confines of her apartment in the Tower.

The Bishop of Lincoln's house stood a quarter of a mile from the city wall, facing Watling Street. Both sides of the road were heavily built-up with rude sheds and wooden dwellings that crowded every inch of the available land between the stately gardens and townhouses of the affluent. Ahead on Isabelle's left, the yellow stone tower of the Templars was completely hemmed in, but beyond the old Templar stronghold, the Bishop of Lincoln's house stood in splendid isolation behind a great stone wall – more a miniature manor than a townhouse.

The party rode through the gate into a flagstone courtyard, and as Isabelle and Matilda approached the sprawling, two-storey home, the steward came out to meet them. At that moment, a young man came striding around the corner of the house from the direction of the stables, a recalcitrant shock of black hair poking from beneath his tight woollen cap.

'Jean!' Isabelle cried in a burst of joy.

Jean d'Erly looked over in surprise and flashed a broad grin as he recognized her. 'Your Ladyship!' he shouted excitedly, running towards her. 'What are you doing here?'

'I was about to ask you the same question!' Isabelle laughed as Jean helped her down from the saddle. As the steward turned to assist Matilda dismount, Isabelle took Jean's hands and stepped back to observe him. 'Is it my imagination, or have you filled out since I saw you last?' she asked gaily.

Jean smiled self-consciously, but not without pride. 'I think so, milady. In Sir William's service, building up your strength is necessary for survival.'

'Well, you don't look any the worse for wear to me.'

Coming up behind Isabelle, Matilda said mischievously, 'Are you going to ask, milady, or will I have to?'

Isabelle shot her a withering look, but before Matilda could embarrass her further, she turned back to Jean and asked quickly, 'Is Sir William here?'

'Of course, milady,' Jean grinned. 'Where I go, he follows.'

'Sir William is with the chancellor at the moment, Lady Isabelle,' the steward interjected, frowning at what he considered Jean's impudence. 'Unfortunately, the chancellor is indisposed with a severe cold, and he has asked you to forgive him for not greeting you himself.'

'If the chancellor is ill, milady,' Matilda said with pretended innocence, 'perhaps we should not impose.' Her eyes crinkled with amusement as Isabelle glared at her.

'No, no, Your Ladyship,' the steward said in confusion. 'You are the first of the guests to arrive – besides Sir William – but the chancellor's secretary, who will be hosting this evening's supper, will be here shortly. Now, if you would be so kind as to follow me . . .'

The steward ushered the ladies into the house, followed by Jean d'Erly. Inside the entrance was a spacious tiled foyer and a wide central staircase leading up to the apartments on the second floor. The steward led them through a doorway on the left into a large, vaulted room that served the same function as the great hall of a castle.

Banquet tables covered with spotless linen had already been set, and meticulously attired servants stood ready to provide the guests with a variety of spiced and mulled wines. In one corner, a musical ensemble had begun to play, a portable organ adding strength to the usual combination of harp, viols and flutes.

As Isabelle entered the room, the household Fool, who was seated cross-legged on a bench beside the fireplace, looked up in mock-surprise. He jumped to his feet and intentionally slipped in the rushes on the floor, falling back with a loud yelp. The impromptu fall was so adroitly done that even the steward, who must have seen the stunt before, could not help laughing.

Isabelle smiled, but the response was mere politeness as she looked in vain for Marshal, barely able to contain her joyous excitement. Her heart pounded with anticipation.

'I'll inform the chancellor that you're . . .' the steward began, but broke off as Marshal came in behind them and greeted them.

A servant was taking their cloaks, but Isabelle was barely aware of removing hers as she looked back towards the door, her breath catching in her throat. Marshal came towards her, smiling, his eyes on her alone, and she went to meet him, momentarily oblivious of the others in the room. Her hands were trembling as he grasped them.

'Lady Isabelle, . . .' Marshal began, glancing self-consciously at Matilda, who was listening eagerly. 'I can't tell you what a great pleasure it is to see you again.'

'Nor I, Sir William,' Isabelle said, wishing everyone else would disappear.

An awkward silence followed, in which Isabelle was painfully sensitive to the attention their encounter had aroused. Simultaneously, she and Marshal said, 'You're looking well.' They laughed together, embarrassed, and Marshal released her hands.

It was then that Matilda redeemed herself in Isabelle's eyes.

'Do you think I might have a tour of the house?' she said to the steward. 'I've always admired it, but only from the outside. I'm sure Sir William and Lady Isabelle would excuse us; they're old friends and probably would like to talk.'

'Certainly, Lady Matilda,' the steward said, graciously honouring her with a title to which she had no claim. 'I'd be happy to show you the house.' He turned to Marshal and Isabelle. 'You might find the chancellor's library a comfortable place to converse until the other guests arrive.'

Marshal glanced at Isabelle, and she nodded.

The steward snapped his fingers and ordered one of the servants to bring wine into the library, which was adjacent to the great hall.

Jean d'Erly, who had been struggling against a grin, cleared his throat noisily and said with exaggerated seriousness, 'If you do not require my services, sire, there are some chores I should attend to.'

'Very well, Jean,' Marshal replied, failing in his attempt to sound natural. 'Please do that.'

Marshal led Isabelle into the chancellor's library and closed the thick oak door behind them. The dim light from the window was augmented by candles, and a fire crackled softly in the hearth. There were two comfortable chairs by the fireplace for the use of the chancellor and a visitor, and a clerk's high stool and writing desk stood by the window. Against the walls were open chests filled with parchment rolls and books.

'Would you like some wine?' Marshal asked.

'No, thank you,' Isabelle said, walking to the fire. She was dismayed by a sudden attack of nervousness. For months and months, she had daydreamed of their meeting again, imagining what she would say, but now the words she had rehearsed so often seemed foolish.

Marshal came over to her and smiled tentatively. Here he was at last, and she didn't know what to say. Their brief time together in Kilkenny now seemed remote and unreal. The reality was that the king had given Helwis of Lancaster to Marshal, and perhaps he had already decided to marry the lady. Why should he not?

'I didn't know until recently that you'd been brought to London,' Marshal said. 'Have you been comfortable here?'

'The Tower is gloomy,' Isabelle told him, 'but the justiciar has been very kind.'

'Good,' Marshal said and cleared his throat. 'Good,' he repeated, smiling awkwardly.

Isabelle could see that he was nervous, too, but was that good or bad? Maybe he was remembering the things he had said to her so many months ago and was now embarrassed by them. Isabelle's tongue flicked out to moisten her lips.

'While I was still at Winchester,' she began, 'the queen told me of your good fortune – that you've received gifts from the king . . .'

'Yes,' Marshal replied. 'He gave me title to the land of Cartmel – and Helwis of Lancaster as ward.'

Isabelle looked away, torn between her pride and her desire to know. She held her breath, hoping Marshal would tell her about Helwis, yet afraid of what he might say.

'I'm not going to marry her, Rusty,' Marshal said quietly. 'I never intended to.'

'Why not?' she asked in a small voice.

Marshal took her hands and held them tightly. The warmth of his calloused palms seemed to course up through her arms.

'Because I don't want to marry anyone but you,' he said.

His words released a flood of emotion in Isabelle, and her eyes blurred with tears.

Marshal was smiling crookedly at her. 'Is the prospect that horrible?'

Isabelle shook her head, wanting to tell him how much she loved him, to tell him that she had prayed he would not marry Helwis and how selfish that had made her feel. She wanted to tell him about Eleanor . . . There was so much she wanted to tell him. 'Oh, Sir William . . .'

'Sir William?' Marshal laughed.

'But I don't even know what your friends call you,' she said, looking up at him shyly.

'Will,' Marshal said. 'At least, they do now. When I was a squire, my nickname was distinctly unflattering.'

'Will,' she said softly, slipping her hands from his and encircling his waist with her arms. Marshal's smile faded, and he took her upraised face between his hands. As he bent towards her, she closed her eyes, and for a long time they were lost in a kiss.

Afterwards Isabelle continued to cling to him, her head pressed against his chest, listening to the thump of his heart. A warm glow suffused her, and she felt lightheaded. 'I'll never marry anyone but you, my love,' she whispered. 'I promise you that. The king can strip me of my inheritance, for all I care, but I'll never marry anyone but you.'

'The king won't be the problem,' Marshal said, stroking her hair. 'At least, as long as the King of England is Henry of Anjou.'

Isabelle looked up at him in surprise. 'Why do you say that?'

'There's desperation in the air, and I find the service of a knight can command richer prizes than I imagined.'

'Don't say that!' Isabelle protested. 'Don't you know how much you're respected? You're . . .' She broke off abruptly, and her eyes widened as the implication of Marshal's words sank in. 'You don't mean . . .' Isabelle said hesitantly, not daring to hope. 'You don't mean the king has offered . . .'

And as Marshal nodded, her heart soared.

'I can't believe it!' she cried joyously, hugging Marshal with all her strength. 'Why didn't you tell me right away? I hoped and prayed, but never really – why didn't you tell me!'

When Marshal did not reply at once, Isabelle looked up at him, and she was taken aback by the strange expression in his eyes.

'What is it? What's wrong?'

'The king will not permit us to marry until the war in France is over.'

'But we can wait, Will,' she said, tightening her grip about him. 'We have our whole life ahead of us.'

'Richard has deserted the king and allied himself with Philip,' Marshal said gravely. 'To make matters worse, His Majesty is ill, and . . . Well, if the King falls, Rusty, I'll fall with him.'

She heard the resignation in his voice, and her hands went cold. Now she understood the justiciar's silence on the news from France.

'But surely it's not hopeless,' she said, clinging fiercely to him.

'Not hopeless . . . But the odds are against us.'

Isabelle felt her knees go weak, and she shook her head dazedly. God could not be so cruel – to give her a glimpse of happiness, only to snatch it away. Eleanor's words came back to her, echoing in her mind: If civil war comes and Marshal finds himself on the losing side, your hopes will die with Henry's cause. No! There had to be a way out for them. There had to be!

From the great hall came the sound of a woman's shrill laughter. The chancellor's guests were arriving. Isabelle wanted to shut out the sound – shut out the whole, uncaring world. She knew what she wanted to say to Marshal – what she had to say – but did she dare?

'I'm sorry,' Marshal said quietly. 'I wish . . .'

'But if you believe Richard will win,' she blurted, 'must you remain with the king? Surely it's not too late . . .'

Her words hung in the air unanswered. Marshal continued to hold her in his arms, but he did not speak. Isabelle looked up at him anxiously, and slowly he released her.

'You want me to go over to Richard,' he said at last.

She heard the disappointment in his voice, and her lips quivered. Why couldn't he understand? If Richard was to be king, what was the point of throwing away their happiness?

'Would it be so terrible to bow to the inevitable, Will?' she implored, not caring that the queen had put those words in her mouth. Eleanor had been right all along.

Marshal turned away and went to the hearth. He picked up the poker and restlessly stirred the logs. 'Would you really have me desert the king?' he asked, staring into the flames.

'I love you, Will,' she said desperately. 'I'm not willing to sacrifice our future to Henry's cause.'

Marshal turned back to face her. 'Is that what you think I'm doing?' he protested. 'I have no choice. Can't you understand that?'

'But you *do* have a choice,' she said, misconstruing his words. 'The queen herself assured me that Prince Richard would welcome you to his banner.'

Marshal's lips twisted into a bitter half-smile. 'So she's worked on you, too. I suppose I should have expected that.'

'But I'm sure she was sincere, Will. If you were to go to Richard . . .'

'The Count of Poitou has already made me the offer,' Marshal cut in. 'I refused.'

From beyond the library door came more laughter and the babble of jocular voices that emphasized the silence in the room as they looked at each other. His eyes pleaded with her to understand, but she could not.

'Why?' she said at last in a choked voice.

'Do you really need to ask why I'll not turn traitor?'

'No, Will. I ask why you choose the king instead of me.'

'Choose?' Marshal said, his voice rising for the first time. 'I swore an oath of allegiance! I *swore* it before God and of my own free will. I cannot violate that oath now; no man of honour could.'

'Honour in *your* eyes!' she retorted. 'If you renounced your allegiance openly, no man would call you traitor.'

She saw him react to the unintended shrillness of her tone. Until that moment, he had been pleading with her; now his eyes hardened.

'I hoped you would understand,' he said stiffly. 'Apparently, I asked too much.'

His sudden coldness cut her like a knife, and she responded without thinking. 'Forgive me for not living up to your standards!' she lashed out defensively.

Marshal opened his mouth to speak, but then he compressed his lips and shook his head. Wordlessly, he turned away. As he walked to the door, Isabelle stretched out her hand, but pride held her back from stopping him. Why couldn't *he* understand?

By the time she dried her tears and entered the great hall, he had gone.

'Are you sure you will not see Sir William, Your Ladyship?' said Hubert Walter, the justiciar's cherubic, wispy-haired secretary. 'He told me that he is leaving London within a few hours.'

'No, Master Hubert,' Isabelle replied stiffly, 'And you may tell Sir William this: Let him come to me when he is girded with an earl's belt. Then I will receive him, and not before.'

'Yes, Your Ladyship,' the secretary said, blinking in embarrassment. 'As you wish.'

As Hubert Walter left Isabelle's chamber, she moved to her window overlooking the Tower's inner courtyard and looked out. She could see Jean standing below with the horses. The ground was carpeted with six inches of fresh snow, which had been falling from the grey sky in thick, wind-driven swirls all afternoon. The winter storm that had been threatening since the day before had come upon them at last.

Isabelle shivered and stepped back, hugging her shoulders, but the draught did not chill her nearly as much as her own despair. She had lain awake half the night, until she had finally cried herself to sleep. Perhaps if Marshal had come in the morning, she would not have refused to see him, but as the lonely, wintry day had worn on, her misery had cloaked itself in anger.

She wanted to wound him, as he had wounded her. She had begged him to put their happiness before his pride, and he had turned his back on her, leaving without a word. Perhaps he had come this afternoon to make amends, but it was too late; she could not forget the look on his face before they had parted the day before. He had made his choice; let him live with it.

'You're a fool, milday,' said Matilda behind her.

'What?' Isabelle snapped, whirling around.

'I said, milady, that you are a fool.'

'How *dare* you speak to . . .'

'Because I've known you since you were a child,' Matilda said, softening her voice. 'You're sending away the finest knight you'll ever know.'

'Mattie, you don't *understand*!'

'But I do understand,' Matilda said, coming across the room and grasping Isabelle's hands. 'Last night you talked and talked, and I listened. How could I not understand? You are desperately afraid of losing him, but is that a reason to drive him away? My God, this world abounds with men to whom a holy oath means nothing, who would prefer your bed and your lands to honour. Is that the kind of man you want?'

'You weren't there, Mattie! You didn't see him – how coldly he looked at me, as if I'd betrayed him. And all I wanted . . .'

'But he's here now, milady! Don't let him go like this. If you do, you'll regret it. You know you will – perhaps for the rest of your life.'

The sound of men's voices drifted up from the courtyard, and Isabelle knew Marshal was leaving. For a moment longer, she hesitated; then she was out the door and racing down the dizzying spiral staircase from her chamber, heedless of Matilda's cry to return for a robe.

You will regret it . . . perhaps for the rest of your life. What if he fell in battle and she never saw him again?

Twice she stumbled and nearly fell, but then she reached the foot of the stairwell, threw herself against the door leading directly to the courtyard, and burst outside. 'Will!' she cried as she saw him riding out through the gate. 'Will!' But her voice was carried off by the wind.

Gaping, the guards at the gate stared at her as she ran across the courtyard and out through the gate into the road beyond, her slippers sinking soundlessly into the snow. Fifty paces ahead of her, Marshal and Jean rode on towards the city, its walls barely visible through the swirling storm.

The wind cut through Isabelle's gown, but she did not feel the cold as she ran blindly after them, slipping and stumbling, the snow flying into her eyes. She cried out again and again, but neither Marshal nor Jean heard her. Desperately, she ran still faster.

But it was no use; the men had spurred their horses into a trot. Pain lanced her side, and she could feel herself slowing down; she could run no farther. As she stopped, gasping, the capricious wind suddenly died, and she called out to them with all her remaining strength.

For an instant, she thought they had not heard, but then she saw Jean rein in and twist around in his saddle. She closed her eyes and clasped her hands to her heaving breast, feeling the snow melting into her hair, and when she opened her eyes again, Marshal was there, looming above her on his horse.

'Will,' she gasped, seizing his leg and holding on as if she were afraid he would ride off again. 'I couldn't let you go without saying goodbye,' she said, blinking at the snow falling into her upraised face. 'I couldn't . . .'

Her words were cut off as Marshal bent down and caught her under the arms. He swept her up into the saddle and enfolded her in the warmth of his robe. 'I love you,' he said softly as they rode back towards the Tower. 'Whatever happens, Rusty, remember that.'

22

Le Mans, June 1189

'God's blood!' Bethune breathed. 'There are thousands out there.'

Atop a wooded knoll six leagues south of Le Mans, Marshal's scouting party looked out over a fog-shrouded expanse of open fields. Below them, they could hear the muffled tread of horses and men and the creaking and rattling of supply wagons – a ghostly army advancing through the mist.

Bethune turned to see Marshal staring at him. 'Why the queer look, Will?'

'Nothing,' Marshal said, shaking his head. 'I heard the same words on another hill once. Gave me a strange feeling, that's all.'

'The Old Man was right,' Harlincourt said. 'The march towards Tours was only a feint. They're going to strike at Le Mans. They must have doubled back yesterday.'

Philip and Richard had moved against Henry in May. Instead of attacking from two directions at once, they had combined forces and struck across the border northwest of Le Mans. They had overrun La Ferte-Bernard and marched south, bypassing Le Mans, apparently intent on attacking Tours. Henry had not been fooled.

'We know they're coming,' Bethune said impatiently, 'so let's go before they reach the main road and cut us off.'

'We don't know their strength yet,' Marshal said. 'We wait.'

Harlincourt and Bethune exchanged looks with the other

knights in the patrol, and Marshal knew they had a right to be concerned. They were not wearing armour.

The king had sent them south in the hours before dawn to locate the enemy, and because speed and range were necessary, they had been forced to ride light. They had already had one close call, nearly riding into the enemy's forward scouts in the fog, but Marshal was determined not to return until he was sure that the entire enemy army was moving on Le Mans.

He had never believed in omens, and he tried to shake off the premonition of disaster that Bethune's first words had triggered. This was another hill in another world, and the army hidden in the fog was not invincible. Yet the feeling of uneasiness would not leave him, and memories of the wait on that desert hill in Palestine came flooding back.

He recalled his rage at the Grand Master's folly, followed by bitter resignation and an empty sense of futility. There had been little fear, for he'd had nothing to lose. Now, however, he had too much to lose, and deep inside, he realized, he was afraid.

His hand strayed to the small parchment roll he carried beneath his tunic, a letter he had received from Isabelle in April, and he smiled to himself.

Isabelle obviously thought he might be illiterate, for she'd had the letter written by a clerk. It was in Latin and phrased in the formal style of a communication intended to be read aloud to Marshal by a clerk of his own. Marshal knew the contents by heart.

> Lady Isabelle de Clare, Heiress of Pembroke,
> Striguil, Longueville and Leinster, to William
> Marshal, Lord of Cartmel and Knight of the
> King's Household, greeting.
>   I have recently been officially informed by
> Master Hubert Walter that His Majesty has
> graciously offered you my hand in marriage, and I
> am writing to confirm to you the great pleasure
> with which I received this news. In choosing the
> foremost knight in the realm to be my future
> husband, the king could not have given me greater
> honour or happiness. Be assured, sire, that I await

the day of our marriage with unbounded eagerness.
I pray that the war that keeps you far from me may
soon be over and that God's purpose will be
revealed in complete victory for His Majesty over
his enemies. I am well in body and spirit, and I
hope that this letter finds you also well.

Each night I pray that Our Lord and Saviour
will watch over you, preserve you and give you
strength in battle. As the Lord looks with favour on
those who seek fulfilment of their prayers through
their own efforts, I am sending my faithful Fulk le
Brun to guard your life as he would my own. I beg
you, sire, for my sake, do not send him from you.

Marshal glanced back at the silent, hulking *serjant*, who
was with them now, armed as always with sword and
longbow. Fulk was a loner, impossible to know, and only
slowly had they adjusted to his dark, brooding presence. Out
of consideration for Isabelle, Marshal had allowed him to
stay, but there were times when Fulk irritated him. Unless
ordered away, he followed Marshal everywhere, like a great,
dark shadow.

The early-morning sun was slowly burning away the mist
enshrouding the enemy. First the banners emerged from the
fog, then the glinting armour of the horsemen, and finally the
entire host of Richard the Lionheart and Philip of France was
revealed, spreading across the fields below, the nearest
elements within bowshot of the knoll.

'That's their whole army, all right,' Harlincourt said. 'Five-
or six-thousand-strong. Satisfied, Will?'

'Yes,' Marshal said, turning his horse. 'We have what we
came for. Let's go.'

'Have our men destroyed the bridge across the Huisne?' the
king asked, wincing as his surgeon probed the edges of an
ugly red swelling on the back of his leg between his calf and
heel. Henry lay face-down on his bed, the mattress sagging
under his weight. His stocking had been removed to expose
the festering carbuncle.

'The bridge went up in flames an hour past, sire,' Marshal
said. 'Prince John's men did a thorough job, and we've driven

stakes into all the fords up and down the river. They are impassable now.'

'Good,' Henry grunted with satisfaction. 'That should hold them for the time being. Richard must have thought he'd catch me napping. Well, I'm not past it yet!'

'I must open your leg again, sire,' the surgeon said. 'There is sign of mortification, and I must cut away the dead flesh and insert a drain. I don't like the way the affected area continues to spread.'

'*You* don't like it,' Henry growled, twisting his head to glare at the surgeon. 'But you love to cut, don't you, Master Gerald?'

'It's necessary in this case, sire,' the surgeon replied defensively.

'All right, all right! Just give me time to get some wine into me, and then you can have your fun. In the meantime, you can wait outside. We have business to discuss.'

'Yes, sire,' the surgeon said, bowing and retiring with his assistant.

With the coming of spring, Henry's fevers had abated, but in their place came another affliction, minor at first and hardly noticed. An infection had set in below the scar-tissue of an old wound. Initially, it had caused no concern, but as the weeks wore on and the inflammation slowly spread and festered, it became clear that the months of fever had dangerously sapped the king's resistance.

Henry rolled over with a groan and sat up, gesturing to his servant to bring the wine. The servant had already poured a cup, and Henry drained it in three great gulps. 'More,' he demanded. 'And keep it coming. When that bloodthirsty scoundrel starts cutting, it's going to hurt like fury. What's the enemy doing now?'

'Making camp in the woodland park on the south bank of the river, sire,' said the Earl of Essex. 'They don't seem to be in a hurry, now they've seen we're ready for them. I doubt they'll make a move before tomorrow.'

Geoffry, the chancellor, cleared his throat. 'Will you be convening the barons this evening, sire? The enemy outnumbers us three to one at present, and we should decide now whether or not we'll defend Le Mans.'

'We'll stand fast, by God,' Henry said, swallowing more

wine. 'I'll hold the council, but I want the issue settled between us here and now. Where's Prince John?'

'He's not yet returned from inspecting the city militia, sire,' Essex said.

Henry nodded. 'Well, gentlemen, I say we defend Le Mans. What do you say?'

'The city is well-fortified, sire,' Essex replied. 'Philip and Richard have the forces to take it eventually, but if they settle in for a siege, they completely lose the initiative and become a stationary target for a counter-attack. My guess is that they will break off their attack; but if they don't, we can bring our own army down from Normandy and trap them between two fires.'

'I agree with Essex, sire,' the chancellor said, 'but it's my duty to point out the risk in allowing yourself to be encircled. We don't know the extent of Philip's own reserves; he may be able to match what we can bring down from Normandy.'

Henry shook his head. 'That's their whole army out there now. Marshal, you've been damned quiet. What do you think?'

'Defend Le Mans, sire. To abandon the city now, after having spent the winter fortifying it, would send the wrong message to those barons who may be attacked next. Our agreed strategy was to defend our strongpoints as they were attacked, rather than to meet the enemy head-on in the open, and I see no reason to reject that plan now.'

'I agree, sire,' William de Sille added, speaking for the first time. He was the castellan of the heavily fortified tower just north of the city.

'That's settled, then,' Henry announced, impatiently snapping his fingers for more wine. 'Marshal, send a message to fitz Ralph to muster the Norman barons at Alençon. They should prepare to march to our relief.'

'Yes, sire,' Marshal said briskly, hoping Henry's combative energy would last.

Relieved that the long months of waiting were over, the king was spoiling for a fight and thinking clearly and decisively; but the ugly infection had evidently become as painful as it was dangerous, and the surgeon's knife might only make matters worse.

'We're fighting a defensive war,' the king said, 'but I see

no need to hide behind our walls and wait passively for the swine to move into position. If they're careless in their approach, we'll attack with a cavalry sortie. Ordinarily, Marshal, I'd let you lead it, but this time I want our men to see me out front. Essex, you'll organize skirmishers to meet them once they reach the lower town. Don't try to hold them back for long; just cut them up a little and then torch the suburbs.'

'Are you sure you want to set fire to the suburbs, sire?' Essex said. It was a sensible move, but Le Mans was Henry's birthplace.

'Yes,' Henry said firmly. 'I hate to do it, but we have to deny them cover. With the lower town razed, we'll have a clear field of fire from the walls.'

Marshal and Essex nodded in approval, but Geoffry looked worried. 'I think you should stay out of the fighting, sire – to give your leg a chance to heal.'

'I've waited for a month, and it's only got worse,' the king said irritably, beginning to slur his words. 'Besides, I'll still have some time to rest. We've blocked the river well enough to stop a crossing in force, so they have no choice but to move south again and use the bridge on the road to Angers. That should give us another full day at least, and probably two.'

The chancellor looked to Marshal and Essex for support, but found none. In the king's place, they would do the same; infection or no infection, Henry should lead his troops.

Henry turned on to his stomach, dropping his empty wine cup on to the floor. 'I'm drunk enough now,' he grunted. 'Clear out now and send in the butcher.'

John returned from his inspection too late for the conference with the king. When he was told by the guard at Henry's door that the surgeon was inside, he did not seek to enter, but waited in the passageway. John was not squeamish; he wanted to speak with the physician alone.

All morning he had driven himself and the men under him at a merciless pace, but although his face was flushed and his undergarments clung to his hot, sweating body, his mind was like ice. He was guided by one imperative – not to be caught on the losing side – and what he had discovered at the river had brought him to the moment of decision.

The door to the king's chamber opened, ending John's restless pacing. The surgeon emerged, preceded by an assistant who carried the physician's surgical chest. John called out to him.

'A moment of your time, Master Gerald.'

The surgeon turned and peered short-sightedly down the passage. Recognizing John, he hurried forward, unconsciously smoothing his grey beard and adjusting his rich silk robe. John caught the flash of gold as the physician slipped his fee into a purse on his belt, and his lip curled with contempt. A physician's ability to cure rarely matched his skill at extracting payment.

'You wish to see me, sire?' the surgeon said, bowing lower than courtesy required. The man was obsequious.

'I want your opinion of His Majesty's condition. Your *true* opinion.'

'The infection is spreading, sire, but I have done what is necessary. I have cut away the dead flesh, inserted a drain and dressed the wound. I have also examined His Majesty's urine and determined that the humours are not in harmony. The black bile is definitely out of balance with the phlegm, and I have prescribed a powder to relieve the obstruction in His Majesty's liver, which is responsible for the imbalance.

'I did not ask what you have done, Master Gerald,' John said coldly. 'Just how dangerous is the infection?'

As the surgeon launched into another evasive speech, John reached out and seized him by the breast of his tunic. '*How dangerous is it?*' John hissed.

The surgeon swallowed convulsively and shook his head. 'It's dangerous, sire, but I can't say what will happen. No one could.'

'But the festering has been getting worse with each passing week. Does that not suggest it will continue to worsen?'

'Ye—es, sire.'

'And if it does?'

'There will be increasing mortification, and fever, too. I may have to amputate.'

'His Majesty will not permit that. Not now.'

'Then, sire,' the surgeon said, 'I would not be responsible for the consequences.'

John nodded slowly. 'I see,' he said, releasing the surgeon. 'Very well, you may go.'

As the surgeon scurried away, John turned and walked off in the opposite direction, heading for his own chamber. He would think a while longer before committing himself, but he knew he had already made up his mind. If he was to switch sides, it would have to be now, when he had something to trade: information. He could send Gerard de Ridefort across to Richard after dark to make the offer. The former Grand Master's defection to the enemy would arouse no suspicion.

Everyone thought the river shielding Le Mans from the enemy was impassable; only John knew that it was not.

At dawn the following day, the Bishop of Le Mans celebrated Mass for the king and his barons and knights. Henry was in a theatrical mood, and he remained in the cathedral until everyone else had left. When he emerged, flanked by Prince John and the bishop, he stood on the steps for a few moments, regally acknowledging the cheers of the knights and soldiers assembled in the square.

He had not donned his hauberk and was dressed in brown hunting clothes. He gave no speech, relying instead on a mute show of nonchalant confidence to inspire his troops. Calling for his horse, he disdained the use of a mounting platform and swung up into the saddle with the apparent ease of a man half his age and weight.

Marshal, astride his warhorse nearby, silently applauded the show, but he was close enough to see the king grit his teeth against the pain in his leg, which was bound with a thick linen bandage that bulged beneath his stocking. The morning air was still cool, but as Henry settled himself in the saddle, Marshal saw beads of sweat appearing on his forehead.

'I'm going out to have a look at the enemy,' Henry said loudly, and Prince John, Marshal and half a dozen barons immediately moved their mounts forward to accompany him.

Henry looked at Marshal and frowned. 'You won't be needing your armour,' he said. 'We're quite safe on this side of the river.'

'I'm sure that's true, sire,' Marshal replied evenly, 'but a hauberk's no problem for me.'

'And I say you don't need it,' Henry snapped. 'Anyone who thinks he needs his armour can stay behind.'

Immediately John and the six barons who had ridden forward to accompany the king dismounted, and their squires hurried to their sides to assist them in removing their chain mail. Marshal remained in the saddle. Henry glared at him, and Marshal tensed, prepared to absorb an insult, but the king left the words unsaid.

As one by one the men who had stripped off their armour remounted, Henry's expression relaxed, and he moved his horse closer to Marshal. 'You and Geoffry are birds of a feather,' he said softly. 'Fussy old women.'

'Yes, sire.'

'Sorry about the scene, Marshal, but my leg is hurting like the devil. You may accompany us as far as the south gate, but no farther. Understood?'

'Yes, sire,' Marshal said, relieved to know that it was pain and not anxiety that had caused the display of ill temper. Still, he thought, Henry was pushing bravado too far. For the king to parade before the enemy without armour might be useful theatre, but Marshal could not approve Henry's insistence that the men with him disarm themselves against their own better judgment.

As the king rode out of the square towards the south gate, the knights and troop captains dispersed to their pre-assigned posts at the wall towers and gatehouses of the hilltop city. Marshal, Bethune and Harlincourt joined the knights assigned to the south gate and followed the king's party. Fulk, as always, trailed Marshal at a discreet distance.

Because the passage across the river had been blocked, the gates were open and the drawbridges down. Le Mans retained a surface normality. Merchants were opening their shops, and the streets were filled with the aroma of baking bread, meat pies and the yeasty smell of brewing ale. Already, the road to the gate was clogged with carts and early-morning crowds; but the traffic in the streets was nevertheless lighter than usual, and there was a noticeable absence of able-bodied men of fighting age, most of whom had been conscripted to man the walls.

The soldiers at the south gate cheered the king as he passed through, and the civilians in the road beyond hastily gave way and joined in the cheering. Below the south gate, the road forked into two highways, one leading southwest to Tours and the other southeast to Angers. The road to Tours had been cut by the destruction of the bridge across the Huisne, and the road to Angers, which ran parallel to the river for some distance, was apparently being shunned by travellers. Only residents of the lower town spreading out below the city were still coming over the drawbridge that spanned the deep moat surrounding the walls of Le Mans.

Marshal ordered the men with him to remain inside the gate, but he proceeded across the drawbridge, allowing only Jean to accompany him. As he reined in his stallion, he saw Henry turn in his saddle and look back to be sure Marshal wasn't following. The king gave Marshal an ironic salute and spurred his horse into a canter, heading down towards the river.

'His Majesty doesn't believe in your cardinal rule, does he, sire?' Jean said, and Marshal looked at him sharply, thinking the remark a jibe. But Jean's expression was serious.

'A king does as he pleases,' Marshal said curtly. 'Let's hope he doesn't come to regret it.'

The suburbs had not encroached on the southern approach to Le Mans, and Marshal had a clear view of the river and the enemy encampment. Philip's white-and-gold silk pavilion had been pitched before the wooded park in which the bulk of his army sheltered, but Marshal could see no obvious sign of Richard's presence. Presumably, he slept as usual in a simple tent, or, because the weather was fair, in the open.

The opposite riverbank swarmed with French soldiers hauling water from the river for domestic chores, and as yet there was no indication that Philip intended to break camp and move south. Marshal frowned. Philip might be a lazy campaigner, but not Richard. Marshal had expected to see them striking their tents by now. Why were they staying put?

He raised his hand to shield his eyes against the sun and watched a detachment of knights across the river riding towards the ruins of the burned-out bridge. In the lead, he recognized the banner of André de Chauvigni, one of Richard's favourites, and his frown deepened. 'What the devil are they up to?' he muttered aloud.

Henry had reached the fork in the road and was leading his party down towards the bridge site, apparently intending to taunt Richard's knights. The knights ignored the king's approach, spread out in a line along the bank and began to probe the riverbed with their lances.

It was then that Marshal noticed the eddies curling around the charred bridge-pilings jutting out of the river – eddies that indicated the swift waterflow over shallows.

'Christ's wounds!' Marshal burst out. 'It's silted up!'

'What, sire?' Jean said, startled.

'Look at that!' Marshal cried in alarm as Richard's knights began to push into the river. 'The bottom's silted up around those pilings. There's a ford there now – the best damned ford they could ask for!'

The king and his unarmed party halted in confusion, barely fifty paces from the river. 'Come back!' Marshal bellowed, but even his powerful voice did not carry the distance. One of Richard's knights had turned in his saddle and was waving his lance, and in response to the signal, trumpets began to blare. In an instant, the enemy encampment was swept into a swarming, swirling confusion as knights and *serjants* rushed for their horses and foot soldiers gathered their weapons.

This was Richard's doing, Marshal was sure. Philip, accepting the river as impassable, would have marched patiently south to the nearest bridge; but Richard had not been content to waste two days, and he had sent out men to find a ford. The only saving grace was that they had not found it during the night, slipped across the river and stormed the walls under the cover of darkness.

The twelve knights fording the river had recognized the king, and now they came charging across in a shower of spray. John turned tail at once, and the king hesitated only a moment before he wheeled his steed about and raced for his life, followed by five of the six barons. The sixth – one Gerard Talebot – stood his ground.

Although the barons had stripped off their armour, they still carried shield and lance, and as the first of Richard's knights burst from the river, Talebot charged and shattered his lance on the opposing shield, slowing the enemy down but not stopping him. As the knights charging up behind spurred their mounts up the riverbank, Talebot, having done what he could, veered off the road and galloped out of harm's way.

'Equip me!' Marshal growled, moving off the drawbridge to clear the path to the gate. Jean drew up beside him, handed over Marshal's shield and lance and lowered the helmet over Marshal's head. As Marshal slipped on his mail gauntlets, Jean lashed the helmet down with quick, practised fingers.

All along the wall behind them, men were shouting orders, and as John, the king and his barons thundered up the slope towards the gate, the bells of Le Mans began to peal the general alarm.

John, hunched low over his saddle, raced straight past Marshal, his cape billowing out behind him, his black eyes wide and fixed on the gateway to safety; but as Henry galloped towards the drawbridge, he flashed Marshal a crooked grin and shouted breathlessly, 'So you were right, God damn it!'

'Skewer one for me, Marshal!' shouted the last of the barons to cross the drawbridge.

Richard's knights, with André de Chauvigni in the lead, were pounding up the roadway, their lances lowered. With their horses burdened by the additional weight of the knights' armour, they had had no hope of catching the king; but they knew the south gate was open, and they were making a bid to force their way in. Brave, Marshal acknowledged, but foolish.

The rush of adrenalin into his system was a release. Forgotten was his premonition of defeat. Once again, he was aware only of the present moment hurtling towards him as he prepared to meet the steel-clad riders thundering up the road. Behind him, he heard a cry, 'To Marshal!' and knew his knights were coming out to join the fight.

As Marshal lowered his lance and spurred his mount into the charge, Bethune surged up beside him, and together they galloped down the roadway to meet the attackers head-on. Fresh horses and the short downhill run gave them the advantage in momentum, and as their lances splintered with ear-splitting cracks against the lead riders' shields, their opponents were thrown back in their saddles. As the lances struck, Marshal and Bethune both swerved their stallions into the enemy chargers, driving them off the road.

Marshal hauled on his reins, and as his mount skidded around, he drew his sword and charged up behind André de Chauvigni, whom he had nearly unhorsed. Chauvigni, off-balance and struggling to regain control of his horse, was too slow in drawing his own sword. As he pulled it free, Marshal's blade flashed down, catching the knight's sword arm just above the wrist. The force of the blow paralysed Chauvigni's nerves, and his sword dropped to the ground.

Chauvigni's companions, intent on crashing through to the gate, had swept past them, only to be met before the drawbridge by Harlincourt and six more of Henry's knights in a crash of shields and splintering lances.

Marshal struck Chauvigni once more, caving in the right side of his helmet, and as the dazed knight reeled, Marshal seized his reins to take him captive. Instantly Jean, who had followed Marshal in the charge, was at his side, and Marshal thrust the reins into his squire's hands.

'Take him into the city,' Marshal yelled. 'He's worth a hefty ransom!'

Bethune had beaten his own opponent into submission, and his squire had taken the captive's reins. The fight in front of the drawbridge had become a wild mêlée as the defenders battled Richard's knights in a press of snorting, plunging stallions. Sunlight flashed on the scything blades, and the vicious ringing of steel on steel rose above the cacophony of tolling bells. It was ten against seven, and the defenders were being forced to the left of the drawbridge and back towards the moat.

Marshal raised his sword, preparing to charge back up the road into the fray, but first he looked down towards the river to be sure they would not be attacked from behind. Troops were swarming across the ford, and a substantial force of knights and mounted *serjants* had already crossed; but the enemy was ignoring the road up to the south gate and was moving off to the right, apparently preparing to invade the southeastern suburbs.

Marshal took in the situation at a glance, but the brief instant of delay cost the life of one of his knights. Even as

Marshal and Bethune dug in their spurs, Hugh de Malaunoi's horse reared up in panic on the very edge of the moat, and a moment later, horse and rider were forced backwards and plunged to their deaths.

Yelling like madmen, Marshal and Bethune struck the attackers from the rear: in an instant, the tide of the extemporized battle turned. One by one, Richard's knights were knocked from their saddles or disarmed. Five knights managed to cut their way out of the trap and flee, but the others were captured and handed over to grinning squires.

The skirmish over, Marshal was the last to come back in through the gate. As he entered, the portcullis was lowered behind him and the bridge drawn up, sealing the gate.

'Well done, Marshal!' the king shouted, riding towards Marshal through the press of soldiers, knights and squires. Henry had put on his chain mail and was wearing an open-faced helmet.

'Thank you, sire,' Marshal said, breathing hard and looking around for Jean. 'I have a present for you. André de Chauvigni. His ransom should be worth a penny or two.'

'Sire!' Jean cried, appearing at Marshal's side, his face crestfallen. 'I lost him.'

'What do you mean, you *lost* him?'

'As we crossed the drawbridge, sire, some fools started dropping stones off the gatehouse parapet. They missed me, but one stone broke your prisoner's arm, and the other struck his horse. The horse bolted, and I couldn't hold it.'

'Well, it's your loss, Marshal, not mine,' Henry said. 'I would have let you keep him. Now, come with me. You're not needed here, and Essex is already being pressed hard in the town below the east gate.'

'Bethune, Harlincourt, Clifford, Quency – on me!' Marshal yelled. 'Dammartin, Plouquet and Canteleu, round up any squads of *serjants* you can find and bring them out through the east gate!'

With Marshal, the four knights and their squires in tow, the king set off at the gallop for the east gate. Barely twenty minutes had passed since the alarm bells had begun to ring, but already the narrow sidestreets were deserted and the shops closed. The main thoroughfare to the east gate, however, was choked with old men, women and children streaming in from the suburb under attack.

A force of one hundred foot soldiers had mustered just inside the east gate, apparently in response to a call for reinforcements, but with no specific instructions. 'What orders, sire?' their mounted captain cried as the king forced his way through the refugees towards the gate.

'Take your men outside and keep the approach clear,' Henry shouted and spurred his horse through the gate. As the king and his knights rode out across the drawbridge, the people in the road beyond raised a feeble cheer.

'They won't be cheering much longer,' the king said grimly to Marshal at his side. 'We'll have to torch the town soon.'

At an intersection one hundred paces below the east gate, Essex waited with a shock-troop of twenty knights, prepared to stop an enemy breakthrough at any one of the dozens of hastily erected barricades blocking the streets in a wide defensive arc.

The pikemen, crossbowmen and *serjants* clustered behind a barricade fifty paces beyond Essex were holding their own for the moment, but were under heavy attack. The steadily swelling battle noise washing up the hill from several directions made it clear that Philip's troops were pressing hard all around the improvised perimeter.

Essex's face was grave as Henry rode up. 'They may flank us soon, sire, unless we commit our reserves.'

'No,' Henry said at once. 'We don't want to waste our strength here. We'll set fire to this area now, and then you can pull back.'

'But the wind is blowing up towards the city, sire,' Essex warned. 'If it jumps the wall . . .'

'The wall is eighteen-feet high.'

'But, sire . . .'

'Damn it, man, we can't give the swine cover right up to the walls, and we don't have all day to decide! We must do it now!'

'Very well, sire. I'll give the order.'

A mounted *serjant* was galloping towards them. 'My Lord Essex!' he cried breathlessly. 'We can't hold our position much longer!'

'Marshal, the barricade is beyond that bend,' Essex said quickly, pointing down the street to their left, which cut across the slope and then turned sharply downhill. 'Can you support it and buy us time to fire the suburbs? I want to keep my own knights here to cover the general retreat.'

'We'll try, sire,' Marshal responded and turned to his knights. 'Helmets and lances!'

'May we squires fight, sire?' Jean pleaded as he handed Marshal his helmet.

'Yes.'

'Thank you, sire!'

Marshal chafed at the delay as the grinning squires armed themselves, but he contained his impatience. He expected to face massed infantry if the barricade should be breached, and he wanted the additional shock value of five more horsemen.

'Let's go!' he cried, digging in his spurs. Followed by his knights and squires, he raced towards the endangered barricade. Behind him, he heard Essex shouting orders to fire the suburbs.

As they neared the turn in the narrow, deserted street, a concerted roar of triumph and blood-lust came from the direction of the barricade beyond the bend, and Marshal knew the enemy was breaking through. His stallion slewed around the corner at full gallop, and he lowered his lance, signalling the charge.

Halfway down the slope, the street was blocked by stacks of barrels and upended carts. Essex's pikemen were still fighting on the flanks, stabbing and slashing at the assault troops scrambling over the barricade, but in the centre the ground was littered with dead and dying defenders, and the enemy was unopposed.

The French troops had righted two of the carts and pulled them aside, and foot soldiers were pouring through the gap, yelling like fiends. Below the barricade, the street was choked with infantry surging up the hill.

But as the ten charging horsemen burst into view above the attackers and thundered down on them, the French battle cries turned to bellows of fear. The nearest soldiers scattered to the sides of the street, and the men behind them turned to club and claw their way back through the gap.

The violent backward thrust of the terrified men set off a wave of panic that rippled outward, sweeping over the press of soldiers in the street below. The retreat became a rout as Marshal and his knights struck the mass of panicky men like thunderbolts, hurtling through the gap and riding down men by the dozens.

Marshal buried his lance in the chest of a Frenchman who had turned to strike at his horse with a pike, and he drew his sword. His knights and squires formed a wedge behind him, and they hacked their way forward ruthlessly, heedless of the screams of the men they felled, driving the bellowing herd of infantry before them.

In less than a minute, the rout had gathered momentum of its own, and Marshal started to rein in. Through the restricted view of his eye-slit he glimpsed a knight and three mounted *serjants* appear at the bottom of the hill, where the street widened into a road leading away from the suburb, but he gave them no heed. They were too few and too late to stem the flood of foot soldiers streaming past them and out into the fields beyond.

Marshal turned in his saddle and shouted to his men to break off the slaughter and pull back. They had won Essex the time he needed; behind them, thick clouds of smoke were already rising into the sky.

'Will!' cried Bethune, who had been fighting close behind him. 'Crossbow!'

Startled, Marshal turned sharply and looked back down the hill. The enemy knight he had ignored was forcing his mount up the street through the fleeing mob, an armed crossbow in his hand. He wore no helmet, and as he reined in and stared up at Marshal, his face contorted with hatred. It was Gerard de Ridefort.

'The bastard must have gone over to Richard!' Bethune yelled, yet even then Marshal didn't realize the danger.

Openly to kill a knight with a crossbow was unthinkable, and Marshal watched in disbelief as Ridefort raised the weapon to his shoulder. But the hate Marshal saw in Ridefort's expression was beyond reason, and suddenly he knew he was going to die.

The range was too short for him to miss, and it was too late to flee. Marshal raised his sword and charged, knowing he would not live to reach his antagonist. The roadway between them was now almost clear, and the French stragglers scattered as Marshal's steed surged into a gallop. Time seemed to stand still as Marshal bore down on Ridefort. He could see Ridefort's glittering eyes lining up the shot, his fingers tightening on the trigger-lever . . .

Suddenly, Ridefort's mouth flew open, and his eyes widened in a look of infinite surprise. Still clutching the crossbow, he toppled from his saddle, a cloth-yard arrow buried in his chest.

Marshal hauled on the reins, but his stallion's momentum carried him past his fallen foe. His knights had followed him in the charge, and the enemy *serjants* wheeled their mounts about and fled, riding down their own men in their haste to escape. Marshal turned his horse and rode back to where Ridefort's body lay spread-eagled in the dust.

It had all happened too fast for him to feel fear. He had experienced only the icy certainty of impending death. But he was still alive, he thought numbly, staring without comprehension at the arrow protruding from Ridefort's chest.

Bethune and Harlincourt drew up beside him, cursing Ridefort's soul, their shock and outrage evident in their unnaturally high-pitched voices. Marshal was not listening. He was looking up the hill to where Black Fulk stood atop the barricade, a longbow in his hand, and now Marshal understood.

Across a hundred miles of land and sea, Isabelle de Clare had reached out to save his life.

23

Essex's fear had been realized. The wind had fanned the fires the defenders had set in the lower town and had carried showers of sparks over the wall and into the city. Fire had broken out at three points inside the southeastern wall, and despite the desperate attempts of the soldiers and citizens to contain them, the fires spread unchecked.

Marshal reeled as he stumbled backwards out of a burning house, choking and gagging on the smoke that filled his helmet.

'Let the damned thing go!' Bethune yelled, tearing out of Marshal's arms the bulky feather mattress that he was carrying. 'It's on fire and suffocating you!'

Marshal retched violently and fell to his knees.

'Get that helmet off him, Jean!' Bethune ordered, and Marshal felt his squire pulling at the helmet bindings. A moment later, his head was free, and he sucked in air in a long, ragged gasp. Blinking to clear his eyes, he got unsteadily to his feet.

The bent, white-haired woman whose mattress Marshal had tried to save was hugging herself and moaning as she watched the blue paint on her tiny house blister and blacken as flames burst through the windows and raced up the façade to merge with the blaze on the roof.

She had managed to save a chair, a few pots and pans and a small mirror, but that was all. She had wasted too much time struggling to pull her bed down from the second floor, and if Marshal had not heard her anguished cries and stopped to help, she might have been trapped.

'Will!' Bethune shouted, remounting his horse. 'There's

nothing we can do here; the whole damned city's going up! We've got to get to the cathedral.'

The street where Marshal and Bethune had halted was already engulfed in flame, and the blistering heat was driving out the last of the householders trying to save their belongings. Marshal stopped a man with a singed beard and eyebrows, who drove an ox-cart piled high with furniture, and ordered him to take on the old woman's few remaining possessions. Then he swung up on to his horse and followed the impatient Bethune towards the cathedral.

'God curse Henry of Anjou!' the old woman shouted wildly after them. 'He's done this to us!'

The woman's curse was all but lost in the chorus of shouts, screams and wails that rose from the city in a unanimous outburst of anger and loss. The sound of human grief melded with the crackle and roar of the widening inferno. Overhead, the sun was dimmed by a black, wind-torn pall of smoke, and everywhere the air was filled with sparks and tiny embers swirling on the wind and falling amid the dazed citizens, who continued to scurry with their pitiful loads through the streets clogged with carts and a menagerie of domestic animals.

Marshal gritted his teeth against the nausea from smoke-inhalation, cursing himself for stopping to help the old woman. Bethune was right; his place was with the king.

The square before the cathedral was packed with soldiers and mounted *serjants*, waiting in subdued silence, staring towards the king and his knights gathered on their horses by the cathedral steps.

'The smoke has driven our men off the southeastern wall, sire,' Essex was saying as Marshal rode up, 'but the fire in the lower town has forced the enemy to retire for the moment. Philip has brought his entire army across the river, but as yet he's made no attempt to encircle the city. We've opened the northwest gate to the people fleeing the fires inside the walls, and the enemy's mounted patrols are not interfering with the exodus.'

Henry nodded, his mouth set in a grim line. His face was flushed, and sweat streaked the soot smudges on his forehead. Although the king still looked resolute, Marshal was worried about his leg. Henry had been in the saddle for hours, and Marshal had no doubt that they would have to give up the defence of Le Mans. The king would have to travel far and fast in the next few days, and if the infection worsened . . .

'We'll have to abandon the city, sire,' Essex said. 'Our food supplies are going up in smoke; there's no hope now of withstanding a siege.'

'You were right about the wind, Essex,' Henry said bitterly, gazing bleakly out over the burning quarter of the city. 'I should have listened.'

Marshal glanced at the chancellor, who looked as if he were in pain as he watched the flames consuming his father's birthplace, and then Marshal looked at John. The prince's expression was curiously detached, as if the disaster did not touch him.

'If we're going to move, sire,' Marshal said, 'we should do so now, before Richard persuades Philip to cut off your retreat.'

Henry nodded. 'Is the road to Alençon open?'

'I've just come from the north gate, sire,' said William de Sille, castellan of the tower north of the city. 'The road was completely clear.'

'Good,' the king said, squaring his shoulders. 'Essex, you and Prince John will take every man who has a horse to ride and make a forced march to Alençon to rendezvous with the barons who will muster there. I'll follow with Lord Geoffry and my household knights to act as a rearguard. We'll have to leave our infantry behind, with permission to negotiate a surrender as soon as necessary.'

'I'll want one hundred men to reinforce the tower's garrison, sire,' de Sille said quickly. 'Philip won't find it easy to take, and the city won't be his until he's forced us to surrender. We'll tie down his army, sire, and give you the time to regroup in Normandy.'

'Thank you,' the king said fervently, gripping de Sille's arm. 'Time is what we need.' He lifted his head and swept the assembled knights with a fierce look. 'We're not beaten, by God,' he called out in a strong voice that echoed round the square, 'and we won't be as long as I have breath in my body!'

The king reined in his horse on the crest of a hill two leagues north of Le Mans, where the road to Alençon entered the forest. He turned for a last look at the city he had abandoned. The flush of exertion had dwindled to bright-red spots in the centre of his cheeks, and elsewhere the skin was unnaturally pale. The king's breathing was always heavy, but now he was panting, and his teeth were gritted in pain.

Marshal, preoccupied with the possibility of pursuit, had not noticed the change. The disaster was sinking in, fraying his nerves and sapping his energy. It had never happened to him before, but he had seen it in others – in men who had too much to lose.

The twenty knights riding with the king had drawn up around Henry as he gazed at the thick black smoke billowing up from Le Mans and spreading across the sky. Gradually, Henry's expression hardened, and his eyes flashed with angry frustration.

'The wind was an act of God,' he hissed. 'God, not Richard, drove me out.' He lifted his face to heaven and shook his fist in rage. 'Why?' he shouted up at the bright sky. 'What kind of God are you to curse me with sons who would destroy me?'

Several of the knights recoiled at the blasphemy and quietly moved their horses away, as if they expected a bolt of lightning to strike from the blue.

'Why, damn it?' Henry yelled again, his face contorted with unreasoning fury.

'He's not likely to answer while you're shouting at him, sire,' Marshal said quietly.

'What?' The king blinked, as if suddenly realizing he was not alone, and then laughed sardonically. 'I suppose you're right,' he said wearily, sagging in the saddle. 'And maybe it wasn't God's doing. Maybe my old friend, Thomas à Beckett, stirred up that wind.'

'I doubt it, sire,' Marshal said distractedly, looking back down the road they had travelled towards a distant dust-cloud. Horsemen were coming, riding hard. 'How's your leg, sire?'

'It feels like it's on fire.'

'We could rig a litter between two horses. It wouldn't slow us down much.'

'No,' the king snapped. 'I'll let you know when I can no

longer sit a horse. So they're finally coming after me, are they?'

'Some, at least. I'll stay here with Bethune and Harlincourt to slow them down.'

'You can have more men, Marshal.'

Marshal shook his head decisively. 'No, sire. Your escort is too small as it is.'

He looked over at Fulk, stoically sitting his horse at the side of the road, his jaw muscles working on a chunk of rawhide. Marshal would have liked to add Fulk to the king's escort, but he knew the *serjant* would refuse.

'All right, Marshal, I'll leave you to it, then,' Henry said, visibly summoning his reserves of strength. 'My leg should hold up long enough for me to reach Fresnai. I'll stay the night at Viscount Beaumont's castle.'

'Very well, sire. We'll catch up with you there.'

The king turned his horse and rode off, and Marshal looked back at the dust of the approaching riders. His mind was clouded with fatigue, and for several seconds his eyes remained unfocused. But then a sudden intuition quickened his pulse. He straightened, and watched the enemy's approach with renewed anticipation.

Marshal drank briefly from his water-bag and handed it back to Jean d'Erly, his eyes fixed on the pursuers galloping up the road from Le Mans.

'No more than four knights,' said Bethune, who had the sharpest eyes. 'The rest are squires and *serjants*.'

'Too few and too late,' Harlincourt said. 'I still can't understand why Philip didn't block the north gate. It's the only luck we've had today.'

'We could forget about these men, Will,' Bethune suggested. 'The way they're pushing their mounts, they won't last much longer, and even if they could catch up with the king, there aren't enough of them to worry about.'

Marshal pointed to a second cloud of dust rising from the road half a league behind the first group of riders. 'More coming – and faster,' he said tensely, and he saw Harlincourt turn to look at him. 'They must be riding light. We'll stay put and hold them all up for a while – just to be on the safe side. It's time to lace helmets, gentlemen.'

The squires moved up beside their masters and handed them their helmets. Just before Harlincourt lowered his helmet, he gave Marshal a sly grin. 'You think Richard's coming, don't you, Will?'

'Maybe,' Marshal said, lowering his own helmet, and as Jean lashed it down, his stomach muscles tightened. Richard *was* coming, of that he was sure.

'Well, he's not in the first group,' Bethune said and then laughed. 'That's Philip de Columbiers in front. I unseated him in a tournament years ago. This is going to be easy.'

'Good,' Marshal said, 'because I want to stage a little tournament right here. You two ride out into the open and place yourselves astride the road, with your squires carrying extra lances.'

'Aren't you joining us, Will?' Bethune asked.

'Not yet,' Marshal said grimly. 'You're the bait; I'm the hook.'

As Bethune, Harlincourt and their squires rode out to challenge the oncoming knights, Marshal moved off the road with Jean and Fulk into cover at the edge of the forest overlooking the slope.

'Now we'll see if Columbiers and his friends are the fools I think they are,' Marshal said to Jean. 'If they have sense, they'll brush right by us.'

The four helmeted knights, leading their squires and a dozen *serjants*, were only one hundred paces from the foot of the hill and still coming when Bethune and Harlincourt halted halfway down the slope and lowered their lances. For a moment, it looked as if Richard's knights might ignore the challenge and charge through the decoys, but an instant later the knight Bethune had identified as Philip de Columbiers reined in and signalled for the others to stop.

'Make way in the name of Richard, Count of Poitou!' Columbiers shouted up to Bethune and Harlincourt.

'This road is closed to traitors!' Bethune yelled derisively, and immediately the challenged knights fell to arguing over which pairs would be the first to break lances with Bethune and Harlincourt.

Marshal shook his head. 'Look at that, Jean, and remember it. Those knights rode out to capture a king, and now they're breaking off the pursuit to accept our challenge. That's stupidity, not chivalry.'

Columbiers and the knight he picked as partner were the first to charge, and Bethune and Harlincourt met them at the bottom of the slope. All four lances shattered simultaneously, and although the enemy knights were thrown off-balance, they stayed in the saddle. Bethune and Harlincourt calmly turned their chargers and rode back up the hill for new lances. Columbiers and his companion returned to their group, and the second pair rode forward to make the next run.

Again the ritual was repeated, and again Harlincourt and Bethune nearly unseated their opponents. Marshal could hear Harlincourt's laugh as they rode back up the hill to prepare for yet another pass. But there was no more time. The second group of pursuers was bearing down on the site of the impromptu tournament.

'That's Prince Richard!' Jean exclaimed, pointing at the unmistakeable figure riding far out in front of the rest.

'I see him,' Marshal said. 'Give me a lance, lad.'

Richard was riding in pursuit with twenty lightly armed *serjants* who wouldn't weigh down their mounts. Richard himself was armed with no more than sword, shield and a foot soldier's steel cap. In his eagerness to overtake his father, he had thrown caution to the winds.

'Prince Richard has no hauberk, sire!' Jean cried.

'He has never learned my cardinal rule,' Marshal said coldly, his rising excitement laced with grim determination, 'but he's about to.'

As Richard rode into the midst of the men who should have been far ahead of him, racing after the king, Marshal heard him bellow furiously, 'What the devil are you doing? God's legs, it's Henry we're after!'

Philip de Columbiers tried to answer, but Richard cut him off. 'Come on!' he cried in exasperation, and, waving his sword, he spurred his stallion into a gallop.

Marshal's pulse was racing, and he took two deliberate breaths, holding himself in check; he wanted to time his charge perfectly. Richard had just won a brilliant victory, but now his recklessness had placed his life in Marshal's hands. The *serjants* Richard had outstripped were fast approaching, but they would be too late to save the Count of Poitou.

Columbiers and his knights had been slow to react, and Richard reached the base of the hill before they came galloping after him. Richard was not suicidal, and he certainly had no intention of charging Bethune and Harlincourt without armour. Realizing he was alone and exposed, he started to rein in.

Now! Marshal dug in his spurs and burst from the forest.

'He's mine!' Marshal yelled to Bethune and Harlincourt, who held their position blocking the road. 'He's mine!'

Richard looked up to see Marshal hurtling down the grassy hillside straight for him. His eyes widened with shock, and his mouth flew open. 'No, Marshal! I'm unarmed!' he cried, starting to turn his horse, but there was no escape.

Thundering down on his victim, Marshal shifted direction to cut him off, his lance trained on Richard's chest. Behind his helmet, Marshal's face was distorted in a wild grimace. Richard, who threatened to destroy Marshal's life, was helpless to defend himself. Helpless! He had to surrender or die, and in the space of three heartbeats it would be over.

But Richard refused to surrender. Instead, he turned to meet Marshal's charge, and in the split-second that remained, Marshal realized he had lost the contest of will. If he killed Richard now, John would be the next King of England. *John.*

With a desperate cry, Richard swung his sword in a futile attempt to deflect the onrushing lance, and his cry merged with a roar of rage and frustration that burst from Marshal. An instant before impact, Marshal shifted his aim and drove his lance into Richard's horse.

The stallion died in its tracks, throwing Richard from the saddle. As Marshal galloped past the fallen prince, he drew his sword and slashed furiously at the nearest of the riders bearing down on him. He knocked a knight from the saddle, and then three *serjants* in quick succession, venting his rage, and the press of onrushing riders broke up and scattered before him.

He wheeled his horse about and galloped back up the road. Richard, who had staggered to his feet, cried out to the knights and *serjants* giving chase. 'Stop, you fools! Can't you see it's an ambush?'

Bethune and Harlincourt, riding with their squires to Marshal's aid, turned and swung in behind him. 'What ambush?' Harlincourt laughed as they galloped up the hill.

But Bethune was angry. 'Why didn't you finish him?' he demanded.

Marshal gritted his teeth and spurred on his horse, pulling ahead of the others. He had no wish to explain himself. He had made his choice, and it was a bitter one.

Isabelle was seated in the shade of a silk pavilion on the bank of the Thames near the White Tower. The riverbanks and bridges were lined with Londoners who had come down to watch the annual tourney on the Thames. Commercial river traffic had been suspended for the event, and the trunk of a great oak tree had been anchored in the middle of the water to serve as a quintain. Upstream from the target, the bright water swarmed with the contestants' swift, light rowing craft.

As Isabelle watched, the latest competitor to try his luck was fast approaching the target. He stood precariously balanced in the prow of a narrow-waisted boat propelled by four oarsmen, a long, slender lance held tightly against his ribs. The rowers had come up to speed, and the boat knifed through the water, froth rising at the bow with each stroke of the oars.

The coxswain guided the boat towards the tree-trunk at precisely the right angle, but the young man in the prow did not have the strength and balance to shatter his lance on the target. The lance flexed for an instant but held, and the force of impact flung the youth over the side. The splash as he hit the water was greeted by hoots of laughter from the spectators, whose mirth only increased as it became apparent that the would-be knight of the Thames could barely swim.

As the boy thrashed desperately in the river, the derisive shouts and laughter swelled along the banks, and the crew of the nearby rescue boat dutifully played to the crowd by delaying the pick-up until the last possible moment. The nobles and ladies gathered under the pavilion where Isabelle sat were well supplied with wine, and they rocked with laughter; but she reacted with only a half-hearted smile.

Normally, she would have enjoyed the show. The tent shielded her from the sun, a soft, cool breeze came off the waters and there was plenty of action. The young men who missed the tree with their lances or who fell back into the boat were instantly seized by their comrades and tossed over the side.

Isabelle had hoped the diversion of the tourney would give her a respite from the worry that hovered constantly near the surface of her thoughts ever since she had learned of the disaster at Le Mans. The news had come three weeks before, but there had been nothing since, and the waiting and wondering were fraying her nerves.

Hubert Walter, the justiciar's secretary, had assured her that the king would quickly rally his forces in Normandy, but Isabelle could not forget that Henry had made Le Mans his stronghold. If Richard and Philip could attack him there and drive him out within two days . . .

Isabelle twisted restlessly on her bench, and out of the corner of her eye she saw the cherubic secretary coming down from the Tower towards the pavilion, as if summoned by her thoughts. She left the tent unobtrusively and went to meet him. In the last few months, they had become friends, and the chubby little man had kept her abreast of events.

The secretary was frowning as he walked, his eyes on the ground, but at her approach he looked up and smiled. 'Good afternoon, Lady Isabelle. Have you tired of the tourney already?'

'Good afternoon, Master Hubert. No, I saw you coming, and thought you might have received fresh news.'

The secretary cleared his throat uncomfortably and glanced towards the river. Isabelle tensed. He was a clever, discreet man and fully capable of hiding his feelings, but he had never pretended with her. His obvious discomfiture could only mean that there was bad news.

'We've received dispatches, Lady Isabelle,' he said, still avoiding her eyes. 'They're fragmentary and somewhat confused, but – well, the situation has deteriorated rapidly.'

The secretary paused, and Isabelle had to restrain herself from pressing him. She could feel her heart pounding against her ribs.

'The king never reached Alençon,' he continued. 'Instead

of proceeding north, where he could have reorganized his defence behind a secure line of fortresses in Normandy, he turned south and made his way with a small party to Chinon.'

'Chinon!' Isabelle gasped. The city was at the southern extremity of Anjou, far behind enemy lines. 'And his army?'

'Still in Normandy, and blocked by Richard's forces.'

'But why did His Majesty turn south?'

'No one here knows for certain. Having arrived at Chinon, he appears to have simply given up. For the last few weeks, Philip and Richard have had a free hand, and without the king's leadership, many barons have surrendered their castles to Richard without a fight. The prince has completely overrun Touraine and Maine. Philip is besieging Tours, and I'm afraid the city may have already fallen to him. For all practical purposes, the king has lost control of everything except Normandy.'

'Where is Sir William?' Isabelle asked anxiously. 'Do you know?'

'He's safe, I assure you. He and the chancellor are with the king at Chinon.'

'But they are cut off, Master Hubert!'

'Yes, but in no immediate danger,' the secretary said, and then he sighed heavily. 'You see, Lady Isabelle, I think the war is just about over. The Archbishop of Reims and the Count of Flanders are going to Chinon to arrange a peace conference. I don't know what Philip's terms will be, but the king has little choice but to accept them.'

Isabelle swallowed, hesitating to ask the question uppermost in her mind. 'Do you think they will try to depose the king?'

To her infinite relief, the secretary shook his head. 'That might be in Richard's mind, but probably not in Philip's. If Philip intended anything so drastic, he would be besieging Chinon to take Henry prisoner. He has emasculated Henry in France, and he would be foolish to put Richard on the throne of England now – even if he thought the English barons would accept Richard.'

Isabelle almost sighed aloud. She cared nothing for the balance of power in France, and now that there would be peace, the king could honour his promise to Marshal.

Her relief was obvious, and the secretary's face clouded.

'I'm afraid there is more to tell you, Lady Isabelle. I said that no one knows for certain why the king suddenly gave up the fight and fled to Chinon, but I think I know the reason. We've received word that the king is ill – gravely ill.'

Isabelle took the shock without flinching, but she could feel the blood draining from her face. 'Are you saying that – that he won't recover?'

'The dispatch is not that specific,' the secretary said, again finding it difficult to meet her eyes, 'but one can read between the lines. I'm very much afraid the king is mortally ill, and I believe he knew that when he went south to Chinon – into the heart of his inherited domains. I think he went there to die.'

Isabelle said nothing, her expression impassive, but she felt her world crumbling. If Henry died, her chance for happiness would die with him.

'I'm deeply sorry,' Hubert Walter said in a pained voice. 'I know how much you hoped the king's promise to Sir William would be fulfilled. There is always the chance, of course, that Richard will honour his father's pledge, but I'm afraid that's . . .'

'Unlikely,' Isabelle said woodenly.

'Yes. Richard is a proud man, and we can hardly expect him to reward the very knight who so recently unhorsed him. It's always dangerous to humiliate an enemy and leave him alive.'

A fresh roar rose from the crowds along the Thames, and Isabelle looked blankly out at the river. Another youth had been thrown into the water. The cheering, carefree crowds and the bright sunlit river seemed to mock her in her misery. The day should have been bleak and windswept, she thought, with black clouds hiding the sun. She felt like crying aloud in her pain. She and Marshal had come so close – so close!

The secretary was watching her with concern. 'It may still turn out all right, Lady Isabelle,' he said, as people do when there is nothing else to say.

'Yes,' Isabelle said distractedly, struggling for composure. She refused to accept passively the destruction of her hopes. She had to keep fighting, no matter what the odds; it was the only way she knew.

'Master Hubert,' she said, drawing herself to her full

height. 'You will kindly arrange an escort for me to Winchester. I am going to see the queen.'

'But I'm not sure the justiciar will allow . . .'

'If what you fear is true,' Isabelle cut in, 'the justiciar will shortly be out of office, and the queen at liberty. *I* am not out of favour with Her Majesty, so I think it would be wise to honour my request.'

24

Anjou, France, July 1189

Few of the wayfarers on the hot, dusty road to Ballan recognized the Plantagenet leopard emblazoned on Henry's banner and so remained unaware that they were seeing the king pass by; his pitifully small entourage numbered only a dozen knights and squires, and a handful of personal servants.

Henry rode at the head of the column, flanked by Geoffry and Marshal. It was not a long ride from Chinon to Ballan, where the peace conference was to be held, but Marshal had not been sure that the king would be able to stay in the saddle. Henry's once-ruddy cheeks were chalk-white, and his face was coated with a sheen of sweat. His infected leg was swathed in bandages that now extended up to his thigh, and the stench of putrefaction enveloped him like a cloud in the oppressive, sultry air.

The king had been riding for some time with his eyes closed, moaning softly, but now he opened them and blinked dazedly. 'Where are we, Marshal?' he croaked.

'We're almost there, sire,' Marshal said, pointing to an abbey on the outskirts of Ballan, set back from the road and surrounded by cultivated fields and orchards.

Henry started to slip sideways in his saddle, and Marshal and Geoffry reached out to steady him.

'Has Philip taken Tours?' Henry asked anxiously.

'Yes, sire,' Geoffry said. 'Two days ago.'

'I knew that,' Henry said quickly. 'Yes, of course. Two days ago. Marshal, what terms does Philip offer?'

'I don't know, sire, but unless they are unusually harsh,

·314·

you will have to accept them. We've lost everything but Normandy.'

The king groaned and closed his eyes again. Marshal could not tell if it was from pain or anguish. The two had merged in Henry to produce a suffering that Marshal could only imagine, and in its presence his own feelings seemed insignificant. This man had been a great king, one who had wished only to live out his reign in peace. Henry deserved better than this bitter ending to his life, dying slowly, deserted by many of his barons and humbled by his own impatient son.

'Marshal!' Henry said fiercely, opening his eyes. 'You've got to help me through this. I'll accept their terms because I have to, but, by God, I'll have my revenge. When I'm well again, we'll fight.'

'I'll do what I can, sire,' Marshal said, glancing at Geoffry. The chancellor's face was ashen, and he looked close to tears.

'They've forgotten they're dealing with Henry of Anjou,' the king growled, drawing strength from anger. 'I'll fight on, I swear I will. I'll gorge myself on war!'

It was the last, defiant growl of a mortally wounded leopard, Marshal thought sadly. Henry was dying, and the king had realized it before any of them. When Henry had awoken in Fresnai the morning after Le Mans, he must have sensed that the infection in his leg had him in a death-grip. It was then that he had suddenly, inexplicably, ignored the pleading of his counsellors and turned south.

But now, goaded by the prospect of humiliation before Philip and Richard, the leopard bared his fangs one last time.

As they neared the abbey, they saw the banner of the king of France marking the conference site at the edge of an orchard outside the abbey wall. They left the highway and rode across the fields towards the trees. No tents had been erected, and only a small group surrounded Philip and Richard, who were sitting on the ground in the shade.

By keeping the meeting as informal as possible and minimizing the number of witnesses, Philip was obviously trying to preserve what dignity remained to his antagonist, and Marshal noted the gracious gesture with respect. It was yet another sign that the young monarch had matured.

At Henry's approach, Philip rose from the robe on which he was seated and came forward with the Count of Flanders and the Archbishop of Reims. Richard also stood up, but he did not come to meet his father. The Count of Flanders had told Marshal that Richard continued to insist Henry was feigning illness to win with sympathy what he could not win in the field.

Philip was clearly shocked by Henry's appearance, and his formal smile of courtesy vanished. 'My dear Henry,' he exclaimed with genuine concern, 'if I'd known you were so ill, I would not have asked you to ride so far.'

'It's of no consequence,' the king grated hoarsely, squaring his shoulders and endeavouring to sit up straight. 'Let's get on with it.'

Richard was looking on with a cynical scowl, and for the first time Marshal fully appreciated the depth of Richard's suspicion of his father. No other man present could doubt that Henry was dying.

'Please, my dear Henry,' Philip said solicitously, 'dismount and be seated on my robe.'

'I didn't come here to sit and pass the time,' Henry said brusquely, drawing on his last reserves of strength. 'I've come to hear your conditions for peace. What are they?'

Philip stiffened momentarily, but then his nose twitched as he caught a whiff of the stench enveloping the king. 'As you wish,' he said quietly. 'I will not keep you long. We have drawn up a list of conditions, which even you may agree are fair. Flanders will read them to you.'

The Count of Flanders unrolled a parchment and cleared his throat. 'These are the conditions for peace, sire,' he said.

'First, you shall renew your homage to Philip of France in a public ceremony, in return for which you will be reinstated as lord of your former domains in France.

'Second, you shall order your vassals on both sides of the channel to swear allegiance to Richard, Count of Poitou, as heir to all your lands in France and to the Kingdom of England.

'Third, you shall immediately surrender Alais of France to a guardian of Prince Richard's choosing and publicly agree to the marriage of Richard and Alais upon Prince Richard's return from Crusade. These are His Majesty's principal demands.

'In addition, you shall pay the French crown an indemnity

of twenty thousand marks to defray the crown's expenses in this unfortunate war, and you shall surrender three fortresses in the Vexin to the custody of the French crown.

'Finally, you shall release from the bonds of allegiance all those vassals who have supported Prince Richard in this war – either openly or secretly – until the terms of this treaty have been fulfilled. Further, you shall swear to take no punitive action against the said vassals at any time thereafter.'

In the heavy silence that followed, the mutter of distant thunder caused several of the knights in attendance to look in puzzlement at the sky. The haze was thickening overhead, and the eastern horizon had a leaden hue, but no thunderclouds were in evidence.

'Is that all?' Henry rasped.

'Those are the terms, sire,' Flanders said, and he glanced at Marshal, as if asking him to assure the king that the conditions were fair.

The terms were more than fair; they were astonishingly lenient. They represented little more than Philip had hoped to achieve a year before through negotiation, and they left Henry's territorial rights intact.

Marshal looked towards Richard, wondering if he had willingly acceded to the terms or if he had been forced to agree. Philip's leniency might appear magnanimous, but it could also be the result of shrewd calculation. To crush Henry's power in France, only to give it to the young, vigorous Richard, might strike Philip as self-defeating. Far better to allow father and son to hold each other in check.

For Richard to give up territory he'd won in battle was distinctly uncharacteristic, particularly since he refused to believe his father was ill. Yet Marshal doubted that Philip could have forced too much on his ally. Perhaps, with his inheritance secured, Richard was more interested in fighting Saladin than in seizing territory in France.

Marshal sighed inwardly, for the terms hardly mattered. Henry was dying.

'I agree to your conditions,' the king said to Philip.

Henry's eyelids drooped, and Marshal reached out to steady him as he suddenly sagged sideways. The king shook off Marshal's arm and straightened up. 'As to your condition regarding those of my vassals who supported my son,' Henry said harshly, 'I will need a list of their names in order to comply.'

'A list has been compiled,' Philip said, and he nodded to Flanders, who stepped forward and handed a sealed letter to Geoffry. 'Since you accept the terms,' Philip continued, 'I consider the war between us at an end. I ask you now to give your son the kiss of peace.'

Henry grunted and nodded in grudging assent, and Richard, totally impassive, came forward for the first time. Gripping the saddle pommel, Henry bent down to bring his lips close to Richard's upraised cheek, but there was no kiss. Instead, Marshal heard the king's fierce but barely audible whisper in Richard's ear. 'May God spare me long enough to have my revenge on you, my traitorous son.'

Richard did not react; he did not even blink. He turned and walked away from Henry with the same unreadable expression on his face.

The mutter of thunder had grown to an ominous rumble, and a wind began to stir the sultry air. The king nodded once to Philip and jerked on his reins, turning his horse. Followed by his knights, he rode away, slumped forward in the saddle.

Two leagues from Ballan, Henry collapsed, and Geoffry only just managed to keep him from tumbling to the ground. One of the king's servants hastily spread a cloak on the grass beside the road, as Marshal and Geoffry eased Henry off his horse. The wind was gusting now and the temperature had dropped sharply, but Henry's face was still beaded with sweat. Even in the open, the stench of flesh rotting beneath the bandages was overpowering.

'God, it's on fire,' Henry gasped, grinding his teeth. 'My whole leg's on fire.'

'Wine!' Geoffry yelled to the servants as he and Marshal carried the king to the side of the road and carefully lowered him on to the cloak.

A small group of travellers was approaching – students and merchants who had banded together for their journey – and the men in the lead slowed their nags as they drew near, curious to know what was going on. With snarled curses, the knights drove them on down the road.

Marshal looked up at the rapidly darkening sky. 'We can pitch a tent here, sire. The storm will break any moment.'

'No,' Henry said weakly. 'Chinon. Get me back to Chinon. I'll be safe there.'

'You *are* safe, sire,' Marshal said, exchanging a look with the chancellor, who pillowed Henry's head in his lap and stroked his father's hair.

'Chinon,' Henry gasped again, and Marshal nodded.

'Bethune! Harlincourt!' he called. 'Rig a canvas litter between your horses for His Majesty.'

The wine arrived, and Geoffry propped up the king as a servant held the cup to the dying monarch's mouth. Henry managed to swallow some, but then he waved the cup away as wine overflowed his lips and ran down into his beard.

A bolt of lightning ripped the sky to the east, followed a second later by a thunderclap that shook the ground. Henry's eyes went wide. 'Am I dying?'

'No, sire,' Marshal said, going to one knee beside the king. 'We'll have a litter rigged in a minute, and then we'll get you to Chinon. You can rest then. The war is over, sire, and your lands are safe. Do you understand?'

The king closed his eyes with a sigh and nodded weakly. 'The list,' he croaked. 'I want the traitors' names so I can curse them. God curse them all!'

'You can read it later, sire,' Geoffry said, tears running down his cheeks.

'The list!' Henry choked.

The chancellor pulled out the letter and tore it open, but his eyes were too blurred to see the names and he handed it to Marshal. As Marshal unfolded the parchment, the first heavy drops of rain began to splatter around them.

'The names, Marshal!'

Thunder crashed directly above them, and several of the horses threatened to bolt. 'The ink will run if the letter gets wet, sire,' Marshal said, swallowing hard. He had seen the name at the top of the list.

Henry struggled up into a sitting position. 'The names!'

'Sire,' Marshal said, looking helplessly at Geoffry, 'the first name on the list is Prince John.'

For a moment Henry stared blankly at Marshal, as if he had not heard, but then his mouth contorted in a silent cry of anguish and he fell back into Geoffry's lap with a long, agonized moan. 'My sons,' he whispered faintly, closing his eyes. 'God, *all* my sons.'

The storm broke upon them then, and as they carried the king to the litter, the rain descended in a torrent.

Two days later, Henry of Anjou was dead.

The barons of Touraine and Anjou began arriving at Chinon early on the day following the king's death. The Earl of Essex had been making his way down from Normandy to give his support to the king at Chinon, and he arrived late in the morning to discover that Henry was past earthly help.

Towards noon, the barons bore the king's body down from Chinon's great rock fortress, down the valley of the Vienne and across the river to Fontevrault. Henry had lavishly endowed the abbey at Fontevrault, and the nuns took charge of his remains.

All afternoon, the assembled knights and barons waited for Richard, to whom Marshal had sent a messenger with the news of Henry's death. Now, as the sun sank towards the horizon, they stood pensively in small groups while the shadow of the abbey church slowly lengthened over them. Marshal waited apart from the others, in the company of Bethune and Harlincourt.

'You'd think it was catching, the way they're keeping clear of you, Will,' Harlincourt said.

Marshal shrugged. He was aware of the occasional furtive look cast in his direction, but he understood and did not mind. 'Who knows? It might be,' he replied. 'Guilt by association.'

'That's a thought,' Bethune said. 'What do you think, Hugh? Maybe we should keep our distance. Our captain may have stepped in shit, but we don't have to let it rub off on us.'

'True, true,' Harlincourt replied cheerfully, 'but I'm curious to see what happens when Richard arrives. It's not every day you get to see a knight pay his respects to a monarch whom he's recently knocked on his royal backside.'

'Stop it,' Marshal said quietly. 'For all practical purposes, Richard is king, and you might as well start thinking and acting accordingly.'

Bethune shook his head. 'You should have attacked him instead of his horse, Will.'

Marshal's mouth turned down at the corners. 'You think so?' Then it would be John we'd be waiting for.'

'When do you think John defected?' Harlincourt asked, and Marshal shook his head.

'I have no idea,' he said.

'Cunning swine,' Bethune muttered bitterly, and they lapsed into silence.

Much of the time they had waited in silence. Every so often Bethune and Harlincourt had tried diverting Marshal with their banter, but each time it had fallen flat. Marshal had wanted to tell them that the effort was not necessary, but he knew they believed his outward calm was a pose. It wasn't.

Marshal had done all the agonizing of which he was capable in the long hours of the all-night vigil that the king's knights had kept beside his body. Marshal had given free rein to second thoughts and self-recrimination, but in the end he had come to terms with himself. Given the chance to relive this past year, he realized, he would do nothing differently.

His pain when he thought of Isabelle was numbed now by fatigue, and eventually, he told himself, it would fade. His hope to win her hand had been a grand, beautiful illusion – an illusion he would have to learn to live without . . .

The Earl of Essex had detached himself from a group of barons and approached Marshal.

'You've been keeping to yourself, Marshal,' Essex said casually.

'Not intentionally, sire.'

Essex smiled slightly. 'No, I suppose not. It's the cloud over your head. It makes people uneasy – especially when they're not all that sure of their own futures.'

'I've nothing to fear from Richard,' Marshal said.

Essex raised his eyebrows. 'Nothing to fear, perhaps, but a lot to lose. Even if he allows you to retain Cartmel, that will still leave you virtually a landless knight. And if he won't take you into his service, you may have to go abroad.'

Marshal nodded, acknowledging the obvious.

Essex cleared his throat in a gesture of uncharacteristic diffidence. 'I've been talking with a number of the barons about your situation, and we are agreed that we owe you more than a fond farewell. If you are forced to go abroad, we'd be grateful if you would allow us to provide you with enough capital for a fresh start – to give you more freedom of action. It would be a loan, not a gift.'

'Thank you, sire,' Marshal said warmly, touched by the offer. 'You'll never know how much I appreciate that.'

Essex smiled wanly and sighed. 'But you won't accept.'

'I can't, sire. I can't accept a loan I might never be able to repay.'

Essex was about to say something more, but at that moment hard-riding horsemen galloped over a rise in the road to the east. Richard had arrived.

The Count of Poitou, accompanied by two of his knights and their squires, drew rein at the entrance of the abbey church. Their horses were lathered with sweat, and their surcoats and cloaks coated with dust. Richard swung down from the saddle, and his eyes swept the gathering, his expression as unreadable as it had been outside Ballan. Yet those who knew him well detected a change in his bearing, a touch of grave dignity that overlaid his customary swagger. Richard the Lionheart was king.

Abruptly, he pointed to Marshal, then to Geoffry, beckoning them to follow him. Then he turned and strode into the church.

Marshal and the chancellor waited at the rear of the church as Richard approached the altar, before which Henry's body lay in state. Richard stopped at the bier and cocked his head to one side quizzically, as if he were still not quite sure his father was dead.

Geoffry, visibly exhausted by grief, was staring at Richard, clearly awaiting some sign of emotion from his half-brother. But there was nothing. Richard sank to his knees and prayed briefly. For what? Marshal wondered. His father's soul? Forgiveness? Or was it a secret prayer of thanksgiving?

It was strange, Marshal thought, that he found himself more curious about Richard's feelings than about his own fate. Wrapped in the candlelit gloom of the silent church, he felt only a fatalistic listlessness.

As Richard rose and turned to leave, there was neither grief nor triumph in his face, only an expression of finality.

Whatever his thoughts during his reverie, he had put the past behind him. He was ready to begin his life.

Richard strode back up the aisle and halted before Marshal and the chancellor. 'When I came across the bridge over the Vienne,' he said angrily, 'the poor of the countryside were still gathered there, waiting for the alms they have every right to expect.'

'The treasury at Chinon is empty, sire,' Geoffry answered. 'We had no money to give.'

'And what about de Marcai?' Richard snapped. 'Surely it falls to the Seneschal of Anjou to see that custom is adhered to. A King of England has died, gentlemen! It is unseemly that no alms accompanied his funeral cortège.'

'Stephen de Marcai's coffers are also empty, sire,' Marshal said stiffly. 'We've had no money for weeks. If we'd had money,' he added pointedly, 'you would have seen evidence of it in the field.'

'None? None at all?' Richard demanded, unconvinced.

Geoffry swallowed, fighting back tears. 'Not even enough to maintain the king's personal servants, sire. Your father died in his sleep, and by the time I discovered he was dead, the servants had already stripped his body and absconded with his clothes.'

Richard blinked, and, for an instant, Marshal thought he saw something akin to sorrow briefly shadow Richard's eyes, but the moment was fleeting. 'Come with me,' Richard said brusquely, and left the church.

Richard ignored the silent crowd outside and led Marshal and the chancellor out of earshot of the others. The sun had set, lighting the western sky a fiery orange, and the Evening Star shone brightly, a brilliant point of light against a darkening blue background. The wishing star. This evening, it seemed reserved for the new King of England.

Richard stopped and turned to Marshal, his hands planted aggressively on his hips. 'You tried to kill me the other day,' he said, 'and you would have, if I hadn't deflected your lance.'

Geoffry caught Marshal's eye, and Marshal had no difficulty reading his expression. *Tact, Marshal, tact.* Richard was trying to save face, and Marshal knew it would be wise to placate his vanity; but he was in no mood to curry favour.

He had fought on the losing side, but he had fought for the right one.

'If I'd wanted to kill you, sire,' Marshal said quietly, 'you would be dead now. I'm still strong enough to direct my lance where I choose.'

Richard's eyes narrowed and his lips compressed into a thin line, but Marshal refused to give way.

'If I had killed you, sire,' he added coolly, 'it would have been no crime, and I certainly don't regret killing your horse.'

For a long moment, Richard stared at Marshal in silence, and Marshal became aware of the barons watching from a distance, clearly expecting an explosion of anger from Richard.

Abruptly, Richard laughed. 'You don't, by God!' he exclaimed, and laughed again. 'Well, better the horse than me. But I'll say this, Marshal: things might have turned out differently that day if I'd been fully armed. A duel between us on equal terms would be an interesting match.'

'Perhaps, sire,' Marshal said, smiling for the first time, 'but I'd prefer not to stretch my luck.'

Even knowing how mercurial Richard could be, Marshal was surprised by the abrupt reversal. Richard now appeared completely relaxed and genial. 'You fought me to the last, Marshal,' he said, 'but I can't hold that against you. Quite the reverse, in fact. You stood by my father long after prudent men were coming over to the winning side. The king always has fair-weather friends, but loyalty like yours is a good deal harder to find. You're as true a knight as I know, and I would have you serve me as you did my father.'

'*Serve* you, sire?' Marshal said, dumbfounded.

'That's what I said, isn't it?'

'It would be an honour, sire, but in what capacity would you have me serve?'

Richard shrugged casually. 'Time will tell, but for the moment you will act as my proxy. I will have to remain here for several weeks, but I want England prepared for my coronation. Tomorrow, immediately after the funeral, you will proceed to England and obtain my mother's release from Winchester. I will give you letters authorizing her to assume temporary control of the government. Then you can see to your own affairs. I'll have no further need of you before the coronation.'

'May I ask, sire,' Geoffry said, 'who the next chancellor will be?'

'William de Longchamp,' Richard said curtly. 'But for the time being, at least, you will retain your ecclesiastical position and honours.'

'Thank you, sire,' Geoffry said.

Richard was about to turn away, when Geoffry cleared his throat.

'Yes?' Richard said impatiently.

'There is one thing I'd like to draw your attention to, sire,' Geoffry said quickly. 'As you've noted, Sir William served your father with honour and great distinction, and in recognition of Sir William's service, the king gave him the heiress of Pembroke, the Lady Isabelle de Clare. I thought perhaps . . .'

Marshal reddened. It was a selfless gesture on Geoffry's part, but pointless, and it embarrassed him. For Richard to forgive his enmity in the war was one thing, but to grant him now the richest marriage prize in England was quite another.

'My father didn't *give* him the heiress,' Richard said sharply. 'He only promised her. The wardship falls to me now, to dispose of as I see fit.'

'Of course, sire,' Geoffry said, glancing apologetically at Marshal.

'You understand, Marshal, don't you?' Richard said.

'Yes, sire. I quite understand.'

'Good,' Richard said sternly, and then, suddenly, he grinned and clapped Marshal on the shoulder. 'In that case, she's yours.'

'Sire?' Marshal said with a catch in his voice.

'Are you hard of hearing, Marshal? I hereby give you Isabelle de Clare – both the lady and her lands. And if you're half the man I think you are, you'll be married and working on a son before I reach England.'

Ignoring the stunned look on Marshal's face, Richard casually clapped him on the shoulder again and walked away to address the waiting barons.

* * *

'I *told* you it was going to rain, milady,' Matilda complained, pulling up the hood of her cloak. 'We'll be soaked by the time we get back.'

'You didn't have to come,' Isabelle said listlessly, 'and a summer rain won't kill you.'

But it had been a bad day to try out her new peregrine, Isabelle admitted to herself, and she'd been wrong in thinking that hawking would lift her spirits – though she couldn't have known she would lose the falcon. Ordinarily, the loss would have upset her, for she had supervised the bird's training herself, but now she hardly cared.

Poor Matilda, Isabelle thought. She had never been fond of hawking, particularly in the absence of genteel male company; but Matilda considered it unseemly for Isabelle to ride out alone, so she had been forced to come along.

They were returning from the hunt along a narrow road paralleling the marshy north bank of the Thames, a league downriver from the Tower. The rain was coming down more heavily by the minute, the drops pocking the river's surface. The rain suited Isabelle's mood.

All London buzzed with excitement at the prospect of a coronation. It was said that a representative of the new king had crossed the Channel and that the queen was at liberty. Isabelle was glad for Eleanor, who was now free after all these years, but she greeted the rest of the news with complete indifference.

The queen had received Isabelle graciously enough at Winchester, and she had listened sympathetically to Isabelle's plea to intercede with Richard. But Eleanor had held out no hope. Marshal had fought Richard to the end, and to the victors, not the vanquished, went the spoils.

Had John shared in the defeat, Isabelle might have at least derived some small, bitter satisfaction from his fall; but he had won the favour of the new king. Eleanor had confirmed the rumours that Richard had received John with honour and given him the kiss of peace.

'Can't we go a little faster, milady?' Matilda said, waving her arm at the rain as if she would chase it away.

Isabelle nodded and was about to spur her mare into a trot, when she noticed that the horse was beginning to limp.

As she reined in, one of the three Tower *serjants* riding escort drew up beside her.

'I think she's thrown a shoe, milady,' he said, dismounting.

Before the *serjant* could protest, Isabelle slipped from the saddle to hold the reins of their horses while he checked her mare's foreleg.

'That's it, all right, milady,' the *serjant* said. 'I'll take off the other shoe to put her on an even keel. It won't take but a moment.'

'You can go on ahead, Mattie,' Isabelle said, looking up at her disconsolate companion.

'It doesn't matter now,' Matilda sniffed. 'We're already about as wet as we can be.'

Two horsemen were cantering up the road from the direction of the Tower, and as they neared Isabelle and her party, they slowed their mounts to a walk. Matilda turned and bent towards Isabelle. 'I wonder what they want,' she said in a stage-whisper. 'The blond one is certainly a handsome devil.'

The *serjant* who had dismounted had fetched a tool from his saddle-bag, and he set to work removing the mare's shoe, ignoring the riders' approach; but the other two *serjants* edged their mounts forward, eyeing the strangers.

One of the riders was tall and slim, with rosy cheeks and yellow, curly hair. His companion was dark, short and chunky. The blond *was* handsome, Isabelle noted idly, but his attire was a shade too flamboyant for her taste. Neither man was armed, nor accompanied by squires, but Isabelle was sure they were knights.

They halted, and the blond bowed to Isabelle and Matilda with an extravagant flourish. 'Fair ladies, please allow us to introduce ourselves. I am Baudouin de Bethune, and my friend here is Hugh de Harlincourt. May we be of service?'

'We're quite all right, thank you,' Isabelle responded. 'My horse threw a shoe, but we'll be on our way in a moment or two.'

'Do I have the honour of addressing Lady Isabelle de Clare?' Bethune asked.

'Yes, you do, Sir Baudouin,' Isabelle said with a tentative half-smile, surprised out of her cheerless mood. 'May I ask how you know who I am?'

'How?' Bethune said in mock-surprise, turning to Harlincourt. 'What do you say, Hugh? Could there be any doubt? The fiery hair, those eyes . . .'

'Lady Isabelle,' Harlincourt said, performing his own lavish bow, 'the good, the fair, the wise and courteous lady of high degree. How, indeed, could that be anyone but you?'

The absurdity of the strange knights' mysterious clowning in the midst of the downpour was too much for Isabelle, and she laughed for the first time in weeks.

'Don't you think, Sir Hugh and Sir Baudouin,' she said lightly, 'that you should tell me why you've sought me out – as you so obviously have.'

'Of course,' Bethune said merrily. 'We've come to fetch you back to the Tower to meet with the king's representative. When we left him, he was mired down in business with Hubert Walter, but he is quite anxious to see you.'

'Yes,' Harlincourt agreed with a grin. 'Quite anxious.'

'The king's representative?' Isabelle said, exchanging a puzzled look with Matilda. 'But why should he wish to see me?'

'I believe it has to do with the marriage Prince Richard – soon to be His Majesty – has arranged for you, Lady Isabelle,' Bethune said.

Isabelle's smile vanished. 'My . . . marriage?' she said in a faltering voice. She had known it would happen sooner or later, but now, before she'd had a chance to adjust?

Harlincourt swallowed his grin. 'That's enough, Bo,' he said quickly. 'Will would have our hides . . .'

'Will?' Isabelle gasped with sudden, wild hope. 'Did you say Will?'

At that moment, she caught the sound of hoofbeats and turned to see a rider galloping towards them.

'Look at the way Will's pushing that horse,' Bethune said, shaking his head. 'We told him we'd find his lady, but some men just don't have any patience.'

But Isabelle didn't hear Bethune, for she was already running towards Marshal, her feet flying over the muddy road.